To

Best Wishes

BOOK ONE

CHRYZINIUM
·THE LAZARUS VI PROJECT·

RICK LORD

Vul-Stream Publishing LLC

Chryzinium: The Lazarus VI Project
© 2016 Rick Lord

Printed in the United States of America,

Cover Design: Vul-Stream Publishing LLC and Timothias Hucklestone

Vul-Stream Publishing
PO Box 13421
Salem Oregon 97309
,
LCCN: 2016944772
ISBN: 978-0-9974611-0-7

In Loving Memory and Dedicated To

George Steinberger
Chuck Hunt

Special Thanks To

Jackie Lord, My loving wife
Cecil and Addy Lord, My Loving Parents
Deborah Warren, Friend and Project Manager
Ed Stiner, Friend and Chryzinium Partner
Sherry Steinberger, Friend and Support
Phillip Wade, Friend and Collaborator
Tim Wade, Friend and Collaborator

Beta Team

Beth Van Noy
Ed Stiner
Perry Grenz
Anne Birch
Suez Smith
Laura Krout
Kevin Van Dyke
Beth Van Dyke

Illustration/Cover Design

Timothias Hucklestone

Editors

Shannon Butcher
Deborah Warren

Book Design and Layout

Luminare Press

Contents

PREFACE

Chryzinium – (Cry-zin-ee-um) AKA, Unibihexium Carbon Particle, is a complex chromium-carbon based element discovered in the Grand Canyon, June of 1996. Despite the fact this extraordinary element has no matching earth-like properties; it is this element that is thought to be the cure-all vaccine for many, if not all, of humanity's life-altering diseases.

If every disease could be completely eradicated with one simple vaccine; it would be a miracle drug sought after by tens of millions of people. However, it is this concept that also comes with many unforeseen negative ramifications.

Health care, being a 4 trillion dollar per year industry, would in no way support such a product on the world market today. Financial institutions would collapse overnight. Healthcare establishments would ultimately crumble. And, because population growth rates would multiply exponentially, there would be a fight for world supremacy, the likes the world has never seen.

Malthusianism – Reverend Thomas Robert Malthus' theory that when population increases at a faster rate than it can support, and unless checked by moral restraint or disaster (disease, famine, or war), widespread poverty and degradation will inevitably result. (Merriam-Webster Dictionary)

Where disease has no consequence, population is no longer controlled by its effects, but only by disaster and those who are in control.

It has been asserted that Chryzinium cures disease by altering the very structure of the human DNA. If that is indeed the case, those taking the vaccine would then not be considered human by scientific standards.

The altering of human DNA would then most assuredly disrupt the very thing that separates humans from other species.

Since the July 4th, 1947 UFO crash in Roswell, New Mexico, a host of breakthroughs within the neuroscientific community has emerged with frequencies never before realized. The reengineering of DNA suddenly became possible.

Scientists concur on one basic principal. Every disease has one common metabolic thread; they can be linked to 39 root allergens. By developing a synthetic DNA that is impervious to all allergies, 140-year, disease-free lifespans are possible.

Modern society refers to them as extraterrestrials. The Bible refers to them as angelic beings and/

or demons. The Native Americans refer them as 'Star People.'

The 'Ancient Ones,' also referred to as the Anasazi, a tribe that inhabited the earth shortly after the fall of man, wrote of these 'Star People' an estimated 12,000 years ago. According to carvings and hieroglyphs found around the world, the Anasazi were said to be the 'great protectors of the land.'

They were thought to have had a deep spiritual respect for the earth. The earth and all its animal and plant life were considered sacred and to be revered as a gift from the stars. Hence, a special energy force from the 'Star People' was given them. They write often of being visited by so-called spirit guides who provided them mystical powers and knowledge.

Because of their beliefs, the Anasazi could actually draw from earths' energy and conjure powers and visitors from the stars. Petroglyphs carved in rock caves all over the world depict a time in which they were guided by the 'Star People.' Anasazi legend refers to these beings as the Shafutah, the same beings of which many present-day Native Americans speak. It was the Shafutah that would come and share advancements far beyond our present-day technologies, including life-enhancing elements, with the Anasazi. It is believed the Anasazi had life spans of 500 to 600 years, respectively. Long before the cretaceous period, just like the dinosaurs, the Anasazi civilization also ceased to exist, not due to a cataclysmic event, but by their own doing.

The Bible speaks of a time before man where void and darkness was upon the earth in Genesis 1:2. There are those who believe that there was a race of beings who freely roamed the surface of the earth during that time. It is these beings that are believed to be demons or fallen angels cast from heaven – The Shafutah. After the creation of man, the Shafutah feared mankind and their ability to think and create for themselves. Their only recourse was to take back what they thought was rightfully theirs. Realizing man's great weakness was lust for power; the Shafutah knew they could destroy the human civilization by giving to man the illusion of power and self-reliance.

SECRETS

Torrential rain falls as though water is being shot from cannons in the sky. Curb to curb rainwater rushes downtown 3rd Street like a river. Christmas decorations dance violently along the main street through town with winds gusting up to 30 knots. The warmer than average temperatures have dampened much of the town's Christmas spirit.

Driving less than 20 MPH, the windshield wipers on Albert's 1947 Chevy Coupe can't keep up. The heavy rain and strong winds hamper his visibility so much that he is forced to pull over to the side of the road.

It has been a rough day for Doctor Albert Hess, and getting home quickly is at the forefront of his thoughts. At 7:15 PM, Albert should have been home 2 hours ago. "With this rain, perhaps it is best I just sit it out till it passes," he says to himself with his thick German accent.

Cautiously, Albert pulls to the side of the road and

turns the engine off. With the wipers stopped, the rainwater washes over the windshield in sheets like molten glass, distorting 3rd Street's lights and business signs.

As he sits behind the wheel waiting for the squall to pass, he begins to feel lightheaded and queasy. "Must be something I ate," he whispers. Looking ahead 50 feet or so, he sees light spilling from the windows of Bea's Diner. The diner's fluorescent sign that hangs perpendicular to the building, swings back and forth with every gust of the strong winds. With the wind also rocking his car, this too wreaks havoc on Albert's unsettled equilibrium.

Even Christmas at Bea's Diner, though whimsically decorated, seems to generate little holiday enthusiasm. With no customers, April has little to do to keep her busy. Sipping from her soda, she leans against the business side of the coffee counter to observe the passing freak storm through the diners' plate glass windows.

Only 21 years old, April Dunn is slender in build and pleasant to the eyes. Her white waitress cap accents her long brown hair as it falls neatly over her shoulders. A white lace apron is deftly tied over her black and white plaid dress. She works four nights a week at the diner. However, during the days, she works in a bakery across town as a pastry chef's apprentice.

Her mother, Betty, was the quintessential, midcentury, stay-at-home mom. For April and her twin brother, Brian, Betty was always entertaining the kids with stories, crafts, and cooking projects. Never did a day go by when mom wasn't in the kitchen with April teaching her the joys of cooking. This was the foundation that gave April her insatiable appetite for baking.

Her father was a detective for the Dayton Police Department, which probably explains her overtly curious nature. Nothing got by April. Her keen eye for details would have served her well as a detective just like her father; had she chosen such a career path.

From early childhood, April always disliked secrets. Birthdays and Christmas were ardently taxing, because of mysteries hidden inside the wrapped gifts. This would drive April crazy. It is that overpowering need-to-know personality trait that makes her who she is.

Two years ago, April's twin brother Brian was killed in an explosion at a construction site in Cincinnati. He was just nineteen years old. Brian was loved by all who knew him. Energetic and fun loving, he was a good, smart, and hard-working kid with a promising future. The accident devastated the entire family and since that horrible day, they have never been the same.

From early childhood, April and Brian were inseparable. They did everything together. The loss of her brother had taken a considerable toll. She needed a fresh start with new surroundings to help her heal and move forward with her life.

After Brian's death, April left her parents' home and set out on her own. She rented an apartment in the small town of Lebanon, 27 miles south of Dayton, Ohio.

Directly across from Bea's Diner, bathed in brightly lit signage, is the Star Theater in all its glory. The establishment's bright white marquis, surrounded in glowing pink and green neon-scrolled tubes, proudly advertises the headline attraction in big black letters, 'The Day the Earth Stood Still,' starring Michael Rennie and Patricia Neal.

Though heavy rain and strong winds blur the sign, dark silhouetted shapes of anxious moviegoers can still be seen mingling about. People wearing wind-torn rain slickers, and useless, back-folded umbrellas, line the sidewalk awaiting their turn to enter the theater. Even for a Thursday evening, the small towns' inhabitants endure the inclement weather just to be entertained for a meager 92 minutes.

April watches the streaming rivulets of rain on the windows as it turns the moviegoers into a moving canvas of indistinguishable shapes and colors. The entrance of a customer breaks her daydreaming and redirects her focus back to her duties at the diner.

Middle-aged Doctor Albert Hess enters as he tightly grasps his black battered briefcase. He is dressed in a soaking wet wool overcoat and Fedora hat. It spills rainwater from its brim as the diner's door shuts behind him. His face shows the beginnings of mid-life aging. The graying in his black hair wisps out from under his hat.

Upon entering, he takes a moment to consider his seating options. April's smile beckons the man to the counter. Taking her cue, the man takes a seat. He holds the leather case close to his chest, as if carefully guarding its contents.

He politely removes his hat. Beads of rainwater on his cheeks sparkle in the glow of the overhead fluorescent lighting.

"Coffee sir?" she kindly asks.

Albert nods yes.

She reaches under the counter and grabs a cup, setting it down in front of him.

"Cream and sugar?"

Albert shakes his head, "No thank you."

She smiles, pours his coffee, and turns to place the pot back onto the hotplate behind her. Albert pulls from his coat a handkerchief. He begins to pat his face dry as April turns back to him.

"Would you like a piece of pie? We have a wonderful selection."

Shaking his head no, he opens the flap of his briefcase and looks inside. He removes a stack of folders and a large, manila envelope. 'Great,' April thinks. 'He's here to do work and drink up all of the coffee. Oh well, at least I have someone to talk to and keep me busy.'

Albert's hands are shaking as he spreads the documents out on the counter. Looking up at April, they lock eyes. Cold beads of sweat begin to form on his face.

April senses there is something terribly wrong. "Are you okay?" she asks with concern.

"Take this and hide it away, don't show it to anyone," Albert says to April sliding the manila envelope toward her. His thick German accent is not what April was expecting.

"What?" April asks.

"Please."

April looks down and notices the bold red words 'Top Secret' that are stamped just below the clasp. Looking back up to Albert she sees he is beginning to sweat profusely now and his face is ashen. His breathing is heavy and his face is becoming drawn and pasty.

"Are you okay? Do you want some water?" she asks, becoming more concerned.

Albert grabs hold of April's hand and looks directly into her eyes with desperation.

"Please!" he implores.

Slowly releasing her hand, his eyes glaze over. He grabs his chest and falls backward, dragging his briefcase and folders to the floor with him.

Hundreds of papers, folders and other documents spill from the briefcase, covering the man and the floor like a large white and yellow paper quilt.

"Oh, my dear Lord!" April gasps.

April runs around the end of the counter and kneels down beside him.

"Hey mister, can you hear me?" she asks, shaking him by the shoulders. Leaning over, she places her ear to Albert's chest. She listens intently, hoping to hear a heartbeat.

"I need to call the police."

In shock, she slowly stands and makes her way back around the counter. Picking up the phone that sits next to the cash register, April dials "0" for the operator.

"Hello, hello, my name is April Dunn. I work at Bea's diner and a guy came in and collapsed on the floor. I think we need an ambulance and probably the police. 2482 - 3rd Street," she informs, then hangs up the phone. She walks over to the counter and looks over to see Albert, appearing lifeless. The color has completely drained from his face. His eyes are still open, and have turned milky white.

Leaning back away from the counter, not wanting to see him, she glances at the 'Top Secret' manila envelope still lying next to Albert's coffee cup. She knows the police are on the way and she is becoming anxious over what to do with the document. Looking around the diner, she quickly considers her options.

Gathering her thoughts, she takes the envelope and opens the clasp. Reaching inside, she removes its contents, folds and places them into her purse that sits under the counter.

Taking the empty envelope back around the counter, she scoops up a hand full of papers and loads them into the "Top Secret" packet and lays it on the floor with all of the other scattered papers, folders and envelopes. Just as she does, the door opens and the police enter. Startled, April stands to her feet.

"I think he's dead."

FIGHT FOR LIFE

Hillsdale Falls is an average sized town of 81,000 people. Typical for Middle-America, the small town is slow-paced but strives to act chic. Lumber was at one time the primary industry until the late 90's; however since then there has been a steady decline in lumber products, due to the constant barrage of strangling regulations.

Yet, the people are resilient and innovative, keeping the town's lifeblood pumping with the continuing growth of high-tech industries coming to the area.

The days are getting shorter as winter approaches. The holidays are at hand and the trees are barren as the icy, 20 degree temperatures grip the town this season.

The Shaes live in an upper class part of town referred to as 'The Heights.' It is an older, affluent part of Hillsdale Falls that has neatly groomed yards, large homes, and high-end cars lining the winding streets. Most of the residences have been remodeled and bring a great deal of curb-appeal to the neighborhood.

The Shaes live in a large Cape Code style house, which is in dire need of upgrades. This is definitely something Rebecca has been fighting Mark for, for years. It is just another costly source of contention in their marriage. Although decorated and furnished nicely, the dingy white moldings, outdated wallpaper and subtle traces of elegant ambience of a time past, blatantly reveal its years of neglect. The kitchen is large, with a center island, tile countertops, and worn cabinets.

Tuesday morning is as predictable as peanut butter and jelly. Rebecca prepares lunches for the kids as her husband Mark rushes about getting ready to leave for work. The day begins early, as it does for most families with two teenagers in school. Rebecca, a stay-at-home mom, is rushing to get lunches together. Her husband Mark is running late. He is an attorney who heads up the Intellectual Properties legal team for SpiresGate, which is Hillsdale Falls' only nanotechnologies super-conductor manufacturing lab.

His high-stress job demands much of Marks' time. With Rebecca's maxed-out credit cards, constant appetite for the latest in fashion, and non-stop shopping sprees, it's hard for Mark to keep up. Even with the Shaes living somewhat beyond their means, Mark is diligent and still manages to squirrel away a little money into a rainy day fund, something Rebecca is always trying to acquire.

As Mark enters the kitchen, he pecks his ritualistic morning kiss on Rebecca's cheek. "Are there any donuts or something quick I can eat?" he blurts out as he grabs his travel mug off the counter and fills it with coffee.

"There's the cauliflower and broccoli salad you tried to poison us with last night," Emily quips.

"Shouldn't you be somewhere?" Mark interjects sarcastically.

"Not time yet."

"No, I mean, isn't it time for you to live somewhere else?"

"Mark!" Rebecca shouts, trying to tame her husbands' sarcasm towards Emily.

"She started it," Mark retorts, sounding petty.

Rebecca shakes her head in dismay over another morning of arguing. Finishing up the kids lunches, she realizes that Taylor has yet to be seen.

"Where's your brother?" Rebecca asks Emily.

"How should I know?" Emily replies with her typical teenage attitude.

Emily is 15 years old. She is tall and pretty, just like her mother. Her long brown hair shines with youth and vitality. Not interested in cheerleading herself, like her mom, she could have easily made the squad just by simply showing up for tryouts. Too much work cheerleading, she often boasts. It would leave her little time to hang with her friends.

It is her extreme good looks and fashionable tastes that put her at the top of the popular list so early on.

However, it's those same attributes that have created the stuck-up fem-fatale she has already become.

Her morning beauty regimen usually takes up to a full hour. Add to that another hour for hair, dressing and primping, Emily can easily spend two hours getting ready for school.

Unfortunately, her investment on outward appearance leaves her with little time for her studies. However, even though she is terrible at most things scholastically, her artistic talent is nothing short of stellar. A love for landscape painting, she is a natural, considering she has had little training. Almost every painting that hangs in her room, she has done herself. Not to mention the artwork that adorns a good portion of the Shaes' home.

Taylor finally enters the kitchen, grabs his sack lunch and begins to dig through the bag, examining its contents. He is about as boy as any boy can be at 13 years old. As it is with many siblings, he and his older sister don't get along. Emily smirks as Taylor enters.

"Here's the spore, now," Emily says maliciously.

"Freak!" Taylor answers back, abruptly.

With coffee in hand, Mark walks to the side kitchen door to leave for work. "I'm out of here. Oh, and I'll be home late. Don't hold dinner for me. Another fire I have to put out before I leave work this evening." The door slams behind him. Rebecca finishes cleaning up after making the kids' lunches. Emily grabs her lunch and heads for the door. Once at the door she stops to inform her mom of a change in her schedule.

"Mrs. Lawson wants me to stay after school so I can help Eugene with his science project."

"Yeah right! YOU? Help someone with a science a project? What a bunch a bull! You can't even boil water without a book of instructions. You just want to hang out after school with your stuck-up friends and smoke," squeals Taylor.

"Shut up, you little roach!"

"You're not smoking are you, Em?" Rebecca inquires with concern.

"No. I'm not smoking."

Emily turns to Taylor and glares at him spitefully.

"I hope not. Come on, both of you get going. You'll be late," says Rebecca.

Emily attends Liberty High School, while her brother Taylor attends Evergreen Middle School. Mom believes Emily and Taylor are both products of teenage hormones gone askew, and hopes they'll soon grow out of it. However, Emily seems to be having a difficult time.

Emily is in her sophomore year and has found her place with those that share her same interests; walking the halls in search of hot boys, wearing the latest in designer fashions, and of course, defying authority. The siblings finally exit their home to suffer the short walk together to their respective schools.

Rebecca finds comfort in the fact that the remainder of her day comes with, at least, some solitude and normalcy. For today, it's Christmas shopping, some house cleaning, and brunch with her girlfriend, Alesha.

Not showing any interest in history class, Emily sits at her desk, bored and distant. There are 26 students in attendance in Mr. Alverez' 3rd period World History class, all of whom are there due to some form of learning disability.

Walking up and down each aisle of desks, Mr. Alverez passes out the graded test papers. As he delivers them to each student, he gives a brief comment related to their associated score.

"Ethan, 'A-Plus,' good job," Mr. Alverez comments.

"Lisa, 'B,' not bad, but you can do better."

"Mr. Spiegleberg, 'B.'"

"And Miss Shae, it's another 'F' for you. Magellan? A jello salad created in Mexico City in 1945? Nice try."

The class breaks into laughter as Emily viciously grabs her paper from Mr. Alverez.

"Quiet!" retorts Mr. Alvarez to the class. "You can come see me after school, Miss Shae."

"I'm not coming to see you after school!" Emily barks back angrily.

"Yes you are."

"No, I'm not! I have plans after school!"

Having had enough of Emily's attitude, Mr. Alverez points towards the classroom door.

"Out! You just bought yourself a one-way ticket to the principal's office. Leave now! I'm not having you disrupt my class with your nonsense anymore!"

"I'm not leaving."

"You most assuredly are, young lady!"

Emily remains in her seat, folds her arms, continuing to defy Mr. Alvarez' demands. Emily glances sideways, seeing her classmate, Samantha, gesturing with an imaginary cigarette between two fingers.

"Go girl! Take a break!" Samantha whispers.

Emily, taking Samantha's cue, grabs her books and her purse. She stands and storms toward the door of the classroom and pushes the door open with a bang. Just as she takes her first step into the hallway, Emily collapses, as if being turned off by a switch. Her head hits the floor with a thud as her books and purse scatter into the classroom and hallway.

Emily's eyes roll back into her head. The class looks on, thinking she's joking around, until she begins to violently convulse. Along with white foam, the contents of her stomach begin to surge from her mouth.

Mr. Alverez immediately runs to her aid, turning her head, preventing her from choking on her own vomit. While checking on Emily, he notices that her body is limp and her face has begun to turn ashen grey. Looking up and down the hallway, Mr. Alverez frantically screams for help.

STEAMERS CAFE

It's 11:22 AM and Rebecca Shae and Alesha Mason are enjoying a visit at Steamers Café. Rebecca and Alesha have been friends, going all the way back to third grade. In fact, Alesha was Rebecca's maid of honor, and vice versa.

Their brunch and coffee ritual began soon after college and continues to this day. Married to Dave Mason, Alesha and her husband many times get together with Rebecca and Mark to entertain and visit. But, the two ladies always carve out some time just for the two of them.

For years, Rebecca and Alesha have been meeting at Steamers Café twice a week for coffee, desert and/or brunch. It's that special time for the two to visit without kids and husbands interrupting. As regulars, Marcus, the café's owner, knows the ladies well.

In his fifties, he is not only the café's owner, he's also the head waiter. With mugs in hand, Marcus brings Rebecca and Alesha their pumpkin spice lattes.

"Can I get you ladies anything else?" Marcus politely offers.

Rebecca and Alesha think for a moment before answering.

"I would really like a slice of cherry cheese cake," Rebecca says with a smile.

"Make that two, Marcus," adds Alesha.

"I shouldn't be eating cherry cheese cake before I eat lunch," Rebecca confesses.

"It's the holidays, live a little! Life is too short to go without dessert." Alesha retorts with supportive permission.

Marcus smiles, "I'll be right back with your desserts."

Rebecca's cell phone begins to ring. Lifting her purse to the table, she retrieves her phone from the leather abyss. As she looks at the phone, she does not recognize the phone number on the caller ID. She shrugs to Alesha and answers the phone.

"Hello? Yes this is Rebecca Shae."

As Alesha looks on, she sees Rebecca's countenance change from puzzled to panic in less than a second.

"Oh no! No! Yes! I'm on my way."

Rebecca ends the call and immediately drops the phone back into her purse. Frantically, she slides her chair back and stands.

"It's Emily, I have to go!"

"What's wrong? What happened?" Alesha asks quickly.

"She's been taken to the hospital. Hillsdale Falls Memorial Medical Center."

"What? What's happened to her?"

"I don't know. The school said she collapsed in the hallway and wouldn't come-to."

"Go! Go! I got this!" Alesha insists.

Without missing a beat, Rebecca quickly exits the café and runs down the sidewalk, heading toward her SUV. Driving away from the curb, she nearly runs into a car while merging into traffic, then she races off down the street.

Rebecca fumbles in her purse for her cell phone and frantically calls Mark. After a series of rings, the call goes to voicemail.

"Hello, you have reached the cell phone of Mark Shae, at the tone, please leave a message and I'll get back to you as soon as possible, thank you."

Frustrated, Rebecca is forced to leave Mark a message.

"Mark it's me! I just a got a call from the school. They're taking Emily to the hospital. She collapsed in the hallway and wouldn't wake up!"

Rebecca pushes the "end call" button and throws the phone back into her purse. "Where the heck is Hillsdale Falls Memorial Medical Center?" She shouts in exasperation. Driving down Center Street, the main street through town, she finally sees a blue hospital sign directing her to turn left. She quickly makes her way to the hospital.

HILLSDALE FALLS MEMORIAL MEDICAL CENTER

It's 12:38 PM, and Rebecca is pacing the emergency room waiting area. Over the intercom is heard, "Doctor Clemons to ER, Doctor Clemons to ER." The large electric automatic doors, connecting the emergency room to the ambulance portage, slide open with a whooshing sound. A gurney surrounded by paramedics, rolls inside. In a race for time, an entourage of paramedics go whizzing by. The ER nurse runs to greet the incoming patient.

"Male, fifty two years old, head trauma, rollover car accident," a paramedic announces.

"Vitals?" asks the ER nurse.

"BP 100 over 60, pulse 56, respiratory shallow."

"Where's my baby? I hate being here. I hate *her* being here," Rebecca mumbles as she makes her way to the information desk.

"The doctor will be here to meet you shortly," she is told.

The sounds of the ER are instilling fear in Rebecca as she waits for word about Emily. She is becoming more panicked as time passes. Finally, running toward the ER from a long hallway, Mark joins Rebecca. She grabs hold of him and they hug long and hard.

"Where is she?" Mark asks Rebecca.

"I don't know?"

"What do you mean you don't know? Is she here or not?" Mark asks in frustration.

"Of course she's here. I just don't know where, here. The lady at the information desk said a doctor would be coming to see me," Rebecca responds.

The ER's two huge doors that lead back to triage swing open. A short, bearded, balding man wearing a lab coat adorned with stethoscope, pocket protector, pens and the standard Hillsdale Falls Memorial Medical Center badge approaches the admin station. With a mere point of a finger, the nurse behind the counter directs the doctor to Rebecca and Mark. With a smile, the doctor approaches the couple.

"Hello, I'm Doctor Ivan Heller. Are you Emily's parents?"

"Yes. How is she? Is she okay? Can we see her?" Rebecca asks anxiously.

"I'm Mark Shae, Emily's father."

"Nice to meet you. How about the both of you come with me?"

"Is she alright? I want to know if she's alright," again Rebecca insists.

"That's what we're going to talk about, and yes, she's alive and stable."

Doctor Heller leads Rebecca and Mark through the ER doors and the triage station.

"Where is my daughter?" Rebecca demands.

"She is currently on the 3rd floor in Imaging. We're going to my office on the 5th floor, so we'll take the staff elevator," Doctor Heller says, leading the way.

Once on the 5th floor, the three make their way down the hallway to Doctor Heller's office. As he opens his office door, he extends his arm as an invitation for them to enter, "Please have a seat." Only Mark takes a seat whereas Rebecca defiantly stands.

Doctor Heller's office is fairly good-sized with a plethora of house plants, plaques and paintings on the wall. A coffee counter and a small fridge, makes his office quite comfortable. Two guest chairs are positioned directly in front of his desk.

"Would you please tell us what's going on with Emily?" Rebecca demands again.

Doctor Heller walks around his desk and sits. Folding his hands, he looks at the anxious couple.

"The truth of the matter is, I don't know what's wrong with your daughter. That's why she's down in Imaging. We've taken a blood sample and are now waiting for the lab results to come back. In the meantime, we are conducting a CAT scan, to see if there's something neurological going on."

"Is she awake? Can we see her?" Mark asks.

"No, she's not awake. She came in unconscious and is still in the same condition. When she's done with her CAT scan, she will be going straight to the ICU. As soon as she's been checked in there, you may see her."

Rebecca and Mark stare blankly at the doctor, in shock. Their lives have been turned upside down in a matter of hours. Rebecca is a strong, resilient woman who has always taken life by the tail.

She was voted class president in high school and graduated from college with honors. Though she traded her business degree for family life, she has always been a woman of strength and control. Even with all of her many achievements, Rebecca is now left feeling hopeless and powerless.

As she stands at Mark's side, her tenuous control over her emotions snaps and overwhelms her. Tears roll down her face as she succumbs to her feeling of uncontrollable despair.

Mark looks up at Rebecca and sees that she is no longer able to keep her composure. Mark stands and puts his arms around Rebecca, consoling her. Looking on, Doctor Heller offers them his office while he goes to check on Emily's status.

"You two stay here and try to relax. I'm going to see

how things are coming along with Emily. I'll be back in just a few minutes. We'll find out what's going on. I promise."

Rebecca nods a tearful, "Okay."

Remembering suddenly that Taylor will be coming home from school shortly, she squeezes Marks hand.

"Would you pick up Taylor from school? I don't want to leave Emily."

"Absolutely," Mark replies softly. He kisses Rebecca on her forehead and gives her a hug.

"Everything will be alright," he consoles.

"Why don't you sit down and try to think positive. Do you want some coffee from the cafeteria?" he asks.

Rebecca shakes her head 'no' to the offer, but does take Mark's advice, and sits in one of the chairs opposite Doctor Heller's desk. She looks up at Mark and cracks a slight smile as he combs through her hair with his hand.

"I'll be back as fast as I can, okay?" Mark softly says to her. Rebecca nods and smiles bravely as Mark turns and exits the office. Rebecca's smile quickly diminishes as her composure dissipates. Fresh tears begin to flow down her cheeks.

PILOTS AND CONSPIRACIES

Walter Cecil Baggerly, 'Baggs' as he's known by many, has always had a profound interest in aviation from childhood. As a boy, he built model aircraft and dreamed of a career in some form of aeronautics. He went on to aggressively pursue his passion, graduating in 1965 with a degree in aeronautical engineering.

Prior to joining NASA, he had flown F-4C fighters for the United States Air Force in Vietnam. During his eight-year stint in the Air Force, he successfully completed 121 air combat missions; accumulating 14 kills. While on active duty, he earned numerous medals, including the Air Force Commendation medal. Given his astounding career and academic credentials, Baggs joined the NASA space program in 1978. During his inaugural flight on August 30, 1983, he orbited earth 98 times. Now retired from NASA, as one of America's first black astronauts and aeronautical engineers, 73-year-old Baggs still enjoys aviation and space travel, albeit, from the comfort of his home. As fate would have it, Springboro, Ohio is not only his hometown from childhood, but also his birthplace.

The last years of his remarkable career had him 'flying' a desk at Wright Patterson Air Force Base. Not far from home, he easily made the commute. Everybody in town knows Baggs. He is a celebrity in his own right. He is, after all, the only astronaut to come from Springboro. Nonetheless, his penchant for all things aeronautical still soars to the present. With his computer and collection of model planes, Baggs' head is always in the clouds.

When he's not flying one of the model aircraft in his prized collection, he spends much of his time consorting with his long-time friend, conspiracy theorist/ UFOlogist, Lewis Warren, another retired aeronautical engineer and pilot. Lewis also worked at Wright Patterson, though some years past. Although complete opposites, Baggs and Lewis have been best friends since the day they met.

Where Baggs is the quintessential neat freak, many wonder if Lewis owns so much as a single comb. Lewis is not one who takes much interest in personal hygiene, dressing neatly, or being polite.

A little on the quirky side, Lewis spends much of his time studying UFOlogy and, of course, anything else strange and unusual. Always a source of entertainment for Baggs, Lewis is fascinated with the weird, the unusual, and of course any new conspiracy that comes across the internet. Despite their differences, Baggs and Lewis have maintained their friendship for more than three decades, proving that opposites do attract.

Three years ago, Lewis managed to drag Baggs along for a trip to the State of Washington's Mount St. Helens, in search of Bigfoot. Baggs refuses to talk about it with anyone out of sheer embarrassment. Lewis's fascination with Sasquatch, AKA Bigfoot, has always been inordinately passionate. But, this particular Bigfoot adventure came from a story supposedly verified by one of his other nutty friends.

As the story goes, a soldier in the National Guard who worked the Mount St. Helens site a short time after the eruption in May of 1980, had an encounter with the elusive beast.

At only 24 years old, Bill the guardsman was allegedly placed on a special cleanup crew far up the mountain east of the crater. A large tent was set up which was guarded by armed active duty soldiers.

Bill and four other guardsmen were brought to the tent and given a military style 'swearing in.' They were ordered to absolute secrecy about what they were going to see. It was even demanded of them not to comment to each other on what they were about to experience.

The soldiers put the fear of God into the five guardsmen. They were given a short briefing and then ordered to forget about what they had just been told including everything they were about to witness.

After what seemed like hours, they were all ordered to get into the back of a truck that was parked 50 feet or so from the tent. The truck had in the back, a large piece of canvas material and two 12 foot long boards. Soon after, a jeep pulled up to the tent door carrying a civilian and another member of the military.

The two men exited the jeep and slowly entered the tent. Within a few minutes the men exited the tent, along with a bipedal creature that stood well over 7 feet tall and covered in matted, brownish-red hair. It was reported that it resembled a beast from X-Men dressed in brown fur. One of its arms was bandaged and appeared to have burns on about 10% of its torso.

The civilian and military men helped the creature into the Jeep's front passenger seat. The civilian climbed in the back, and the military man drove. They pulled in parallel to the truck with the five guardsmen in the back. The men, even though ordered not to speak, couldn't have if they had tried. They were completely speechless.

Bill spoke of the creatures eyes. They drooped sadly, and pain could be seen in its face. As the jeep pulled away, the Guardsmen's truck followed. They drove for about a half hour and stopped at an outcropping of rocks where a small cave could be seen about 50 feet away.

Parked within a few feet of the jeep that carried the creature, they could hear the men and the creature speak. However the language was not English and in fact was not of any known dialect they had ever heard. He commented on how it sounded like gibberish.

Then without warning, the creature let out a screeching roar. Though startled, there was no verbal response. It was dead quiet as they sat in utter disbelief. After a few minutes the jeep drove off and the Guardsmen followed directly behind.

Four other stops were made where the exact same routine took place. But on the last stop, after the creature's howl, there were cries heard coming from behind a few large boulders. These were not ordinary cries, but cries that one would expect to hear coming from a wounded animal.

It was then they were ordered out of the truck. The Guardsmen were told to get the two long boards and canvas from the back of the truck. Hiking to the boulders, the men were to construct an oversized stretcher with the materials they had in hand. Led by the civilian, the men took the makeshift stretcher behind the rocks to where they heard where the cries were coming from.

Another creature just like the one sitting in the jeep, lay on the scorched ground badly burned and bloodied. Only this creature was closer to 10 feet tall. Weighing well over 500 pounds, it was clear why the special guardsmen were sequestered. They needed the man power to lift the enormous injured beast into the back of the truck.

Back at the tent, the guardsmen carried the beast

inside. Set up like a hospital, the inside was not at all what one would expect. Medical devices, hospital gurney, operating room lighting, and medical staff swarmed the interior like an emergency room.

After the men had carried the beast to the operating gurney, the men were promptly ushered out and ordered back to the truck. A high ranking military official approached the men and thanked them for their service. He went on to tell them that these creatures are inhabitants of the mountain and wish no one any harm. "They just want to be left alone," He sternly informed the men. He asked that their secrecy be regarded in good faith.

From there, the men were driven back to the camp at the base of the mountain. Supposedly, Bill told the story to a friend of Lewis' some 30 years later while lying in a hospital bed dying of cancer.

Stories like this only fuel Lewis's imagination. It was this ridiculous, unexplainable story that led Lewis to drag Baggs to Washington in search of Bigfoot. As expected, the trip to the mountain with Baggs proved futile. They brought back nothing but dozens of mosquito bites and a bag of supposed Bigfoot 'scat,' of which Lewis still maintains is authentic. Even though Lewis may come off as eccentric, Baggs enjoys his comradery and enthusiasm for the unknown, nonetheless.

BAGGS' HOUSE, EARLY SATURDAY MORNING

For Baggs, the day starts as it always does with two cups

of coffee, two strips of bacon, two eggs, two slices of wheat toast, and a glass of tomato juice. The sun rises brightly in Springboro, shining through the glass panes of the kitchen's French doors. Fall is quickly turning into winter.

What few leaves do cling to their branches easily break free with the slightest of breeze and float down, bouncing off the glass like large burnt orange snowflakes. The crisp late fall air is perfect flying weather and Baggs is eager to head to the park and pilot one of his favorite aircraft models.

Placing his breakfast plate into the sink, Baggs exits his kitchen and quickly walks into his living room. Even though Baggs' home is militarily immaculate, it is quite large in size and located in an older neighborhood of similar homes.

The home is of a craftsman-style build, but from the outside it is not much to behold. However, on the inside, the home is spacious and ornate. 1414 Havelock Lane has been his home from birth. Although his mother passed away some 23 years ago, Baggs has stayed true to his birthplace, always upgrading and taking care of the old home.

His passion for aircraft shines through with his extravagant taste in decor. His living room resembles that of an aviation museum for model planes. The huge room displays more than a dozen of his favorite flying models, most of which hang from the beams of the knotty pine ceiling. Suspended overhead by at least 5 feet, his planes appear to race through the sky, though frozen in flight.

The 12 foot long oak table that sits against the far wall displays a few of Baggs favorite flyable treasures. Carefully gazing over his collection, Baggs finally reaches for one of his prized radio-controlled planes. The World War II, twin engine, B-25 Mitchell bomber is a spectacular miniature replica of the real deal. But, before Baggs can grab it and head out the door, his cell phone begins to ring.

He sighs begrudgingly and walks over to his phone lying on the end table. Picking up the phone, he reads the caller ID and grimaces as he sees it is once again Lewis on the other end. Baggs answers the call with a bit of trepidation. He knows full well Lewis is not one for short, concise conversations. 'How long will this take?' Baggs thinks to himself.

"Hello Lewis," Baggs answers abruptly.

"Are you at your computer?" Lewis says, excitedly.

"No I'm not, I'm going flying. Why, what's up?"

"There's something you have got to see."

"Is this something I can look at a little later?

"Yeah, but you gotta see this. Call me when you get back."

"Okay, fine," Says Baggs as he quickly ends the call.

He takes a short breath and sighs. He then stuffs his cell phone into his shirt pocket, returns to the table, and picks up his World War II bomber and radio control unit. With his plane and radio in hand, Baggs exits his front door and quickly walks to his truck. Opening the tailgate and canopy lid, he carefully places the plane and radio inside the already gear-packed truck bed.

Grass Park isn't really a park but a nice sized vacant area of land that lies just eight minutes from Baggs' home.

Lacking trees, shrubs, or dogs, Grass Park makes for an ideal miniature airport for any model airplane enthusiast. Even though his hobby is illegal, Baggs doesn't worry much. Authorities turn a blind eye on his model aviation activities due to his long-time celebrity astronaut status.

The breeze is light and the temperature is a cool 46 degrees, perfect weather for flying. Without hesitation, Baggs fires up both engines on the vintage warbird. Quickly checking wind conditions, he points the aircraft into the wind. Stepping back a few feet, he positions the radio control unit in front of him. With both hands firmly holding the radio, his thumb pushes the joystick forward for full throttle.

Like a pair of bumblebees on steroids, the engines scream to life. Within 50 feet, the majestic flyer is well into the sky. He banks the airplane to the left and then to the right. Across the sky the bomber races with pin-point accuracy. Commander Baggerly has been flying radio controlled model planes for decades and it shows. He masters the plane like the well-seasoned pilot he is.

Off in the distance a young girl approaches, pushing her flat black Stingray bike toward the makeshift airfield. She is all but four-and-a-half feet tall, wearing pink coveralls and dirty white sneakers.

If not for the blond ponytail and pink attire, one would swear the child was a boy. Lit by the orange glow of the low-laying sun, her freckled face and tomboy appearance comes into Baggs' line of sight.

Standing just a few feet from Baggs, she drops her bike to the dirt and walks over to stand by him as he flies his plane. Briefly Baggs looks at the girl, making sure she is a safe distance from flying aircraft. He smiles at her, expressing his generally kind, warm personality. She smiles back, but quickly takes interest in what he has in the sky.

Back to the controls, Baggs hears one of the plane engines sputter. Looking back down to the girl he says, "Not very good gas mileage, this thing. I'm going to have to bring her in so she doesn't crash. Many lives at stake, you know?" Baggs jokingly remarks.

Carefully he readies the plane for landing just as the other engine begins to sputter. "Uh Oh!" he says. The model plane continues to descend as he turns the craft onto its final approach. The warbird is lined up and ready for landing when both engines quit. "Dead stick," he says to the youngster. "Dead stick is when you have to land without power."

He flips a switch on the radio and the miniature flaps lower, slowing the twin engine masterpiece to a manageable landing speed. Within a few seconds the

B-25 Mitchell Bomber touches down with exact precision. "Problem with dead stick landings is, now I have to go fetch it." he says to the little girl.

"Is it hard to fly?" she asks.

"No. Not once you learn how. Just like with anything, once you know how to do something, and you practice, it becomes easy."

"I'd like to learn how to fly that."

"You would? Well, you might have to enroll in flight school?"

"Flight school? Is that what you did?"

"Yes. I have to go get my plane, but you can walk with me if you'd like."

The two walk off together to retrieve the bomber. Once at the landing site, Baggs picks up the plane and begins the trek back to base camp for the model. As the two walk, the young girl doesn't take her eyes off the plane.

"You wouldn't happen to have a couple of nine-sixteenth box-end wrenches, do you?" asks the young girl.

"Excuse me?" Baggs responds.

"A couple of nine-sixteenth box-end wrenches, damn chain fell off my bike and if you've got some tools, I can fix it. Even a couple of crescent wrenches will work."

Despite her use of expletives, Baggs is impressed by her mechanical prowess.

"All I have is a pair of needle-nose pliers and a few very tiny wrenches and screwdrivers. Don't need big tools for small planes like this."

"Hmmm. Those aren't going to work," the girl replies.

After a few moments of contemplation, the girl continues.

"How long are you gonna be out here? Maybe I can catch a ride with you. So I don't have to push my bike all the way home."

Baggs stops what he's doing and smiles at the little girl.

"I don't think your mother would appreciate you being dropped off by a stranger," he says with parental concern.

"She's not going to care. What's your name?" asks the girl.

"Walter Baggerly. My friends call me 'Baggs' for short."

"Baggs is a funny nickname."

"Yes it is. I agree," he says with a chuckle.

"Well Mr. Baggs, my name is Marty. Marty Milner."

"Marty! Well that's an odd name for a girl."

"Ya, I suppose. But see? Now we're not strangers. Besides, I know you. You live across the street from me."

Baggs looks surprised.

"You do? I don't think I've ever seen you before, Miss Marty."

"That's because you're not paying attention to the world around you."

"Where do you come up with this stuff? How old are you anyway?" Baggs asks, stifling a laugh at Marty's sardonic wit.

"Ten. I turned ten on July 23rd, and what do you mean, where do I come up with this stuff? What stuff?"

"I don't know. You just sound very grown-up for a 10-year-old."

"That's what everyone says. So, what do you think? Can I catch I ride with you?"

"What about your mother?"

"What about my mother? She's probably still in bed. Besides she doesn't care what I do."

After carefully assessing the situation, Baggs relents.

"Okay, but we're going to have to make room in the back of my truck for your bike. I have a lot of my airplane stuff in there," Baggs informs Marty.

"No worries. Whenever you're ready, we'll hit it," Marty says self-assuredly.

Baggs shakes his head, and chuckles.

"Well, in your words, let's hit it, then!" Baggs responds.

Together, they begin the task of unloading the back of the truck and rearranging Baggs' flight gear. Within a few minutes the two have the truck reloaded. Last in is Marty's bike, dangling precariously halfway out the open back hatch. The two get into the truck and drive off.

BAGGS' HOUSE

With a bounce and rattle, Baggs' truck pulls into his driveway and comes to a stop. Marty is the first to disembark. Just as Baggs' feet touch the driveway, Marty is eagerly at his side. Slowly, Baggs walks to the back of his truck and retrieves Marty's bike. Setting the bike down on the driveway, Marty takes hold of the handlebars to begin her trek home.

"Thanks for the ride, Mr. Baggs," Marty says sincerely.

"No problem, it was nice meeting you. And it's just plain Baggs. No Mister."

"Baggs it is."

Baggs looks on, amused as Marty pushes her disabled bike across the street. The young girl's vivacious personality is bigger than life. Her way with words and the way she commands a conversation is humorous and refreshing. Once Baggs sees that Marty is safely across the street, he continues the chore of removing his plane from the back of the truck. Finally, with gear in hand, Baggs walks up the brick pathway to his front door and enters.

It's 11:40 A.M. and Baggs has settled into his home office. Oak bookshelves line the walls. Books on aviation, space and history fill the shelves; even a few books and magazines written on UFOlogy and conspiracy theories clutter the room. Many of which have been given to him by Lewis.

Baggs sits at his desk waiting for life to come to his computer. With a wiggle of the mouse, his computer screen display blinks on with its colorful, personalized, aviation wallpaper. As the screen illuminates his face, Baggs remembers the earlier call from Lewis. "Better find out what Lewis wanted to show me," he mumbles to himself. He retrieves his cell phone from his top shirt pocket and with a single swipe of his thumb, the call to Lewis goes through. Lewis immediately answers.

"I thought you'd never get back," Lewis says, annoyed.

"What's up?" Baggs interjects, not giving in to Lewis' impatience.

"Are you by your computer?" asks Lewis.

"I'm right here. What do you have?"

"I just sent you a link. Check this out."

Baggs quickly opens his email and clicks on the message from Lewis.

"I've got it," he retorts.

"Open the link and look at the picture full screen," Lewis insists.

Baggs clicks on the link and a landscape picture of the Grand Canyon appears on the screen.

"See what I'm talking about? If that's what I think it is, it has to be the biggest UFO I've ever seen. It must be 10 miles across!" Lewis continues.

Baggs settles back into his leather chair as he studies the image before him.

"Interesting. Where'd you get this?" He asks.

"It was taken by a tourist last month. It was circulated around a few of the UFO publication websites."

Baggs continues to study the image. Leaning in closer to the screen, he scrutinizes the minute details.

"Do you have some time to get together?" Asks Lewis.

"Right now?" Baggs grumbles.

"Yes now, we need to call Sy and see if he can meet us at the coffee shop."

"You call Sy. I want to look at something here. I'll call you back," Baggs says and ends the call.

Baggs slides his chair back from his desk, stands and walks over to one of his many bookshelves and begins searching for, what he believes, is a connection to the image Lewis sent him.

Usually, it's Lewis that comes up with these crazy conspiracies and cover-ups. But now, Baggs is thinking Lewis may have something here. In fact, he knows so.

Searching the bookcase for a particular folder, but not finding what he's looking for, Baggs takes a breather from the hunt to think. Leaning back onto his desk, he clicks the mouse to print the image from his screen.

"Hmmm, I wonder if it's..." Walking to an adjacent cabinet he pulls out a yellow folder, "Ah Ha." Adding the printed photo into the yellow folder, he calls Lewis.

After Lewis answers, Baggs says, "Lewis, I have something here you need to see. Did you call Sy?"

"Ya, he can meet with us if we go now."

"Well come and pick me up. I'll be waiting," Baggs says, ending the call.

Knowing Lewis doesn't live too far away, he gathers up his leather flight jacket and hat and puts the yellow folder into his briefcase.

Just then his doorbell rings. "Already? That was fast," Baggs says to himself entering the living room. "Come in," he shouts walking to the door. The doorbell rings again. "Oh for crying out loud!" Baggs quickly opens the front door. Ready to blast Lewis for not coming in, Baggs looks down to see Marty standing in the opening. She holds up a small box wrapped in pink birthday wrapping paper.

"I thought you might need this," she says confidently.

Baggs takes the small package from Marty. Bewildered, he shakes the box, lifting it up to his ear. The box is heavy for its size.

"Just open it!" Marty barks.

Baggs carefully peels back the wrapping. It is a super deluxe curling iron. Baggs cracks an auspicious but quizzical smile.

"I don't know if you know much about us black folk, but we do just fine in the curly hair department."

"That's not what it is. I just used the box."

Baggs chuckles and opens the end of the box. After tipping the box on end, an old 8 inch crescent wrench slides into his hand. Puzzled, he looks at Marty.

"If all you've got is a pair of needle-nose plyers, I figured you needed some man tools. This will get you started," Marty smartly replies.

Marty looks around Baggs, and takes a peek into his house. Seeing the plethora of model aircraft, she pushes between Baggs and the door and storms into his expansive living room. Baggs spins around to try and intercept her before she accidentally breaks one of his prized planes. Before he is able to stop her, Marty picks up the single-engine Great Lakes biplane replica that sits on the long oak table.

"Marty, put it down. Please don't touch the planes," Baggs says as calmly as possible.

Realizing that she has crossed a line, she carefully places the aircraft back on the table.

"Sorry," she says apologetically.

Baggs slowly takes a seat on his ottoman, "We need to put you through flight school, first."

"Really?" exclaims an enthusiastic Marty.

"Really! But not now, I have to leave for a little while. I'll be back later, how about then we can get you started, if it's okay with your folks."

"Just mom. I don't have a dad. Well, I have a dad, I just don't know him."

"Tell you what, what about coming by this afternoon and I'll give you your first flight lesson over some milk and cookies?"

Just then, there is a light tap at the door. Lewis pops his head in the doorway mid-conversation.

"Make that a beer and you've got a deal," Marty says smartly.

Marty turns to leave and walks towards the door. As she does, she stares Lewis down, as though deciding whether or not he meets her approval. Making a brief assessment of the old man she warily approves and carefully scoots by him running toward her house.

"Have a few beers with the kids? Why not?" says Lewis jokingly.

"There will be no beer. Just milk and cookies. She

lives across the street. I think she comes from a pretty depressing home. No father and her mother doesn't seem to care too much what the kid does. It's really rather sad," Baggs sighs and starts out the front door. "Let's go."

POLINKA'S COFFEE SHOP

Polinka's is a hole-in-the-wall coffee shop on the edge of town. Baggs, Lewis, and Sy meet there often to talk shop. It is now just past one in the afternoon, and Lewis and Baggs have secured for themselves their usual table, a booth in the back corner of the restaurant.

Donna, the owner's daughter, is one of only two wait staff who works there. She is 38 years old and has worked for her father since she was young. She knows Baggs, Lewis, and Sy well. With a coffee pot in hand, Donna approaches their table.

"Just coffee, I suppose?" Donna says with sarcasm.

"Yeah, Sy will be here shortly," Lewis announces.

"Yeah, I figured that," Donna replies.

Donna pours three cups of coffee, leaving each a napkin and a spoon. From her apron she pulls out a handful of dairy creamers and places the small plastic condiments on the table.

"If you need anything else, you know where to find me," Donna says as she walks away.

Lewis, like Baggs, was also a pilot, however, not an astronaut. Lewis was one of the first pilots to fly the much-coveted Galaxy C5A back in 1969. His exceptional career as a transport pilot for the Air Force is overshadowed by his crazy conspiracy philosophies and unkempt appearance.

Baggs removes the yellow folder from his briefcase and places the closed folder on the table. Taking one of the creamers, Baggs empties the contents into his cup of coffee.

"I think we should wait for Sy," Says Baggs while he stirs his coffee.

The door's bell jingles and Sy enters the café and takes the seat next to Lewis, across from Baggs.

"You're here. Good. Baggs wasn't going to show me anything till you got here," Lewis says impatiently.

Baggs greets Sy with a simple nod and his usual friendly smile. Sy is in his late 40s. His full name is Simon Lazlo, but his friends call him Sy. Being a well-established jet propulsion lab technician, he speaks often about witnessing strange clandestine government operations at his workplace, Wright Patterson Air Force Base.

Sy is also known for being eclectic and verbose, which makes his tales amusing entertainment for Baggs and Lewis.

He is married to Norma, who is also a scientist and lab tech who works on the base. However, Baggs and Lewis have never met or seen Norma. Sy and Norma live in a large, beautiful home within a gated community at the other end of town. Dual income and no kids provide for them amenities that many with children can't afford.

Lewis and Sy crossed paths five years back at a UFO sightings conference in Chicago, another silly event Lewis continues to attend year after year. Realizing that they were from the same town, Lewis and Sy quickly became friends. Lewis introduced Sy to Baggs at Polinka's where the three have been meeting ever since.

As soon as Sy settles, Baggs slides the yellow folder to the center of the table. Lifting one corner, he pulls out the printed image Lewis sent him earlier. He spins it so Sy and Lewis can get a good look.

"Have you seen this before?" Baggs asks Sy.

Sy takes the photograph in hand and carefully looks over the details of the image. After a couple of moments, Sy shakes his head, placing the image back on the table.

"Where'd this come from? Where'd you find this? Who took it?" Sy asks, inquisitively.

"Lewis sent it to me this morning. A tourist captured the shot at the Grand Canyon, about a month ago."

Sy can't take his eyes off the image.

Baggs begins to smile, and with a nod he says, "Check this out." He pulls out an old newspaper clipping and places it on the table, rotated so that both Lewis and Sy can see the clipping clearly.

"See, look at how similar they are," Baggs says.

Lewis investigates the clipping for himself. Holding the paper clipping and printed computer image side by side.

"The newspaper picture was also taken by a tourist, from Grand Canyon Village, Arizona," Baggs says softly.

Rick Lord

Both Lewis and Sy look at the images, quiet and stunned.

"Identical. Only the newspaper picture was taken back in 1954," Baggs reveals.

PATH TO POWER

Anthological literature, even though still considered modern day philosophy, originates from the Elizabethan period.

John Dalberg Acton, or Lord Acton, was an English Catholic historian and Moralist of the late nineteenth century. It is he who is often quoted as saying, "Power tends to corrupt and absolute power corrupts absolutely. Great men are almost always bad men." It is this quote that best sums up the notion that the unbridled drive for power is the Achilles heel of any government.

STATE OF HUMANITY, PRESENT-DAY

With systematic abhorrent decline, the world has finally plunged itself into chaotic revolution. Violence is prevalent, many people hide away secluded in their homes. As nations fight against nations in record numbers, all-out nuclear war is only a matter of time, unless great change happens soon.

Hunger, famine and, disease plague every continent

to degrees never imagined. Terrorism has grown routine; and people traveling, no matter the destination, are apprehensive. On a near-daily occurrence, rumors of world war are at the precipice.

Class warfare, race relations, and religious groups clash with violent upheaval, week by week. The gap between the haves and the have-nots has never been so wide. Taxes are at an all-time high, while decent-paying jobs are at an all-time low. Corporations and manufacturing have long since relocated to other countries in search of lower operating costs.

Despite the repeal of the 2nd Amendment, the right to bear arms, gun violence is still America's number one killer. There are the few that have hidden away their guns, but to be caught with a firearm comes with serious penalties.

Governments of every nation have become so corrupt, no statesman is safe in public. The fear of reprisal, violence, and even the possibility of assassination have made the politician's life a high-risk position. Only but a few representatives actually care much about upholding the Constitution and its principles.

Backdoor deals and shady government cover-ups are commonplace. A country once admired, coveted, and cherished as the shining, city on a hill has declined to mere mediocrity, lack and third-world status. While its people struggle, the government grows with decadent elitism, continuing its scandalous appetite for more power. The great America of yesteryear is no more.

Located in the U.S. Capitol building, Kevin Rhodes' office is a hundred plus feet down the long brightly lit marble corridor.

Amanda Sykes is on her way to a previously scheduled meeting taking place in Kevin's office in just a few minutes. Amanda was appointed to the secret Lazarus VI Project at its inception. Her prior position with the Department of Defense makes her well qualified for the job of Deputy Director of Security.

At 27 years old, Amanda is in a league all of her own. She graduated summa cum laude from Harvard University. Her military career earned her Army Ranger Tabs, and she went on to become a Navy Seal, an accomplishment achieved by only eight other women.

Amanda's hair swings to the staccato beat of her black designer pumps. Walking fifty feet down the polished white marble corridor, she finally arrives at Kevin's office door.

Aside from her impressive resume, Amanda is a statuesque 5 feet, 11 inches tall. Slender, shapely and in perfect physical condition, Amanda could have easily chosen a career in modeling. High cheek bones, olive complexion, full supple lips, and a gorgeous smile are all framed in long full brunette hair.

It is however the highly-educated, militarily-trained internal workings of Amanda Sykes that truly set her apart. Dedicated and regimented, she has worked hard to earn her place as an extraordinarily talented intelligence officer for the U.S. Government. Trained as an Intelligence Officer for the Department of Defense, her position as Deputy Director of Security for the Lazarus VI Project could not be more appropriate.

Amanda taps lightly on the door while at the same time entering. She steps inside the plush, ornately-decorated office of Kevin Rhodes. "Good morning gentlemen," she greets.

Kevin Rhodes, Lon Thompson, and Pat Vance all acknowledge Miss Sykes with cordial nods. Enveloping the room with her enigmatic presence, she sets her laptop case down on a cherry wood coffee table directly in front of a long overstuffed brown leather couch.

Sharing the couch with Lon Thompson, Amanda composes herself at the opposite end. She retrieves her laptop from the computer bag.

Originally appointed by President Adam Parkston for the position of Secretary of Health and Human Services, Kevin Rhodes held the position for only eight months. During that time he was surreptitiously repositioned as Chief Liaison Officer for the Lazarus VI project.

It was his connection and association with the powers that be at M-PAC laboratories that proved advantages for his title re-designation. His new-found position with the controversial program is making him both admired and hated among his colleagues.

Already enlisted to the project are a few, hand-selected top government officials. Kevin's job has been to assemble a special committee for the project. And that special committee must include congressional support.

Kevin Rhodes, Amanda Sykes, and Lon Thompson are in charge of the screening process. The challenge has been, convincing those they select to sign a non-disclosure agreement. Anyone divulging information to the public or to the press would be catastrophic.

With a bigger-than-life personality, Kevin has made his position well recognized within the dog-eat-dog Washington machine. He has one objective; initiate and implement the Lazarus VI Project as quickly as possible, at whatever cost.

Considered quite handsome, with dark wavy hair and greying temples, his 6 foot, 3 inch stature and deep radio announcer voice feed his narcissistic personality. Kevin has been married for 22 years to Linda, his stay-at-home wife and mother to their two teenage boys. Kevin spends little time playing the role of husband or father.

His syrupy-sweet, condescending persona can only be described as sickening. A majority of the women that truly know Kevin steer clear of him like the plague. There are those who have yet to observe his woman-izing antics and who fall for his disgusting, plastic Hollywood-type charm.

Ironically, it is that same sleazy persona that has helped propel Kevin from a short term quasi-position of Secretary of Health and Human Services to Chief

Liaison Officer for the Lazarus VI Project.

Kevin's office appears as though he has been there for years. Oversized brown leather couch and chairs, ornate teak tables border a nine by twelve foot Persian rug. It is an office setting fit for any proud CEO managing a Fortune 500 company. On the end tables, warm light spills from three gold and black onyx lamps.

Kevin is clearly a man who has a propensity for the finer things in life. Collectable artwork, including a gold-framed original by Van Gogh, garnish the Wedgewood grey and mahogany wood-trimmed walls. His lavish office more resembles an Oxford library than that of a government servants' place of legislation.

Kevin rests against the front of his four thousand dollar leather-topped executive desk. With his arrogant, power hungry persona leaching out of every pore, he lights his Cuban Belicosos Finos cigar. As Kevin takes his first puff, white smoke billows, forming a white cloud of importance surrounding his head. If only there was a mirror for him to validate the man of great power he believes himself to be.

Lon Thompson, Director of Homeland Security, sits at one end of the long leather couch. At 6 foot, 2 inches and as thin as a light pole, Lon's voice is oddly deep and graveled for his stature. As Amanda settles in, he politely offers introductions.

"Amanda, across from you is Secretary of State, Pat Vance, I don't know if you two have formally met," Lon asks. Amanda smiles and nods.

"Yes, I know who you are, nice to formally meet you."

Pat Vance is in his late sixties. Standing at only 5 feet, 6 inches when wearing lifts in his shoes, Pat thinks too much of himself, like many of his fellow politicians. He is pleasing to the eyes, despite his age and small stature. He has a full head of white hair, trimmed and combed to perfection, contrasted by his fake tan. He smiles at Amanda, revealing his obviously-bleached white teeth.

"Very nice to meet you formally, as well," Pat says to Amanda with a wink. His movie star-like persona, self-assuredness, and political status are all tools he uses to convey his importance to anyone he may encounter.

His heavy makeup and light dusting of translucent powder are his attempt to turn back the clock on his nearly 70-year-old face. Should the opportunity arise, Pat is always ready for any impromptu on-camera interview. This might explain why Pat spends such an inordinate amount of time hanging around the Capitol's news-camera-laden rotunda.

Beginning to feel a little uncomfortable with Pat's leering stare, Amanda breaks her silence.

"Whoever does your makeup should be fired. You look like you belong in a casket," she says with uncanny wit.

Pat's arrogant flirtatious smile immediately fades to embarrassment. Clearing his throat and a fiery attempt at redirection, he asks gruffly.

"When are we going to get this show on the road?"

"We're waiting for Byron," Kevin says, exhaling another puff of cigar smoke.

Amanda looks on quizzically as she does not know who Byron is. "Byron Sutter, House Ways and Means Committee," Lon interjects.

Amanda acknowledges with, "Oh, Okay."

Kevin continues with another puff from his cigar. Amanda indiscreetly covers her mouth and nose, offended by the heavy smoke in the room.

"Is there a window we can open?" Amanda asks pleading for fresh air. "The cigar smoke is making me sick to my stomach."

Kevin obliges by extinguishing the cigar in an ashtray on his desk. The room remains uncomfortably quiet as the team awaits Byron's arrival. As usual, Byron is late to the meeting. Finally, the office door opens and Byron enters. He carries his briefcase under one arm while ending a cell phone call with the opposite hand. Byron clumsily enters, accidently slamming the door behind him. "Sorry," Byron says.

Byron takes a seat in the leather chair next to Pat Vance. Byron sets his briefcase down while getting settled. Kevin nods to Byron with a slight smile.

"Would anyone like a cup of coffee? Water? Brandy?" Kevin offers his guests. No one accepts Kevin's offer. Pat looks down at his watch, sending out an obvious signal that time is of utmost importance.

Taking the cue, Kevin begins with introductions, "Byron, you know Lon and Pat. Across from you is Amanda Sykes, she is Deputy Director of Security. Amanda, this is Nevada Representative Byron Sutter.

He's Chairman of the House Ways and Means Committee."

"How do you do, I don't think I've ever seen you around," Byron says to Amanda.

Amanda responds with a soft voice, "I guess you can say I work mostly behind the scenes."

"Now that everybody has been introduced, let's get down to business."

Kevin hands to Byron the non-disclosure agreement. "We need you to sign this, Byron." Byron takes the form and looks it over briefly.

"Why am I signing an NDA?" Byron asks.

"We're forming our committee for the Lazarus VI Project and everything we discuss about the project must be kept confidential from here on out. Okay with you?" Kevin asks.

Byron appears a bit perplexed as he carefully looks over the document. After a few moments, he finally concedes and signs the form and hands it back to Kevin. Kevin picks up a manila folder from his desk. Before handing the folder to Byron he reiterates.

"Again, just for the record, what we are going to be discussing today is for your eyes and ears only. It is imperative nothing is to be said about any of this beyond this room. Is that understood?"

Byron shrugs with apathetic agreement as he is still in the dark over what exactly the meeting is about. Kevin then passes the manila folder to Byron.

Kevin asks Byron. "Have you ever heard of or know

anything about the Lazarus VI Project?"

Byron shakes his head, implicating 'No.'

"Our meeting here today is for your benefit, Byron. I think you'll appreciate what we have to share with you. Have you ever heard about a vaccine called Chryzinium?"

Byron again shakes his head.

"If there was a vaccine that cured every disease, would that be of interest to you?" Kevin asks. "What if I told you there was such a vaccine? Would you want to hear more about it?" Kevin continues.

Byron says, "Yes, I'm interested."

"Byron, this is an opportunity like no other. We believe what we have here is a vaccine that will end most, if not all, disease as we know it. If that's the case, don't we owe it to the American people to get it out there and save lives?"

Byron nods, 'Yes.'

"The Lazarus VI Project was developed so we can get this amazing vaccine into the hands of those who need it most. If we can truly help those that are diseased, shouldn't we? But, why not use this as an opportunity to secure our ailing healthcare program at the same time? Federal Health Pay (FHP) is a disaster. It has led to national budget deficit issues that are crippling our country. If properly implemented, the project could fix healthcare and eliminate the national deficit in as little as 42 months."

Byron looks over the few pages that are in the folder.

As he thumbs through the documents he begins to shake his head. "I don't know what any of this stuff is. What are we talking about here?" Byron sits up in his chair and continues, "With all of the pork spending, entitlement programs and over-inflated federal expenditures, we're financially drowning. It's not the deficit I worry about, it's the debt. He retorts with political indignation.

Kevin has conveniently loaded the folder with an abundance of nonrelated documents to confuse Byron. They all pertain to the Lazarus VI Project, but they are completely out of context.

Kevin smiles and responds with his usual sarcasm. "That's exactly what I'm talking about. We have no way out as it stands. Even if we had a 100 percent tax rate, we wouldn't be able to pay the debt down. But with the implementation of the Lazarus VI Project we can fund it all, while at the same time helping good Americans enjoy healthy lives. You want to hear more?" Kevin asks Byron.

"Where are you going with all of this?" Byron asks, annoyed.

Kevin continues. "The program is simple; it's merging the Chryzinium vaccine with a one-of-a-kind atomically powered micro Radio Frequency Identification implant. An R-F-I-D chip."

"Seriously, there isn't a person alive that would go for having a RFID chip put in them," Byron says with outrage.

"This is where I think you're wrong," Kevin says smugly. "If you had a dying loved one that had only weeks to live, you mean to tell me you wouldn't agree to a little implant for a new lease on life? Hell, you'd do the implanting yourself. We're not talking about a microchip they use for cats and dogs. This thing is about as high-tech as you can get."

Byron looks over the paper work in the folder trying to make sense out of the contents. It is obvious to Lon and Kevin, Byron is carefully contemplating the proposal.

Lon reaches down alongside the couch and picks up his briefcase. From inside he pulls out a large portfolio. He opens the portfolio to the third page and spins it around so Byron can see the graphic on page 3.

The word 'Vul-Stream' boldly titles the top of the page. Under the title, printed in color is an artist rendition of a micro-sized ID implant chip.

The enlarged technical illustration is of a transparent capsule, resembling a capsule that one would take orally. However, it is made of a very delicate crystal-like glass and capped on both ends with anodized black micro-conductors. The atomically powered black circuit board appears to float within the center of the transparent envelope. Its actual size is ten times smaller than a grain of rice.

Byron reaches out and takes the artwork in hand, carefully studying the graphic while sitting back into his seat. After a moment, Byron lowers the portfolio, slowly shaking his head, disturbed.

Kevin smiles at Byron, "Electro Linear Infusion. It's the first-ever atomic RFID chip."

Byron knows the RFID chip conspiracy has been around for years, but now he understands that this is becoming a reality.

With a vaccine such as Chryzinium coming to the forefront, the frenzy would result in financial chaos. Pharmaceutical companies worth hundreds of billions of dollars would be in ruins. Medical research laboratories and manufacturers of medical equipment would dry up overnight. The financial world as we know it would be strained beyond repair. Not to mention the population explosion that would inevitably take place.

The European Union, Canada, South America and the United States formed the World Health Organization for one cause. Their promise was to fight world hunger and global disease. With Chryzinium, the cure for disease is now for the first time a real consideration.

From day one the challenge has been to create a sufficient funding avenue by which healthcare is not only affordable but can also maintain some form of profitability. As it is now, the system is far from sustainable and continues to run in the red year after year.

Kevin's proposal would guarantee a sizable return on the initial investment. The Lazarus VI Project is poised to take over the present healthcare system with the added benefit of making tremendous profits. Along with a technological oversight control implementation, the project would grow exponentially.

"Byron," Kevin directs. "Please take out the one-page summary of the project and read it. It's titled 'Summary,' you can't miss it. Please read it for yourself. This is a great program."

Byron finds and removes the summary from the clutter of the folder. While Amanda, Lon, Pat and Kevin look on, Byron takes a few moments to read about the Lazarus VI Project.

LAZARUS VI PROJECT SUMMARY

After extensive studies concerning all aspects of implementing this type of a cure-all vaccine to the public, it was determined a system for tracking and monitoring recipients of Chryzinium, would also be required. This simple device will monitor and track those in the new system via a personal FHP member number.

As each participating individual is monitored and tracked via their personal Vul-Stream RFID code, he/she would be charged accordingly for the vaccine depending on income level. This would create a revenue stream that by design is fair and equitable. The revenue would be automatically drafted and go straight into the FHP system on a predetermined monthly schedule.

As more individuals are diagnosed with disease, more will request the Chryzinium vaccine. All revenue from the project would be earmarked solely for

M-PAC Laboratories, pharmaceutical companies, medical research labs, and many other medical facilities nationally.

The plan includes merging these entities with the program to further the production and distribution of the Chryzinium vaccine and the Vul-Stream chips.

Currently it is M-PAC Laboratories that is solely responsible for the development of Chryzinium and Vul-Stream. Soon, the need will outgrow supply, not just nationally, but globally.

A sworn commitment from a select group of governmental committee members is all that is required to initiate a successful launch of the project.

Project implementation is pending.

After Byron finishes reading the plan, he looks up with concern and asks warily, "How much will the vaccine cost? Do we know it's safe?"

"We're running trial tests as we speak. We should be complete in a couple of months. If the Chryzinium vaccine does indeed prove itself to be a viable healthcare product, we are creating the most effective healthcare program known to mankind. This makes Vul-Stream an acceptable means by which we can monitor the program's success.

Normally I would say this is a perfect time to run a proposed trial period through Congress to prove the viability of the Lazarus VI Project, as a whole. But, I know Congress will not see it that way. Not yet, anyway," Kevin states.

Prior attempts to pass a bill requiring an implant RFID chip have failed miserably. And even with the new vaccine and all it has to offer, the proposition would still fail, at least on the Senate floor. Kevin believes and is betting, the public would agree to an RFID chip if there was a chance to live a long, disease-free life.

"Congress would never sign into law a requirement for the American people to get any RFID chip shoved into their hand, foot, arm, leg, forehead, or wherever," Byron responds.

"Byron, you're absolutely right. With Congress the way it is, the backlash would be unimaginable, it would never pass. But, if we let the people decide, we'd be circumventing Congress all together."

Byron is becoming disturbed as he is actually considering this absurd proposal.

"Where did this Chryzinium vaccine come from? And again, how do you know it's going to be safe for everyone?" Byron asks.

"Good questions. Now we're getting somewhere," Kevin says, smiling self-righteously before continuing. "Chryzinium was originally developed, or should I say, discovered by a government scientist while working at the Los Alamos National Laboratory about thirty years ago. I have been to the M-PAC Laboratories on numerous occasions, isn't that right Amanda?"

Amanda nods and smiles agreeing with Kevin.

"Their top priority has always been public safety. Why do you think it's taken 30 plus years to develop? Like I said earlier, the beta-testing program is well underway and so far the results are proving to be a hundred times better than expected," Kevin takes a moment before continuing. He has Byron eating out of the palm of his hand.

"Our biggest concern is M-PAC. Will they be able to develop the vaccine in mass quantity? Will they be able to keep up with production demands? In time, without the help of other labs throughout the country it may be destined to fail just by attrition. That is why we have to act now. The vaccine is now able to be duplicated, and to be frank, the President wants this, and he wants it now. He is staking his reputation on this entire project."

Byron is now beginning to understand why he's been invited to the meeting. He will be the cushion between the opponents and the proponents. The plan will be to ram The Lazarus Project down the throats of every American via executive order. In other words, President Parkston will bypass Congress all in the name of legacy.

Kevin smiles and continues, "The Lazarus VI Project is only for a temporary trial period and only for a select group of individuals. If the vaccine works as well as promised, we'll go before Congress and get an approval vote then."

Byron thinks carefully about what has been shared

with him. He looks around at Lon, Pat, and Amanda, hoping to garner some visual support.

"What do you want me to do?" Byron concedes.

"I need you to get Phoebe on board with this, but only when the time is right. Phoebe doesn't know any of this yet and I want to keep it that way. At least not until just before Parkston and I meet with the Lazarus VI committee members. And that includes you. I want Phoebe there at the meeting however, I don't need her banging my door down before then. I know her. She'll think we're out to steal every single person's privacy. And I know she would be the first one to run to the press. We can't have that.

"Lon, Amanda and I, as well as a few others, are going to the M-PAC Lab. We're giving you and some of the others that are on the committee a first-hand look. I want you to go with us. I even want Phoebe to come along. What do you say?" Kevin asks.

House Republican Leader Phoebe Wescott has but one friend on Capitol Hill, Byron Sutter. Unfortunately for Byron, she's not in attendance at this meeting.

After a moment of consideration, Byron nods, 'Yes.'

Frustrated and anxious over hearing all of this, Byron stands, throwing the Vul-Stream conceptual art book onto the coffee table in front of him.

"I don't know. I have to think about all of this," Byron says while standing and walking toward the door.

Lon's face is resting in his hands as he realizes, Byron is not yet totally convinced. Lon intercedes, "Look, it's already in the works and it's going to happen. We need to know you're with us."

Kevin makes a quick glance to Lon and Amanda. He then shouts at Byron, "Sit down, please!" Amanda abruptly stands and meets Byron at the door. Just as Byron opens the door, Amanda reaches out with her right hand and pushes the office door shut.

Byron looks at Amanda, confused. He turns and looks at Lon and Kevin anxiously. Lon holds his arm out, directing Byron to return to his seat.

Putting her arm around Byron, Amanda walks him over to his chair. Looking directly at her, Byron asks, "Who are you, anyway? What's going on here, Kevin?" Amanda doesn't say a word as Byron reluctantly sits.

Byron turns to Pat Vance hoping for support, "Pat, what's going on here? Are you going to stand by and just watch what's happening without saying something?"

Pat coifs his white hair, "I don't like it, I don't like it one bit, but it has to be done. I'm sure we'll all be glad we did this," Pat admits.

Byron shakes his head, disgusted, "So am I the first out of 535 of us in Congress to be forced into agreeing to such a project? Are you strong-arming everyone into the program like this?"

Amanda walks back over to the couch and takes her seat. Byron looks over to Amanda and then back to Kevin, hoping to hear an explanation.

"Who is this lady to be pushing me around?" Byron demands.

"Byron, we want the best of the best. It is you and others like you who believe in the Lazarus VI Project that can get this thing up and running," Kevin placates.

"Who says I believe in the project?" Byron asks snidely.

"Oh, come on. I saw it in your eyes. We have a chance to save hundreds of thousands of lives, and you know it. That's why you're here. We value your expertise and your ability to talk to others. In fact, when the time comes, we need you to talk to Phoebe Wescott. We need her too," Kevin pacifies.

"The fact is, Byron, Phoebe is not going to listen to me. She hates me, you know that. We don't need all of Congress, we just need you and Phoebe. When the time is right, I want you to sell the project to her," Kevin says.

Lon leans up and sits on the edge of the couch. He looks directly at Byron, "You're going to have to make her see what we see, plain and simple. We need you because you and Phoebe are friends. It's more than saving lives and revenue; it's also a national security issue. There's a lot riding on the project; a lot more than you can imagine. I cannot have her or anyone going to the press about this. From here on, Byron, the security of the entire project lies directly on you."

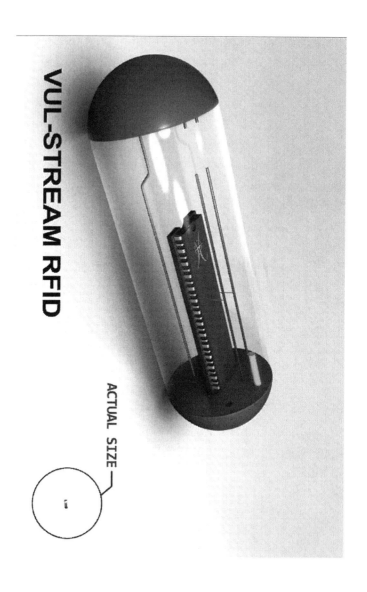

VUL-STREAM RFID

ACTUAL SIZE

Rick Lord

DESCENDING
PLIGHT

John Gussman, single and only 29 years old, is considered the nation's top biochemist at the National Scientific Laboratory in Los Alamos, New Mexico. With three degrees in biochemical engineering, John's renowned scientific acumen earned him great prestige within the industry. This year is momentous for John. Authoring five published research papers pertaining to biogenetics, John is at the top of his game.

A devoted believer in creationism, John spends much of his off-duty time researching biblical science. With his vast scientific intellectual prowess, he uses expertise in archeology and human genetic mapping to support his beliefs. However, it is his interest in theology that many times puts him at the brunt of much scrutiny among his peers.

An accomplished pilot and single engine airplane owner, John often flies to Arizona's Grand Canyon area to dig and explore. Specifically, he searches for evidence to substantiate his belief that there is, indeed, a God, and it is He that is the creator of the universe.

Hiking, or riding by pack mule, he and his close friend, Arnie Swinth, often spend weekends exploring the Grand Canyon and outlying desert areas. At least twice a year the two take archeological excursions together traveling to destinations they consider to be hotspots for proof of creation.

John has recently learned of a cave that supposedly hosts intriguing petroglyphic carvings of a race of giants that once roamed the earth. John is on his way back to the Grand Canyon to see this cave for himself.

It's Friday, June 27th, 1996. John's four-day hiking trip has finally arrived. A few days in the canyon to do what he loves – hiking, exploring caves, collecting rocks, and discovering artifacts. It is 6:00 AM, John is at the airport prepping his single engine bush plane for the 175 nautical mile trip to Tusayan.

Arnie resides in the town of Tusayan, Arizona, a small town south of the canyon. Arnie and John have been planning this trip to hike to the bottom of the canyon for months. This time they plan to enter the canyon via the South Rim.

Arnie, an astrophysicist and archeologist, lives only a few miles from the Grand Canyon Tusayan airport. Tusayan is approximately 7 miles from the South Rim and 2 miles from the park entrance.

Once in the air, John's flight is scheduled to take only an hour and a half. The flight has been smooth with no headwinds that would slow him down. The time is 8:10 AM and John is rapidly approaching Tusayan.

Arnie sits in his truck drinking a hot cup of coffee. Parked just off the airport tarmac, he waits patiently for John. At last John's plane makes a shallow bank to the left just beyond the canyon rim. John has lined up his plane for a straight-in approach to runway 21. Arnie watches as the white-and-black bird touches down.

John taxies the plane to the transient parking area designated for visiting aircraft. Shutting down the engine, and unbuckling his seatbelt, John pops the door open and steps out of his plane. Wearing sunglasses and a tan ball cap, John turns and pulls his oversized backpack from behind the pilot seat.

Only 5 feet, 9 inches tall, John easily makes up for his average height with his broad shoulders and well-toned muscles. John's masculine physique, good looks, and rugged outdoorsman appearance are not what one might expect a scientist to look like. Along with his charming, boyish smile, it's hard to believe John has remained single all these years.

Looking to the far side of the parking area, John sees Arnie's truck parked on the grass. Locking and securing his plane, John heads towards the truck toting his large pack and sleeping bag. John approaches Arnie's truck and throws his survival gear into the back. Walking back around the truck, John opens the door and climbs inside.

"You made it," Arnie says.

"Did you think I wouldn't?" John smiles and they shake hands.

"Every time I watch you come in, it makes me wish I could fly."

"You can; just takes lessons."

Arnie shrugs, starts the truck and the two drive off toward the canyon's park entrance.

The South Rim is where many of the canyon's spectacular viewing sites are located. However, the two men are on a quest, not a sight-seeing tour. Looking into the back of the truck through the rear window, John sees all of Arnie's junk. Backpacks, shovels, picks, inflatable rafts, and dozens of rocks picked from the side of cliffs litter the bed of the truck.

"I see you brought everything you own for the hike down," John sarcastically comments.

"I'm not taking all that with me. I'm leaving most of it in the back of the truck."

"Are you sure?" John exclaims, again being sarcastic. "I hope we're not riding mules down, again."

"No mules, not the way we're going. Gonna be a long hike to Chuar Butte. We're gonna take Desert View Drive east to Comanche Point and hike down from there."

"Comanche Point was off to my left as I flew in. Isn't Chuar Butte where one of the airliners that collided back in the 1950's crashed?"

"Yup," Arnie says.

Arnie is 14 years older than John and worked at Los Alamos National Science Lab with John until he retired early a year ago. Greying around the temples, Arnie is beginning to show signs of sun damage to his face.

Arnie's tan face and arms stick out from his worn tee-shirt. Riddled with holes and stains, his shirt depicts a very faded American flag printed on the front. Good companions with a propensity for the peculiar, Arnie and John travel often together.

Last year was a trip to Mount McKinley, and the year before that it was a trip to Nepal. John has hiked the Grand Canyon before, but he has never made a four-day long excursion with the extreme conditions they're about to experience.

The sky is clear and the temperature is already a blistering 88 degrees. The drive along Highway 64 takes only about 20 minutes to reach Comanche Point. It's the hike down and back that'll take a majority of their time.

Comanche Point jets out of the western face of the Cape Solitude Plateau. Hiking down to intercept Beamer Trail for the long hike to Chuar Butte is no easy task. This is especially so when hiking down from that location, unless, of course, one is highly experienced and in top physical condition like John and Arnie.

Arriving at the 4x4 trail head to Cape Solitude Plateau, Arnie drives the rutted path as far as he can. Unable to go any further, Arnie pulls his truck off to the side.

"I thought you were going to buy a Jeep?" John asks.

"Yeah, one of these days I will. It seems I only need one when I'm with you."

John and Arnie both exit the truck and walk back to the bed. John grabs his backpack and sleeping bag. Arnie rummages around in the back of the truck. He grabs his backpack and sleeping bag combination and his favorite hiking stick. Carved and hewn from solid hickory, Arnie hikes nowhere without it; especially now that he is getting older.

The men gear up and ready themselves for the long, arduous hike down. Strapped to their belts are their water canteens, Bowie knives, and side-arms.

"You have your compass?" John asks Arnie.

"Yeah."

After adjusting their packs, they begin their trek down. For this estimated 18-mile hike, the treacherous terrain, snakes, scorpions, coyotes, badgers, and mountain lions are the least of the two hikers' concerns. It's the heat Arnie and John dread. The water they bring is the only water they'll have until they reach the Little Colorado River.

No other souls occupy the trail they are blazing. No city slicker tourist would be foolish enough to take on such a mission. Nonetheless, the untamed landscape of the 6000-feet deep canyon is majestic and awe-inspiring beyond words.

However, the four-day hike before them is daunting. The surrounding cliffs of the canyon begin to tower higher and higher above them with each passing hour. The magnificence and splendor of the canyon engulfs their keen senses in a way that can only be expressed as spiritual.

This is what it must feel like to walk the surface of an alien planet. The wildlife, while indigenous to the area, would no doubt appear unfamiliar and strange to most.

Frightened by human presence, snakes slither back under their rocks, and scorpions dart across their path, cautiously ready to defend their territory as the two slowly hike down the inhospitable landscape.

Every hour the two take time out for a much needed rest. Carefully rationing their water, John and Arnie each take small sips. Drink just enough to stave off dehydration, no more. Removing it from his pack, Arnie takes his plastic pouch containing his hand selected ingredients of trail mix and chocolate chips and eats small portions.

The only other food they bring is dry packaged goods and freeze-dried foods. Just add water, heat and eat. Their Bowie knives and side-arms are their only protection from predators. It's a much unique type of self-defense when hiking in such extreme conditions. After the short 15-minute break, the two weekend archeologists are back on their journey downward.

"When we get to the fork where the Little Colorado and Colorado River meet, we'll be just below the wreckage of the 1956 airliner crash on Chuar Butte. The crash site is a thousand feet up the face," Arnie says.

"I've always wanted to see that," John says with excitement.

"Just west is Temple Butte where the Pan Am Constellation crashed," Arnie adds.

With each passing hour, the men descend another 400 feet lower into the canyon. The temperature grows more intense throughout the day. As their trek continues, the canyon's temperature exceeds 110 degrees.

The end of June is probably not the best time to hike to the floor of the Grand Canyon. But for John and Arnie, it's the only time available for this trip. Even though John is in excellent shape physically, and well prepared for the 120 degree temperatures they expect. Arnie is older and slower.

As the two hike down, Arnie is already thinking about the trek back up to the top. Having done this before, he knows all too well, the stresses on his body will be taxing. This is a new hike for them. The two have never descended to the canyon floor via Comanche Point.

"Coming back will be fun," John says sarcastically.

"Yeah, we'll have to be aware of our time spent on the floor. The hike back will easily take two, if not three, times as long."

Eleven hours have now passed, and the men have finally reached the Little Colorado River. It's close to sundown up on the rim, but down in the canyon, it's already twilight. The two unpack and ready themselves for the first night of their adventure. Both John and Arnie are prepared for the cool nights and bring down-filled sleeping bags that are not only lightweight but plenty warm.

Sterno is the hikers' choice for cooking. Open the can, light it with a match. With a few small rocks surrounding the can of Sterno, a small pan will easily sit over the top of the flame. Add some stream water and a couple of freeze dried pouches of chicken, potatoes and stuffing, and a much desired dinner is ready for the hungry hikers to enjoy.

The night air cools quickly. Now that the men have finished eating, they bed down to get some much needed rest for the next day's 7-8 hour hike to Chuar Butte. Even though Chuar Butte isn't their ultimate destination, it's is a great spot to use as a base camp.

They are exploring the rumored petroglyphs located in two caves just opposite the northeast side of Chuar Butte. This is something that has been exciting John's curiosity for months. This is his reason for the expedition. As he lies there, warm in his sleeping bag, he hears Arnie beginning to snore. The trek was indeed exhausting but John's adrenaline still courses through his veins.

The petroglyphs he's heard rumor of are Egyptian. They tell of a race of giants believed to be those who were of the biblical 'Nephilim' (angels cast out of Heaven). It is these giants who were supposed to have roamed the earth long before the great flood of Noah's time. They are believed to be the offspring of the Nephilim.

If this is true, it confirms there was a great flood,

and of course reasonable proof of the Bible's account of creation. Soon, John's eyes also begin to close as exhaustion overcomes him.

FIRST DAY ON THE FLOOR

As daylight breaks over the canyon floor, John's sense of smell awakens him from sleep. Arnie is already awake, and has coffee cooking in the small cook pan. Arnie sees John's eyes blink open.

"I'm making coffee," Arnie says.

The aroma of freshly-brewed coffee is too great a lure for John to ignore. Finally sitting up, he struggles out of his sleeping bag. Sleeping fully-clothed not only saves time getting ready, it's a matter of survival. There's no telling what could come upon them during the night.

It's only a matter of time before the heat of the day cloaks the canyon floor. John stands and stretches, taking in the fresh morning air. Reaching down to his pack, John takes the short line loose that holds his tin cup. Holding the cup out, Arnie pours him a welcomed cup of hot coffee.

"We're going to have to get a move on if we're going to make any time before the heat," Arnie declares.

Not being much of a morning person, John quells the prattle by sipping his hot brew while taking in a panoramic view of the canyon floor. Something catches John's eye off in the distance – a silhouette of what looks like another human being.

"We're not alone," John says with his garbled morning voice.

Arnie takes this as a cue to also stand and look where John is gazing. The figure is hard to make out, but it does look like there is another person in the canyon. He or she must be at least a quarter of a mile away from John and Arnie.

"By himself? Can't be. No one in their right mind would be down here by themselves," Arnie says with concern.

"We're heading that way, so I guess we'll see," John replies.

John finishes his cup of coffee and shakes out his cup. Tying the cup back onto his pack, John begins the task of stuffing his sleeping bag back into its tiny nylon sheath. Once Arnie finishes eating his trail mix, he is also ready to go, having his backpack loaded. With the Sterno now cooled and put away, Arnie takes his empty canteens to the river to replenish.

In just a matter of minutes, John follows suit and walks to the rivers' edge and refills his water supply. Jerky and dried fruits are John's preference for sustenance. With jerky in mouth, John is ready and eats on the go.

The objective is for them to reach the Colorado River, at a place they can set up a more permanent camp. A quick dip in the river will certainly help cool and refresh, if they can get there early enough.

Along the way, they'll stop for their 15 minute rest,

and snack on some trail mix. Too much food on the stomach while hiking makes for a lethargic journey. However, now on level ground, the hike is a bit more tolerable, though the uneven terrain still plays havoc on their ankles and knees.

It's not quite 9:00 AM, and the temperature is already in the triple digits. Another long day of hiking is ahead for the two adventurers.

The human figure Artie and John thought they saw earlier is nowhere to be seen. The canyon is notorious for playing tricks on the mind, especially so when reflected heat rises from the ground. Was there really somebody in the distance, or was it an early morning mirage? All they can do is wonder. Chatter among the men is minimal. It is essential that they utilize their energy wisely.

Eight hours later, they reach the confluence of the Little Colorado River and the Colorado River. The Beamer Trail parallels the south side of the Colorado River heading west. However, John and Arnie will be heading east along the south side of the Colorado the following day. Still early, they make for themselves a place to set up camp.

"We have one day to find the caves, that's it," John points out as he strips the pack from his shoulders.

"We'll head out at day break," Arnie confirms.

As the two set up a place to bed down, John sees just beyond an outcropping of rock, the figure of a man. He's only a couple of hundred yards away. John points the man out to Arnie. Arnie turns and looks intently for a couple of moments.

"He's Indian," Arnie announces. John is relieved to know Arnie sees the man as well. Placing both index fingers into his mouth, John lets out a screeching whistle in hopes of getting the gentleman's attention. Slowly, the man turns. Looking up onto the low, flat plateau, the man reacts to John's call with a wave. John waves back to the gentleman.

"He seems to be by himself. That's odd," Arnie observes.

"Maybe he'd like to join us for dinner," John suggests.

"Crap, I think he's actually heading our way. We're not a restaurant you know," Arnie says, rolling his eyes.

John and Arnie continue to set up their camp. Arnie breaks out the can of Sterno to heat their supper. He picks up a few rocks to build a cook surface for the small sauce pan. John unloads his pack, searching for something tasty in the freeze-dried aisle. Arnie reminds John they only have enough rations for their allotted time in the canyon.

John responds with a more neighborly approach, "We should at least offer him something if he's hungry."

Arnie doesn't feel it is their responsibility to feed other campers; especially those hiking the floor of the Grand Canyon. "I would think since this guy is hiking around down here, he'd certainly have brains enough to bring his own grub," Arnie grumbles.

John removes from his pack two packages of the

noodle and chicken entrees and hands them to Arnie. Pouring water from his canteen into the pan, Arnie mixes the evening meal in with the water, heating it over the makeshift stove.

Just as the noodle and chicken feast begins to steam, the stranger steps up over the layered rocks. His high cheek bones and reddish complexion, proudly represents his Native American descent. His long white hair is pulled behind his head and lying on his back as a beaded ponytail tie gathers his mane back away from his craggy face.

Standing slightly taller than five feet, the old man smiles and with a big grin says with a hint of Navaho in his voice, "Smells like dinner."

John stands and greets the old man with a handshake and a smile.

"Would you care to join us?" John offers.

John looks back and smiles at his companion, who is sitting on his pack stirring the stew in the pan. "This is a good friend of mine, Arnie."

Arnie looks up at the old man, forcing a smile. The stranger smiles back, stretching out his hand for a handshake, which Arnie now feels obligated to return.

"How do you do? They call me Sani," the stranger introduces himself.

Arnie immediately retorts, "Does that mean hungry, me wantum food?" John gives Arnie the look of shame. Sani responds with a smirk.

"No, Sani means 'old man.' I'm from the Navajo

Indian Painted Desert Reservation. It is east of the canyon."

"Nice to meet you. Please have a seat," John offers.

"Thank you kindly, I think I will sit with you. But no thank you on the food; I have dried deer meat in my pack," Sani says as he sits.

John turns back to Arnie, "He's got his own food."

Arnie smirks. Sani takes off his pack and sets it down on the ground next to him.

Sani looks at Arnie with an odd stare. When Arnie looks up at him, Sani makes his offer. "Wantum smokem peace pipe? Tradum puff on pipe for biteum of stew," Sani retorts with his own sparkle of sarcastic humor. Sani is on to Arnie's grumpy ways. Sani laughs.

"No worry, pale face, me not wantum hand out," Sani says, exaggerating his native tongue jokingly.

Chuckling, John follows suit and seems to relax. Trying to make light conversation, John asks Sani if he knows the area.

"Of course he know the area, he just told you he's from the Navajo Painted Desert Reservation. Do you think he was on his way to the mall and made a wrong turn?" Arnie quips and smiles at John with a cocky 'gotcha' look on his face.

"You come to hike the Grand Canyon. Not many people today come to experience the great beauty of the land," Sani states.

"We're here to explore the caves of the Egyptians. Tomorrow, we're hiking up the Colorado River, heading east. Are you familiar with the caves?" John asks Sani.

With a bewildered look on his face, Sani responds, "Yes but why are you hiking up the river that way? Hard to get to caves going that way."

"I thought you knew where these caves are," Arnie says to John.

"I do," John defends. "Sani, why can't we get there hiking along the Colorado River heading east? I have my map. Let me show you."

John opens the back panel of his backpack and pulls from it his map. John folds the map into a square, exposing the thin red line marking their intended pathway to the infamous site. John points out the marked trail to Sani.

"This won't get us there?" John asks.

Sani tilts the map to get a better look. John points to the red line, showing Sani their planned route. Sani looks to John and smiles, "Much easier to get there from Little Colorado River."

Taking the map, Sani taps with his weathered brown index finger at the point of confluence of the Little Colorado River and the Colorado River. Sani slides his finger back up the Little Colorado an inch or so. "Go up this way. Much easier," Sani tells John.

John looks at the map, studying carefully the pathway Sani is suggesting. John looks to Sani, and with a quizzical look, asks him the question that has been on his mind, "Have you seen these caves before?"

Sani nods yes. John smiles with a deep sense of relief.

"If the stories are true, the trip will definitely be worth the effort. Supposedly there are markings on one of the cave walls depicting giants. Have you seen them?" asks John.

"I have seen them many times. But, you should know, they are cursed."

"What?" Arnie shouts.

Sani smiles, "No, cave not cursed. I just screw with you."

Arnie laughs.

Sani continues, "Caves are there. You will find them interesting."

John smiles at Arnie, delighted by what the old man has just verified.

Sani smiles and slowly stands to his feet. "I should be going," he says to the men. "Thank you for your kind hospitality. You have a safe journey."

John stands as well to see the old man off. "You down here in the canyon for just the day?" John asks.

"No, I'm down here for a while. Much to do," Sani says softly. The old man picks up his pack and throws it over his shoulder. John nudges Arnie to say something.

"See ya' around, old man," Arnie finally says.

"You can count on it, pale face," Sani replies, laughing. He turns and walks to the rock ledge and disappears out of sight as he climbs back down off the plateau.

"Finally. Let's eat and get some sleep. It's going to be an interesting day, tomorrow," Arnie says to John.

The two will cross the Little Colorado approximately

400 yards south of the confluence of the Colorado River. The hike to the caves will take a half a day. The climb is less difficult going the way Sani instructed, and this comes as good news.

Nonetheless, it will certainly be worth whatever the effort is, knowing for sure that the caves do indeed exist. For them to see the mysterious petroglyphs will be a once in a lifetime opportunity.

The next morning, John and Arnie quickly gather and pack their supplies. Getting prepared for another day of hiking comes with a special air of excitement this early Sunday morning. Barely daylight, the two set out on their quest, munching on their trail mix and dried meat breakfast.

Crossing the Little Colorado has its obvious risks, but, by backing up the river a few hundred yards, the men are able to cross without the use of rafts. However, they do plan on getting plenty wet. Even early in the morning, the cool water will be refreshing.

Nearly to the opposite side of the Little Colorado, Arnie slips on a rock and tumbles into the water. The fall causes Arnie to let go of his prized walking stick. Quickly regaining his footing, Arnie gingerly stands. He realizes his treasured cane is now floating downstream, heading straight for the mighty Colorado River. There is nothing he can do. He watches as his hiking stick floats away.

"Not much of a walking stick if it doesn't keep you from falling in the river," John laughs.

"Yeah, ha ha. Thanks," Arnie responds with subtle indignation.

Arnie is soaking wet from the chest down. His backpack is drenched, but the heat of the day should dry things out. Fortunately, Arnie always ties his sleeping bag to the top of his backpack, keeping his bedding completely dry.

Blazing a new trail over such uninhabitable terrain is exhausting even for the most physically fit. But doing so with 40 pound packs and 10 pound gear belts is grueling.

Still, they are resolved to climb cliffs and rock faces. However, this is nothing compared to going by way of the Colorado River. For this, they are thankful for Sani's wisdom. The extreme conditions still wear heavy on the men. Stopping every so often to recalculate their heading, the men use the time to rehydrate and replenish their energy with trail mix, proteins, and granola.

Three and a half hours into their journey, they have finally come to their final climb. From this point, they hike to the top of a narrow plateau to an outcropping of layered rock. The two ancient caves should be located on the northeast face of the rock. A short climb of thirty more feet should bring them to the entrance of the caves.

Thankfully, they will not have to scale a sheer 90 degree cliff. The face of the final climb provides a more attainable 60 degree ascent. The face is mostly igneous rock with crevasses to use as handholds and footings. Not needing to carry all of their supplies with them to the top, the men leave their packs at the base.

The only item John insists on bringing along is his camera, and five extra rolls of film. Carefully buttoned and secured in the top pocket of his cargo shirt is the camera. John has divided the five rolls of film in the rest of his pockets. This leaves John's hands free for the climb. Arnie wears his jeans, tee shirt and his hiking boots. 'Hike light' has always been Arnie's motto.

Readying himself for the climb, John looks over at Arnie and notices he is sitting on the ground and leaning against the cliff face. He looks as though he is not feeling well. His face appears pale and pasty.

"Are you okay?" John asks

Appearing dazed, Arnie says in a weary voice, "I don't feel too good right now." He dips his head down between his knees.

"What's wrong?" John asks, walking over to him.

Arnie does not respond.

"Hey are you getting sick? You wanna rest for a while?"

Arnie raises his head slowly. "I don't know, I just feel real light-headed."

"You want some water?"

Arnie places his head between his knees again. John is becoming more concerned over Arnie's condition. He's thinking he may be suffering from heat exhaustion, or maybe worse.

With no trees to provide shade, John walks over to their stack of supplies and from his pack he removes a small blue tarp. With sticks and rocks, John creates a rudimentary awning to help shade Arnie. He hopes removing direct sunlight may help.

More than an hour has passed, and Arnie is still not showing signs of improvement. John is becoming a bit more frantic. Arnie isn't responsive and is now curled up in a fetal position. The color in his face has turned ashen and his lips are a greyish-purple color.

It is becoming gravely obvious that Arnie is in need of medical attention. John makes the difficult decision to go in search of help. He remembers that Sani said he was going to be in the canyon for a while. If John could just find him, Sani might be able to help.

John takes Arnie's sleeping bag and covers him and then uses his own sleeping bag as a pillow for Arnie's head. Taking from Arnie's belt 2 canteens of water and some granola, he places them directly in front of Arnie's face so he can see that they are within reach. He takes Arnie's 38 revolver and lays that in front of him as well.

"I don't know if you can hear me or understand me, but I gotta go get help. Here are some supplies. I'll be back as soon as I can, okay?" Arnie still does not respond. Even though his eyes are open, he lies motion-less and shivering.

Taking with him a minimal amount of supplies to expedite his journey, John turns and looks back at his buddy one last time before heading back down. John reluctantly begins his long trek to the river's confluence in hopes of finding Sani.

John climbs down the last of the layered rock formations onto the small beach that parallels the east side of the Little Colorado River. He finds himself almost at the same location where he and Arnie originally crossed the river earlier that day.

Already the day is waning. There is no way he'll make it back before nightfall.

John wades once again across the river to get to the west side. It's the only way back to where the men last saw Sani. John begins his hike towards the confluence. The hike is taking its toll. Even though in good health, his body is in dire need of rest. From a controlled hiking pace to a walk that's more of a stumble, John trudges onward.

John hears something off in the distance. It sounds like a man singing and howling. Is he so exhausted he is hearing things? John can do nothing but continue on, in hopes it is someone who can help.

Rounding an outcropping of rocks that about puts him into the river, John's attention is suddenly diverted when he sees the glow of a fire off in the distance.

"That's where the whooping and hollering is coming from. Great, the crazy Indian is six sheets to the wind! The old man is half in the bag on fire water. He's not going to be in any condition to help!" John mumbles, exasperated.

Sani stops dancing long enough to recognize John approaching. He waves at John and hollers, "Hello, my friend!"

Cautiously, John approaches. He sees in the bonfire light, Sani has a walking stick that looks oddly like the one Arnie lost to the river earlier that day. The golden brown hickory-wood walking stick is as recognizable as a 1963 Corvette Stingray. 'He must have fished it out of the Colorado River. Obviously accomplished while still sober,' John thinks to himself.

Out of breath, John blurts out, "Arnie is sick. Can you help me? Or are you too drunk?"

Smiling back at John oddly, Sani responds.

"Drunk? Who, drunk? I no drunk. I no touch spirits," he laughs.

Both relieved and surprised, John apologizes, "I just thought the way you were dancing around and whooping and hollering, you were, I don't know, having yourself a little party."

"I have party, yes. But no need spirits to have party. Just need big fire and new walking stick."

"Yeah, I can see that," John says sheepishly without mentioning to Sani the stick's previous owner.

"You say friend is sick. Where is he? What's wrong with him?"

"He's on the ledge just below the caves. I don't know what's wrong with him. He's not doing good, I can tell you that."

"Well, let us go."

"It's getting dark," John informs.

"Yeah, that is what happens when sun go down, it get dark. That why I have fire stick. You have fire stick?"

"What? A fire stick? No, I don't have one."

Sani walks over to his backpack and pulls out his fire stick.

"You no have fire stick?"

John is somewhat amused by Sani's sarcasm.

"Ah, fire stick. You mean flashlight. Yes I have a flashlight."

"Well, let us go to friend. We see what is wrong."

Sani walks over to the fire and kicks the logs around, spreading them out to extinguish the fire. Then he picks up his pack and throws it over his shoulders. With his new walking stick and flashlight in hand, Sani begins hiking up the Little Colorado River.

John takes a deep breath and prepares his mind for the long hike back to Arnie. Turning on his flashlight, John follows behind Sani, slowly catching up to him.

"Maybe one of us should go get help?" John asks.

"No talk, walk," Sani retorts.

John rolls his eyes and follows the old man's lead.

ARNIE'S LEDGE 3 ½ HOURS LATER

Although it is dark now, Sani and John have managed to make their way in spite of the treacherous journey. Breaking over the layer of rocks that rim the ledge where Arnie lays, Sani and John finally emerge. John points his dim flashlight at Arnie and immediately realizes he hasn't moved an inch.

John yells out to his friend. "Arnie, I found Sani.

You okay? Can you hear me?" Arnie doesn't move or respond to John's voice.

Fearing he may be dead, John and Sani quickly walk over to where Arnie is lying. John kneels down to check Arnie's wrist for a pulse. Sani asks John, "Is he alive?"

"Yeah, he's alive. I don't know what's wrong with him. I thought it might be heat exhaustion. But, not if he's still like this."

Sani reaches down and peels Arnie's eyelids open. He takes a moment to study Arnie's condition. He turns to John and asks. "When last time he eat?"

"I don't know. This morning, I guess. Why?" John asks.

"I think he has the Sugars."

"The Sugars? What are the Sugars?"

Sani smiles at John and says softly, "Diabetes."

"He's not diabetic."

Sani looks back down at Arnie again. "Hmmm! I think he has the Sugars."

"How would you know he has the Sugars, I mean, how do you know he's diabetic?"

"His breath. Smells like fruit."

Sani removes his pack and sets it on the ground. "Hold fire stick."

John takes hold of Sani's flashlight and shines it into his backpack for him, while Sani digs around inside.

"Why you come down here in canyon not prepared? He could have died. Hiking canyon in his condition, he should know better. The Sugars is bad disease, nothing to play around with."

"I don't think he's got diabetes. Or the Sugars, or whatever it is you call it," John argues.

Sani removes from his backpack a small leather pouch. Unraveling the thin leather tie, Sani pulls from the pouch a few small leaves. Removing another smaller pouch, Sani opens it as well and puts several leaves into it and shakes the pouch vigorously.

He removes the leaves and places them into the palm of his hand. Each of the leaves have a shiny, light powder coating on them. Holding in his palm the leaves, he asks John to drop a small amount of water from the canteen onto the leaves.

Sani, clasping his hands together and in a rotating manner, he carefully rolls the leaves into a small ball. Taking the wet ball of leaves in between his forefinger and thumb he carefully opens Arnie's mouth and inserts the ball of leaves between his cheek and lower gum.

"He needs to keep leaves right where I put them. Don't let him spit out. He will come around in a few minutes. As soon as he does, get yourselves some rest. Sleep tonight here and head back to top of canyon in morning. You hear me?"

Dumbfounded, John has no choice but to concede with an agreeing nod.

"I see you down here again, I shoot you both with bow and arrow," Sani threatens as he repacks his pouches.

John looks around where Sani is kneeling and observes, "You don't have a bow and arrow."

"I very resourceful, I make one. Then shoot."

Despite the situation, John chuckles.

Sani stands to his feet and asks, "You got any food?"

"Yeah, we got food, just no Sterno. It got wet when Arnie fell in the river."

"Sterno? What Sterno?"

"It's what we cook with. It provides heat," John responds.

Sani looks on with disgust, "You not know how to make fire?"

"Well, kind of, just never had to before. Rub sticks together right?"

"You got matches?"

"They got wet, too. Once they dry out they might still work."

With exasperation, Sani continues. "Ay, Ay, Ay, Tenderfoot! Here, I show you how to make fire."

Sani bends down and reopens his pack. He reaches inside and grabs a small object.

"Open your hand," Sani insists of John.

John complies, and Sani drops into his palm an old worn Zippo lighter with 'Grand Canyon' engraved on the face. John looks up at Sani, disappointed.

"A lighter? Some Indian you are," John quips.

"You wanna spend night rubbing sticks together, be my guest Kemosabe. Lighter much faster. Gift shop sell these for $15.00. A little high priced, but what you expect for tourist trap?"

Sani closes his backpack and stands just as Arnie begins to come around.

John looks over at Arnie and then looks up at Sani, "What was that you gave him?"

"Old Indian remedy."

Arnie begins to fumble with his tongue and the foreign material he has in his mouth.

"Keep that in your mouth. No spit out. Leave between cheek and gum all night. You hear me?" Sani sternly says to Arnie, leaning over him.

Arnie reluctantly repositions the ball of leaves in his mouth as directed by Sani. "Yeah," Arnie says with a garbled voice.

Sani shines his flashlight into his own face so Arnie can see him clearly.

"Hey it's you. What are you doing here?" Arnie asks, recognizing Sani.

"I should ask same question. You very sick man. Should be dead. You have the Sugars. Diabetes. You know that?"

"Yeah, how'd you know?" Arnie asks.

"Sani know much. Remember what I say, you two meatheads get out of here and get to top in morning. Drink much water and eat on way up."

"You knew you were diabetic and you didn't tell me!?" John asks Arnie, angrily. Arnie doesn't say a word.

Directing his next question to Sani, John continues.

Rick Lord

"What about his blood sugar?"

"Just go quick, like water down mountain stream. There, I speak Indian for you. Make pale face happy," Sani laughs. "He'll be fine tomorrow."

Sani stands and dusts his pants off. "I go now," Sani smiles as he grabs his pack, walking stick, and flashlight. "I will see you again, my friends." He walks off, soon disappearing into the darkness.

"Was that my walking stick?" Arnie asks.

"No, it's his walking stick now."

"When we get back, you're seeing a doctor. I can't believe you'd risk hiking down here as a diabetic!" John reprimands.

Arnie lies back with his arm over his forehead.

"I'm going to take your pillow. It's my sleeping bag."

Arnie carefully and quietly climbs inside his own sleeping bag. John does the same.

"This is my last hoorah," Arnie confides.

"It's not your last hoorah, you just need some medical help."

"No, it's my last hoorah," he reiterates.

"Just see a doctor. Okay?"

"I have been seeing a doctor. I have pancreatic cancer."

"What?"

"I'm dying. They gave me less than a year," Arnie admits.

"Why didn't you tell me?"

"I knew how much this meant and I didn't wanna disappoint you."

"How are you feeling now?"

"A lot better. I guess whatever this stuff is that the old Indian guy gave me is working."

"Yeah, go figure. Well, what do you say we get a little shuteye and in the morning we get the heck out of here?"

GENETIC TRANS-MUTATION

MK-ULTRA, HISTORY OF MADNESS

M-PAC is an acronym for MK-Ultra, Passive Atomic Chemical. MK-Ultra was a classified name from Germany's 1929 scientific project created to explore the possibilities of genetic purification.

The scientific processes that initiated the pursuit of genetic purification actually began in the city of Freiburg im Breisgau, in the state of Baden-Württemberg, Germany in 1929.

While pursuing medical studies at the Albert Ludwig University of Freiburg, Heinrich Stoll was experiencing major breakthroughs in the sciences of genetic reengineering during his final years at University. His reputation as a student there was generally upstanding, but he excelled especially in the fields of chemistry and biochemistry.

Upon graduation, Heinrich was invited to attend a lecture by Richard Kuhn at Kaiser Wilhelm Gesselschaft for Medical Research in Dahlem. Richard Kuhn had become a renowned advocate for the studies and hopeful implementation of *Genetic Purification* through chemical remapping using a mixture of synthetic and organic base elements.

It was there that Heinrich had the opportunity to study at the Institute of Anthropology, Human Heredity, and Eugenics. As a result, he learned primarily through his collaborative efforts with other scientists developing and implementing acute scientific systems and ideologies. This, he believed to be for the greater good of mankind.

In March of 1934 MK-Ultra faded into obscurity. However it was at that time that Heinrich was approached by an assistant of Richard Kuhn in regards to a recently established branch of the institute for advanced biochemical testing, referred to as "Research Unit C."

This is where he was able to get a strong foundation in the metabolic sciences of genetic reengineering. Unfortunately, it was Kaiser Wilhelm Gesselschaft that also functioned as a front for a number of secluded groups in collaboration with the Third Reich. It is this reason that led to the facilities' clandestine operations due to its connection to the "Für Immer" project.

Through this branch of the institute, Heinrich was able to collaborate with the extremely knowledgeable

Professor Otto Lutz. It was Lutz who was instrumental in the creation of Unit C. His knowledge of genetics and feverish desire to construct a superior, Aryan race was the driving force for this unit.

During this period, genetics became quite popular for both scientific discussion and exploration. Even though genetics was still in its primitive state, it did lead to many early developments that laid the groundwork for future breakthroughs in metabolic restructuring.

In fact, it was these very breakthroughs that led to the reemergence of MK-Ultra in 1945. It just so happened to coincide at the same time there was a multinational push to find a cure for chronic rheumatic diseases plaguing people in that era.

In order to accelerate the process, Unit C conducted a series of scientific tests to determine positive or negative consequences, if any, by utilizing a newly manufactured compound element. Combining transuranic sulfides to a prime element was, at first, more about disease control than anything else.

The findings were astounding. A new compound element termed CTS-235, the scientific classification for Chromium Transuranic Sulfide, was discovered. By adding chromium, thought to be the missing agent, something quite unforeseen resulted.

Unfortunately, the compound fell far short of its anticipated disease-curing abilities. However, its combined properties demonstrated something remarkable. At the very least, the element proved that human DNA structure could be manipulated. In fact, CTS-235 could alter DNA to the point where it could more easily accept a replacement synthetic version DNA, if such a structure could be produced.

Even though control of disease was a secondary benefit of the scientific research, the idea all along has been to create a super race of humans. And could a super race of humans be born out of a synthetic DNA? When their findings proved DNA could be manipulated via CTS-235, MK-Ultra mysteriously vanished into thin air. And Unit C ceased to exist. Interestingly, Professor Otto Lutz also disappeared. However, Richard Kuhn and Heinrich Stoll met their demise in August of 1946, at the hands of a faction who were tied to remnants of the Third Reich, for reasons unknown to this day.

It was a multi-government, resurrected, scientific offshoot of MK-Ultra that operated from 1945 to 1965. It was referred to as MK-Ultra SA, which emerged out of the Middle East. This mindset was quickly adopted throughout Europe and the United States. It was thought at that time their efforts to create a super-human race was within reach.

President Harry S. Truman demanded that scientists from Russia, Germany, and the Middle East come to investigate the cause of the July 4th, 1947 UFO crash in Roswell, New Mexico.

These scientists, with backgrounds in dark-matter engineering, served in positions on the U.S. scientific research team, known as "Majestic 12." During the foreign scientists' time in New Mexico, UFO studies would dominate the 1945 to 1965 MK-Ultra SA program.

The U.S. had other concerns. What if a super race could be achieved, and what would this do in terms of the military force, whether it be our side or the enemy's? Some believed the two middle-Eastern scientists were basically hired as spies by the United States to research the goings on with MK-Ultra SA.

Even with supported efforts from German and Russian scientists, MK-Ultra SA's attempts continued to fail miserably. However, genetic purification was not their only goal.

During the winter of 1965, the efforts of Majestic 12 brought forth again the highly-controversial reemergence of CTS-235. Shortly after CTS-235 was reintroduced, MK-Ultra SA was once again surreptitiously terminated. And the scientific teams from abroad drifted into historical obscurity.

In the late 1990s, the Unibihexium Micron Particle was discovered. Not willing to curse the new discovery with the ill-fated MK-Ultra designation, the U.S. government formed M-PAC ("MK-Ultra Passive Atomic Chemical") as a cover. The discovery of the Unibihexium Micron Particle virtually changed chemical science from the ground up. Reengineered by M-PAC in 2001 by renowned scientist, Doctor Sigmund Hess, Unibihexium Carbon was created making the element replicable in mass quantity. MK-Ultra was, in a sense, back. However, construction for the M-PAC facility didn't begin until May of 2004 and was not completed until January of 2010.

It was the discovery of Unibihexium Carbon Particle that was determined to be the missing element necessary for the illusive fountain of youth serum. It was that missing element, Unibihexium Carbon that was responsible for reenergizing the defunct MK-Ultra program, putting it back on the scientific radar.

'Unbihexium Carbon Particle' or 'UBH' was accidentally discovered in the Grand Canyon by Doctor John Gussman, who gave the element its name. Ironically, it was he who received the notoriety for this great scientific breakthrough just by being in the right place at the right time.

Later, Doctor Sigmund Hess, used the element in combination with CTS-235 to form a vaccine called 'Chryzinium.' Oddly, Doctor Hess is one of the founding pioneers of the 1967 MK-Ultra program. He now holds the position of head physicist and is in charge of operations at M-PAC Laboratories.

Doctor Hess is tall, slender, grumpy and not well-liked. At 72 years old, he is often thought of as a present day Adolf Hitler. This due primarily to his rigid, iron-fisted rule over the facility, his thick German accent, and, of course, his Nazi-like beliefs.

M-PAC LABORATORIES

For years, the existence of Area 51 was denied by our government. That is, until lately. Now they have come clean. In fact, they not only acknowledge Area 51, but have revealed that it is a primary detachment for Edwards Air Force base, even posting signs stating such.

Now the same deceptions are being circulated for mysterious M-PAC facility. It is spoken of in conspiracy circles as a Dark-Government Laboratory hidden somewhere in the southwestern desert.

According to the few clandestine documents accessible because of the Freedom of Information Act, we now know the obvious. Our own government claims there is not, nor has there ever been, an M-PAC laboratory facility. However, plenty of eyewitness accounts suggest otherwise.

That being said, there is some proof the facility does exist. There are the occasional leaks from the inside and a tiny piece of evidence popping up every now and then that does verify its existence.

It has been said M-PAC lies 100 feet below what many believe to be Dreamland (Area 51). It spans 2 football fields in length and width, with 40 foot ceilings in the main bay. The massive complex has only been seen by those who work there, a select group of scientists and a few government officials who have visited the site.

The only way in and out of the site is by air. Those who have had the privilege of flying to the facility can only speak of desert landscape below, just before the plane windows are blacked out.

It is interesting that Area 51 would be considered

the most probable location for M-PAC. It is the only government facility in the desert that has a landing strip long enough for jet transport planes and an overly large hangar. The hangar incorporates ultra-high security, ten-story elevators and NORAD (North American Aerospace Defense Command) caliber tunnels that stretch for miles underground.

Witnesses state that the only entrance to the lab itself is by way of 'the Dove.' These are M-PAC's private, unmarked planes similar to the surreptitious Janet airliners that transport workers to and from Groom Lake on a near-regular schedule. The Dove is rumored to be the only access for M-PAC Scientists, employees, and the occasional visiting dignitary.

THE M-PAC FACILITY

Twenty feet above the main lab floor, three quarters of a mile of steel-grated catwalk surround the bay. Armed military personnel, scientists, and lab technicians traverse the sterile, underground compound around the clock, seven days a week.

Armed guards, wearing grey anti-contamination uniforms, carry their weapons in the ready, keeping vigilant watch over the premises at every corner of the complex. Perched 30 feet above and in the center of the bay, armed guards occupy an overhead watchtower with a 360° vantage point. With their birds-eye view of the lab, they keep the underground facility secure with the strictest of rule.

All visitors, whether government or otherwise, must carry top-secret clearance credentials to enter. Only the purple marked areas of the skywalk are divided into Sectors 1 and 2. It is only these areas that visitors are permitted to enter.

Three armed guards are appointed to every six visitors. No visitor is allowed to venture anywhere on their own. Guard supervision is mandatory at all times, including bathroom facilities.

Sectors 3, 4, and 5 are only accessible by those who carry the highest of Top Secret security authorizations.

Project scientists and lab technicians work in the main bay below. Wearing white anti-contamination suits, they communicate with each other via sign language, unintelligible to visitors to the lab.

Like watching a choreographed rhythmic dance, the team of 35 to 50 men and women silently mill about their respective work stations. The polished white floors mirror the hundreds of yards of clear tubing in which a transparent pinkish/grey liquid flows.

From large sterile polished aluminum vats, four-inch glass pipes stretch back and forth connecting containers to pumps and then on to other containment vats throughout the facility. The web of clear tubing carrying the liquid can easily be thought of as pop art gone awry. The high-pitched whine of pump motors vibrate the steel grated structure above.

Polished stainless steel entry doors, spaced every 60 feet, line the outside of the catwalk. Each door is marked with a sequential numeral beginning with the number 210. Under each numeral is a hieroglyph type symbol referred to as the sign of the Shafutah. In fact, the sign of the Shafutah insignia marks all equipment and is even etched in floors. The strange insignia adorns every upper left crest pocket of all uniforms within the facility.

At the far end of the bay, a bright red beacon rotates, announcing the start-up of the turbine generators. The generators charge huge banks of batteries, which power centrifuges and water-cooling pumps at the far end of the bay.

Exiting room 210, Doctor Thomas Ecklund walks hurriedly toward the metal stairs leading to the lower floor. Immediately following Doctor Ekener, Doctor Sigmund Hess exits the same door, heading the opposite direction along the catwalk.

Door 216 slides open as Doctor Hess approaches. He enters the dimly-lit room and takes a seat in a black swivel chair that sits directly in front of a bank of three video display monitors. Just beyond the monitors, clear plastic drapes the far wall. Construction on a new part of the facility is underway, disrupting the doctor's space.

Mounted flat into the desk top in front of him, a flat control console, housing an assortment of knobs and lighted buttons, lies at his fingertips. A joystick protrudes from the left side of the controls.

Taking the joystick with his left hand, he begins to maneuver the remote camera mounted at the other end. Known to those within the facility as "Satan's Eye,"

Camera 22 is located 50 feet below the main bay. It is there the camera keeps constant vigilance on the highly radioactive room referred to as the "Bell Cell." It is in this deadly, radioactive room where Unibihexium Carbon is atomically refined.

The monitor on Dr. Hess' left shows an image of a set of digital displays, as he pans camera 22 to the left. Dr. Hess leans in toward the monitor to take a closer look. With his right hand, he takes his index finger and pushes a small, white, square button. The image on the screen is magnified 10 times its original size.

He observes the reading displayed on the video screen. The image on his monitor is that of an electron spectrum analyzer. The analyzer depicts a small digital screen that portrays a set of red, flashing, sequential numeric values.

The spectrum analyzer readings a range from 0.00135 to 0.00141. As he studies the readings, he presses the talk button on the console, engaging the small microphone that is directly in front of his mouth. With his thick German accent, he makes his announcement over the bay's intercom system. "Wilhelm Avercamp, Wilhelm Avercamp, come to two one six, schnell!"

Within seconds, the door of the control room opens and Wilhelm Avercamp enters. "I don't understand, the readings, they haven't changed! They haven't gone up or down in more than an hour," Doctor Hess says, angrily. Avercamp walks over to where Hess is sitting and leans in toward the monitor so he can better read the numeric values.

After giving careful thought to what he is observing, he turns to Hess. "I don't think the numbers are correct. I think it's the analyzer that is giving false indications. Look at the other monitor."

Doctor Hess turns to look at the center monitor. The image on the screen depicts the bluish glow of water from 30-feet-deep, Olympic-sized swimming pool. The massive tank cools the hundreds of nuclear reactor rods encased in tubes that reach from the bottom to the top of the reservoir.

"If there was problem, we'd see the same reading here. There's nothing wrong," assures Avercamp.

Hess is still not satisfied with Avercamp's diagnosis. "If that is indeed the case, I want the analyzer pulled from the Bell Cell and replaced. I will not rely on assumptions. I want to know for sure what's going on in there."

Avercamp quickly complies with the Doctors orders, "I'll have it replaced immediately, Doctor Hess." Avercamp turns and exits the control room.

Satisfied with this response, Hess swivels his chair around and stands to his feet.

Only half of Room 216 is a control room with monitors and electronic gadgetry. The other half is a private lounge area. It is in sharp contrast to the technical side of the room. Separated by a heavy, floor to ceiling burgundy velvet drape, the lounge resembles a stateroom more than an office.

It is decorated with teak and mahogany walls and fine paintings. A large faux window displays a back-lit landscape image of an open field. Throngs of butterflies in flight are projected in 3-D, giving the window a sense of depth and realism.

Leather chairs, a table, and a lamp surround the center of the room. Doctor Hess enters and sees the silhouette of a man sitting in a brown leather chair. Walking to a bureau cabinet, Doctor Hess removes a syringe from the top drawer. Rolling up his left sleeve, he gives himself an injection. Afterward, he turns to the gentleman in the chair and smiles, saying softly, "Just a short time to go, Master."

LIFE ALTERED

THE FEDERAL HEALTH PAY SYSTEM

Federal Health Pay (FHP) is a government, single-payer healthcare system. It was implemented during the time when public outcry over the complexities and high expense of the previous government healthcare system created heavy financial burdens on families. Unfortunately, this new system is proving to be even worse.

The government pays for doctor visits, hospital visits, surgeries, and lab work. However, the average out-of-pocket expense is still 35 percent due primarily to co-pays. Not to mention, there is a national flat tax of 6 percent based on gross income.

Even this is not enough to support the overstressed FHP system. Waiting times for surgeries can be as long 2 years depending on age and income level.

Prescriptions, however, are paid by an adjusted co-pay system which is based entirely on income. The concept is simple, the higher the income, the higher the co-pay. Because not all pharmaceuticals are FDA-approved, many may come from other countries and are not covered by FHP.

The advantage being that any out-of-country (OOC), non-approved pharmaceuticals can still be legally purchased. The caveat: OOC pharmaceuticals are purchased at the buyers own risk and can only be distributed by an authorized FHP physician. If there are complications due to the administration of a particular pharmaceutical classified as experimental, all healthcare costs from that point on, are then the sole responsibilities of the using individual and/or family member.

HILLSDALE FALLS MEMORIAL MEDICAL CENTER 1:55 PM

A small storage room marked 'Staff Only' is just a few doors down from Doctor Heller's office. The room is crammed with a single round table, four schoolroom style chairs, and volumes of medical journals stacked on shelves. An old hospital computer and black desk phone sit on the table.

Too old to be suitable for staff use, the archaic electronics are no doubt discards after the hospitals' technological upgrades. The overhead fluorescent lights cast their brilliant glow, yet leave the storage room void of any sense of warmth or comfort. Much of the 5th floor staff use the room to sneak away and make private calls or take short naps.

A few of the hospital staff actually use the room

to conduct research. However, in Doctor Heller's case, he is there to conduct a very important private phone conversation.

He sits hunched over the table while cupping his cell phone with both hands, carefully concealing his conversation. After a few moments of discrete dialog, he completes his call. Settling back into his chair, he thinks carefully about the lucrative circumstances that have been presented him. Resolutely, he stands and exits the room.

Rebecca paces Doctor Heller's office, her mind occupied with concerns for Emily. She observes the doctor's many certificates and acclamations adorning the office walls. Her anxiety is mounting by the minute as she waits for the doctors' return.

Rebecca removes one of the certificates from the wall to get a closer look. Just then, Doctor Heller enters his office. Rebecca turns and hands Doctor Heller his framed document, irritated with how long it's taking to see Emily.

"I want to see my daughter. Where is she? Take me to her. Now!" Rebecca demands.

Politely taking the certificate from Rebecca, Doctor Heller smiles and waves his arm in a pleasant gesture towards the door, "Come with me."

Doctor Heller takes the lead, "We're taking the elevator to the 6th floor, ICU." He explains. Down the hall and to the right, they reach the elevator.

At the 6th floor, the elevator doors open and Rebecca

and Doctor Heller emerge. With urgency, they walk towards Emily's room.

"It's on the right, room 611," Doctor Heller informs Rebecca.

Approaching the door, Doctor Heller stops, "Before we go in, understand, she's got a lot of monitoring equipment attached to her. We are still waiting to hear from imaging. We're monitoring everything we can right now."

Just as they are about to enter, a female nurse approaches them, hindering their entrance.

"Doctor Heller, the results from imaging just came in. I accessed them from the computer in the room. They are on the screen now."

Doctor Heller nods and smiles, "Thank you. Let's take a look and see if they've found anything." Doctor Heller and Rebecca finally enter.

ICU, ROOM 611

Emily is surrounded by monitors displaying her vital signs. Blood pressure, pulse-rate, and oxygen levels depict a very alive young girl. However, the wires and tubes attached to her, make her resemble a machine. A clear tube is taped to Emily's face as it extends into her mouth and down her throat. An intravenous line is taped to her wrist feeding her electrolytes.

Emily shows no sign of consciousness. The room is filled with the sounds of her respirator and the rhythmic blips emitting from her heart monitor.

Rebecca walks over to her comatose daughter. Tears again begin to flow down her cheeks. She covers her mouth, stunned. She extends her hand forward and gently brushes Emily's hair back from her forehead.

Doctor Heller has taken a seat at the computer screen that is mounted to the wall via an articulated arm just above the small rolling desk. Pulling it closer, he studies the screen intently. After a few moments of careful examination, he turns his attention to Rebecca.

Rebecca looks over to Doctor Heller. She can tell something is terribly wrong.

"What is it? Tell me what's wrong with my girl," she demands, her voice quivering.

"Is your husband coming back soon?"

"Why, what's the matter with Emily?"

It's never easy for a doctor to inform anyone of bad news, especially when it concerns a child. Doctor Heller clears his throat and again asks, "When's your husband returning? I need to talk to both of you."

Rebecca is becoming irritated by the doctors' stall tactics. "Tell me now. I want to know what's wrong with her."

Doctor Heller finally concedes and quietly says to her, "Emily has a brain tumor."

Rebecca stands as still as a statue. It is as though she didn't hear a word the doctor said. It takes a moment for the news sink in before Rebecca can speak, "You must be mistaken."

She slowly turns back to her daughter in shock.

"I wish I was," Doctor Heller says, standing to his feet.

Rebecca leans down carefully embracing Emily amongst all the wires and tubes that drape over her. Just then Mark enters, escorted by the same nurse. Turning to Mark, Rebecca begins to cry as she explains to Mark with her voice shaking.

"She has a brain tumor."

"What? No, no, no!" Mark exclaims in shock.

Doctor Heller interjects, "The tumor is small, but what troubles me is the location. I'll be honest. Treatment for any brain tumor comes with a huge amount of risk and possible lifelong neurological complications."

"What do we do?" Mark asks.

"In Emily's case, any surgical procedure is going to be invasive, to say the least. There will be a greater than average chance she will experience serious complications. But I don't know for sure, not everyone experiences the same side effects. So it's impossible for me to predict a sure outcome, no matter what the treatment. I want to talk to both of you about something. Would you follow me back to my office?" he asks sympathetically.

Mark and Rebecca both look at Emily, still reeling from the shock of the news. Rebecca wipes the tears from her cheeks with her hand. Mark puts his arm around Rebecca to comfort her.

"Where's Taylor?" Rebecca asks Mark softly.

"He's downstairs in the waiting area," Mark replies.

"Can we leave him there?" Rebecca asks the doctor.

"He'll be fine; I'll send Nurse Sprague down to get him some snacks."

The three exit ICU and head back down to Doctor Heller's office.

DOCTOR HELLER'S OFFICE

Mark, Rebecca and the doctor enter. "Please, have a seat," Doctor Heller offers. Numb from the news, Rebecca sits slowly. She is no longer combative and demanding, but is now subdued and quiet.

"So what do we do? What options do we have?" Mark asks.

"That's what I'm going to discuss with you. I had my suspicions. That's why I left you earlier, Mrs. Shae. I went to go make a phone call."

Doctor Heller takes a seat in his large, leather chair. He folds his hands in front of him and leans forward on the desk.

"There is something new, a new program, a new vaccine. In fact, the vaccine is so new; Emily would be the first person ever to have it administered. I think Emily fits the criteria," Doctor Heller explains.

"So, what is this vaccine?" Mark asks.

"Its clinical name is 'Chryzinium.' It's thought to be a kind of miracle cure. Since this has never been tried on anyone, we don't know what complications or side effects there may be, if any," Doctor Heller continues.

"How do you know about this vaccine, whatever it

is you call it, and how do you know it'll work?" Mark asks with concern.

"The scientific community has been working on the vaccine for a number of years and it is very promising. However, the FDA has not approved it yet. They are waiting for reports back on beta test subjects. Emily would fall into that category. Even though lab tests prove excellent, I don't know what to expect until we administer the vaccine and see what it does. Like I said, our only other alternative is surgery. I'm afraid the prognosis using an operative approach is not a good one," he hesitates before continuing.

"Something you need to know, whether Chyryzinium works or not, the cost is steep."

"How steep? What do you mean by steep?" asks Mark.

"The cost is fifty thousand dollars."

"What! We have to pay fifty thousand dollars to have my daughter become a guinea pig for some pharmaceutical company? I don't think so!" Mark retorts.

"Wait a minute, she's my daughter too. I have a say in this! We'll find the money if that's what it takes," Rebecca fires back at Mark.

"Where?! You spend every dime I make on God knows what! We don't have fifty thousand dollars. We don't even have 5 thousand dollars!"

"So what, Emily is just left here to die? I don't think so!"

Mark is feeling the pressure, he is between a rock

and a hard place. As Mark contemplates the options, he sits back in his chair, rubbing his forehead.

Doctor Heller explains, "There's one more thing. If Emily receives the Chryzinium vaccine, she'll have to receive an RFID implant, so that the manufacturing lab can monitor her progress. A tiny micro-processor would be inserted into her right hand at the time of the procedure."

"That seems a little odd. I've never heard of anything like that," Mark interjects.

"Nobody has. This is cutting-edge technology," Heller responds.

"I know there is much to consider," Doctor Heller pushes his chair back from his desk and stands. "I'm going to step out so you can discuss this in private." The doctor steps out from behind his desk. He reaches into his lab coat pocket, and pulls out a small pad of yellow sticky notes, writes on one, and hands Mark his private cell number.

"You two take whatever time you need. Call me when you've made a decision," Doctor Heller tells Mark and Rebecca. Then he quietly exits his office, closing the door behind him.

As soon as he leaves the office, Mark argues with Rebecca, "So is Emily now a specimen? One of their lab rats?"

"You heard the doctor, the only other option is surgery. What if Emily comes out of that a complete vegetable? Is that what you want?"

"Of course that's not what I want! Don't be ridiculous! I just don't like the idea of our daughter being used as a Guinea pig. And then having the nerve to charge us fifty thousand bucks? Are you kidding!?"

"Well since surgery is out of the question, what else are we supposed to do? Let her die!? All you care about is money?"

"Says the woman who spends money like a drunken sailor. I can't keep up with you. I'll never make enough money for you. Will I? Besides, it's not about the money. It's about using a drug on our daughter that hasn't even been proven and then charging us for it."

Suddenly, loud weeping and talking in the hallway interrupt their debate. Mark steps to the door and peeks out the small square window. Not able to see well enough, he cracks the door open to garner a better look.

Mark observes five family members, embracing as they walk. He watches as they make their way down the hall. As the family disappears around the corner, Mark slowly closes the door. He realizes he has just witnessed a family that has lost a loved one.

With a deep sigh, Mark walks back to Rebecca. He places his hands on her shoulders.

"Okay, let's do it. Maybe it'll work. I just hope this is the right thing to do."

Rebecca's hand reaches up and takes hold of Mark's hand with a comforting gesture.

Mark walks around to face Rebecca. Locking eyes, he asks one more time, "You sure you want to do this?"

Rebecca shrugs with a reluctant response. "I don't know what else to do." Mark nods his confirmation.

"I'll take a second mortgage out on the house. I'm sure we have enough equity to make it work. Okay?" Mark suggests.

Rebecca smiles, wiping the tears from her cheeks.

Mark pulls loose his cell phone from his belt case and calls Doctor Heller to inform him that they've made a decision.

Mark sits down beside Rebecca, taking her hand in his. Rebecca looks to Mark and cracks a slight smile. But, her smile turns to panic as she realizes she has completely forgotten about Taylor.

"Where did you say Taylor was?" she asks.

"I left him in the waiting area downstairs. I couldn't bring him up. He wasn't allowed up here."

"I'm sure he's allowed here in the doctor's office. He's just not allowed in ICU. What were you thinking!?" Rebecca says, annoyed.

"Hey, I wasn't brought here to the doctor's office; I was brought straight to ICU. No kids allowed in ICU."

Both Mark and Rebecca are feeling the stress of all that has happened.

"I'm sorry I snapped, I think you should go get him, no telling what mischief he's gotten into down there."

"Let's wait for Doctor Heller; I'm sure he's fine."

Doctor Heller softly taps on the door and enters the office, "So, have you decided how you'd like to proceed?"

Rebecca and Mark respond in unison, "Yes."

Doctor Heller walks around his desk and takes a seat.

"We want to try the vaccine," Mark informs the doctor.

"I'm sure you've made the right decision. Just so you know, it will take 24 hours to get Chryzinium sent to us from the lab."

Rebecca and Mark nod with approval. "How long until it takes effect?" Mark asks.

Doctor Heller responds with a shrug. "Not sure, maybe a day, a week, a month, I don't know for sure."

"Seems a little iffy for a drug you claim is all that and a box of donuts," Mark replies sarcastically.

Doctor Heller smiles and responds as kindly as he can.

"I understand your frustration, Mr. Shae. And I wish I could give you a definitive answer. However, since we've had no prior beta test subjects, we have no way to predict the time of efficacy. Considering the great risks of our alternative, brain surgery, I believe this new vaccine may be our best option."

Rebecca flashes Mark a scowl.

"That's what medical science is. We practice medicine. And I emphasize 'practice.' We exercise what we know and experiment with what we don't know. Sometimes we get lucky and get it right, and other times we're wrong."

Mark looks over to Rebecca for visual conformation to make sure there are no doubts. With a sigh she concedes, "We don't have any other choice. I'm not going to let them carve up her brain. She's my baby. I want her back," Rebecca begins to cry.

"Is any of this covered by Federal Health Pay?" Mark inquires.

Heller shakes his head. "Unfortunately, no. FHP only covers FDA-approved pharmaceuticals. Let me correct myself. The procedure and hospital fees are covered, less any co-pay, but not the vaccine itself."

"How does this work? Will the lab bill me?" Mark asks.

"Make the check out to me, and I'll forward the money electronically to the lab with my FHP authorization identification."

Reluctantly, Mark reaches into his coat pocket and retrieves his checkbook.

"Make it out to 'Doctor Heller'?" he asks.

"Doctor Ivan Heller, please."

"Why not make it out to the hospital?" Mark asks warily.

"I told you, in cases like this, payment must be made to the lab directly, and that can only be done by an authorized FHP physician."

Annoyed, Mark resolutely tears the check out and hands it to the doctor. Heller quickly glances at the check and puts it into his top desk drawer.

"Give me a few days. I have to secure a loan. I'm taking a second mortgage out on the house. I can get SpiresGate to cover the check until that happens," Mark informs the doctor.

"As soon as we get the vaccine, I'll call you and we'll get her going on it immediately. Go home and get some rest. Nothing we can do until the vaccine arrives. She'll be in good hands, I promise," he consoles the apprehensive couple.

Doctor Heller stands, walks around his desk and opens his office door. Rebecca and Mark slowly stand. "Can we see Emily again before we go?" Rebecca asks.

"Of course, just know she's not going to be any more responsive."

"We won't be long; our son has been down in the waiting area all this time," Mark informs.

SATURDAY, OCTOBER 17TH, SHAE RESIDENCE

Saturday morning is usually filled with TV noise and controlled chaos at the Shae house. Today is different, though. Rebecca is at the hospital with Emily, and Mark is at home, working in his office. Taylor is upstairs in his room playing on his computer.

No word as of yet when the Chryzinium vaccine will arrive at the hospital. It was supposed to be delivered yesterday. Anxiety and frustration has overwhelmed the family for three agonizing days.

As one of the attorneys for SpiresGate Technologies, Mark keeps busy, despite the demands of their daughter's condition. Rubbing his eyes from exhaustion, he stumbles from his desk and walks to the kitchen to pour another cup of coffee. Wearing only his boxer shorts and a tee shirt, Mark shivers.

He tries with futile resolve to fight off his feelings of helplessness. His daughter lays in ICU in a comatose state, not to mention, he's just shelled out fifty thousand dollars in hopes of bringing her back to full recovery. As he pours himself a cup of coffee, Mark hears his cell phone ring at his desk.

Leaving his coffee on the kitchen counter, Mark quickly runs to his office. Reaching over, he fumbles to pick up his phone, but the call has ended. Mark checks his caller ID. Sure enough, it was Rebecca. Mark hits the redial button, returning her call. Immediately, Rebecca answers.

"It's here!" she announces excitedly.

Mark responds, "On my way," ending the call. He scrambles around his office, picking up his clothing that lies in disarray on chairs, tables and the floor.

Mark dresses as quickly as he can. He glances at the clock on the wall, 10:20. Mark yells from his office up to Taylor.

"Taylor, I'm going to the hospital!"

"Okay," Taylor shouts back.

HILLSDALE FALLS MEMORIAL MEDICAL CENTER, 11:15 AM

Just as Mark enters the ICU, he quickly walks down the hallway, and enters room 611, where he meets up with Rebecca and Doctor Heller. "Finally, I thought you had taken the 50K and headed to Cabo."

Doctor Heller ignores Marks callous remark. Rebecca stares at Mark, embarrassed.

"What? I'm sorry," Mark tries to recover.

Dismissing the cognitive dissonance that now envelopes the room, Doctor Heller breaks the tension by explaining the ramifications of Emily's upcoming procedure.

"The Chryzinium vaccine is administered intravenously. It is a slow, steady drip that will enter Emily's bloodstream during a period of 15 hours. No dramatic response is expected right away. However, our hope is that she regains consciousness, and then we can go from there. You can either stay here, or go home. It's up to you," Doctor Heller concludes.

"We'll stay, we want to see her," Rebecca says.

ICU, ROOM 611

The Shaes look on as Nurse Maggie Sprague enters Emily's room, carrying a small white cooler. She sets the cooler down on the tray next to Emily's bed. Opening the cooler, Maggie removes a large syringe containing a clear, pinkish-grey liquid.

A saline bag hangs from an infusion pole just behind Emily's head. Nurse Sprague looks to Doctor Heller and asks him, "Are we ready?"

Doctor Heller gives her a go-ahead nod. Maggie complies and injects the liquid into the saline bag. In a matter of seconds she completes her task, quickly packs up the small cooler, and exits the room.

Turning to the Shaes, Doctor Heller clears his throat, "That's all there is to it. Now we wait."

Rebecca and Mark walk to Emily's bedside. Rebecca takes Emily's hand and smiles. "I believe," she whispers. Mark brushes back Emily's hair. He leans over, gently kissing her on the forehead.

Mark puts his hand on Rebecca's shoulder. "You gonna stay?" he asks.

"I'm not leaving her."

Doctor Heller checks Emily's vital sign monitor for any abnormalities. Pleased by the readings, he turns to the Shaes and smiles with assurance. "You can stay if you wish, but, I expect it won't be for quite a while until we see anything. I'll be here checking in on her throughout the day; if you want to go home and get some rest, now's the time."

"You sure you don't want to come home and at least freshen up?" Mark asks.

After a brief moment she concedes. "Yeah, maybe a shower and something to eat would be good."

"Call if there's anything," Rebecca insists.

"Absolutely," Doctor Heller affirms. Rebecca and Mark hesitantly leave Emily's side.

SHAES' HOUSE, SATURDAY, 6:49 PM

Taylor sits at the kitchen island eating his hot dog and French fries, which he has skillfully prepared for himself. Though burnt to a crisp, the cinders are suitably smothered in ketchup.

Taylor devours his juvenile delicacies in seconds despite their unappetizing condition. Finishing the last bite, he wipes his mouth on his sleeve and heads to the refrigerator. Taking a big gulp from the half gallon of milk, Taylor belches loudly just as Rebecca enters, "What are you doing? Use a glass."

Not acknowledging his mothers' demands, he shrugs her off uncaringly, returning the carton of milk back to the refrigerator shelf. He grabs an apple off the end of the counter and quickly exits, leaving in his wake a kitchen disaster of teenage enormity.

Rebecca shakes her head in revulsion as she gazes over Taylor's mess. She begins taking charge of clean-up detail until her cell phone begins to ring. She grabs it from the counter quickly and recognizes it is Doctor Heller calling.

"Hello? Yes, we're on our way, thank you. Thank you." Rebecca ends the call and shouts to Mark who is in the other room. "We gotta go to the hospital! It's Emily!"

HILLSDALE FALLS MEMORIAL MEDICAL CENTER, 8:15 PM

Rebecca and Mark enter the ICU, both excited and anxious. Doctor Heller, Nurse Maggie Sprague along with Doctor Levi Mintle, Doctor Brad Nunenbush, and Doctor Carly Stinson surround Emily's bed.

Surprised, they see Emily sitting up. Joining the huddle of professionals that surround her daughter, Rebecca is able to make eye contact with her daughter.

"Emily!" Rebecca shouts. Pushing her way through the wall of hospital staff, Rebecca gets to Emily's side.

Seemingly awake and alert, Emily cracks a slight smile. "Can I get a drink of water?" Emily asks with a dry hoarseness to her voice. Nurse Sprague quickly accommodates Emily's request. Carefully, the nurse places the plastic straw up to Emily's mouth.

"Oh baby, you're okay," Rebecca exclaims. Tears of joy stream down Rebecca's cheeks as she leans over and embraces her daughter. Mark also pushes in to see his girl.

"You gave us quite a scare, sweetie," Mark says softly. Mark looks up and makes eye contact with Doctor Heller, "It didn't take 15 hours, after all."

Doctor Heller interjects, "She has to stay on the vaccine intravenously for 15 hours. She just woke up earlier than we expected."

Rebecca wipes the tears from her cheeks with a tissue. "Does this mean she's going to be alright?" she asks.

The Doctors' colleagues, who have come to witness the miraculous effects of the Chryzinium vaccine, congratulate Heller with a pat on the back and shaking of hands.

After the accolades, Doctor Heller asks the group for some privacy so he can talk with Mark and Rebecca alone. Obliging the doctor's request, the team, including Nurse Sprague, politely exit the room while also shaking hands with Mark and Rebecca on their way out.

As the door closes, Doctor Heller redirects his attention to Emily's many monitors. After a quick scan, Doctor Heller smiles at Emily. "How do you feel, young lady?" he asks. She lightly nods an 'okay.'

"How did I get here? I'm in the hospital, right?"

"Yes, you're in the hospital. Your brain decided to shut off for a little while," Doctor Heller answers, fielding her question.

Emily responds, "I'm hungry." Rebecca begins to laugh and cry at the same time hugging Emily endearingly. She is euphoric over what she feels is an incredible miracle.

Doctor Heller calls from the intercom that is incorporated into Emily's bed. "Nurse Sprague, would you come back to room 611?" Turning his attention back to Rebecca and Mark, "We're going to go to my office after the nurse gets here."

Rebecca notices Emily's right hand is heavily bandaged and asks, "What's this?"

"It's the RFID monitoring microchip that we implanted. It's what we'll be using to gather data on how she's doing."

"Will she always need the implant?" Mark asks.

The doctor pauses for a moment before answering. "Yes, it's part of the program. I'm afraid she'll be living with the implant for the rest of her life."

Nurse Sprague enters the room.

"I didn't mean for you to leave, Nurse Sprague. I'm taking the Shaes down to my office. I want someone in here at all times," Doctor Heller requests.

"Yes Doctor, I'll be right here."

Doctor Heller smiles and gestures for the couple to follow him.

Arriving at his office, Doctor Heller opens his door for the Shaes to enter. The three take a seat. "Can we take her home?" Rebecca asks bluntly.

Doctor Heller shakes his head, "We're going to have to keep her here for observation for at least a week. We're sailing in uncharted waters right now with this new vaccine. We don't know what to expect. Tomorrow is Monday, and we're going to begin running a battery of tests. We need results from those tests, and results take time. So, she's going to have to stay here until we're finished." Doctor Heller pauses for a moment.

"I know it's not going to be easy, but I need you both to keep quiet about the Chryzinium vaccine. No talking with friends or other family about the vaccine, and that includes the press. We don't need or want any unnecessary attention right now. You can come and visit as much as you want, but mums the word for now. Is that understood?" Doctor Heller implores Mark and Rebecca.

The doctor removes a one-page legal contract from his top desk drawer. "I need the two of you to sign this."

He hands the document to Mark.

Mark unfolds the paper and reads the top of the page: "Non-Disclosure Agreement."

"A Nondisclosure? You're kidding, right?" Mark blurts.

"No. Both of you need to sign this. This is all new territory, and we can't afford any publicity. Absolutely no information can be leaked about any of this."

After slowly scanning the document, Mark reluctantly signs the agreement. He slides the document over to Rebecca and she follows suit with her signature.

"I hope this is worth it," Mark says under his breath.

"She's your daughter! Of course it's worth it," Rebecca responds bitterly.

MARKS OFFICE, SPIRESGATE TECHNOLOGIES

It's Monday afternoon, and Mark is finishing up some last-minute paperwork before leaving for the day. With Emily in the hospital, Mark has not been spending much time at the office, and work is piling up. Unexpectedly, there is a tap on his door. The door opens and Carol Hoecker enters. She sits in the chair in front of Mark's desk and crosses her long legs.

"Can you meet with me for lunch tomorrow?" she asks.

Mark is a bit surprised by her proposal and takes a moment before answering.

"Why?"

"I'm meeting with Doctor Heller and we want you to join us."

ANATOMY OF A CRASH

Baggs' Monday evening rituals are as predictable as sunsets. Just as he climbs into bed, readying himself with one of his favorite aviation magazines, he realizes he's forgotten to take the garbage out to the curb. "Will I ever learn?" Baggs mumbles to himself as he reluctantly throws back his comforter. Tossing the magazine to the side, he swings his legs over, steps directly into his slippers and stands with a groan.

Tuesday is garbage day, and as always, the garbage men come before the break of day. Even though Baggs has lived in the same house his whole life, he still forgets from time to time.

The air is cool and crisp as Baggs steps out his front door. Warmly wrapped in his black terrycloth bathrobe, he ventures onto the front porch. He takes a moment to inhale a deep breath of the cool night air. Now acclimated to the briskness of the evening, he continues on with his chore.

He walks around to the side of the house and drags the cumbersome garbage can to the curb. The one good thing about this unwelcomed inconveniency, it gives him the opportunity to take a moment to gaze up into the clear night sky.

Baggs is reminded time and again of the magnificent wonders of the universe. He is in awe of the brilliance of the twinkling stars. It's as if they are beckoning him to come and dance among them once again. "I so miss flying," he reminisces to himself in a soft voice.

As his eyes drop from the sky, landing back on the realities of life on earth, he begins his trek back to the house. It is the faint sound of his phone ringing inside that breaks his trance-like state.

"Of course, you call now. It's got to be Lewis!" he grumbles. Stepping up his pace, he finally enters his bedroom.

Just as Baggs reaches for his phone, it stops ringing.

He throws his robe over the foot of the bed and carefully slides off his slippers. With his bare feet, he arranges the slippers with military precision before sliding back into the comfort of his bed.

Propping himself up against the pillows stacked against the headboard, he reaches over and grabs his reading glasses and cell phone from the night stand.

Perching his glasses on the bridge of his nose, he views his caller ID. "I knew it," he mumbles. Redialing the number, Baggs returns Lewis' call.

After only two rings, Lewis answers with urgency, "Hello Baggs."

"What's up?" Baggs asks.

"I was thinking about the pictures. You said one was taken in 1954, while the other picture was supposedly taken just a couple of months ago. That means, whatever that thing is, it's been there for a while. Are you familiar with the midair crash of United Airlines flight 718 and the Super Constellation TWA Flight 2 over the Grand Canyon back in 1956?" Lewis asks.

"Yeah, of course. Why? Now what?" Baggs answers with a hint of dread.

"We should get together with Sy again. He still flies and probably has a current aeronautical chart for the area. I have a hunch there may be more to that crash than what's been told," Lewis says convincingly.

Baggs realizes Lewis is leading into another one of his crazy theories, something Lewis does quite often. Shaking his head, he reluctantly concedes.

"Okay, you got me. What are you getting at?" Baggs asks, quizzically.

"I want to meet with you and Sy as soon as possible," Lewis insists.

"So you want me to call Sy and drag him over here now? I'm in bed."

"Not tonight, but tomorrow?"

Baggs pauses for a moment before continuing. "He's your friend. You introduced him to me, remember? Why don't you call him?"

"Yeah, I know, but for some reason he takes you more seriously."

"Yeah, I wonder why," Baggs says with sarcasm. "Okay, fine, I'll call him. How about ten hundred hours at Polinka's."

"Ten hundred hours tomorrow sounds good. Make sure you have him bring his plotters and a current aeronautical chart for the area. There is vitally important stuff I've discovered," Lewis says before ending the call abruptly.

"Yeah, I'm sure it is," Baggs says to himself, shaking his head with irritation.

Baggs sets his phone down on the nightstand and with a sigh, he mumbles to himself, "I swear the guy's got a screw loose. What ridiculous theory has he come up with now?"

POLINKA'S CAFé, OCTOBER 20, 10:00 AM, SHARP

Baggs enters Polinka's with his briefcase in hand. As always, he comes wearing his flight jacket adorned with NASA patches, wings and squadron affiliations, proudly commemorating his numerous and remarkable aviation achievements. Of course, he's the first to arrive. And as usual, he takes his seat at the booth at the back of the diner. As though programmed, Donna walks over with three coffee cups in one hand and a coffee pot in the other.

"I take it Lewis and Sy are coming? Can't have a meeting of big thinkers without the rest of the brainiacs, can we?" Donna says, exuding her dry sense of humor.

"Late as always," Baggs says to himself, looking at his watch. Just then, the diner's doorbell jingles. Together, Lewis and Sy enter, both carrying their briefcases. Donna fakes a welcoming smile as they approach the table.

With his weathered face, rough hands, and out-doorsman persona, Sy doesn't fit the appearance one would expect of a lab technician. Ironically, Lewis is pretty much the same. In fact, he even looks somewhat like an older version of Sy.

"Gonna have to start charging you all rent if you keep using my café as your office," Donna jokingly informs the group while placing cups on the table.

"We do pay rent. We pay dearly for that brown stuff you call coffee," Lewis quips.

"He said it, not me," Baggs informs Donna, pleading innocent.

Donna pours coffee into the white ceramic cups, spilling a small portion of Lewis' coffee on the table. "Oops, my bad. You need anything else, you know where to find me," Donna laughs. She walks back to the counter, leaving the conspiracy nuts to their business.

The three men settle in the best they can, despite being cramped by briefcases and coffee cups. Lewis takes his napkin and wipes up the coffee that Donna spilled in playful retaliation.

"So, what's up? What crazy theory were you leading to last night about the 1956 airliner crash?" Baggs asks Lewis while pouring a steady stream of sugar into his coffee.

"Crash, what crash?" Sy asks with a snap of his head.

"Don't ask me, ask him," Baggs points at Lewis.

"Did you bring a current Grand Canyon aeronautical chart?" Lewis questions Sy.

"Yeah," Sy responds, while beginning the arduous task of opening his flight-case in the tight space of the diner's booth. Leafing through a collection of aeronautical maps, Sy retrieves the Grand Canyon chart Lewis requested.

"So, what's this about an airplane crash?" Sy asks.

Grabbing the map from Sy, Lewis unfolds the colorful chart and spreads it out over the already-cluttered tabletop.

The best he can, Lewis leans up and over the map, carefully analyzing its topography. With his right index finger, he pushes down hard over the area marked 'Painted Desert.' Looking up to Sy and Baggs, Lewis begins to explain his theory.

"Sy, I don't know if you know any of this unless you've read much history on famous airliner crashes. On June 30th, 1956, two airliners departed Los Angeles International Airport. Of course, LAX wasn't much for international flights back then. In fact, there were just over a hundred commercial flights in the entire state every day. Compare that to the sixteen hundred flights that come and go per day now.

"Anyway, United Flight 718 and TWA Flight 2 both departed LAX within a few minutes of each other at about 9:00 AM. By 10:30 AM, they were both lying in pieces at the bottom of the Grand Canyon. Long story short, they collided with each other midair.

"What would cause two small planes in a great big sky to occupy the same place at the same time? The odds are astronomical. United flight 718 was a DC-7 and TWA Flight 2 was the real cool-looking three-vertical-tailed Lockheed Super Constellation.

"The way investigators tell it, the Constellation made a VFR request for a change of altitude from 19,000 feet up to 21,000 feet because of weather. Basically, it put them in the direct path of the DC-7. The DC-7 ran right up its tail. The DC-7 crashed into the side of Chuar Butte and the Connie crashed just below Temple Butte, killing all 128 souls on both planes."

Sy and Baggs both stare intently at Lewis, captivated by the chilling tale. "Yeah, I remember hearing about that. So what about it?" Sy asks.

"Yeah, I gotta hear this too," Baggs retorts with skepticism.

"I'm glad you asked. You're gonna love this," Lewis says with a Cheshire cat grin. Lewis asks Baggs to retrieve the manila folder containing the photos Baggs brought to the meeting the day before.

Opening the folder, Lewis removes the pictures. "Either of you recognize where the picture in the newspaper was taken?" Lewis asks, holding the picture up with his left hand.

"Yeah, it says in the article it was taken at the Grand Canyon," Sy continues, being somewhat condescending.

Lewis again smiles, but this time he does so now holding up the new photo that was taken just two months earlier. Like a crash investigator, Lewis places the photo over the map. The same area he believes the strange anomaly is pictured as hovering.

"Whatever that thing is, it's hovering over the Painted Desert and has been for who knows how long. Obviously, it was there in 1954 as witnessed here in the newspaper article. Right?" Lewis asks, holding up the other photo. He then points to the map as he continues.

"This here is called the Painted Desert Line. The Painted Desert line is a waypoint airliners used for navigation back then. It was what they used for time and distance ground tracking.

"As the story has it, Captain Jack Gandy, pilot of the TWA Constellation, requested a change of altitude from 19,000 feet to 21,000 feet, but was denied. Shortly after, he requested one thousand feet on top. On top of what, I ask? In other words, was he asking for permission to get on top of clouds? I don't think so. I believe he was, in a sense, subverting the then fledgling aircraft collision avoidance system to gain a better perspective of the Grand Canyon for the passengers' viewing advantage.

"They did things like that back then. They thought nothing of turning a cross country commercial flight into a sightseeing excursion for passengers. But…" Lewis pauses for dramatic effect.

"But what?" Sy demands.

Baggs is still skeptical as he takes a moment to digest Lewis's story. After a sip from his lukewarm coffee, he clears his throat. "By all means, please continue. I gotta know where you're going with all of this."

Lewis smiles, "Some of what took place that morning is documented by actual radio conversations between Gandy, the TWA pilot, and the TWA ground operator. There were indeed thunderheads and cumulous clouds over Arizona. This is what crash investigators say caused the two planes to collide. One or both planes were hidden from each other by cloud cover.

"But witnesses on the ground say the clouds that morning at the time of the crash were reported over Grand Canyon Village, not over the Painted Desert. In fact, the storm was reported to be moving northwest, away from the canyon at 10:00 AM. So how could it be, the TWA pilot was skirting around clouds or thunderstorms that were now behind him?"

After taking a sip of coffee for himself, Lewis continues.

"Like I said, one or both planes were over the Grand Canyon doing what all planes did back then. They were sightseeing for passenger thrills. But, every pilot knows you don't go sightseeing in a thunderstorm, even back then.

"Both flights would have requested changes in heading and altitude if there was even a hint of foul weather ahead. Neither would have been anywhere near the Grand Canyon, or at least near where they said they were, if bad weather was ahead.

If you read the articles about the crash, they all say the same thing. Bad weather was the probable cause of the crash. But, eyewitness testimonies on the ground say the storm was moving northwest away from where the two planes collided. So what was it one or both pilots saw that morning? Did Gandy really see thunderheads? I don't think so.

"Read here. The eyewitness testimonies of those who have actually seen whatever that thing is. They all describe it the same way. It looks like a giant spiral of grey, like thunder clouds. But, the cloud takes on a metallic sheen. What kind of clouds take on a metallic sheen? Whatever it is, it appears to have mass, as solid and real as the coffee cup in my hand. Witnesses say it kind of materializes out of thin air. One minute it's there, and then the next it's gone.

"I think both pilots, at the same time, witnessed this thing becoming visible right in front of them and it scared the tar out of them. Enough so that both pilots took evasive action causing them to cross each other's path."

Lewis crosses his arms over his chest and sits back into his seat, proudly.

Sy and Baggs look on silently, not knowing for sure

how to react. Baggs is genuinely intrigued.

"I want to see whatever that thing is for myself," Lewis announces as he taps his index finger on the map.

"Oh boy, here we go," Baggs mumbles to himself.

Baggs really can't dispute the theory Lewis has come up with because he doesn't know enough to make a cognitive judgement either way. Sy, on the other hand, appears uneasy and stirs in his seat. He may as well have just been presented a piece of an actual flying saucer.

The ramifications and magnitude of such a theory is mind-boggling. Interrupting the bizarre conversation, Donna approaches the table with coffee pot in hand.

"What a mess you got here," she exclaims.

LIFE FLIGHT

The low sun on the horizon brings its orange, early evening radiance to Springboro. A single desk lamp glows as Baggs sits in his office chair. As usual, his reading glasses ride low on his nose as he leafs through one of Lewis' old UFO magazines.

Out of all of Lewis' past conspiracy notions, Baggs is more than intrigued by this latest theory. Indeed, he even thinks Lewis may be on to something.

Given the new concept presented him about the possibility of alien craft hovering over the Arizona desert, Baggs finds himself questioning his own beliefs. His mind races with questions about the universe, and mankind in particular. What are all of these UFO sightings about? Where do they come from? Why are the UFOs here, and why are so many people seeing these things?

As Baggs sits in thought, the more troubled he

becomes. For the first time, he has been presented with information and evidence which contradict his own principled beliefs.

Baggs was raised in a family that didn't go to church or have much in the way of organized religious affiliations. However, his mother did speak often of stories in the Bible, and she occasionally read from the Good Book. Many times, she lovingly warned young Walter in her sweet, southern accent, "Always be prepared to meet your Maker."

His mother's influence is probably the reason he has always accepted creationism as his scientific answer to the existence of the universe. God created everything, end of story.

But still, he knows enough to know there's nothing in the Bible that speaks of aliens or alien craft visiting from other planets. Therein lies the contradiction. Baggs is beginning to wonder if stories of Jacob's ladder or Ezekiel's Wheel could be biblical references to alien space craft.

Thumbing through his collection of aviation periodicals, Baggs can't help but think introspectively about life, earth, heaven, and hell. And now a very real possibility that aliens from outer space actually exist. How does that all fit in to the grand scheme of things?

Breaking the silence of the afternoon and interrupting his thoughts, the doorbell rings. After letting out a subtle sigh, Baggs sets aside the magazines and removes his reading glasses from his nose. He stands with a weary groan and slowly walks out of his office to answer the door.

As he cracks open the door he sees standing before him a four-and-a-half-foot-tall zombie.

"So, what do ya' think?" asks the young zombie.

"Hello, Miss Marty," Baggs smiles from ear to ear.

"Hey, how'd you know it was me?" Marty responds smartly.

"Not a whole lotta' zombies your size in the neighborhood these days."

"Well, did I scare you?"

"Oh yes, very scary. But, you're a little late for Halloween."

"I know, just fooling around with Roxy's makeup."

"I see," Baggs replies with a hint of trepidation. Why on earth would she make herself up that way?

Little Marty stands quiet for a moment as her demeanor begins to change. Baggs senses there is something wrong. He looks over the top of her head across the street to her house, and notices her mom's dilapidated car is not in the driveway.

"Are you at home alone?" Baggs asks.

"No, my mom's boyfriend is there."

Hearing this, Baggs becomes suspiciously concerned, but does not quite know how to address the situation. Looking to get more information from Marty, Baggs does his best to question her in an unassuming way.

"When do you expect her to come home?" Baggs asks nonchalantly.

"Not till late, she bartends tonight."

"What's your mom's boyfriend's name?" Baggs carefully pries.

"Vernon. Can I come in?" Marty asks while barging in and walking around Baggs.

Despite the cold breeze blowing in through the front door, he makes the decision to leave the front door wide open, hoping the young sprout leaves just as quickly as she entered.

Becoming more emboldened and upfront with Marty, Baggs decides to put aside niceties in hopes of getting some much-needed answers.

"So does Vernon take pretty good care of you when your mom's at work?" Baggs asks.

"What kind of plane is this?" Marty asks, circumventing the question.

"It's a powered glider. Where does your mom work?" Baggs continues.

"She works at the Blue Pearl. So, if it's a glider why does it have a motor?"

"I tell you what, how about after you get out of school tomorrow I meet you at Grass Park and we can fly the glider? I'll show you why it needs a motor."

"Actually, I think that works just fine with my schedule," Marty responds with her adult-like persona.

Turning from the table, Marty walks over to Baggs and smiles at him endearingly. "Can I fly it, maybe?" she asks in a hopeful tone.

"You bet. In fact, let's start flying lessons tomorrow."

Excited about her upcoming adventure, Marty walks back to the front door and begins to exit. As she crosses the threshold she turns back to Baggs. With a twinkle in her big zombie eyes, she smiles and waves just before running across the street back to her house.

It has become apparent to Baggs that Marty isn't going to share too much about her home life. There is a child in Baggs' life he is beginning to care about, for the first time.

FAIRMONT ELEMENTARY SCHOOL, 2:45 PM

Within a nanosecond of the ring of the school bell, pint-sized people of all nationalities emerge from the buildings like ants streaming to a picnic. Hopping on bikes, climbing into buses and cars, and walking along sidewalks, the little munchkins enthusiastically scamper to their destinations.

Marty is no exception as she rides off quickly on her flat black Stingray bike. Blond ponytail flying behind her, cuffed blue jeans, dirty white sneakers, and blue down jacket, all announce unapologetically she is all tomboy.

Her grungy, overstuffed backpack strains her shoulders as her hands grip high on the handlebars. Peddling as fast she can, she rides hard to her rendezvous with Baggs. Today is the day she is going to learn how to fly!

GRASS PARK, 3:00 PM

It's at least two miles from the school to Grass Park, but Marty made it in only fifteen minutes. That's got to be some record! Racing across the field, she sees Baggs off in the distance, prepping the bright white and yellow glider for flight.

Sliding her back tire in the dirt, she quickly brings the Stingray to a stop. Without even a moment of hesitation, she drops her bike and unceremoniously dumps her backpack to the ground. "I'm here!" Marty announces loudly.

Baggs stands proud with his kind, grandfatherly smile and twinkling eyes. He welcomes the young pilot-in-training with a polite, "Hello." Without missing a beat, he hands her the radio used to control the glider. "I see you made it," he says (as if there would be any doubt as to her making it to her very first flight lesson).

He is happy to see his new friend. A warm feeling of being with a kindred spirit floods his soul, knowing he now has someone young to teach and with whom he can share his life experiences. Never having his own children, Marty is like a gift from God.

"You still have traces of zombie makeup around your left eye. You need more soap and water," Baggs informs Marty.

Then he realizes it isn't makeup he sees, but bruising. "What happened?" Baggs asks, suddenly concerned. A rage is beginning to well up from the very pit of his stomach as thoughts of abuse race through his head.

Marty smiles, "I hit my eye on the handlebar yesterday."

Baggs looks carefully at her eye, still suspicious, "Is

that why you weren't in school yesterday?"

"No. There was no school yesterday," Marty replies, matter-of-factly. "Hey, are we going to fly or are we going to chitchat the day away?"

Not totally believing Marty, Baggs relents and drops the subject for the time being. "Okay, let's fly this thing," Baggs says as he readies the glider.

With a flip of a switch on the plane and on the radio, Baggs begins Marty's first flight lesson.

"Before we take to the air, it's important we check to make sure the aircraft is worthy to fly," Baggs says while positioning himself behind Marty.

Grasping onto the radio with his hands over Marty's hands, Baggs operates the joysticks so she is able to understand how they magically move the planes control surfaces.

"Watch the plane's wings. When we move this stick back and forth, it operates the planes ailerons. Those are the small flaps you see on the big long wing. The ailerons are what cause the plane to bank right and left. That's referred to as 'roll.'

"The stick under your right thumb operates the rudder. The rudder steers the nose of the plane right and left. That's called 'yaw.' That's the short tail that sticks up on the back of the plane. And if you move the same stick forward and back, that operates the elevators. Those are the small flaps on the wings at the back of the plane. That's what makes the plane go up and down. It's referred to as 'pitch.' Go ahead and move those around a bit so you get familiar with how they operate and feel, okay?"

Marty takes the controls for herself, moving the joy sticks while studying the plane's control surfaces. "The left stick doesn't do anything when I move it back and forth," Marty warns Baggs, concerned there may be something wrong.

"That's the throttle control. Once the motor is running, the back and forth movement of that stick will adjust how fast the propeller spins."

Satisfied by Baggs answer, Marty continues practicing for a few more moments. Eager to get the plane in the air, Marty looks up at Baggs.

"I think we should take her up," Marty states.

The child's impatience and excitement for action outweigh the boredom of learning Bernoulli's principal of flight.

"I agree, let's take her up," Baggs chuckles.

Baggs reaches down and with the flip of another switch on the plane; the small electric motor begins to spin the propeller. He takes the radio from Marty, while at the same time picking up the glider. With a quick snap of his wrist, Baggs launches the plane into the air. As he pushes the throttle forward, the tiny motor screams to full power and the plane is instantly aloft.

Baggs reaches back around from behind Marty, positioning the radio control directly in front of her.

"Take your hands and work the radio control with me," he instructs. Marty eagerly complies and reaches up and grasps the radio over the top of Baggs hands.

Her small thumbs rest gently on top of his. Feeling the movement of the joy sticks underneath, Marty is amazed by how such little pressure on the joy sticks can move the big plane up and down and right and left so easily.

"Doesn't take much, does it?" Baggs asks.

Marty is fascinated. Very gently he slides his dark weathered hands out from under Marty's hands. Like letting a child go for the first time riding a bike, Marty now has total control of the plane. Baggs reaches down and with a flip of the switch, the motor shuts off. High in the air the plane's nose gently drops toward the ground.

"Just let go of the sticks. Let the plane do what it wants to do. It wants to fly. All you have to do is correct its direction, up or down, left or right," Baggs instructs. Again, he gently places his hands over the top of Marty's small hands and together they fly the glider around and around till finally it loses much of its altitude.

"It's time to bring her in for a landing," Baggs informs Marty. Together with Baggs guiding the plane, they bring the big white bird in for a landing. Smoothly the plane skids across the grassy field until it comes to a stop.

"Wow that was great, let's do it again!" Marty shouts.

Baggs grins endearingly at the young aviator. For the next hour and a half, Marty and Baggs fly the glider over and over, draining one battery after the next until all are dead.

"It looks like we're done here. And, I might say, you have done a fantastic job. You're a natural at this," Baggs says with pride. "Time to head back and get all these batteries on charge."

The sun has begun its descent behind the surrounding hills, and the air temperature is dropping quickly. "Can I hitch a ride with you, Baggs? That is, if you're going my way," Marty asks.

Baggs quickly considers her request, "Yeah sure, help me load up. We can throw your bike in the back like we did before."

In a matter of minutes the two head off down the road for the short trip home. Arriving at his house, Baggs sees Sy's brand new, custom, black mid-life-crisis-mobile sitting parked out front at the curb.

Carefully, he backs his truck into his driveway. As he does so, he sees what he guesses to be Marty's mother standing at her car with the hood up.

Baggs is not sure what to expect from her when she sees Marty getting out of his truck. "Is that your mom?" Baggs asks before Marty exits.

"Yup," Marty replies.

Putting the truck in park, Marty exits the passenger door and runs across the street yelling, "Roxy, I'm learning how to fly!"

"Did she just call her mom, Roxy?" Baggs says under his breath while exiting the driver side door. Sy exits his car and walks over to meet Baggs.

Baggs sees Marty and her mom walking back across

the street towards him. "This should be interesting," he mumbles.

"What?" Sy says, unaware of what is going on.

"Nothing. What brings you here?" Baggs asks, diverting his attention to Sy.

"Oh, I just wanted to talk to you about something. Who's the girl?"

"Neighbor girl. I'm teaching her how to fly the glider."

"Really?"

Baggs walks toward Marty and her mother, meeting them at the apron of his driveway. Sy follows along.

"Hi, I'm Roxanne, Roxanne Milner," Roxanne says lighting her cigarette as the two approach.

"I see you've met my little runt, Martha. She wanted me to meet you."

Baggs smiles politely. "Hi, Roxanne, I'm Walter Baggerly. My friends call me Baggs, and this here is a good friend of mine, Simon, we call him Sy."

Roxanne may have been at one time pretty, but her rough, haggard appearance makes her look older than she actually is. She easily looks to be in her late 40s and could be considered anorexic as she leans her frail 90 pound frame onto one hip.

Her short, bobbed, badly-bleached blond hair looks atrocious as her bangs highlight the dark circles around her eyes. It is obvious that cigarettes, booze, and her fast-lane lifestyle have taken their toll.

"Baggs. Interesting nickname. My friends all call me Roxy," she retorts while exhaling clouds of cigarette smoke from her mouth and nose.

"Marty, I told you, I go by Marty," Marty fires back, correcting her mom.

"She hates Martha. I don't know why. It's my grandmothers' name. I don't care; I call her Martha or Runt, just to get her goat. Ticks her off, huh baby? I've been here eleven years and I don't think I've ever met you before. My granny left me this place when she died. I've been here ever since," Roxanne says with a smokers rattle.

"So where do you go to school?" Sy asks Marty, trying to be polite and include himself into the conversation.

"Fairmont Elementary. I'm in the fourth grade. Baggs is teaching me how to fly," she says proudly.

"So I heard. You know who this is teaching you how to fly, don't you? This is Walter Baggerly. Commander Walter Baggerly, the astronaut," Sy informs Marty.

"Well I'll be damned, an honest to goodness spaceman living right across the street," Roxy says, coughing up and spitting out a wad of phlegm onto the sidewalk.

"You're an astronaut?" Marty says, excited to hear this interesting news about Baggs.

"Probably long before my time. I'm only 29," Roxanne interjects.

Baggs is pretty shocked to hear that Roxanne is only 29 years old, but he just smiles, trying his best not to be impolite.

"Imagine an astronaut living here in this dumpy

neighborhood," Roxanne continues with tactless delivery.

"Been here all my life. Astronauts may go far, but the pay isn't all that great. Besides, I like the character of these old Craftsman style homes. Cozy feel to them," he softly interjects.

"I work at the Blue Pearl Bar. Come on in and let me buy you a beer sometime," Roxanne offers.

She looks down at Marty and grabs her by the back of the neck.

"Speaking of which, I gotta get to work. I need you to help mama with the car. Damn thing won't start again."

Taking another puff from her cigarette, Roxy redirects her conversation back to Baggs, "Like I said, come in for a beer sometime. On me."

"Thank you."

Coughing up another phlegm-ball and spitting it onto Baggs driveway, Roxy continues.

"If the runt here gets under foot, just boot her out. She shouldn't be over here bothering you, anyways."

"No ma'am, she's no problem at all. She has a real fascination for airplanes. Thought I'd teach her some of the ups and downs of flying. No pun intended," Baggs says with a chuckle.

Judging by the blank look on Roxanne's face; she doesn't get the pun. Clearing his throat, Baggs asks. "If that's okay with you, that is?"

Roxanne looks down at Marty while at the same time answering. "As long as she does her chores and it keeps her away from my beer, I don't give a rip. Like I said, if she gets under foot, a good swift kick in the behind usually moves her out the door pretty quickly," Roxanne says to Baggs, dragging Marty across the street.

"Come on home and help mama get that piece of junk running."

"Nice to meet you!" Baggs hollers insincerely to Roxanne.

Marty stares at Sy's car intently as they walk back across the street. Marty then turns back to Baggs and she gives Baggs the thumbs-up sign, as if saying, 'Cool, you got mom's approval.'

Baggs and Sy walk back up to the truck so he can unload. "What a piece of work she is," Baggs exclaims. Turning his attention to Sy, he asks, "So, what brings you over to this part of town?"

Sy dismisses the question with a shake of his head. "Not important right now. I wanted to talk to you about something, but it can wait."

It is becoming obvious to Baggs that something is bothering Sy.

"Kind of got lowlifes for neighbors," Sy remarks.

"She's a good kid. Just got dealt a bad hand when it comes to parents."

Unloading Marty's bike from the back of his truck and pushing it to the side of the house, Baggs glances over to Marty's house, once again. Marty climbs up under the hood of her mom's old sedan and shouts to her, "Now!" Roxanne turns the key and the starter cranks and cranks and then with a cough, the engine comes to life with a sputter and a cloud of white smoke.

From under the hood, Marty operates the throttle, gunning the engine, bringing it to full life. Returning to idle, Marty climbs out from under the hood. Pulling the prop rod, she lets the hood slam shut.

Roxanne slams the car door shut and without so much as a wave or a thank you, she drives off in a roar.

Marty walks back across the street to Baggs house. Baggs has managed to pull Marty's back pack, bike, and his glider from the back of his truck.

"You need help with any of this?" Marty asks Baggs politely.

Baggs smiles at Marty. "No worries, I got it, besides, I got Sy here to help. Right?" Baggs glances at Sy.

"I rolled your bike over by the side of the house. And here's your backpack," Baggs says.

"Well, I better go, you heard Roxy, I got chores to do."

Baggs nods to her. Sy then asks, "So, you call your mom Roxy?"

"Yeah, she doesn't like me to call her mom. She says it makes her feel old. So I call her Roxy. Besides, that's what her boyfriends call her."

"Well you have a good night, okay?" Baggs says while he and Sy take his plane and radio up the porch to his house.

"You too," Marty responds. Throwing her backpack over her shoulder, she wheels her bike back across the street to her house.

Turning back to Baggs, Marty shouts, "We going flying again?"

Baggs smiles back at his new protégé, "You bet we are." Baggs watches as she turns and pushes her bike across the street.

Baggs and Sy slowly enter his house and place the glider and gear back onto the long table. Baggs' happy demeanor slowly begins to subside as he contemplates the deplorable lifestyle Marty must be forced to endure. His heart is heavy with concern.

"I gotta head home. I'll talk to ya later, okay?" Sy says. Baggs nods 'okay' as Sy exits the front door.

VUL-MATTER: DARK ENERGY REVEALED

Emitting from tectonic plate fracture points; vortices and ley lines are proven to have higher than normal levels of electromagnetic energy. NASA has also proven that certain 'earth waves' are linked to the human energy field. In other words, the nine major points of the human Chakra draw energy from these vortices and ley lines.

There are 11 major vortices and 29 minor vortices around the planet. Interestingly, major and minor vortices coincide with each other at varying levels and types of energy. Consequently, energy fields can be at odds with each other. If positive energy vortices exist, is it reasonable to assume there are negative energy vortices as well?

There are as many as 28 lightning strikes per minute

where Venezuela's Catatumbo River and Lake Maracaibo meet. Most scientists believe that this anomaly is due primarily to the topography and peculiar weather patterns around the area.

However, French-born geophysicist Lorenzo Pegallio discovered that the high volume of lightning strikes around Lake Maracaibo are not strikes at all. In fact, these so-called lightning strikes do not originate from clouds, but are high-energy bursts escaping earth's core. Pegallio believes it is dark energy being released into the atmosphere.

He ascertains that there are 39 areas around the globe where these dark energy vortices exist. And they are not always associated with vortices and/or ley lines. Using electromagnetic measuring equipment, Pegallio exposed a phenomenon referred to as 'black lightning.' It is this black lightning or dark energy that is now referred to as 'Vul-Matter.'

The mythical character Atlantes, a powerful sorcerer featured in the "chansons de geste" (French medieval epic poetry), was thought to have garnered his powers from dark energy. It is also thought, early Egyptians and pre-cretaceous civilizations used dark energy to precisely cut and transport mammoth stone monoliths. They knew how to defy the power of gravity.

Sixty five million years ago, Anasazi lore speaks of having harnessed the power of dark energy as well. It is they that made contact with beings of the dark energy sub-world realm, the 'Shafutah.' Ancient Petroglyphs document that the Shafutah were able to create form and mass out of thin air. In addition to defying gravity, they also possessed medicinal capabilities that far exceeded even modern-day science.

Doctor Albert Hess referred to dark energy as Vul-Matter. His findings proved there is a dark realm to all energy. There is a negative for every positive; a yang for every ying, and an evil for every good. Even Newton's 3rd law of motion, 'for every action, there is an opposite and equal reaction,' proves these theories factual. There is a positive and negative force greater than man that shares our universe.

The Roswell, New Mexico alien space craft crash of 1947 and the 1966 Kecksburg, Pennsylvania UFO crash are just two of countless verifiable instances of unearthly occupation here on earth. However, not from outer space, like many believe, but from earth's abyss, where dark energy (Vul-Matter) resides. In fact, cloud rings that appear to have mass and density are witnessed as materializing all around the globe.

For more than a hundred years, UFO sightings have been increasing at an alarming rate. Some call these signs of the times; the looming great apocalypse. Some even believe them to be signs of the prophesied return of Jesus, the Christ King. This is often referred to as 'signs in the heavens.'

The slow but steady rising of the Shafutah through the ages has been well documented. Lest we forget:

Nero, Caligula, Attila the Hun, Grigori Rasputin, Joseph Stalin, and Adolf Hitler.

Through the ages, the Shafutah have been analyzing the people. Evil rulers challenge man's influences, endurance, and will. For millennia, the Shafutah have been preparing for the New Solution – the New Era where they have total supremacy. Thriving off humanity's thirst for greed and their lust for power, there has been but one missing factor for total dominance. Technology.

For the Shafutah to manifest itself as an absolute global power, technology must be at its pinnacle. The Shafutah must have a device that is sustainable, and upon which mankind must depend – completely.

The early 1800's was the beginning of the industrial revolution. Since the Wright Brothers' first powered flight took place December 17th, 1903, twelve men have landed on the moon, the SR71 flew across the United States at 2,193 MPH, and there is now an International Space Station that orbits the earth at 17,150 MPH. That means that on the space station, the crew witnesses one new sunrise every 92 minutes.

Hundreds of millions of cell phones are in the hands of almost every human old enough to speak. They are not just phones, but technological wonders. The majority are hand-held computers, capable of taking and sending still images and real-time video around the world in mere seconds. News of the next major terrorist attack is known worldwide in minutes. Computers are the very lifeline to mankind's very existence. Technology now grows at an exponential rate, beyond anyone's expectations in decades past.

Now is the era of technology. Now is the time for the Shafutah to rise. The Shafutah will reemerge once again to rule. Referred to as 'Strikes,' ancient writings of the Shafutah are often mistaken as early hieroglyphs from Asia Minor. However, one such carving discovered in the late 1800s depicts actual verses written in Gaelic. The script is believed to be early satanic worship. Carved in one stone found 6 miles southwest of Letterkenny, Ireland, the Strike is translated, '*Quoro 6:66* – She shall bring forth a Queen, and it is She who will bear the prince of darkness in man form, whom will rule over all the nations.'

INDOCTRINATION

House Republican Leader Phoebe Wescott is short, feisty, and dressed for business. She wears well her stylish but conservative Ann Taylor tweed suit, her shiny, copper hair in a sleek bob. Her look fits her spirited Irish temper. The 5 foot, 2 inch congresswoman is well known as one who is not always easy to work with and for her propensity to debate.

She has a tendency for doing government business strictly by the book. While considered an asset by some, she is an iron gate for others. A hard right conservative, she understands and knows the Constitution to the letter.

Serving in Congress for 23 years, Phoebe has been known to move heaven and earth to see to it that the Constitution is always upheld as written. "It's not a wishy-washy, living, breathing document as some believe it to be,' she has been quoted saying many times.

Her office is as bland as a beige 1990 mini-van compared to Kevin Rhodes' office. Her desk is schoolroom metal grey. Her other meager furnishings are only there if they serve a purpose.

A large Bible sits on a stand just to the side of her desk reminding those that enter that she stands for biblical principles. 'Tax-payers shouldn't be paying for lavish amenities. They sent me to Washington to work on their behalf, not to lord over them in luxury,' is a message she speaks loud and clear to her not-so-humble colleagues.

It's 2:15 PM and Phoebe works diligently without so much as a lunch break. With her head buried deep in her work, there is a light tap on her door. All who know Phoebe know good and well that one is not to simply barge in, but to knock first. Still, it is best to wait to speak to her when her door is open. Aggravated by the interruption, she rubs her eyes and lifts her head.

"Come in," she calls with a hint of irritation.

Byron Sutter, House Ways and Means Committee Chairman, slowly opens her office door and sticks his head inside. "Are you too busy to talk?" Byron asks.

"I'm always too busy to talk," she retorts, taking a breath and removing her glasses. Realizing a break from her papers is certainly due, she invites Byron into her office.

Byron takes a seat at one of her old chairs that sit directly in front of her desk. Just by looking at Byron's countenance, Phoebe can tell he has something serious on his mind.

"What is it?" she asks, taking a sip from her cold cup of tea.

"Have you heard of the Lazarus VI Project?" he asks.

Phoebe leans back in her chair folding her arms in front of her and smiles, "Why do you ask?"

"I'm supposed to talk to you about a proposed project that's being discussed tonight at the White House. The Lazarus VI Project. I don't imagine you've heard about it."

Phoebe takes a deep breath before answering, "As a matter of fact, I have."

Byron looks surprised. After what was told him in Kevin's office just a few days prior, he was certain the Lazarus VI Project was classified Top Secret and no one knew of its existence.

"So what have you heard?" Byron asks.

"Enough."

"How did you hear about it? I was told this was all Top Secret. Kevin forced me to sign a confidentiality agreement."

"Oh, for the love of Pete, Byron, you gotta know by now the people here keep secrets like four-year-olds. In fact, word has it you wear old man, tidy-whitey under-wear," Phoebe says with a snide smile.

She leans over and opens her right top drawer. Digging through the stacks of paperwork, she pulls out a thin manila folder and throws it on top of her desk in front of Byron.

Opening the folder, he sees that it contains a six-page synopsis of the Lazarus VI Project, the same documents he read earlier.

"Believe it or not, I do have friends," she snaps.

Byron takes the pages, browsing them lightly. Sliding the pages back into the folder, he places the folder back onto Phoebe's desk.

"You weren't supposed to know anything about the Lazarus VI Project. They asked me to be the one to fill you in, but not until just before the committee meeting. They were afraid you'd go to the press. They want to keep it hush-hush for now."

"Of course they do! When's the meeting?"

"This evening. They want you to come. They want you on the committee. Since you already knew about the project, why didn't you go to Kevin or go to the press?"

"Timing, Byron. Make no bones about it; I have every intention of going to the press. Just not yet. I know full well how they plan to force the project on the American people, but as God as my witness, I'm going to stop them dead in their tracks long before that happens."

"They invited me to the M-PAC Laboratory and they're inviting you too."

Byron reaches into his jacket pocket and hands her a special invitation signed by none other than Kevin Rhodes and President Parkston.

"Are you going?" Byron asks as she takes the invite from him.

"You bet I'm going. I wouldn't miss that for the world.

You can't fight the enemy if you don't know the enemy."

This was not at all what he was expecting to hear from Phoebe. Phoebe and Byron have been friends for many years, but even this comes as a shock to him. After a moment of awkward silence and knowing she is eager to get back to work, Byron stands and heads to the door. Phoebe stops him with a clearing of her throat. She reaches into her top desk drawer and removes a small thumb drive and holds it up.

"It's all right here. I own them," she says, self-assuredly.

"I hope you know what you're doing," Byron cautions Phoebe as he exits.

OVAL OFFICE, WHITE HOUSE,
WEDNESDAY EVENING

Washington DC is experiencing abnormally warm temperatures this holiday season. Heavy rain, thunder and lightning have been plaguing the area this particular Wednesday evening.

The Oval Office is bustling with those that are Lazarus VI committee members and a few that are not yet, such as Phoebe Wescott. President Parkston and Kevin Rhodes are hoping to solidify the project once and for all this evening with unanimous support.

The time has finally come for Chief Liaison Officer Kevin Rhodes and President Parkston to clear the air once and for all concerning this very controversial proposal. Unfortunately, Kevin Rhodes has not arrived, thereby delaying the start of the meeting.

President of the United States, Adam Parkston, Homeland Security Advisor Lon Thompson, Vice President Jay Hammond, Secretary of State Pat Vance, National Security Advisor Steven Van Noy, House Republican Leader Phoebe Wescott, House Ways and Means committee Leader Byron Sutter, Chairman of the Federal Reserve Colin Franky, Congressional Budget Office Representative Paula Slater, CDC Director Doctor Corina Mendez, Secretary of Defense Chuck Hunt, and last but not least, Deputy Director of Security Amanda Sykes, are those who are in attendance so far.

With the project not yet proposed to Congress, the atmosphere is still somewhat polarized. There are those in favor and those against the implementation of the much-debated Lazarus VI Project. The project has been kept quiet publically and for good reason.

President Parkston is becoming uneasy with the banter that is becoming more intense. Most of it is derogatory remarks coming from Phoebe Wescott. That being said, he makes the executive decision to proceed with the meeting despite the absence of Kevin Rhodes.

President Parkston clears his throat and calmly addresses the room, "Excuse me everyone."

The room immediately settles. Just then, Hayden Ross, the White House Press Secretary, enters the room through the curved Oval Office door.

Extravagantly dressed, wearing a black tuxedo, white silk shirt and patent leather shoes, Hayden makes his impromptu entrance oddly dressed for the occasion. Waving his hand to gain attention from President Parkston, a few of the attendees mock his choice of formal apparel, not knowing he has other places to be.

"A little overdressed, aren't you Hayden?" Lon Thompson asks with a condescending chuckle.

"Another black tie press dinner. And for steak and lobster, I'd wear a kangaroo suit and pink tutu," Hayden responds with his typical, yet witty, press secretary prowess.

President Parkston acknowledges Hayden's wave and walks over to where he restlessly waits at the door. They whisper into each other's ear, keeping their conversation private. Within a few seconds, Hayden exits the Oval Office just as Kevin Rhodes enters, barging his way in through the half closed door.

"I was beginning to wonder if you were going to make it," Parkston remarks anxiously.

"Sorry, the traffic is crazy tonight and the weather isn't helping. My apologies, Mr. President. Everyone," Kevin says graciously.

"Well, come on in and let's get this thing going," Parkston insists, trying to move the evening along.

As Kevin enters, he immediately sees Phoebe Wescott sitting on the couch next to Byron. Knowing he's up against an evening of opposition, Kevin makes his way to the coffee cart. Kevin pours himself a cup of coffee and President Parkston brings the meeting to order.

"I know there are some who have concerns about the Lazarus VI Project. That's why I believe it's imperative that all the cards are laid on the table, so everyone is up to speed.

"Trust me when I say, I too would much rather be at home with my family tonight," Parkston says, trying his best to placate any animosities for being there. President Parkston then continues.

"I have been working hard with Kevin on this project for some time now. But, he knows better than I, the intricacies of this fascinating program. That being said, I'd like for him to present the Lazarus VI Project in detail to all of you. Kevin, if you don't mind would you?" President Parkston yields the floor to Kevin.

Kevin takes a sip of his coffee and begins.

"It is a foregone conclusion we have dug ourselves into a financial hole that even the Congressional Budget Office agrees will take decades to climb out of. Am I right, Paula?" he asks CBO Representative Paula Slater, of who nods in agreement.

Kevin continues, "It is no secret the healthcare system we currently have in place is not working. Despite co-pays and taxes, the current FHP is unable to sustain itself. Not to mention, the country's financial deficit and debt are completely out of control.

"I'm here to tell you that Lazarus VI is a project with heart and soul, a viable way to solve many of the health issues we're facing today. With the Chryzinium vaccine, tens of thousands of lives will be saved. Children diagnosed with terminal cancer will be cured. Loved ones suffering from Alzheimer's cured. Multiple Sclerosis, Diabetes, Parkinson's disease and a myriad of other diseases would be cured by one simple vaccine.

"This is a program that will change our healthcare system for the better, once and for all. However, the issue here is not only the vaccine itself, but the way in which we as a country can further benefit from its miraculous powers."

Phoebe, unable to contain her disdain for the whole project, interrupts, "You mean capitalize on it! Don't you, Mr. Rhodes?"

Kevin fires back. "Yes! As a matter of fact, I do mean capitalize on it, Ms. Wescott," Kevin cuts her off before she can excite the others with probing questions.

"I think Ms. Wescott's real concerns come from the idea that a microchip implant would accompany the vaccine. I think that has been the concern all along from many who have opposition to the project. Please, you have to carefully consider what we are offering.

"It is that little ID chip that makes the Chryzinium vaccine work. And yes, there is a RFID chip being developed and tested to monitor those who take the vaccine. However, I can promise you, there is no plan to leash or link poor Americans to an electronic tether so we can spy on them. The chip is for monitoring purposes only.

"With a new vaccine such as this, there are many biological parameters that need to be monitored for individual safety. I've seen the device and can attest to the fact that it is as harmless as a cell phone.

"That being said, M-PAC has developed the very first atomically-powered RFID implant referred to as Vul-Stream. I believe with Chryzinium and Vul-Stream together, we can help solve all of our current healthcare challenges. Hence the Lazarus VI Project.

"The new RFID chip, along with its amazing atomically powered technology is far beyond anything ever imagined. Even though M-PAC provides the processor and atomic element, it is actually being manufactured off-site at a mid-west super conductor nanotechnologies plant. And I might add, that plant is now employing more than 1,500 individuals. How's that for stimulating the economy?" he says with a laugh.

"We must have a system in place that monitors, controls and retrieves vital data. Not to mention, we'll need a program that will recoup revenue invested. Pharmaceutical companies, doctors, hospitals, and even the economy as a whole, will lose billions when Chryzinium is introduced.

"Do you realize our healthcare programs hold the diseased hostage? We don't cure diseases; we provide maintenance drugs, so people, at best, can only cope with their diseases. Our present system is as evil as the day is long. It profits by preying on the sick, and this has to stop. If it takes the Vul-Stream RFID chip implanted into every living, breathing soul to stop the madness, so be it.

"I believe we have a moral obligation to the people

to offer cures for disease, but more importantly, we have an opportunity to put this country back on the fast track to financial independence. That's only if we start thinking outside of the box. I believe the technology we have at our fingertips addresses those concerns most exceptionally.

"Vul-Stream is not some scary anti-privacy electronic leash tying people to some supercomputer. Granted, it sounds radical. It is radical. But it's also necessary.

"As more and more people take the Chryzinium vaccine, pharmaceutical companies lose revenue, healthcare facilities lose revenue, and taxable dollars dwindle away. We must charge appropriately for the vaccine.

"M-PAC is willing to work with our government on the program. They are ready and willing to implement a system that helps individual people and our great nation as a whole.

"Our country salivates over cutting-edge technology! What's more technological than a smart, shiny RFID chip in your hand that contains your vital health records in case of an emergency?

"A chip that is your personal ID. A chip that is your health record, debit card, credit card, and driver's license all contained in a computer that is smaller than the head of a pin. The cost of the massive database is astronomical, and with Chryzinium, the cost can be absorbed by the new health plan.

"I have been working closely with M-PAC for a couple of years now. Both Chryzinium and Vul-Stream,

I believe, will prove to be huge successes in their own right, technologically speaking.

"We need to be ready this time. How many of you actually use the US Postal Service to mail letters? You don't. You use email. That alone is a perfect example of technology catching the Federal Government with its pants down, costing our government trillions of dollars. Are we going to be so foolish as to let this slip through our fingers too? I think not!"

Kevin looks around the Oval Office. He has everyone's attention. All eyes are on him and it appears they're all eating out of the palm of his hand. Like a televangelist bringing his flock to the altar, he sets the hook.

"Chryzinium has just been administered for the first time outside of laboratory walls to a young girl who suffered a massive brain tumor just a few weeks ago. Not only is the tumor completely gone, all indications are that she is doing just fine. In fact, she is now at home recovering. What about others? When do we get a chance to share the miracles of Chryzinium with others?" Kevin asks in closing.

Like a viper, Phoebe can't hold her tongue any longer and interjects with venom.

"Why don't we see Margaret Billings or Bob Martinson from the FDA here? Why is that, Mr. Rhodes? Is that because Chryzinium has yet to be approved? There's been no mention of its chemical properties and what problems it may create in the future. If Chryzinium really does what you say, won't we end up with an overpopulation problem? We'll have people living to a 150 years old. What good is it to live to a 150 with no food?"

Kevin smiles as he continues in hopes of quelling Ms. Wescott's concerns.

"Chryzinium doesn't come from the USA and is not subject to FDA guidelines or approvals."

Phoebe finally jumps to her feet, as she is ready for a fight.

"Is M-PAC located here in the U.S.? Because I have an invitation to visit the lab with you, I might add. Are we leaving the country? Because if we are, I'll be sure to bring my passport."

"Yes, the lab is located on U.S. soil. However, the prime element that makes up Chryzinium does not come from the USA, Ms. Wescott. So you should know, we don't need FDA approval."

"You're kidding, right? You're playing semantics, here. This is the problem with you; all of you who are buying into this!"

She makes a sweeping point with her outstretched arm to everyone in the room for effect, and continues, "A bunch of half-truths, all sewn together just so you can push your own agendas!"

"May I continue? Mr. President?" a doe-eyed Kevin pleads.

"Let's just wait until we get the whole story. Then we can discuss all of the implications. Do you mind, Ms. Wescott?" President Parkston urges while motioning for her to be seated.

Phoebe unwillingly concedes, settling back into her seat. She fires a smoldering 'will you please DO something' look at Byron. He bows his head and doesn't say a word, even in her defense. Kevin walks toward the serving tray and refills his coffee and takes a sip before continuing.

"M-PAC was able to implant a beta version Vul-Stream chip into the girl. With Vul-Stream, M-PAC is able to monitor all of her vital signs right there from the lab."

"Where did the name Vul-Stream come from?" Secretary of Defense Chuck Hunt asks.

"The manufacturer of Vul-Stream owns the trademark on the name. Our agreement with the manufacturing company restricts us from divulging its name or location. Once everything is set in place, and I do mean everything, we can then proceed with the project for a select few that are in critical need."

"How long will that take?" Chairman of the Federal Reserve, Colin Franky, asks.

"As soon as we get the green light from M-PAC, we carefully go from there one case at a time." Kevin answers.

"Would this be voluntary?" Secretary of State, Pat Vance, asks.

"It is all voluntary. No one will be forced into the program if they don't want to be a part of it," Kevin answers.

"You said the cost of the database would be astronomical. Why would we need something that huge if this is all voluntary?" Phoebe cross examines. "Help me understand, Mr. Rhodes. We have a vaccine that could possibly cure all diseases. And for anyone who takes this vaccine, all they need to do, is agree to a chip implant, am I correct? What if they get a doctor to dig the thing out or God forbid, they cut their own hand off? Now they have the vaccine for free. Has anyone given any thought to that?"

"No one is going to have the chip cut out of their hand. That's absurd. You gonna give up your cell phone or your computer? Of course not. It'd be the same thing. And even if they did dig the chip out, M-PAC would know about it immediately. And I'm pretty sure very few would actually consider cutting off their own hand. For what reason? Look I'm not going to keep answering these types of questions. You've made it clear, Ms. Wescott, you are opposed to the whole Lazarus VI concept, I get it. Duly noted. Can we PLEASE move on?" Kevin says defensively.

Kevin glances towards Parkston for intervention but instead locks eyes with Amanda Sykes. Kevin has had enough questioning from Ms. Wescott. Amanda gives a barely discernable nod of understanding in return.

"You say there's a fee associated with the vaccine along with a monthly charge for the chip. Do you know what that will be?" National Security Advisor, Steven Van Noy asks.

"Thank you Steve! We don't know what that charge will be just yet. How much would you pay to have your daughter cured of cancer? How much would you pay to cure yourself of cancer?

"We know there are going to be fees associated with the Chryzinium vaccine and the Vul-Stream chip. Hospitals will still need to exist as there will still be broken bones, scrapes and bruises. Our hope is doctors will only be needed for injuries. And as far as healthcare dollars, hospitals, doctors, surgeons, pharmaceutical companies will all be subsidized by the Lazarus VI Project.

"The monies generated will not only fund those entities but, hopefully provide enough to pay down our ever increasing national debt. You can see why this is a win-win!" Kevin says enthusiastically.

The room is quiet for a moment while they process the information. Phoebe looks over to Byron hoping to get some kind of inner message from his body language. But there is nothing. Byron sits stoic and glazed over with no tell-tale expression.

This is not typical of Byron, and Phoebe knows too well. Byron has always been an open book when it comes to body language. Not satisfied with the explanation of how the project is designed to work, Phoebe attacks once again.

"Mr. Rhodes. If this is all voluntary, how does all this translate to dollars and cents when it comes to revenue? Unless the cost is so absolutely horrendous, are there really that many diseased people in the country that would be able to afford it? Or are there designs on making the Lazarus VI Project mandatory someday?"

Byron Sutter finally breaks his silence, "I think if Chryzinium is what they say it is, people will be lining up around the block to get the vaccine."

The room falls to dead silence for a moment as all eyes, including Phoebe's are on Byron.

President Parkston takes the opportunity to shut the meeting down by making a closing statement.

"Kevin is right; we can't allow another technological breakthrough to slip through our fingers. That is why I have no choice but to sign into law the Lazarus VI Project via Executive order.

"The law will be temporary and in effect for 42 months. This will give us enough time to examine closely the pros and cons of such a program. I believe that this is the only fair way we can put an end to non-factual conjectures. I must remind you, that you are all a part of the Lazarus VI committee and under a subsequent gag order. This must be kept silent until further notice. No leaks. No press. Period."

"I knew it!" Phoebe says venomously under her breath.

President Parkston hearing her remark responds to her accordingly.

"Did you have something to add, Ms. Wescott?"

"I hope you know what you're getting us into."

That said, she turns sharply and exits the room.

The room remains very quiet. Kevin glances over to Amanda who makes her way to the door and exits, following Phoebe.

HOME FOR THE HOLIDAYS

The wipers dance back and forth swiping tiny dry flakes of snow from the windshield. The Shaes' drive home is slower than usual due to Hillsdale Falls' first snow of the season. Rebecca repeatedly turns around to look at Emily sitting quietly in the backseat. With every glance she can't help but smile.

After nearly two weeks in the hospital, Emily is finally on her way home. She knows that what has taken place can only be explained as an honest-to-goodness miracle. People don't usually recover from brain tumors without surgery. And yet now, Emily is tumor-free and as good as new without so much as one incision.

Rebecca is close to euphoric over Emily's amazing recovery. Turning back to her, Rebecca reaches out and gently takes hold of Emily's hand. Emily returns a subdued smile.

Emily continues her dazed look as she turns to Taylor. Sitting next to her in the backseat, Taylor plays his favorite game on his phone. Curious, Emily leans into to her brother, "What are you doing?" she asks softly. He doesn't break his concentration and without giving a single thought to his sister's question, he ignores her.

"Taylor, Emily asked you a question. Are you going to answer her?" Rebecca asks.

"What? I'm playing a game. What's it to ya?" Taylor snaps back.

"Taylor! That's no way to talk to your sister. You apologize to her."

"Sorry," Taylor mumbles unconvincingly.

Forgetting the question she asked Taylor, Emily turns her attention back to the drive home. Remembering the gift she received from Nurse Sprague, Emily removes from her pocket a small, iridescent blue MP3 player.

Pulling the ear buds free from the case she plugs them firmly into her ears and settles in for the drive home. Gazing out the window, she quietly takes in the scenery as if what she is observing is all new to her. Her eyes are fixed as she softly hums a tune.

THE SHAE'S HOME 3 DAYS LATER

Unfortunately, due to Emily's stint in the hospital, the holidays have been put on hold. Thanksgiving has come and gone, and the Christmas season is now in full swing. Rebecca has no choice but to resolve herself to the fact that if they were going to enjoy any of the holidays this year, at least some preparation must begin soon.

It's 10:00 AM Tuesday morning and Taylor is already at school. Mark has gone to work and Rebecca stays home watching over Emily who must remain home from school until she gets cleared by Doctor Heller. No better time than the present to get started on some much-needed Christmas decorating.

Rebecca digs through the Christmas boxes she has brought down from the attic. She removes strings of lights, strands of garland, and her expensive collection of Saint Nicks to display throughout the house.

Rebecca takes solace in the decorating process with a cheerful, grateful spirit this season. Ironically, this is the one time during the year she and Emily actually spend time enjoying each other's company. In fact, many of the ornaments that hang from the tree are handcrafted by Emily.

Rebecca smiles as she holds in front of her one of Emily's favorite ornaments. It is a clear, hand-blown glass ornament that Emily hand-painted. Inspired by their Christmas vacation in Aspen three years prior, the scene on the ornament is of a snow covered chalet decked with Christmas lights, surrounded by snowy pines. It has all the detail of something that could have been professionally-crafted.

The house is beginning to take on the appearance of a Santa's village explosion. With all that Rebecca has removed from boxes and strewn throughout the living room, there is little room to walk.

Emily enters the living room from upstairs and stops to watch her mother digging and sorting through the holiday trimmings.

"Hey sweetie, how are doing this morning?" Rebecca asks.

"I'm okay. I'm hungry," Emily replies stoically.

"You want me to fix you something?"

Without answering, Emily turns and walks towards the kitchen.

Rebecca has noticed that Emily isn't too interested in Christmas decorating just yet. Nor is she displaying any of her usual uncooperative teenage antics. Since being home, Emily has been sedate and withdrawn, behavior traits she has never had. 'It's most likely a side effect from the medication,' Rebecca thinks, reassuring herself.

Rebecca continues with her décor activities and reaches into a box for garland. Festooning the stair banisters with fir boughs and tiny lights, the house is finally starting to look like Christmas. After applauding her own work, Rebecca calls excitedly to Emily.

"Emily, do you want to give me a hand decorating? Christmas decorating will give us something to do together. It'll be like old times. You can help me with the other banister."

No answer. Rebecca stops what she's doing and strains to listen for any feedback. Hearing Emily foraging in the kitchen, she breathes a sign of relief. Still, she has heard no verbal response, so Rebecca decides to go check in on her.

Even though spacious and attractive, the older Cape Cod style house still retains mid-century swinging café doors that separate the kitchen from the living room. They are not to Rebecca's liking, but until she gets the remodel she's been begging Mark for, 'it is what it is,' as they say.

As she gets to the kitchen, she slowly pushes the café doors open. Rebecca covertly takes a peek at Emily.

Emily is sitting at the kitchen's large island with her back to Rebecca. "Hey sweetie, did you hear me? Do you want to help me decorate?"

Rebecca walks around the island to better face Emily. Dumbfounded, she can't believe her eyes. Directly in front of Emily is a bloodied package of raw hamburger meat. Without acknowledging her mother, she rhythmically shoves clumps of the raw meat into her mouth, one small handful after the other.

"Honey! Sweetie! What are you doing!? You have to cook that," Rebecca gasps, quickly pulling the package away from Emily. Trance-like, Emily slowly lifts her head and with a blank expression, "I'm hungry," she says in monotone.

"I know you're hungry baby, but you can't eat raw meat like that. It's not good for you. Here, let me make you some blueberry pancakes," Rebecca takes the raw meat away from her and stores it back into the refrigerator.

Shaken and speechless, Rebecca fumbles about gathering the ingredients to make pancakes. While at the same time she is now keeping a watchful eye on Emily.

Stone-faced and disconnected, Emily sits motionless on the counter stool. Rebecca can't help but make mental notes about Emily's strange behavior. "Weird," Rebecca mumbles to herself. "Who does that? Who eats raw meat? Definitely some issues we'll be discussing with your doctor."

After Emily is fed a proper breakfast, Rebecca carefully leads Emily into the living room.

"Let's decorate together, okay?" Rebecca says, as she hands Emily one end of garland so she can untangle the other. As she does, Rebecca notices the bandage on Emily's right hand is contaminated with hamburger blood. "Oh, we need to change your bandage. It's all bloody."

Back at the kitchen sink, Rebecca carefully removes the gauze that encases Emily's hand. "Does it hurt?" she asks. Emily shakes her head, 'no.' Layer by layer, Rebecca peels the gauze away.

"Doctor Heller told us that we were supposed to wait until your doctor's appointment on Friday to have the bandage changed."

Again, Emily doesn't respond with words, but acknowledges her mother's remark with a slight smile. "Evidently, he didn't take into consideration you might contaminate the thing while eating half a raw cow!" Rebecca jokes, hoping a little levity will help bring Emily out of her lethargy.

The final layer of gauze comes off exposing the area of the RFID chip implant. The wound can barely be seen. A prick of a rose thorn would do more damage. A small dark spot in the skin between the thumb and the forefinger are the only indication of an 'incision.'

"All of this bandaging, for this? They're kidding, right?" Rebecca cleans Emily's hand.

"You know what? I'm going to leave the bandages off. Just keep it clean and dry, okay. I'm not going to reapply all this bandaging for that little thing," Rebecca declares. Throwing the bandages into the trash can under the sink, she leads Emily back out into the living room.

"You know, you might be able to start back to school next week. If all goes well with your check up," Rebecca says encouragingly.

"I'd like that," Emily says softly, finally breaking her silent spell.

"You talk! I was beginning to think you couldn't speak," Rebecca breathes a sigh of relief.

With a little coaxing, Rebecca is able to get Emily involved with some of the decorating. Slowly, Emily takes on smaller tasks, setting small miniature Saint Nicks throughout the house, weaving more twinkling lights into the garland along the banister and hanging the wreath over the fireplace.

After an hour of helping decorate, Emily begins showing signs of fatigue. Being careful not to overwork her daughter, Rebecca clears a spot on the sofa for Emily to rest. Without aversion, Emily accepts the offer and lies down on the couch. Within minutes, she is fast asleep. Taking the quilt from the hall closet, Rebecca covers her up. Looking at her daughter sleeping soundly, she takes a moment to relax a little herself.

As soon as Rebecca finds a comfortable seat, the doorbell rings. Rebecca rushes to the door, hoping to answer it before the bell rings again, possible waking Emily. She pulls the front open and Alesha stands holding a box with two large dishes inside.

"I made some chicken fried steak and a green bean casserole for you guys," Alesha proudly announces.

"Oh, how sweet of you! Come on in," Rebecca whispers, parting the way for Alesha's entrance. "Just need to be quiet, Em's asleep on the couch."

The two quickly pass through the living room and enter into the kitchen. "So, how is she?" Alesha asks while placing the box on the counter.

"She's okay. It's a miracle. She's walking and talking. It's like nothing happened."

"I wish she was awake. I have something for her," Alesha says.

"More? You brought us dinner. That was plenty. What do you have for Emily?"

Alesha removes from her shoulder bag a small plastic zip lock bag. Inside the clear baggy is a small silver heart shaped locket. "You remember this?" Alesha asks holding it up in front of Rebecca's face. Taking the plastic bag, Rebecca immediately recognizes the small silver charm.

"I gave this to you for your sixteenth birthday," Rebecca says, amazed Alesha still had it after all these years.

Rebecca removes the locket from the baggy and holds it up by the thin delicate silver chain. Taking the locket in hand, she opens it and reads the tiny inscription engraved inside, "*Love is Eternal*."

"I always felt bad about having this. You said your grandmother gave this to you. But, you wanted me to have it. I think it belongs to Emily, now."

Rebecca embraces Alesha tightly as tears roll down her cheeks. "You give it to her, okay?" Alesha continues.

"Oh, are you sure, Leesh?"

"I'm sure. And, enjoy the dinner. You know I make a mean green bean casserole!"

"We will. Thank you so much."

"Okay, I gotta meet Dave at Steamer's. We're looking at getting a new car for me. Christmas present! Yay!"

"Oh fantastic! Go crazy girl, have fun!" Rebecca dabs her tears from her face.

Alesha grabs an apple from the fruit basket on Rebecca's counter. With a big smile, she exits out the side kitchen door, waving to Rebecca with apple in hand. Rebecca looks down at the locket. Her emotions get the best of her as fresh tears trickle down her cheeks once again.

SHAE'S HOUSE, 7:52 PM

It's getting late in the evening, and Mark still hasn't

come home from work. It's not like Mark to stay out late without calling. Rebecca, Emily and Taylor have just finished the dinner Alesha prepared.

Because of Emily's condition, she is allowed a temporary reprieve from many of her daily chores. Of course, this does not meet with Taylor's approval. Tonight, he will have to clear the table and load the dishwasher. Again!

"I don't know why Brain-Fade can't at least help clear the table. It's not like she's a vegetable," Taylor gripes loudly.

"Taylor Michael Shae!" Rebecca snaps. "That's not how you speak to your sister! Ever! You hear me?"

"I wasn't talking to her. I was talking to you," Taylor retorts.

Unexpectedly, Emily speaks softly, "I don't mind. I can help."

The kitchen is instantly silenced. Rebecca is almost troubled to hear such kind words come from Emily. It's not like her to be so respectful. Taylor is also speechless, hearing his sister offer to help. He stares at her in disbelief.

This is a side of Emily the family hasn't heard from in a very long time. It's not often a kind word is heard coming from either sibling's mouth, at least for the last couple of years.

Mark's headlights flash through the Shaes' kitchen windows, startling Rebecca. "About time," Rebecca mumbles under her breath. Mark barges in through the side kitchen door.

"Where have you been? No call. No text. No nothing," Rebecca grills Mark. "You missed a wonderful dinner that Alesha made for us!"

"Put some coffee on. Carol is coming over."

Ignoring the interrogation, Mark helps to tidy up the dinner dishes in preparation for his guest.

"Wait, what? Who's Carol?"

"Carol from work. Carol Hoecker. Please, just help me make this place somewhat presentable. Make some coffee."

"Why is this 'Carol' person coming here?"

"Dad's got a girlfriend," Taylor chides, in singsong fashion.

"Enough out of you, mister! Go disappear some-where," Mark snaps.

"Well, who is she?" Rebecca presses. "I should at least know who I'm making coffee for on such short notice."

"She's head of research and development and we've got a situation with our trademark application. Every-thing I have for the application is in my office here at home and we have to have this fixed and in the mail tonight. So please help to make her comfortable. She's coming here as a favor."

"Fine, fine!" Rebecca says coolly as she prepares the coffee maker. Just then the doorbell rings. Turning to Emily, Mark gives her a kiss on the cheek, "Come with me sweetie." Putting his arm around Emily, he leads her to the living room.

Christmas decorations and boxes still lie about in

disarray. Ignoring them, Mark sits Emily down on the couch and as though speaking to the family dog, he tells her to stay. Mark reaches the front door and pulls it open quickly.

"Carol. Please come in. Please excuse the mess. We're decorating for Christmas."

Carol Hoecker enters the Shae home. She is tall, graceful, physically fit and strikingly beautiful. Not quite 30 years of age, she wears an impeccably tailored navy blue pant suit. A white ruffled blouse softens the neckline. Her long brown hair is wrapped in a loosely-coifed bun.

Soft tendrils that have escaped the bun fall around her face. A perfect shade of pink accents her full lips. The pant suit only emphasizes her long legs as she makes her way into the foyer. With a stunning smile she greets Mark. "Good evening Mark. This is a lovely home you have."

"Thank you. This is my daughter. Emily, this is Carol Hoecker from work," Mark says clearing his throat.

Rebecca enters the living room just then. "And this is my wife, Rebecca," Mark continues. Carol flashes her perfect smile at Rebecca and extends her hand for a friendly handshake. Rebecca obliges with her best 'I'm not at all intimidated by you' face.

"Hello, welcome to our home," Rebecca says, maybe too sweetly. Trying not to stare, she asks, "Would you like some coffee?"

"That would be wonderful. Thank you. Black please."

"No problem! Just give me a couple of minutes," Rebecca is trying her best not to say anything condescending. With a fake smile and a quick turn, she pushes through the swinging doors to the kitchen.

Taylor comes into the living room looking for his sister with the intention of getting her to make good on her offer to help with the dinner dishes. That is until he feasts his pubescent eyes on Carol. "Oooolala," Taylor announces loudly as he checks out the long-legged beauty standing in his living room.

"Oh brother," Mark mumbles, shaking his head with embarrassment.

"Carol, this is our son. Taylor, this Carol Hoecker. She's an associate from work. We have work to do, so go back in the kitchen and get your chores done," Mark emphasizes with 'the look.'

Taylor, getting the message loud and clear, signals to Emily to come and help him. Mark intervenes, "She stays here on the couch. Just go do your chores. Now!"

Taylor reluctantly turns back toward the kitchen, but not without one last ogle at Carol. She smiles at him and with a cute wave, she says sweetly, "Nice to meet you, Taylor."

Rebecca relaxes her demeanor and enters the living room with a tray bearing the coffee.

"Coffee's ready!" Rebecca announces.

"Oh, I am terribly sorry, actually, I think I better decline that coffee, after all. I have an early flight tomorrow, and I won't be able to stay that long. I'm so sorry to put you out. Silly me!" Carol genuinely apologizes with a sweet smile.

"Oh, what a shame," Rebecca lies. "I totally get that. I'll get out of your hair so you two can get your business done."

Turning on her heel, Rebecca disguises her annoyance with a pasted-on happy hostess face. She reluctantly leaves the room.

"Let's go back to my office; I have all of the paperwork in a folder in my desk," Mark says, moving the evening along. Mark leads Carol back to his office, closing the glass French doors behind them.

Quickly returning to the living room, Rebecca decides now would be a good time to start picking up some of the decorations that are strewn about. Of course, the task doubles as a reason to surreptitiously keep an eye on Carol and Mark.

SHAES' HOME, LATER THAT EVENING

Rebecca is in bed with the covers pulled up around her. The lamp on her side of the bed is off, leaving Mark's lamp as the only light in the room. Slowly the bedroom door opens and Mark quietly enters. He tiptoes into the room, trying not to wake Rebecca.

"I'm awake," Rebecca announces curtly. Her unexpected statement startles Mark, causing him to run his little toe into the bench at the end of the bed.

"Ow!" Mark grits his teeth and grabs his foot as the pain ripples up his leg. Mark quickly hobbles to the bathroom to check his toe for damage and get ready for bed. Seeing the damage is only superficial he strips off his pants and slips into his pajama bottoms.

After brushing his teeth and killing as much time as possible, he begrudgingly emerges from the bathroom quietly, trying to slip into bed unnoticed. Not wanting to close the evening with a bunch of interrogative dialog, Mark hopes to simply turn off his light and go straight to sleep.

"So, how come I've never heard of this Carol lady before? And what took so long? I thought she was here to pick up some papers and then leave," Rebecca asks.

"And so the evening begins," Mark whispers to himself.

"What?" Rebecca asks.

"Nothing. I told you, Carol works in research and development. There are a lot of people that work at SpiresGate, you know that. I've never had to work with her before. That's why I've never mentioned her before. Okay? Some of the papers were incorrect and we had to redo them."

"Do you think she's pretty?"

"What? No. I mean, I don't know. I haven't noticed."

"Oh come on. You mean to tell me you haven't noticed how gorgeous she is?"

"Well, yeah, she's pretty. But not as pretty as you."

"Hmmmm," Rebecca says through pursed lips.

Mark reaches over and shuts the light off in hopes that the interrogation is finally over.

Rebecca breaks the silence again, "She kept staring at Emily. You didn't say anything to her about what was done, did you?"

"Of course not, nobody knows a thing."

"She acts so subdued," Rebecca softly confesses.

"Carol?"

"No, not Carol, Emily."

"Maybe this is the real Emily. Maybe the tumor was causing her to be aggravated all the time and we're just now seeing the normal Emily."

"Maybe," Rebecca mumbles, trying to be convinced.

Mark and Rebecca lay in bed quietly for a few minutes. It is possible Rebecca is satisfied with Mark's explanation about Emily. At least she hopes so. After a moment of quiet, she continues.

"I walked in on her while she was eating from a package of raw hamburger meat."

"Who was eating raw hamburger meat!?" Mark asks.

"Em. Who do you think? I walked in on her while she was in the kitchen today. I thought she was making a sandwich or something. Instead, she was sitting at the island eating from a two pound package of raw hamburger. With her fingers. Like it was a bag of chips."

"Maybe there's something missing in her diet. I wouldn't worry about it. We see the doctor on Friday. We'll ask him. I'm sure everything's alright."

"You know the bandage the doctor put on her right hand? I had to take that big thing off. She got hamburger blood all over it."

"Yeah?"

"Well that great big bandage did nothing more than cover up a tiny poke in the skin. Not even so much as a stitch."

"You worry too much. You know how doctors over exaggerate everything they do. Remember when I broke my toe? They put a cast on my foot. Like they're probably going to do again tomorrow," Marks says sarcastically referring to his new toe injury.

"Maybe you're right."

"Of course I am. Everything is fine. You've been under a lot of stress. Get some sleep, okay?"

INTELLECTUALLY SPEAKING

The days are getting colder and even though snow has been light so far, it's only a matter of time before the measurable snowfall of winter makes its appearance. Shoppers and travelers scurry about trying to beat its imminent arrival.

Emily's first few days home from the hospital have been interesting. But, the house is finally decorated and even some of the Christmas shopping has been done. Emily has not been all that much help. But, all things considered, she is at least stable.

Today, Emily goes to the doctor for her first scheduled checkup since being released from the hospital. With Taylor already at school, Mark and Rebecca are getting ready for their drive across town for the 10:30 AM appointment at Doctor Heller's office.

As has been the issue all week, Emily seems to be disconnected with her surroundings, and cannot seem to stay focused. Without a doubt, Rebecca has every intention of voicing her concerns and getting some much-needed answers from Doctor Heller.

"Emily, are you ready, sweetie?" Rebecca calls to Emily from downstairs.

There is no answer, and even though Rebecca is frustrated that she has to run back upstairs to check on her, she does so out of concern. Rebecca taps on Emily's door and slowly enters her room. To her surprise, Emily is dressed and is sitting at her vanity brushing her long brown hair.

"Emily, you didn't answer me. Did you not hear me?" Rebecca asks, a little annoyed she climbed all the way back upstairs for what appears to be for no reason. Still, Emily does not answer.

"Emily, are you listening to me?" Rebecca again asks, sounding a bit more aggravated. Still not getting a response, she walks over to Emily and taps her on the shoulder. Emily spins around in her seat. Looking up at Rebecca, she quickly removes the ear buds from her ears and smiles.

Rebecca is somewhat relieved, "No wonder you aren't hearing me, silly! Time to go, okay?" Rebecca's initial fears are put to rest. Her daughter just needs her tunes.

"I was downstairs calling for you. Your father's in the car waiting for us."

"I'm ready," Emily says. She stands and grabs the small music player from her vanity, stuffing it into her purse and exits out of her room. Rebecca shrugs and follows close behind.

"Teenagers! Gotta love em!" Rebecca mumbles to herself as she follows Emily out the door.

HILLSDALE FALLS MEMORIAL MEDICAL CENTER, 10:30 AM

Mark, Rebecca, and Emily stand in front of Doctor Heller's office door. "This is it, right?" Rebecca asks Mark.

"Yeah," Mark says impassively.

Mark taps lightly on Doctor Heller's door. A faint "Come in," is heard from inside. Opening the door, the three enter the doctor's office.

Doctor Heller, Nurse Maggie Sprague, Doctor Levi Mintle, Doctor Brad Nunenbush, and Doctor Carly Stinson are present as the Shae's enter.

Doctor Heller re-introduces those in attendance. "You remember my colleagues?"

Rebecca and Mark nod and smile, "Hello again."

From behind his desk, Doctor Heller stands and addresses Emily, "How are you feeling?"

Emily smiles and responds politely, "I'm fine."

"Good!" Doctor Heller acknowledges. "Nurse Sprague and the other doctors are going to take you to the examination room to draw some blood and perform a few tests. Doctor Heller smiles reassuringly, "That is, if that's okay with you, Emily?"

She nods obediently to the doctor.

"Come with us, dear," Nurse Sprague grasps Emily's hand, leading her and the entourage of doctors out of Heller's office.

"Please, have a seat," Doctor Heller offers the Shaes. "Can I get you anything? Coffee, water?"

Rebecca and Mark both decline the offer with a soft, "No thank you," and take their seats in the chairs opposite Doctor Heller's desk. His demeanor more serious now, Doctor Heller addresses his first topic of concern.

"You have to leave the bandaging on Emily's hand. You took it off. Why?"

"I'm glad you asked that," Rebecca answers. "She got it soaked. You know how?" she asks, annoyed. Doctor Heller nods for Rebecca to continue.

"I walked into the kitchen the other day and she was sitting at the island eating a two-pound package of raw hamburger meat. I removed the bandage to change it because it was soaked with hamburger blood. A little strange, yeah?"

"It's no doubt the medicine. She's probably lacking in iron."

"Okay, why all the bandaging for a tiny little poke in her hand? I mean forgive me, I'm no doctor, but six yards of gauze for a pin prick seems a bit much, so I left the dressing off."

Doctor Heller smiles slightly, "I can see why you'd be a little mystified. The bandaging does more than protect the wound. It's primarily there to keep out ultraviolet light. The RFID chip in her hand is very delicate and sensitive to sunlight, even when indoors, during this period of the healing process.

"She needs to stay heavily bandaged for at least two weeks until the tissue around the implant completely heals. If the bandage does get wet or contaminated, re-bandage it with fresh gauze as soon as you can. About ten to twelve layers will do just fine. I'll be sure to send you home with an ample supply. You have been giving her the medication, correct?"

"Yes, of course," Rebecca responds. "So what's this medication for, anyway?"

"What Emily has in her hand is a foreign object. The body's natural response is to reject it. That could result in infection and a host of other complications. We don't want that. The Rozonothal helps the body accept the implant. How long that takes, we don't know. It's entirely up to Emily's metabolism."

"Is this medication also responsible for her docile behavior? I mean, she's like a completely different girl. She's passive, non-confrontational, easy-going, and pleasant to be around."

"You make it sound like that's a bad thing," Mark interjects.

"It could be the drug," Dr. Heller continues. "It could be the vaccine. Or, it could be that the tumor caused a neurological aggravation in her brain which affected her behavior. Now that the tumor is gone, you may be experiencing the 'normal' Emily. What I'm trying to say, as things stand right now, we don't know yet. How about we pull her off the Rozonothal after Christmas? That should give her body plenty of time to properly accept the implant. Okay?"

"I told you, there was nothing to worry about," Mark reassures Rebecca.

"As soon as they're done with the tests, you'll be free to go," Doctor Heller says in closing.

He stands and steps around the side of his desk, "I'm a phone call away. Anything you need, don't hesitate to ask. Okay?" He places a comforting hand on Rebecca's shoulder, and she smiles.

"Thank you, doctor. Oh, one more thing. Would it be okay if Emily goes back to school? She's getting bored hanging around the house and she's missed so much school already. I think it would do her some good."

Doctor Heller pauses for a moment to consider. "I tell you what. Once we get results back from the tests and if everything looks normal, then yes. But only on a light duty basis. No P.E. If she's not feeling well, you must be able to get her home right away. Is that doable?"

"Yes. How long before we'll hear back on her labs?" Rebecca asks.

"She's not leaving here today without all the labs completed and in my hands. And that's what they're doing now. So we'll all know how she's doing before you leave."

"So she can go back to school Monday?"

"If everything checks out, I don't see any reason she couldn't go back then," Doctor Heller says optimistically while walking to the door. "I'll be back in a few minutes. It shouldn't take much longer. You two sit tight and we'll see how things look," Doctor Heller leaves and closes the door behind him.

Rebecca looks at Mark and smiles. Mark on the other hand looks disconnected and withdrawn.

"You didn't say much," Rebecca comments.

Mark doesn't respond. He removes his cell phone from his coat pocket and checks it for the fifth time with a quick glance before returning it back to its place.

Rebecca takes Mark by the hand and squeezes it tightly. "You okay? What's the matter?" she asks softly.

Mark nods with a 'nothing, I'm fine' dismissal.

LIBERTY HIGH SCHOOL, MONDAY MORNING

Returning to high school after her stay in the hospital has made Emily a bit of a celebrity within her circle of friends. As soon as Rebecca drops her off in front of her school, Emily is mobbed by friends, acquaintances, and well-wishers. After close to a month out of school, Emily has much to catch up on.

"What happened to you? Are you alright? Are you going to die?" are all questions Emily is being asked, even before she takes her first step into the building.

Before Emily gets overwhelmed by all the attention, Christie Lee, one of the school administrators, comes to her aid. Waving off the entourage of curious students that surround Emily, Christie quickly escorts Emily into the safety of the school office.

"Hello Miss Shae," a familiar voice greets from just inside the vice-principal's office. Mr. Alverez, Emily's world history teacher, peeks out from behind the office door and smiles at Emily who stands quietly behind the office counter. "Welcome back. How are you feeling?" he asks with genuine concern.

Smiling back at him, she responds with a soft, "I'm fine."

"Good, good! So glad to hear that. You have some catching up to do, Miss Shae. I'll see you in class," Emily resumes the process of checking in at the administration desk.

First period is study hall; a class Emily has often ditched. Her best friend and co-conspirator, Samantha, meets Emily in the hallway just outside the school office.

"Em! You're back. I missed you," exclaims Samantha, giving Emily a big hug.

"Hi Sam," Emily says, somewhat indifferent to Sam's affection.

"Hey, let's grab a smoke before Brown's class," Samantha says, grabbing hold of Emily's arm to lead her off school grounds.

Pulling away, Emily stops, "I don't want to."

"Woah girl! What happened to you? You get all religious or something?" Samantha teases.

"No. I just don't feel like smoking right now. That's all," Emily says simply. Throwing her book bag up over her shoulder, she walks off, leaving her bewildered friend standing in the hallway.

World history class begins in a few minutes. As students file into the classroom, Emily is already at her desk. With earbuds in her ears, she listens intently to her MP3 player. Samantha takes her seat next to Emily just before class begins.

"Hey, you okay?" Samantha asks. Emily doesn't hear Samantha. She sits quietly thumbing through her textbook. The class chaos is settled quickly by the entrance of Mr. Alverez.

"Good morning, students. Please open your textbooks to page 401."

Mr. Alvarez notices Emily looking down at her book with her earbuds in her ears. Walking to the front row of desks where Emily is seated, he gently pulls the headpiece from her ears.

"Class time, Miss Shae. And I promise you this. You can't afford to miss even one second. So I suggest you pay close attention from here on out. Do we understand each other?"

"Yes sir," Emily responds. Snickers and laughter from the other students meet with a cool disapproving glare from Mr. Alvarez and are quickly silenced.

"Now, let's get started, shall we?" Looking around the class, Mr. Alverez delivers his first quiz question of the day, "We know the Spanish-American War took place in 1898. And we also know it took place between the United States and Spain. Mr. O'Day, will you please tell us the reason for the conflict?"

"We weren't happy with the way they made their tacos?"

Subdued laughter erupts.

"Enough! No, Mr. O'Day. You have confused Spain with Mexico. Spain is not now, nor has ever been known for its tacos. It is clear you did not read Chapter 17."

Without raising her hand, Emily interrupts to answer the question.

"The Spanish-American conflict of 1898 began with the sinking of the U.S.S. Maine, a warship. It was never really clear how it sank, but there were speculations, and for good reason. It was believed the Spaniards were responsible. Anyway, there was an immediate outcry from the people to do something about it. You see, Cuba had been struggling for independence from Spain for over three years. There was a lot of anti-Spanish rioting, so the U.S.S. Maine was sent there to protect U.S. citizens and property. But, the Maine was mysteriously sunk right there in Havana Harbor.

Soon after, the U.S. Congress granted the President, William McKinley, use of force to ensure Spain's complete withdrawal from Cuba, while at the same time, relinquishing any U.S. intentions of annexing Cuba.

Spain declared war on the U.S. and then the U.S. declared war on Spain. So we sent a naval squadron of battleships into Manila Bay and sunk the anchored

Spanish fleet all in one morning. We kicked their butts. We won. The Spanish American war was over."

The entire classroom stares blankly at Emily.

Mr. Alverez, at a loss for words, is unsure how to respond.

"So…." clearing his throat, Mr. Alvarez replies, "Ms. Shae. You know something about the Spanish-American war? I'm impressed. Is this something you learned about because of family history?"

"No sir. Just something I happened to know about," Emily replies politely.

UNEXPECTED TRUTHS

Baggs' phone is positioned conveniently on the nightstand less than two feet from his ear. The old astronaut snores through its incessant ringing. After eight rings, the phone is programmed to go straight to voicemail, and finally does. Seconds later, the phone begins another bout of impatient rings.

Awakening with a start from his REM sleep and with robotic precision he reaches over and grabs the phone from the nightstand. Pushing the talk button, he places the phone up to his ear without opening his eyes. "Hello!" he says groggily.

"I need to talk to you. In private. ASAP," the voice announces on the other end.

"Who is this?" Baggs inquires, shaking off his lethargy.

"It's me, Sy."

"Sy? What's up? What time is it?"

"Not here, not now. Pick me up at my place in an hour."

Squinting at the clock on his nightstand, Baggs waits for the numbers to focus before responding.

"It's 5:45 in the morning! You want me to pick you up at a quarter to seven? You're kidding, right?"

"No. I'm not kidding. Be here in an hour. Don't be late," Sy responds brusquely as the call ends with an audible click.

"Hello?"

Realizing that Sy ended the call, Baggs sets his phone back down on the nightstand. "What the heck?" he mumbles. Throwing back the covers and begrudgingly climbing out from the comfort of his bed, Baggs slides into his slippers and slowly scuffs his way to the bathroom.

Sy's Home, 6:45 AM

Baggs pulls his truck into Sy's circular driveway at precisely 6:45 AM and parks in front of the spacious entryway.

Designed with huge white columns that support the circular driveways' overhang, Sy and Norma's residence could be featured in a home and garden magazine. Baggs' aged truck is an obvious eyesore against the backdrop of the elegant architecture and pristine landscaping.

Before having a chance to shut off his engine, Sy exits the large, ornate, wrought-iron front door and immediately jumps into the passenger side of Baggs' truck.

"You have your cell phone on you?" Sy questions Baggs, skipping any pleasantries.

"Yeah, of course."

"Turn it off. And don't just put it on silent. Shut it down completely. Please."

"Fine," Baggs concedes as he reluctantly removes his cell phone from his jacket pocket and powers it off. Once the screen goes black, he shows it to Sy. "There."

Satisfied, Sy waves his hand, motioning Baggs to drive. "Let's go," he instructs with a sense of urgency.

"Go where?"

"Just go," Sy says. "I'll give directions while we drive."

Sy has always been a bit on the gruff side, but not without his fair share of tall tales. Baggs can see why Lewis and Sy hit it off. Most times, Baggs and Lewis take his stories with a cautious grain of salt, but the gravity in Sy's voice at present makes Baggs intrigued.

At the end of Sy's long driveway, Baggs stops for direction.

"Left, right? Which way are we going?"

"Right. Go up to Tamarack Trail. We'll head over to North Park."

"So what's up? Is there something wrong?"

"I need to talk to you about something, okay?"

"Okay," Baggs acknowledges and heads right onto the sloping residential street.

Ten minutes later, Baggs is driving slowly along the park's edge on Tamarack Trail. "Just pull over here," Sy instructs. Baggs brings his truck to a stop next to the curb.

"Okay? So, what's going on?" Baggs asks while turning to face Sy directly.

"You know where I work. But what you don't know, is what I work on or with."

Baggs replies impatiently, "Yeah, I do know."

"No Baggs. You don't know. I work at the Pentagon. I just fly in and out from Wright Patterson."

"I've been to your office at Wright Patterson. I don't recall you ever saying anything about your office at the Pentagon." Baggs is wondering where all of this leading and beginning to wish he was still in his warm bed.

"I have an office there on the field of course, but that's not where I do what I do."

"I thought you worked as a technician in the jet propulsion lab. Now you're telling me you have an office at the Pentagon? Forgive me if I find all of this a bit off the radar," Baggs says sarcastically.

Sy pulls an envelope from his jacket pocket, "Take this and read it." He hands the document to Baggs. Taking the unsealed envelope from Sy and removing the single sheet of paper, Baggs looks it over half-heartedly. The letterhead displays the logo for the United States Department of Homeland Security.

Looking at the envelope, Baggs reads that it is addressed to Simon Lazlo's office at the Pentagon. Baggs thinks to himself, 'Wow, this guy's good. He's managed to create pretty authentic-looking letterhead, envelope, addresses, and everything. If this is some kind of a prank, this guy's got to be the king of crap.'

"So you want me to read this?" Baggs asks blandly.

"I've been invited to Los Alamos National Laboratory in New Mexico, January 31st, for a one-day seminar. The head speaker is a doctor who is a leader in the studies of chromium transuranic sulfides, CTS-235, and Unibihexium carbon – DNA altering compounds.

"Listen, I know of this guy. He's been around a long time and I think you need to hear what he has to say. There are some pretty far-out ideas being presented, and some of it has to do with what you and Lewis have been talking about. The Grand Canyon sightings."

"Why aren't you going?"

"Norma and I are leaving."

"Leaving? Where are you going?"

"Listen, the less you know about me right now the better. Take the invite here and go to this thing. This letter and a form of ID with my name will get you in."

"Does anyone at this so-called summit know you? You do realize we don't exactly look alike. And I am 'Commander Walter Baggerly.' The astronaut. The once-famous BLACK astronaut!"

"I don't think anyone there knows me personally."

"Well someone there will no-doubt know me. I'm not a celebrity or anything, but I have been on the news, and in a few newspapers here and there. Most assuredly, someone there would recognize me. And what do you mean you're leaving?"

"Like I said, there's some pretty bizarre things happening and Norma and I have decided to pull up stakes and get out of Dodge for a while. Send Lewis. We can make up some ID for him and he can go in my place."

"Lewis? Are you kidding? He wouldn't last ten minutes without getting into trouble. And now we're getting into the fake ID business, great!"

"Kids do it all the time. Not hard to make up a pretty convincing ID. Especially with the printers they got now-a-days."

"I don't know, Sy. This is a little much for me to take in. And who is this speaker guy anyway? How do you know of him?"

"Please, Baggs. You've been a good friend. I need you to believe me. I'm on the level here, okay? There are some radical things going on with the government you should know about."

Baggs takes in a deep breath. With a pause, he looks over to Sy.

"You're totally being straight with me? Right? No bull?"

"As God as my witness. Oh, and one more thing, watch your backs. You guys have been delving into some things that could easily arouse the interest of those who could become a problem for you."

"It sounds like you're telling me we may be subjected to men in black SUV's following us around. Is that why we're out here? Is that why you told me to turn off my phone?"

"I'm just saying, be careful. You're going to learn some things that only a very select few know. What Lewis and you have been investigating with all of the Arizona UFO stuff? It's getting close to raising a few eyebrows."

"That's just great; Lewis gets me into something else. I better not end up in an abandoned warehouse with some goon interrogating me with electrodes and probes," Baggs says while starting up his truck.

Baggs continues, "I take it we're done here? No, let me rephrase that. We are done here. I'm taking you home. I think I've heard enough. I gotta think about all of this."

LEWIS' HOME, 8:30 AM

Looking like a garage sale explosion both inside and out, Lewis' home is cluttered with junk from the front yard to the backyard and everything in-between. In his front room dressed in boxer shorts and a T-shirt, Lewis digs for a small clock-spring hidden somewhere in several boxes of aircraft parts, instruments, and gadgets.

His propensity for tinkering with all things mechanical keeps him plenty occupied with his vast collection of NASA discards.

When he's not reading the latest UFO conspiracy magazine or watching some rerun UFO show on cable, Lewis tinkers with his collection of parts and pieces that most people would find absolutely useless. His dream is to stumble onto the next great invention or discovery of the century. Whatever that might be.

'Mad Scientist' would be an understatement. Since retiring, he has built for himself a treasure trove of possibilities created primarily via his vast collection of steampunk junk.

The doorbell interrupts his search, and Lewis slowly straightens his creaky stiff knees to a standing position. "Hold your horses! Gimme a minute!" he shouts toward the door. Navigating his house is never a small feat.

After stepping over and around boxes of junk, airplane parts, cables and nests of wiring, Lewis makes it to the front door. Opening the door, he is greeted by a bewildered-looking Baggs.

"Baggs! What are you doing here? Come on in," Lewis offers.

Baggs peeks inside the partially open door, observing the quagmire of wall to wall junk. "Holy crap! How do you to live like this? Is that a glider cockpit in your den? There's even more junk than the last time I was here," Baggs shakes his head as he enters.

"We need to talk. Is there a place we can sit?" Baggs asks doubtfully.

"Yeah, in the kitchen. Follow me."

Lewis carefully leads Baggs through a narrow trail of debris to where a small kitchen table and a couple of chairs border the room's one bare wall. Clearing two old pizza boxes and a half-dozen empty soda cans from the table, Lewis offers Baggs a chair.

"You want some coffee or something?"

Baggs wipes the crumbs from the wooden dining chair before sitting. Seeing the unsanitary condition of the kitchen, Baggs declines, "No thanks."

Sitting opposite Baggs, Lewis turns his attention to the reason for the visit. "So, what brings you here, and so early in the morning? Everything alright? You look like you've just seen an alien."

"Okay, first off. How well do you really know Sy?" Baggs asks.

"Oh, I don't know, well enough I suppose. He's a bit out there, but fun to talk with, why?"

"Did you know he works at the Pentagon?"

"No, but I do know he's pretty involved with some of the higher-ups in the propulsion lab. So I wouldn't be surprised."

"Just out of curiosity, have you ever met his wife?"

Lewis sits in thought for a couple of moments. "No, I don't think I have, why?"

"I don't know. He hit me with some pretty bizarre stuff this morning and I'm just wondering how well we really know him. I mean some of what he comes up sounds like nonsense."

"I'm not sure it is nonsense. You know as well as I do, this isn't the same America we grew up in."

"Well, he got me out of bed this morning to show me this," Baggs removes from his top jacket pocket the envelope and letter from the office of Homeland Security addressed to Sy. Opening the envelope he removes the letter and hands it to Lewis. Pulling his reading glasses from the top of his head and placing them on the bridge of his nose, Lewis reads the letter.

"Yeah, so. It's an invite to some scientific hub-bub at Los Alamos. So what's the big deal?" Lewis asks.

"Sy had me pick him up at his place first thing this morning. Had me turn off my cell phone and then drive him over to North Park. It's like this big secret meeting where he shows me this letter. But that's not the big deal. The big deal is, he and Norma are moving away for a while, leaving town.

"He's freaked out about something. He wants us to go to this thing. He says we need to know what's going on, and there's intel concerning the Grand Canyon sightings. He wants you to go in his place," Baggs tells Lewis.

"I don't look anything like Sy. And aren't they going to be checking IDs?" Lewis reacts.

"Are you kidding me? You could be his father. And besides, no one there knows what Sy looks like, so they wouldn't suspect anything if you showed up with a passable ID badge."

"This sounds a little out there, but, okay," Lewis responds.

Baggs continues, "I drove around for 45 minutes after dropping him off, thinking I might be crazy for even coming over here. I don't know, I think maybe we should go. Sy seemed very nervous about all of this. Oh yeah, he said for us to be careful and to 'watch our backs.' That we're getting too close to something we're not supposed to know about. I don't know, what do you think?"

"Heck yeah! This will be a kick in the pants. I've got a buddy who does graphic art stuff. He owes me one. I know I can get him to make me up a pretty decent ID."

"Yeah, that's exactly what I was afraid of."

"Afraid? You can let them strap your butt to a rocket built by the lowest bidder, but you're afraid of this?"

VENOMOUS

It never fails, there's always that one house in the neighborhood where the lawn is never mowed. The garbage cans are over-stuffed. Old Christmas lights from years past hang forgotten from one side of the roof. The paint is peeling and the shrubs are overgrown and unkempt. That's the Milners' home.

Even though the homes in the neighborhood are of the older Craftsman style, the neighborhood is well-kept. The pride of ownership is evident in the meticulously landscaped yards, white picket fences and cheery, brightly painted mailboxes. Except Roxy and Marty Milner's home.

Roxanne was not brought up well. Her parents were both killed in a car crash, leaving Roxanne's grandmother, Martha Flynn, to raise Roxy from the early age of five. Martha absolutely loved Roxanne. Martha willed all of her earthly possessions to Roxanne upon her death, which came suddenly from a heart attack at only 66 years of age.

Martha was a good woman with a generous spirit; maybe too generous, considering the effect it would have on her granddaughter. She doted on Roxy, spoiling her literally rotten. Martha did not teach her about the ramifications of bad decision-making, finances, getting a good education, goal-setting, or real life in general.

In junior high, Roxanne ran with the degenerate. She dropped out of high school in the eleventh grade and had already earned herself a small but permanent rap sheet for petty crimes. Public intoxication, minor in possession of alcohol, and shoplifting. Roxy was too young and irresponsible to appreciate the inheritance left to her by her benevolent grandmother.

Roxanne never married, but has had a steady stream of 'boyfriends.' She ended up pregnant and giving birth to Martha when she was only 19 years old. Barely an adult herself, Roxanne has always felt resentment at being burdened with child-rearing at such a young age.

Roxy sees young Martha as an inconvenience. With another mouth to feed, Martha is an albatross around her neck. Roxy's method of parenting is pretty much hands-off. Give the child plenty of chores and send her outside as much as possible.

Martha, a namesake of her grandmother, is a kind and inquisitive child. She is also known to be somewhat of a mechanical genius. Her aptitude for visualizing the mechanics of almost anything with moving parts is uncanny.

Roxy only acknowledges her daughters mechanical prowess when it comes to keeping her junk car running.

It is 4:15 in the afternoon and Marty arrives home from school. Ditching her bike on the front lawn, she runs up the rickety steps and into the house.

She's hungry and heads straight for the kitchen. First looking for sustenance in the cupboards, she finds nothing appetizing. She then opens the refrigerator and pokes her head deep inside. Pushing cans of beer aside, she reaches all the way to the back and grabs a package of American cheese.

As she begins to pull her head out from the refrigerator, with cheese grasped tightly in her hands, the door is suddenly slammed shut on her head. Marty immediately cries out with pain.

"What's with all the banging around, huh?" the offender asks maliciously before kicking the refrigerator door closed on her again.

Marty cries out louder, "Ow!" Falling to the floor, she grabs her head and turns to see Vernon standing over her. The package of cheese has fallen to the floor. Vernon's dirty boot kicks the package of cheese slices up against the lower cabinets, spreading the slices all over the kitchen.

He reaches down and picks Marty up by her hair.

With his breath smelling of old beer and cigarettes, he screams, "How many times do I have to tell you to keep it quiet when you get home, huh? What's with all the banging?"

With the back of his right hand, Vernon smacks Marty across the face, cutting her brow just above her right eye with his gold nugget pinky ring. Marty squeals out in pain, falling to the floor again in a heap. "Get this mess cleaned up!" Vernon shouts as he opens the refrigerator door, grabbing himself a beer.

Marty begins picking up the dirty slices of cheese. Tears flow down her cheeks and blood drips from her brow and onto the floor.

Dressed in a dirty white tank top and grubby jeans, the lanky, six-foot tall Vernon Kootsmier sits at the kitchen table and opens his can of beer. "Knock it off, before I give you something to cry about! You're bleeding all over the floor. Clean it up," he snarls.

Marty picks up the cheese, trying not to cry. With her right arm she tries to wipe the blood from her brow. Vernon stands and grabs a dishtowel from the oven handle and throws it to the floor in front of Marty. "I said clean up the mess!" he commands, then belches loudly as he exits the kitchen. From the other room, Marty hears him turn on the TV.

No longer hungry, Marty tosses the cheese into the kitchen trashcan. Holding the dishtowel to her forehead, she takes another towel from the refrigerator handle and begins wiping the blood and tears from the floor.

Baggs sits at his computer in his office, trying to find any information he can concerning the scientific summit. Dismayed by his lack of results, Baggs slides his chair back away from his desk and rubs his tired eyes. The doorbell rings. Standing and exiting his office, he pulls the front door open. Sy stands close to the door jamb looking anxious.

"Surprised to see you here. Come on in," Baggs offers, opening the door wider. Sy quickly makes his way into Baggs home while at the same time pulling from his jacket pocket an overstuffed business size envelope. Sy puts his right index finger up to his lips making the 'quiet' sign.

He hands the envelope to Baggs while at the same time pointing to the back. Written faintly in pencil it reads 'Everything you need to make ID.' Baggs nods an affirmative. The doorbell rings again. Seeing the color of Sy's face drain to an ashen white, Baggs motions to him to head into the other room.

Sy quickly ducks into Baggs kitchen. Once Sy is clear, Baggs opens the door. Standing at the front entrance is Marty. The side of her face is red and puffy and the cut above her right eye is smeared with drying blood. Baggs' heart just about stops as he sees Marty's injured condition.

"Oh no! What happened?" Baggs gasps. Marty tries her best to fight back the tears. Baggs reaches his hand out and gently takes hold of her face turning it to get a better look.

Rick Lord

"Come in, come in," he gently asks Marty, grabbing a few tissues from the box on the lampstand.

Marty begins to cry as she enters his house. Baggs places his arm around her comforting her as he closes the door and hands her the tissues.

"This was no accident was it? Who did this to you? Your mom? Your mom's boyfriend?"

Marty nods her head. "Vernon," she reveals, sniffing and blowing her nose.

Sy is standing in the kitchen doorway. "Need to call Child Protective Services," he tells Baggs.

Baggs glares at Sy and is quiet for a moment, "Not right now, okay?"

"You can't leave her there if she's getting abused. And who's this Vernon guy?" Sy asks.

"Her mom's boyfriend," Baggs replies softly.

"What are you going to do about it?" Sy asks as he enters the living room.

"We're not talking about this right now," Baggs says with finality.

"Okay fine. I left the 'you-know-what' on the counter next to the microwave. I gotta go," Sy walks over to Baggs and Marty. He gives Marty a pat on the shoulder before quietly exiting the front door.

"Let's take a look at that eye of yours, alright? How about you stand in front of me while I sit over here on the couch?"

Marty wipes the tears from her eyes and cracks a slight smile as she sits on the brown sofa. Baggs turns on the side lamp and lifts the lampshade to direct the light onto Marty's freckled face. He slides his reading glasses over his nose. "Hmmm. Not too bad. I don't think you'll need any stitches."

"I'll be alright," Marty says bravely. "I've had worse."

Baggs chuckles lightly, "You are quite the little lady Miss Marty. I'm going to get a washcloth and clean you up a little, okay? Just to be on the safe side."

Baggs returns with a warm damp washcloth and gently cleans the wound and surrounding area.

"You know, I should call the police. What this guy did to you is wrong. He belongs in jail."

"No. Don't! They'll take me away again."

"Again? Has this happened before?"

"They'll take me away for good this time. I don't want to leave. You don't know what it's like. It'll just make it worse. Please!"

Baggs leans back into the couch to think. He is deeply concerned about what has been happening. Her safety is paramount. What if this monster were to kill her? All of the 'what if' questions are flooding his mind.

"You don't want me to get help?" he asks, again trying to do the right thing.

Marty nods her head 'no.' "Please don't call the police," she pleads.

Baggs concedes, "Okay, but I'm really worried."

"I'll be okay, I promise."

Marty cracks a smile and gives Baggs a hug around his neck. Baggs tries his best to fight back his own tears. After the big hug, he gets up from the couch and offers Marty some milk and cookies as he walks towards the kitchen.

"Hey, are you all ready for Christmas?" Baggs asks, while taking the milk from the refrigerator.

"Cookies are in the big brown bear jar on the counter. Why don't you grab the jar and meet me at the table," Baggs suggests.

"Today was my last day of school. I'm off for Christmas break. Roxy doesn't do Christmas because she's always working. Sometimes she gets me something and says it's from Santa Claus. But, I know there's no such thing as Santa."

Together, the two sit across from each other at the kitchen table dunking their cookies into their milk. Baggs knows all too well cookies help put a smile on any child's face.

"You know, I don't celebrate Christmas either. I mean, I guess I celebrate it in my heart, but I don't decorate or anything like that. No one to decorate for," Baggs confesses. After grabbing another cookie, Baggs eyes grow big.

"I have an idea. What do you say we celebrate Christmas together? You and me. We can get a tree, set it up right over there in the corner of the room. We'll get some lights, some ornaments, and tinsel and we'll do it up right. What do ya say? You can come over Christmas morning. And something tells me Santa just might show up. Especially if we give him reason to. You like that idea?"

Marty's face lights up, "Can I help pick out the tree?"

"You bet! And I think we should go right now while the picking is good. Is your mom home?"

"No, she's at work; she won't be home till late tonight."

"So it's just Vernon there now?"

"Yeah."

"Well then, how about you let me put a bandage on that eyebrow and we go find ourselves a Christmas tree?"

"Yay!" She says taking another drink of her milk. Baggs and Marty walk out the door with tears long forgotten. He knows the longer he can keep Marty away from home, the safer she'll be.

DEAD BIRD

Known as Montgomery County Airport, the airport facility mainly serves corporate and personal aircraft. Although it has instrument landing facilities, there is no control tower. The public facility is relatively small and is home to many privately-owned aircraft.

Lewis just happens to be one who owns a single-engine plane. Dry, safe, and secure from the elements, his prized aircraft has been stored in a hangar there for more than 20 years. When not cruising around the debris field he calls home, Lewis can usually be found puttering around with his airplane.

A couple of honks of the horn announces Baggs' arrival. Lewis opens the small man-door to the hangar. Soaking up the last vestiges of warmth from the truck's heater, Baggs reluctantly shuts the engine off and exits into the frigid, mid-day cold. The freezing air bites at his face, making his nose run and eyes water. Baggs runs to the door and quickly enters the shelter of Lewis's hangar.

"Check it out. I got it laminated and even slotted for a pocket clip and everything," Lewis announces as he presents his new faux government-issued identification badge.

Baggs takes the ID and scrutinizes it carefully. His involvement with the illegal charade fills him with a foreboding sense of dread. They could both easily end up in prison for counterfeiting a government-issued ID, a distinct possibility he tries hard not to think about.

"Looks pretty convincing, I hope it works. So what's up?" Baggs asks, handing the badge back to Lewis.

"Come here and look at this," Lewis says with excitement. Stepping over and around boxes of nuts, bolts, and airplane parts, the two make their way to the passenger side of Lewis's plane. Missing gauges, loose wiring, and broken plastic are the sad remains of the once regal, instrument-laden panel.

The once-majestic red and white plane is now covered with years of dust and grime. Its original, beautiful red and grey interior has long since been stripped bare. Seats, carpet, trim, and seatbelts lay about in piles of disarray around the plane's fuselage.

"I think I can easily get this thing in the air by the middle of January," Lewis says, pointing at a box containing a variety of new instruments lying on the cockpit floor. As Baggs stands under the wing, all he can do is shake his head in disbelief.

Searching hard for any sign of mechanical integrity, Baggs only sees carnage. The old metal bird has flat tires, a missing propeller and engine parts, and a cockpit that's being used for storage. It hasn't seen blue sky in years.

"Why?" Baggs asks with curiosity.

"What do you mean, why? I'm going to Los Alamos right? At the end of January? Well, I'm not driving there, I'm flying," Lewis proclaims.

"In this? You can't fly this thing. It's a heap of scrap metal. It's no more airworthy than a grand piano. Look at it. It's Christmas Eve; you couldn't have this thing ready to fly ten Christmas Eve's from now.

"And even if you did get this thing running, you wouldn't make it to the end of the runway without killing yourself. How long has it been since you've actually piloted an airplane? Ten, eleven years? You're out of your mind. Besides, I'm going with you and I'm not going in this. We're flying commercially, I've already booked the flight."

"Why are we both going?" Lewis asks.

"I know you. Left to your own devices, you'll be in jail in two shakes of a lamb's tail. Then what? I'm going along. Besides, I'm renting a car when we get there, we can drive over towards the Grand Canyon when you're done with the meeting. Maybe we can see that space craft thing. Whatever it is."

Baggs walks towards the door of the hangar and stumbles over more debris.

"I'm going home," he says, tracing his route to the door carefully. "I'm having Marty over for Christmas and I need to pick up a few things. Why don't you come over tomorrow morning and have some cookies and eggnog with us. It'll be festive and probably the last Christmas we'll have this side of Folsom Prison."

"Ha ha, funny. You do Christmas? Wow! This kid's got hold of you, big time."

"Yeah, bring her a little present, okay? She's a good kid and could use some special attention."

MERRY
CHRISTMAS
MARTY

BAGGS HOUSE, CHRISTMAS MORNING

Awakened by the pounding of a small fist on the front door and the repeated ringing of the doorbell, the chirp of the bedside alarm is no match. "What the…" Baggs mumbles as he's startled out of a sound sleep. Looking over to his nightstand, the blurry, green LED display on his clock reads 7:05.

With a groan, Baggs swings his legs out from under the covers and slides his bare feet directly into his slippers. Rubbing the sleep out of his eyes and grabbing his robe, Baggs shouts, "Coming!" and shuffles his way to the front door.

'Ding dong,' 'ding dong,' continues the doorbell. Baggs releases the deadbolt and opens the door. Marty dashes into the house, along with a blast of brisk morning air, and heads straight for the Christmas tree. "Good morning to you too," Baggs sarcastically chuckles.

"You're going to have to give me a minute to start the coffee pot, okay? No coffee, no Christmas."

Ignoring Baggs, Marty has planted herself in front of the Christmas tree and is reading the gift tags on the presents. "Can I plug in the Christmas lights?" she asks.

"Yes!" Baggs shouts from the kitchen, giving the okay. Marty plugs in the lights. 'To: Marty, From: Santa' the tags on the presents read. One by one, she lifts the brightly-wrapped boxes and with a slight shake, she tries her best to guess what they might contain.

Baggs enters with coffee cup in hand and watches Marty from the arched entry. He stops to take in the scene, amazed at how well the tree turned out. Shiny ornaments and tinsel glimmer as they reflect the colored lights wrapping the tree.

But the look on Marty's face outshines everything. Slowly, Baggs walks in and sits on the ottoman by the tree, "We did good kid, didn't we? Tree looks really nice." Turning back to Baggs, Marty nods and grins from ear to ear.

"Is your mom okay with you being here for Christmas morning?"

"She and Vernon are asleep. They didn't get home till 3:00 AM," Marty replies, still testing gift density and weight.

"You were there last night? Christmas Eve? By yourself?"

"No biggy. I watched TV. I fell asleep on the couch. Roxy woke me up and sent me to bed when they got home. They were at a party."

Trying not to display any emotions of outrage, particularly at this time, Baggs quickly changes the subject.

"Well, what are you waiting for? Start opening!" Baggs says with his own childlike excitement.

Without a moment of hesitation, Marty begins opening one of her presents. Baggs stops her suddenly, "Hold on!" Marty reluctantly stops unwrapping and holds on tightly to the partly opened package with a sigh.

Baggs shuffles back to his room and grabs his cell phone from the nightstand and returns to the living room. "Okay. Go ahead!" he invites her, now that the camera on his cell phone is ready.

Like a proud grandfather, Baggs takes picture after picture as Marty opens her gifts. So far, it's a backpack for her books, a winter coat, a stocking cap and a new tool box.

"But, I've already got a tool box," Marty says with a quirky smile.

Baggs smiles as she opens the toolbox. Packed neatly inside are an assortment of small tools. Inside are needle nose pliers, small wrenches and a plethora of other small tools.

Perplexed, Marty turns to Baggs, "I think Santa thinks I'm a radio repair man. What am I supposed to do with these, they're tiny?"

Baggs smiles conspiratorially, "I think they're intended to accompany another present, which in fact, Santa left for me to watch until Christmas. Give me a second, I have to go get it," Baggs says slyly as he heads into the back room.

He reemerges with a long rectangular box wrapped in bright red and green foil paper. "Better see what this is," he announces as he hands her the big box.

Marty's eyes grow wide as she exclaims, "Wow, it's huge!" Taking the package, she begins tearing through the wrappings. "No way! It's a radio-controlled glider. Wow! This is cool! Now you can teach me to fly my own!" Baggs eyes glisten with joy as he watches her excitement.

"I think you missed one," Baggs points to the back of the tree.

Army crawling to the back side of the Christmas tree, Marty extracts the final gift. The box is small but heavy. First, she looks at it, bewildered. Then, she tears the wrapping paper open, exposing its contents.

"A cell phone? My own cell phone? Are you kidding? I've never had a cell phone. Ever!" she exclaims with a big smile.

"That gift is from me," Baggs says kindly. "Whenever you need a friend, or someone to talk to, or you need help, you just call me or Lewis, okay? This is our secret. Don't let Vernon or Roxy see it. Promise me. I just want you to always be safe. If anyone tries to hurt you, you call me. Promise?"

"I promise," Marty says.

"I already programmed it with my cell number and Lewis's cell number. Press Baggs for me and Louie for Lewis. I wouldn't say anything to Lewis about us referring to him as Louie. It'll be our little joke on him, okay?"

Marty laughs and nods okay. Surrounded by her presents, wrapping paper, boxes and bows, her big smile begins to fade.

"I know there's no such thing as Santa Claus. Thank you Baggs. Best Christmas ever."

As she slowly surveys all of the presents and wrapping paper glistening under the tree, a tear begins to roll down her cheek. Baggs looks at her and is puzzled. "What's the matter?" he asks.

Sadly, she looks up at him. "I didn't get you anything," she confesses, as more tears well up in her eyes.

Baggs smiles, "Wanna bet!? You gave me the best gift ever?"

"What do you mean?" she asks.

Baggs holds out his cell phone and begins showing Marty the pictures he took of her while she was opening her presents.

"You see. You gave me some pretty great memories. The neat thing about fond memories, they're something you can always take with you, everywhere you go. They're gifts that last forever."

Marty suddenly wraps her arms around Baggs' neck. He squeezes her back fondly and then, standing to his feet, he takes Marty by the hand.

"What do you say we make some blueberry pancakes? Heavy on the blueberries and lots of whipped cream?"

"Oh yeah! Works for me! I'm starving," Marty responds while rubbing her tummy.

'Ding dong,' 'ding dong,' the doorbell chimes again. Before Baggs can get to the door, it bursts open, with Lewis carrying in a large, poorly-wrapped box. "Ho! Ho! Ho!" Lewis hollers, doing his best Santa impression.

Lewis sets the package down on the couch and looks directly at Marty. "If you're Marty, which I think you are, then this here present, is for you."

Marty looks at Baggs for some validation. Baggs just smiles and shrugs.

"Go ahead. Open it," Lewis continues enthusiastically.

Marty begins tearing through the wrapping paper, exposing the long, unmarked cardboard box. She looks up at Lewis, confused, "What is it?"

Baggs notices the copious amount of tape Lewis used to package the gift and retreats briefly for a box cutter. Lewis looks down at Marty with a big grin, "This, my little lady, is something every self-respecting American needs."

Baggs reenters the room with a box knife and begins cutting the tape from the ends and sides of the box. Following behind, Marty peels back the cardboard, exposing a long, military-looking cylinder. Pulling the strange object from its wrappings, Marty lifts it up, bewildered.

"It's an RPG! A Rocket-Propelled Grenade launcher!"

Lewis announces proudly.

"Are you kidding me? You got her an RPG? Have you lost your mind?" Baggs glares at Lewis.

"Is it real?" Marty asks excitedly.

"You bet it is!" Lewis boasts, with his hands on hips.

"I don't believe it. Where'd you get this?" Baggs shakes his head in disbelief.

"I've had it a long time. Hey, this thing is worth a lot of money," Lewis continues.

"Yeah, on the black market! You don't give a kid a grenade launcher for Christmas, unless you live in Iraq!"

"No, it's cool. I like it," Marty says propping the weapon up onto her shoulder.

"See! She's a natural," Lewis responds, smiling.

"I suppose you have grenades for stocking stuffers?" Baggs interjects sarcastically.

"No, not with me. They're back at my place."

Rolling his eyes, Baggs gently takes the RPG from Marty and sets it down on top of the box. "We're going to make pancakes. Maybe lock the door, you can join us," Baggs sternly says to Lewis.

"Fake IDs. RPGs. I'm going to be the first astronaut in prison," Baggs mumbles as he walks to the kitchen.

DECEPTIVE
ORIGINS

In 1953 several European countries convened in Belgium and initiated the first-ever international conference to include heads of state from around the world. The initial agenda was to prevent another world war, fight global hunger, and to better understand multiculturalism.

Their concept was to develop an organization whose ultimate plan was to create a one-world government. Their initial motivation was to create a fundamentally basic social, religious, and economic system that would hopefully help prevent many of the world's past tragedies. However, it has since developed ulterior motives.

Now grown to more than twenty countries, the conference is still held annually. It now consists of the who's who of the wealthy elite from around the world, rather than just heads of state.

Even though the event is off-limits to the media and outsiders, leaked conversations from a few within the clandestine group have revealed a nefarious philosophy. Of late, population control has been the zenith of their agenda.

How many people on the planet before there's not enough food? The gap between the haves and the have nots would grow exponentially, resulting in a world-war of epic proportions.

Soon after the formation of Germany's National People's Army in 1956, an impromptu summit was held in Weiss Baden, Germany.

During a radio interview concerning the conference, assistant to the Minister of Defense, Adolf Grenz, accidentally commented openly on air, "The only way to control population is to control disease, by controlling all medical and scientific advancements."

LOS ALAMOS, NEW MEXICO, JANUARY 30TH

It's a chilly 36 degrees Fahrenheit in Los Alamos. The skies are clear with a light 3 to 5 knot breeze. At an elevation of 7,320 feet, the city is quite a bit higher than what Baggs and Lewis' hometown, which is only just above 700 feet in elevation. The air feels thin for the old guys, but at least there is no snow, and none is predicted for their short, five-day stay.

At 3:50 PM, they finally arrive at their hotel room. Lewis does not take well to commercial air travel and has been complaining almost non-stop since they landed.

"Over seven hours travel time to get from Dayton to Albuquerque with not one, but two stops along the way. And then we spend another hour and a half of driving a rental car the size of an egg to get here. We could have walked faster. I'm exhausted!" Lewis continues his grumbling while unpacking his small carry-on duffle bag.

Baggs chuckles and shakes his head. Since the seminar was scheduled for Saturday, they were forced to deal with frenzied Friday commuters heading home for the weekend. Even Baggs feels a fair measure of fatigue from the trip.

He pauses from unpacking to watch Lewis. Without shame, Lewis removes only one pair of briefs, one pair of socks, a wrinkled pair of slacks, a wrinkled button-down shirt, a wadded-up grey blazer jacket, and a small toiletries case from his duffle bag.

"And now we're staying at the illustrious Aladdin Motor Inn Motel. It smells like dirty socks in here," Lewis whines.

Baggs cannot help but wonder if Lewis realizes it may be his own dirty socks he smells.

"You are aware that you're going to a fairly significant science seminar tomorrow, right?" Baggs reminds Lewis.

"Yeah. Why?"

"Well, if you're wearing what you just pulled out of that bag, you'll look more like a dumpster-diving hobo than a fellow scientist."

"Are you kidding? Scientists all dress in slacks and sport coats."

Baggs shakes his head in disdain, "Never mind. I'm going to go pick up our package before they close. Be back shortly."

THE ALADDIN MOTOR INN MOTEL, 6:00 AM, JANUARY 31ST

Before the sun rises, Baggs' cell phone chirps the morning wake-up call. Rolling over, he grabs it from the nightstand to shut off the alarm. Clearing his throat, he hollers to Lewis, who's still asleep in the double bed next to his, "Hey, get up, it's time."

Lewis slowly rolls over and acknowledges Baggs with a disapproving groan, "It's still dark. What time is it?"

"Time to get up. Come on. We've got a lot to prepare for. You can take the first shower," Baggs offers.

Lewis stumbles out of bed and slowly shuffles into the bathroom.

Baggs stretches, swings his legs out, and steps directly into his slippers.

"Must make coffee," Baggs says with determination.

With the shower running and the coffee brewing, Baggs begins the task of getting ready for the important day ahead. Retrieving the box he picked up the day before, he opens it and removes a small envelope containing Lewis's falsified identifications, a pair of shoes, a long-wired mini microphone and a roll of medical grade adhesive tape.

The shower shuts off and Lewis exits the bathroom wearing an old worn out pair of men's white jockey underwear. "Come on!" Baggs winces. "Put a towel around you. I don't want to see that."

"What? I'm putting my pants on, if you don't mind," Lewis says nonchalantly.

"No you're not! Here. I picked this up on the way back from getting the package yesterday."

Baggs hands Lewis a small travel iron. "Cover up those white chicken legs, and put a towel on the table over there, and start ironing the wrinkles out of your clothes. You're not going there looking like you slept in a cement mixer. We need you to blend in. Remember? You have used an iron before right?"

Lewis responds with a sheepish shrug and an exasperated, "Fine!" Covered with a towel and another spread across the small dinette, Lewis clumsily irons his clothes.

"Have you ever wondered why a jet propulsion lab tech would be summoned to some weird, invitation only, scientific shindig at the Los Alamos National Laboratory?" Lewis asks while ironing a pant leg.

"Don't put your pants on yet, you need to run this wire up your leg first. And yeah, I've been wondering that from day one. Maybe some of the far-fetched crap he tells us isn't so far-fetched after all," Baggs replies.

Lewis grabs the wire and tape from Baggs.

"Leave just enough slack to plug into the right shoe."

"Ya, I got that," Lewis sits on the edge of his bed and begins taping the slender audio wire to his right leg. "I shaved my legs and my chest so the tape will stick."

"I don't need to know that. Just tape the wire in place real good and don't tape over the microphone. And you didn't have to shave both legs, just your right and only where the tape goes. Seriously? Why would you shave both legs? Never mind, I don't wanna know," Baggs retorts, repulsed.

"Yeah, I couldn't remember what shoe has the recorder. Pretty cool set up, though, huh?"

"Let's just hope this thing works like it's supposed to. No cell phones, cameras, or recorders. Just ID and the letter and that's it. If they get suspicious get the hell out of there. Find a phone and call me ASAP."

"So what are you going to do while I'm gone? I'll have the rental car."

"Speaking of which, it's in my name, so be careful. I'm just going to wait for you to get back or call. I'll be on my computer for the most part. Come on. Hurry up with that thing, you need to get going."

LOS ALAMOS NATIONAL SCIENCE LABO-
RATORY, 7:45 AM

Lewis drives up to the visitor center and exits the economy rental car. With false credentials in hand, he approaches the information desk.

Without question and with a pleasant smile, the nice lady politely hands him a map of the facility. In red highlight, she charts the route to building 4200, the lecture hall. Feeling confident now, Lewis drives the highlighted route to his destination.

Once at the correct parking lot, Lewis steels himself and walks to the entrance. An official looking man asks for his ID and invitation letter.

Lewis calmly presents them. The gentleman visually scans the documents and hands them back to Lewis. The A-frame sign on the right side of the door reads in bold block font, 'NO CELL PHONES, CAMERAS, AND/OR RECORDING DEVICES OF ANY KIND.'

After being checked in, Lewis enters the hall quickly looking for a seat toward the back. Surprisingly, only about 40 people are in attendance. Not the big crowd he was expecting, or wanting. Minimizing any chance of someone trying to speak to him, he keeps a hand-kerchief in hand.

As Lewis picks his way through the seating aisles, a fellow scientist approaches offering a friendly hand-shake. Covering his mouth with his handkerchief, Lewis whispers, "laryngitis" and the man quickly backs away covering his own mouth. 'Whew!' Lewis thinks as he finds a seat in the back of the lecture hall and sits as low as possible.

Two taps on the microphone announce the start of the seminar.

A black-suited man at the podium announces, "Excuse me, ladies and gentlemen. If you would all please find your seat, thank you." The sound system squeals with high pitched feedback.

The lecture hall lights dim. A spot light draws all eyes to Doctor Sigmund Hess as he steps up to the podium.

Doctor Hess is in his mid-seventies and wears a 1930s-style brown suit, white shirt, and dark tie. His out-of-date clothing, wingtip shoes, and thick German accent catch Lewis by surprise. If Lewis didn't know better, he would think he's just been transported back in time to World War II.

"Good morning everyone, it is good to see all of you. Please know that today is for you. A big salute to all of you for all your hard work on the Lazarus VI Project."

"I'd like to thank all of you for coming. I know many of you traveled quite a distance to be here today. I'm honored that you have come. I look forward to speaking with each and every one of you personally later today." Doctor Hess pauses to take a small sip of water from the glass resting on the podium.

'Great, this clown might know Sy,' Lewis thinks to himself while slouching lower in his seat. Becoming more paranoid, Lewis is beginning to sweat and is strongly considering leaving before he is discovered.

Taking a deep breath, he reaches down to turn on his shoe recorder. At the toe of his right shoe is a tiny switch that activates a digital recorder. Lewis hopes to record the speech to a flash drive hidden in the heel of his shoe.

"Many have asked, and we understand some of you are wary of the intricacies of the Lazarus VI Project. Many of you are interested in how we developed the vaccine. I know most of you have been working on the project for some time, but only in minute, unrelatable applications. I hope today to address your concerns."

Doctor Hess picks up from the podium a hard-wired remote for the archaic screen projector. Lewis is miffed by the old technology being used for the presentation.

With a push of a button on the remote, Doctor Hess queues up an image on the large screen. The first slide displays an illustrated helix graphic of a basic human DNA strand.

"As I'm sure you all recognize; this is a cross section of a typical human DNA strand. This is the helix of the 23 pairs of chromosomes that are excusive to each one of us."

Hess brings up the next slide. The second illustrated image looks very similar to the first image.

"The question has always been, is it possible to replace human DNA with a synthetic version? The answer is, yes. Through the immense efforts of bio-chemists and geneticists over the last, believe it or not, 80 years, science does continue to prevail.

"Understand that DNA sequencing has only been mappable since the mid 1980's. So why should it be necessary for science to produce a synthetic hybrid replacement DNA? We have no choice. The human race demands it. We are under a plague of what is referred to as 'Genetic Load.' Allow me to explain using a simplistic example.

"Print out a single page document. From that one document make another copy, from that copy make another copy, and so on. Continue the process over and over one hundred times.

"By the time you get to the one hundredth copy, what you end up with is a copy of a copy that suffers from severe degradation.

"That is exactly what has been happening to the human race for millions of years. That is why cancer is at an all-time high. Diabetes. Parkinson's disease. Down syndrome. Cystic Fibrosis. And the list goes on.

"All of these are at near pandemic levels because we have reached that one-hundredth copy, relatively speaking. We are producing degraded copies from what was once a perfect human specimen at the time man evolved. We are now in a sense, reverse evolving.

"What we needed was a way to develop a new copy reproduced every time. We need new DNA strands that are perfect and reproducible. DNA that is genetically reproduced as a perfect first copy every time.

"In 1996 the late scientist by the name of John Gussman discovered a prime complex element referred to as Unibihexium Carbon Particle. Amazingly, this element does what we've been seeking for decades. Its properties help to create the very synthetic human DNA we have needed for so long. Not only is it a prime element for creating synthetic DNA, it has the capabilities of regenerating itself over and over again.

Even though this discovery was purely by accident, it is also remarkable in the fact that it was found right under our noses on the floor of the Grand Canyon. Once processed, Unibihexium Carbon Particle is, in fact, the missing link necessary for creating synthetic DNA."

Doctor Hess clicks to the next slide showing a periodic chart with an additional element added to the bottom (UBH). He clicks to the next image. The word 'Chryzinium' in bold, dark green letters spans the screen against a bluish black field.

"So what is Chryzinium, you ask? To put it simply, Chryzinium is the compound derived from Unibihexium Carbon. It is a manufactured DNA, comprised of complex and simplex elements which analyzes the human body's metabolic structure. It regenerates cell tissue and replaces human DNA with an absolutely pure, synthetic proxy DNA, if you will.

"It does what man has been desiring for centuries. It promotes the resetting of the human biological clock. In other words, the vaccine has the capability of virtually destroying disease at the root by remapping the human DNA structure in repetitive sequential order, thereby continually rebuilding a perfect, youthful, and healthy helix of 23 pairs of chromosomes.

"All disease is a derivative of only 39 root allergens. Every disease is an allergic reaction to something various human bodies cannot tolerate. What we believe Chryzinium is capable of accomplishing is nothing short of miraculous. It creates a substitute human DNA that is proving to be immune to those 39 root allergens."

Hess pauses briefly to click to the next slide, showing an illustration of the chromosome helix broken into several parts.

"So how does Chryzinium accomplish this? Human chromosomes are tipped with telomeres, which protects the chromosomes from damage. As humans age, the telomeres become worn, exposing those chromosomes to damage over the years.

"Through an enzyme catalyst found in Chryzinium, the DNA sequence is exponentially increased, thereby completely rebuilding the telomeres synthetically and repetitively. Tests are proving it actually has the capability of resetting the biological aging clock along with making DNA programmable.

"However, it was the discovery of the transuranic element CTS-235 that is and has been the sub-catalyst necessary to make DNA changes viable. We knew it to be the necessary component for whatever element that had the potential of remapping human DNA. The CTS-235 catalyst was integral for the human metabolism to accept a replacement synthetic DNA.

"That discovery actually took place in 1965. However, it was the rapid progression of scientific technological developments over the past eight years that enhanced the active catalyst. In other words, it is that very element necessary for allowing the altering of human DNA.

"CTS-235 allows human DNA to accept, with greater liquidity, Chryzinium's synthetic DNA-altering properties. But beyond that, it is those properties responsible that allow us to now produce Chryzinium as a vaccine that can be administered in mass quantity.

"As you are aware, we have been conducting human beta tests. This of course must still remain confidential. The beta testing is not only proving successful, but is also proving to be relevant for the programmable reengineering of DNA strands. I can promise you this, Chryzinium will be the breakthrough vaccine of all time.

"This leads me to our next big breakthrough. And that is an individual processor which is based on an atomic programmable biometric. You all know it as Vul-Stream, the first atomically-powered, implantable RFID chip.

"Firstly, it allows doctors to carefully monitor the Chryzinium recipient's medical status twenty-four hours a day, seven days a week. And secondly, we now have a device that reprograms DNA to fight diseases, viruses, and/or bacteria. This, as you know, is currently in the final stages of programming."

The next image Doctor Hess brings up is an illustrated graphic of Vul-Stream; a detailed, expanded depiction of the first micro-sized atomic RFID chip.

"Chryzinium, together with the implantation of this

tiny micro monitoring device, is the foundation of the Lazarus VI project. Healthcare as we know it will be forever changed. Ladies and gentlemen, this is what we've all been working on for so long; the Lazarus VI Project."

Hess clicks his remote and proceeds to the next slide which reads, 'Lazarus VI Project.'

"I am very proud to be involved with this monumental program as well as having the honor of working with all of you.

"Along with the support and backing from the United States Government and the World Healthcare Organization, I must also applaud a small group of scientists and doctors assigned to the project for their commitment to Lazarus VI.

"Without their dedication and persistence, I can assure you this remarkable breakthrough would not have been possible. Unfortunately, due to their schedules, they cannot be here with us today."

Doctor Hess clicks to the next image which depicts a strange looking symbol with the word 'Shafutah' directly underneath.

"Shafutah, which in English simply means 'Health, Peace, and Unity.' This symbol represents our commitment to humanity and our commitment to the Lazarus VI Project."

Doctor Hess clicks to the next image which is a head shot of the founder of the Lazarus VI Project, Adiv Zahim (pronounced, Adeev Zaheem).

"Ladies and gentleman, Adiv Zahim. You may have

heard of him as being the grandfather to Lazarus VI, but as you can see, he does not look at all like a grandfather."

The audience laughs at Doctor Hess' joke. From his youthful appearance in the photo, Adiv is likely in his mid-forties, with jet-black, slicked-back hair.

His complexion is a perfect bronze and his eyes are coal black. His chiseled facial features and captivating smile make him a man who could easily find himself on the cover of any Hollywood fashion magazine.

Hess clicks to the next image. The image is that of an old black and white photo of Doctor Albert Hess taken back in the late 1940's.

"And yes, for those of who don't know, Doctor Albert Hess is my father. My father was responsible for creating many of the processes used today for engineering genetic modifications.

"He, of course, is responsible for many other notable scientific breakthroughs and discoveries during his time. For this and many reasons dear to me, I give special recognition to my father, Doctor Albert Hess. I strongly doubt we would be this far ahead scientifically without his tremendous scientific contributions."

"One by one, the audience begins to stand to their feet and applaud, giving homage to a man they believe has contributed so much. Lewis however, stands just long enough so he doesn't draw attention to himself.

One more click of the projector and the head shots of seven highly-regarded team members appear together in one image. One after the other, Hess reads off the names corresponding with each image.

"Doctor Ivan Heller, who heads up our neurological department. Doctor Levi Mintle, research scientist and lead technical advisor for Vul-Stream. Doctor Brad Nunenbush, Doctor Carly Stinson, and Bio-Chemist Margret Sprague, who make up our programing and data recovery team.

"Wilhelm Avercamp, whom is in charge of our dark energy impulse generators and oversees our radiation lab. And last but not least, Doctor Edward Stiner who is my right hand at M-PAC Laboratories as my personal Operations Tech Supervisor.

"Like these great scientists I have just mentioned, your contributions to the technological aspects for this incredible program are also very much appreciated. On behalf of the Lazarus VI Project leaders, I thank you for your help concerning the implantation of the Vul-Helix engineering platform you have all worked so hard on.

"And because of your hard work, you have been invited here so I can personally award each and every one of you a Certificate of Achievement for your part in this incredible program.

"In just a moment, each of you will be taken backstage and photographed. Along with your certificate of appreciation, you will also be given an honorarium plaque with your picture to be placed on a dedicated wall, not only here at the National Science Lab, but also at the M-PAC facility.

"It is you who are the charter scientists of the Lazarus VI Project. I ask you to please stand again and give yourselves a big round of applause."

Lewis has been in a state of alarm since the meeting began, but now he is terrified. He can't believe what he has just heard. Besides that, there is no way he is going to wait around to be photographed as Simon Lazlo.

He quietly exits his seat and slinks out of the lecture hall trying his best not to be noticed. Once outside, and as fast as his old legs can carry him, Lewis scrambles to the rental car, gets in and drives out of the lecture hall parking area.

THE ALADDIN MOTOR INN MOTEL, 9:20 AM

'Bang,' 'bang,' 'bang,' on the door of room number 107 at the Aladdin Motor Inn Motel. "Let me in. Baggs! It's me. It's Lewis. Let me in!"

Baggs, surprised to hear Lewis, hurries to open the door. "What are you doing here? Didn't you go to the lecture?" Baggs asks. Lewis rushes in, panicked. Baggs whispers, "Great! You got caught. You got caught, didn't you?"

"No, I didn't get caught, but we gotta get out of here," Lewis answers quietly, grabbing his duffle bag.

"Woah, wait, tell me what's going on?"

"For starters, the speaker, this Doctor Hess guy was going to take my picture and give me a certificate of appreciation for my hard work on the Lazarus Project. That's not going to work. Look, let's just get out of here. Head to the canyon. Head to the airport. I don't care. Let's just get the hell out of here. I'll fill you in on the way. You're not going to believe any of what I just got through listening to."

"Did you record any of it?" Baggs gathers up his belongings as quickly as possible.

"Of course I did. At least I think I did. That's if my shoe did its job."

Within minutes the two are on the road, heading out of town.

"I'm starving, let's stop somewhere and get breakfast," Lewis suggests.

Baggs looks over to Lewis sitting in the passenger seat and remarks, "Obviously not too hellish of an experience if all you can think of is food. Just a minute ago you can't get out of town fast enough and now you want to stop and eat? What is it? Drive or eat?"

"Eat! Let's get some breakfast. Maybe someplace on the way out of town. I'll fill you in on some of this stuff when I get some food in my gut."

"Okay fine. Food it is. But, I think we should concentrate on getting out of town first. I have my suspicions you didn't leave quietly. They might be on the lookout for a tiny, bright yellow, whatever this thing is we're driving. It's only 45 minutes to Santa Fe. I know a place where we can eat there." Lewis agrees and begins to relax some.

"Since we'll be on the road for a while, plug that flash drive into my computer and get me my headphones. I want to hear what went on there at the meeting. At least I'll know what it is that got you so freaked out."

DESTINATION ASH FORK

RIALTO CAFÉ, SANTA FE, NEW MEXICO

The Rialto Café is a hole-in-the-wall breakfast and lunch eatery. With only six tables and a four-stool counter, the small café does well for itself for being so far off the main Highway.

Good food and hefty portions have been bringing in steady customers for more than 19 years. Baggs and Lewis drive into the dusty, half-paved, half-dirt parking lot. Baggs removes his headphones as Lewis begins to wake from catching up on some much-needed sleep.

"Good thing you left when you did. You could have been busted, big time."

"You think? So how did it sound?" Lewis asks rubbing his eyes.

"Not too bad, other than a lot of rustling from your shirt."

"It must have been me scratching. The tape made my skin itch."

"Sure it's not all the hair growing back?" Baggs replies sarcastically.

"Hilarious. So what'd you think?"

"I'll tell you what I think. But, before we go inside, I'm calling Sy to find out what the heck all this is about?"

Baggs speed dials Sy. After only two rings, Sy answers his phone.

"Hello Baggs."

"Sy. Hey, just so you know, we've got questions. A lot of questions."

"Yeah, I figured as much," Sy whispers.

"Do exactly as we planned. Call me back as quick as you can," Baggs responds, canceling the call.

"Is he heading to your place?" Lewis asks.

"He better. Let's go in and eat, we can talk more inside," He says to Lewis exiting the car.

They enter the café and take a seat at one of the tables. Between the breakfast rush and lunch rush, the café has only two other individuals sitting at the counter. The interior walls are dingy yellow trimmed in dirty, off-white, Spanish style woodwork.

Every wall in the small café is festooned with framed photographs and memorabilia of pilots, aircraft, and rockets. Lewis gazes at the walls decorated by images of the who's who of aviation fame.

"Since this place doesn't look to be on the main drag, I take it you've been here before."

"Yeah, a couple of times. Good food here."

Juanita, who is in her mid-sixties, walks up to the table and sets down a couple of old one-page menus and two red plastic glasses of water. "Hola. Buenos dias. You want coffee?" she asks, with her thick Hispanic accent.

"Yeah, that'd be good, thanks," Baggs replies kindly with a smile.

As Lewis continues looking around at the restaurant's historical pictures, he suddenly recognizes a picture he has seen many times before. He stands to his feet and walks the few feet to the wall where the image hangs. With a smirk he turns back around to Baggs.

"This is you. This is the same picture that's in your office," Baggs raises his eyebrows and motions for Lewis to sit back down. Lewis walks back over to the table and takes his seat.

"Yeah, it's me. Don't say anything. Don't make a big deal about it, please?"

Smiling at Baggs with a goofy grin Lewis comments "I'm sitting here with an honest-to-goodness celebrity. Don't worry, no one would recognize you. You didn't age well," Lewis teases.

Baggs frowns. Not especially amused. "Look who's talking! Put a sock in it," Baggs barks. Lewis continues to snicker.

"Anyway," Baggs changes the subject, "as soon as Sy gets to my house, he should call."

"You think Marty will hear the honk?" Lewis asks.

"I hope so. It's Saturday morning. Wait a minute, no

it's not. It's 10:40 AM here. That means it's afternoon there. She might be at the park or who knows where. Great!"

With two hot cups of coffee in hand, Juanita arrives at the table. Lewis takes the opportunity to be blunt, as usual. He asks Juanita, "Have you ever heard about or seen the big spaceship looking thing that's been seen hanging over the Grand Canyon?"

Baggs places his hand on his head with embarrassed frustration.

"Oh, El Halo de Diablo? The Devil's Halo. No, I have not seen it. It's nothing though. Just clouds that only look like a ship from space. You can no see it from here anyway. It only can be seen from other side. Something with the weather over there."

"The other side? The other side of what?" Lewis asks.

"You know? Other side. From the canyon side, you have to look back this way. If that is what you are looking for, then good luck. It is just a big grey cloud. You want breakfast or lunch?" Juanita asks pulling out her order pad.

"Huevos Rancheros, for me," Baggs replies

"Sounds good. Me too," Lewis echoes.

Juanita walks off with order in hand. "I don't get it. Some of this adds up and some of it doesn't. I thought we were going to learn something about that 'Devil's Halo' thing, or whatever it is, at the conference. Instead, we hear talk of synthetic DNA and RFID chips. Pretty scary stuff if it's all true," Lewis states, sipping his water.

Pulling into the driveway and parking directly in front of Baggs' truck, Sy shuts off the engine of his shiny black sports car. Sitting there for a moment, he hesitates to honk as planned. A sudden tapping against the passenger side window startles Sy.

He gets out of the vehicle and looks over the top of the car. Marty looks across at Sy. He greets her with an awkward, "Hello again."

Marty smiles at Sy and without reservation exclaims, "Wow! You got a Maserati GranTurismo? Cool. Will ya take me for a ride?"

Sy is not much of a people person, let alone a child person, but even he is impressed that she appreciates his prized possession. "Thank you. But, don't touch please!"

Marty grimaces with disappointment. She's not too sure about Sy yet. Still, any friend of Baggs is a friend of hers.

"You remember I'm supposed to use your cell phone when I get the cue from Baggs. Do you have it?" Sy asks.

Marty looks across the street, making sure that both Roxy and Vernon are still gone. After seeing that the coast is clear, Marty walks around between Baggs' truck and the front of Sy's car. She looks over to Sy as she pulls the phone from the inside pocket of her new coat.

"Well if you want it, come and get it. You have to at least meet me half way," she says, holding the cell phone down out of sight. "Don't want anyone knowing I got this, so get over here get it and be nonchalant about it," Marty orders smartly.

Sy is a little taken aback by her snarky wit. Walking around the car, he takes the phone from her.

"I'll be in Baggs' backyard. Come get me when you're done. And be quick about it. His number is in the contacts. And be careful with my phone," Marty turns and walks up the driveway and into the backyard.

Sy watches Marty walk off and does a half-hearted salute. Marty only has two contacts on her phone, Baggs and Louie. Sy pushes Baggs' contact and the phone immediately connects.

RIALTO CAFé, SANTA FE, NEW MEXICO

Baggs and Lewis are gorging themselves on generous portions of Huevos Rancheros when Baggs' cell phone rings. Baggs recognizes the caller ID. "It's Sy," he says to Lewis, who looks on with a mouthful of food. Baggs answers the call.

"Hello, Sy?"

"Yeah, it's me."

"Give us a minute; we're in a café in Santa Fe. We'll go out to the car where we can talk," Baggs says. He motions to Lewis, 'it's time to go.'

"I'm not finished," Lewis whines with his mouth still full of food.

Baggs reaches into his pocket, pulls out 2 twenty dollar bills and puts them on the table.

"Juanita, I'm sorry. We need to go. Emergency."

"You want doggie boxes?" Juanita asks.

"No. But thank you. It was very good," Baggs says as he heads for the door.

"Adios, Señor Baggs. Maybe you stay longer next time. We catch up," Juanita smiles, waving to Baggs. Lewis stands, still chewing his food and wiping salsa off of his face with his napkin.

"You two know each other?" he asks Baggs as they head for the door. Baggs nods and waves back to Juanita before exiting the diner.

He gets into the car and switches the phone to speaker so he and Lewis can both hear and talk to Sy.

"I'm here, can you hear me?" Baggs asks Sy as Lewis opens the car door and climbs into the passenger side.

"Yeah I'm here," Sy says. "I didn't expect to hear from you so soon."

"How's Marty? She okay?" Baggs asks

"Yeah, she's fine. She's in your backyard."

Lewis leans into the phone for volume emphasis. "You didn't tell me they were going to take your picture and give you some ceremonious plaque. That would have been handy information to have!"

"Who was the speaker?" Sy asks.

"A guy named Doctor Hess. Sigmund Hess, I think was his name."

"Yeah it was Sigmund Hess, Lewis recorded the speech. At least some of it," Baggs interjects.

"The reason you and the other scientists were invited there was so they could honor you monkeys for your contribution to the project. Some Lazarus thing they got going on. They're taking pictures of every one there. That means you, not me. If you're a jet propulsion lab tech, what part do you play in all of this? This Hess guy was talking about some pretty scary stuff," Lewis excitedly replies.

"It's called the Lazarus VI Project," Sy replies.

"Yeah, well there was nothing said about whatever that thing is that's been seen over the canyon. People here think it's just some strange weather anomaly. A cloud formation. They call it the Devil's Halo," Lewis says.

"It's not a weather anomaly. You said you guys were heading to the Grand Canyon to see for yourselves, right?"

"No, we're heading home. I'm not driving all the way over to the Grand Canyon just look at a bunch of clouds. I think we're done here. Nothing to see. We'll be talking to you about all of this DNA and RFID stuff, though. Laser, Lazarus program thing, he was talking about; what do you know about that?" Baggs asks.

"We'll talk when you two get back. If you had stayed at the seminar, you would have learned a lot more."

"If I had stayed, I'd be on my way to prison!" Lewis exclaims.

"Listen, there's someone you need to see while you're there. He's about an hour west of Flagstaff. A little town called Ash Fork. You have to speak to this guy. I know him, he's a good guy and can answer some of your questions," Sy insists.

"Are you kidding? We're six or seven hours away from Flagstaff, and this guy lives another hour beyond that? We won't get there until mid-night. Who is this guy, anyway?" Baggs asks.

"His name is John. John Gussman. He lives a little north of Ash Fork. He's a miner."

"A miner? You want us to go see a rock hound?" Baggs asks, annoyed.

"John who? Wait a minute. Did you say John Gussman? That's the dude Hess spoke of as being the discoverer of that CRY-Crap whatever it is," Lewis continues.

"Chryzinium. You have to talk to this guy. And no he's not a rock hound. He'll be able to fill you in on what this is all about. He knows what's going on and yes he knows about the Devil's Halo. And it isn't some weird cloud formation. I can promise you that."

"Fine. You have this John guys address?" Baggs asks begrudgingly.

"No address. He lives in the backcountry just north of Ash Fork. I hope you have a decent-size truck with four-wheel drive."

"Yeah, we're good," Lewis responds, winking at Baggs as they sit in their tiny, two-wheel-drive rental egg.

"I'll send you his GPS coordinates."

"Heck yeah! Send 'em, we'll talk to him," Lewis responds enthusiastically.

Baggs shakes his head. "Here we go again," he mumbles. "Let me talk to Marty, would you?"

"Yeah sure, hold on."

Sy walks to the backyard gate and sees Marty sitting on a rather large tire swing. Sy hollers at her, "Hey, Baggs wants to talk to you."

"About time, it's freezing out here. We could have had this little talk in that fancy car you drive. But no, let's chit-chat the day away in the freezing cold," Marty says, jumping from the swing and running to the gate.

Eagerly, she grabs her phone, "Hey, Baggs. When are you coming home?"

Baggs voice is faintly heard coming from the small speaker, "Not for a few days. You doing okay?"

Marty's exuberant smile quickly turns sad, "Yeah, I'm okay. Hurry home. I miss you."

"I miss you too. You be careful. Okay?"

"I will. I love you," Marty says to Baggs as she hands the phone back to Sy.

"Text us the coordinates. Hey, does this John guy have a phone?" Baggs asks Sy.

"Yeah, but let me make the contact. He's got guns, so be careful. He'll shoot to kill if he doesn't know who you are."

"Oh, good. It just keeps getting better. Seven, eight more hours of driving. Four wheel driving the high desert in January, and now guns?" Baggs grumbles.

"Just holler my name. He knows me. And he knows I'm on his side. That should tell him you're friend not foe," Sy says, ending the call. Sy looks down at Marty.

"Does your mom know you're over here?" Sy asks her.

"No. She and her boyfriend are gone. Why?"

"My car's unlocked. Jump in. I'll take you for a quick ride. I need to use your phone again to text Baggs directions. Deal? Just don't touch anything!"

Marty breaks out with a huge grin. She runs to the car and jumps into the passenger seat. Sy takes a deep breath, walks to his car, and slides into the driver's side seat.

THE ALPHA DIMENSION

Kevin's office is lit only by his desk lamp, computer screen, and rays of sunlight that spill in through the slats of the dark teak shudders that dress his office window. The light blue haze of cigar smoke fills the air as Kevin sits at his desk filling out security documents.

Each of those scheduled for the trip to M-PAC have been carefully chosen as per governmental position and importance to the project. Since it is Kevin who will oversee the special M-PAC journey, the arduous task of applying for security clearances for each visitor lies solely on his shoulders.

Eight were originally scheduled for the flight down. Besides Amanda Sykes and Kevin Rhodes, the entourage is to include Director of Homeland Security Lon Thompson, National Security Advisor Steven Van Noy,

Secretary of Defense Charles Hunt, CDC Director Corina Mendez, and Chairman of the House Ways and Means Committee Byron Sutter. Even Phoebe Wescott was to join the team however; a last-minute family emergency has waylaid her plans for the trip.

Though her support for the project has been less than favorable, Phoebe's participation was just as necessary. It was hoped that if she saw firsthand the impressiveness of the facility, she could be possibly swayed. Phoebe Wescott and Byron Sutter are the only two invited who hold elected congressional seats.

It is they who would help present the project to their party after it was signed into action. In other words, soften the outrage of the inevitable executive order. Not to mention, it would hopefully quell much of the negative backlash from Phoebe. It has been feared that she would be the one who would leak to the press the project, regardless of her confidentiality agreement.

It was her abrupt departure from the Oval Office meeting three weeks ago that put doubts in Kevin's mind whether she could be trusted. Maybe it's a good thing, for the project's sake, that Phoebe won't be joining the team for the trip to M-PAC after all.

Notwithstanding, the main purpose of this visit is to introduce these top officials to M-PAC and the Lazarus VI Project. It is this specially-formed committee that is hoped will validate M-PAC as a trusted lab. In other words, have they mastered a vaccine that will indeed cure disease? Can they prove a viable RFID chip will do what is expected without endangering the public, and of course, can they deliver as promised?

The team departs from Ronald Reagan Washington National Airport in the morning and there is still much to prepare. M-PAC has more security walls than any other agency or entity. No one gets in without proper Top Secret clearance via M-PAC's own meticulous screening processes.

Even though the entire M-PAC facility is off-limits without proper authorization, there are areas that are accessible via a less stringent security level classification. However, there are ultra-high-security areas that many don't ever get to witness. Even Kevin must apply for this special Top Security clearance with each and every visit he makes to the lab.

With the lower level security credential, one is offered the basic no frills, low informational tour. Still impressive, it's not a tour that goes behind closed doors. It is these low risk classifications that are given the purple 'B-Sector' credential.

They are permitted only in sectors 1 and 2, the areas designated by purple marked walkways and purple signage in plain view on walls, halls and doorways. Even at this lower level of security; the scrutiny for background is extensive.

The M-PAC facility is much the same as the Special Access Program. With strict security and firewalls, M-PAC is virtually impenetrable.

There are areas within the facility that are so sensitive that even people who have Top Security clearance credentials cannot gain access to these areas unless they receive a special indoctrination classification. And those are only given on a one-time, need-to-know basis.

Unlike a typical governmental Top Secret classification, which is a blanket security credential, the facility maintains compartmentalized project analyst security credentials that far exceed Top Secret.

Special Security Officers (SSOs) are assigned exclusively to various departments of operation. Not even between SSOs are they to share information concerning their department. Each area of operation is independent and exclusive unto itself and considers all information highly sensitive.

All employees must undergo a periodic background information investigation. Also, random polygraph tests are given along with the occasional visit to 'The Chair.' The Chair is a term that refers to hypnosis treatment. It is hypnosis applied old school via Sodium Pentothal, (truth serum) and can be expected at any given time without warning.

Sensitive information compromise is an imprisonable offense classified as a class one felony of which is plainly decreed throughout the facility. Even military Generals, governmental dignitaries, and visiting scientists must endure an extensive background check with each and every visit.

With a light tap on Kevin's door, Amanda Sykes enters his office. Her impeccably tailored grey suit moves in complete unison with her equally impeccable figure. Amanda takes a seat on Kevin's couch and crosses her long legs. It is Kevin's cue to edge over and turn on his sticky charm.

"You certainly know how to make grey look good. You should let me take you out to dinner some time," Kevin leers at her as he uses his favorite pick-up line.

"Mr. Rhodes, you are a real piece of work, you know that? Why would you want to take me out to dinner, anyway? You're not going to get anywhere with me. So why not save your money. I think it would be best if we kept our business on a professional level. Don't you?" Amanda says with a smirk. "I have my manifest list and need to crosscheck it with yours."

"You are one tough chick. I was just trying to be cordial, that's all, 'Ms. Sykes,'" Kevin replies, drawing out her name for emphasis. Amanda's face shows no emotion.

Trying to recover his composure he finally retreats and switches to the business at hand, "I emailed you the list earlier this morning."

"I need the hard copy hand-delivered directly from you. Security policies. You know this." Amanda stands in one fluid motion and walks over to the window to look through the teak blinds at the manicured common area. Kevin ignores the fact that Amanda makes him feel subordinate.

"How'd things go back at Vul-Stream's tech lab?" Kevin asks.

"Fine. The transfers are going through as planned. The tech team are expected to make the last three downloads during the next three weeks."

Kevin revisits his previous offer using a more business-like approach.

"Perfect. Well, look, since dinner is a no-go, would you care to join me for lunch? Strictly business of course," he flashes his most charming smile for effect.

"I already have plans," Amanda says flatly. "Maybe your wife would like to go to lunch with you." Not waiting for an answer, Amanda turns away from the window and walks to the door.

Amanda continues, "I'm going to the airport. The Dove is due to arrive at 0830 tomorrow and security is there now at the hangar doing their security sweep. Like I said, I need your copy of the manifest. I trust nothing has changed?"

"No. Nothing has changed, Ms. Sykes." Kevin mutters.

"Good. I'm almost finished with background checks for the flight."

Amanda snatches the folder from Kevin's grasp. "Be sure to let everyone know they need to be at Ronald Reagan National Airport, hangar 7 at 0930 for check in. The plane departs at 1030 sharp." Turning with military precision, she exits Kevin's office.

Kevin is left standing behind his desk feeling frustrated and defeated. Twice this Amanda chick has shot him down like a lone goose at a duck hunt.

At 36,000 feet, the team of seven begin their rapid descent into what is believed to be Nevada; the undisclosed location of M-PAC. The white, unmarked, business-class jet referred to as 'The Dove' makes the 1,800 mile flight to M-PAC in approximately three hours.

Sitting at the rear of the jet, Kevin managed to acquire the seat next to Amanda. Not one to be denied, Kevin has every intention of continuing his quest to charm the beautiful Amanda Sykes before the day's end. After light talk concerning the upcoming events of the trip, Kevin tries yet again to win her affections.

"You know, we have an open marriage. My wife and I," he whispers seductively.

Amanda turns to Kevin and responds with a smile and a voice like silk, "You never mentioned that. Well, that changes everything. As long as there isn't going to be any repercussions from the missus, then maybe we can see what develops." With a bat of her gorgeous eyelashes, she licks her supple lips and smiles seductively at Kevin.

Kevin smiles back, pleased he believes he may have finally made some headway.

"When we land, and before they take our cell phones, I'll just give, what's her name again, your wife, oh yes, Lisa, a call, and just make sure she's okay with all of this. If that's okay with you Mr. Rhodes?"

Kevin's composure crumbles and he begins stuttering. "I mean, well, it's kind of a 'don't ask, don't tell' rule we have." Kevin's attempt at back pedaling, fails miserably as beads of sweat form on his forehead.

"Hmm. I thought so," Amanda responds indifferently. Embarrassed, Kevin quietly settles back into his seat with a defeated scowl.

The Dove has two pilots and two flight attendants who service the passengers of the enigmatic aircraft. Not your typical flight attendants, but Secret Service agents. While they are plenty capable of passing out peanuts and serving coffee, they are well accomplished in maintaining any necessary security measures as well.

They both wear small, gold and black engraved name badges and are referred to only by their first names, Joe and John. As the Dove begins its descent, they begin their pre-landing procedures.

The steeper than average rate of descent is typically unnerving to first timers. This is evident by the concerned looks on the faces of the passengers.

Joe stands at the front of the cabin and removes the in-flight microphone from the small control panel. With a soothing British accent, he reassures the passengers that the flight is going as planned and for all to relax. He also makes clear there will be upcoming procedures that must be followed precisely.

Indirect blue cabin lights come on as the clear windows illuminated from the daylight outside, shift to opaque. The passengers are now unable to see the rapidly approaching desert below.

The soothing British voice comes over the in-flight

speakers again. "Everyone securely fasten your seat-belts please. If you begin to feel queasy, as mentioned before takeoff, airsickness bags are located inside your right armrest. We will be on the ground shortly." The passengers take a moment to fasten their seatbelts and settle in for landing.

Joe continues his well-rehearsed landing procedure.

"Once the aircraft lands, and even after we come to a complete stop, you must remain in your seats, with your seatbelts securely fastened. After landing, we will be connected to an aircraft tug that will tow the Dove into the hangar.

"Once inside the hangar, we will disembark the airplane two at a time. You will do exactly as instructed. When told to do so. I will instruct two of you to unfasten your seatbelts and stand. My colleague, John, will then escort those two off of the plane. Once they are securely off the plane and John returns, I will instruct two more of you to unbuckle and stand. John will then escort them off of the plane. We will disembark in that manner until the aircraft is clear, does everyone understand?"

The passengers all nod their heads in compliance. Joe hangs up the small microphone and takes his seat in a small jump-seat just below the microphone's control panel.

At an ear-popping rate of descent, the plane dives from the sky. At last, the Dove touches down, transitioning smoothly from flight to ground roll. The plane travels down the runway for what seems like an eternity.

There is no way to determine the actual speed or direction of the plane due to the lack of any outside visual references.

Passengers can feel that the plane is now slowing and turning off the runway. It taxis for another few minutes, and then finally comes to a smooth stop.

Joe unbuckles his seatbelt and stands at the front just as John approaches from the rear. Slowly and methodically, John checks to make sure everyone has remained buckled securely into their seats.

After his inspection, he nods to Joe. Joe proceeds, reaching over to the control panel to take the microphone off of its clip. He continues his instructions to the passengers.

"Welcome to M-PAC everyone. Just sit back and relax. It will be a few moments before the tug takes us to the hangar," Joe says, keeping his tone pleasant and matter of fact.

Kevin has been sulking ever since being shot down again by Amanda. More than once now he has felt the distinct sensation of how a rabbit must feel in a lion's den. Being toyed with, then ripped apart and eaten, is not his idea of fun. And he doesn't like the feeling one bit, and certainly not something with which he's accustomed.

Within just a couple of moments, the sound of the tug is heard connecting to the front wheel of the plane. A slight jerk is felt and the aircraft is in motion once again.

One after the other, the jets engines shut down

and the interior lights flicker as the auxiliary power unit takes over powering the planes electrical systems. The plane comes to a stop. Another jerk and the plane begins rolling again, only this time in reverse. The plane then stops once more.

The electric motors that power the large hangar doors are heard as the hangar is slowly closed off to the outside world. Placing the com-set over his ears, Joe changes the channel on the console to speak to the ground crew.

After a short exchange of words, he nods to John. John then opens the plane's door. Hanging up the microphone and headset, Joe walks to the first two passengers in the forward seats. Charles Hunt and Steven Van Noy are the first to be instructed to unbuckle and stand.

John moves in quickly. He faces the two men as they stand, and he ushers them to the aircraft door and carefully leads them off the plane. Forty-five seconds later, John returns and steps back into the plane. Joe moves to the next two to deplane. The military-like procedure continues until Kevin Rhodes and Amanda Sykes are last.

As they exit the plane, they are ushered into the brilliantly-lit hangar. As per their previous visits, they are instructed to follow a bright yellow painted line that leads them to a pair of double-hung steel doors. Over the top of the doors a tongue-in cheek-sign reads, 'You are about to enter the Alpha Dimension,' meant as a light-hearted gesture. Beyond the doors are the three elevators going down to the lab.

The others have already gone down and Kevin and Amanda are attended by one guard. "Good to be back," Kevin says to the guard with a pompous smirk. "We can handle it from here if you want."

Without emotion or eye contact, the guard ignores Kevin. As soon as the elevator door opens, the guard pushes Kevin rudely into the car and turns to offer a gentlemanly hand to Amanda to guide her into the elevator.

"Hello again, Ms. Sykes," the guard says kindly. Amanda flashes her perfect smile. "Hello to you too, Todd," Amanda says politely.

Kevin looks on, indignant and humiliated.

The elevator door closes and the car begins its rapid descent. A moment of weightlessness is felt as the elevator drops downward at two stories per second. Shortly, the elevator brakes engage, slowing the elevator to an uncomfortably quick stop.

The doors snap open with a 'whoosh' exposing a stark, two-tone grey, military type reception area. Though small, it is clearly marked as a high-security area.

On the walls are glaring warning signs. 'Absolutely No Photography,' 'No Recording Devices of Any Kind,' and threats of 'Bodily Harm and/or Death if Caught Entering Unauthorized Areas.' Somewhat superfluous, since anyone allowed entering is stripped of all they own and are under constant supervision.

One at a time, the visitors are each taken into another security chamber referred to as 'Peeping Tom,' a nickname given to the machine by those who work at the facility. It is like an airport security X-Ray scanner on steroids. 'Peeping Tom' scans for any foreign objects outside or inside the body.

Whether the foreign material is made of cloth, metal, wood, plastic, carbon fiber, clay, fiberglass, plaster, or explosives, it will be detected.

Before entering, one must completely strip of all clothing, shoes, jewelry, glasses and even false teeth. All belongings are to be placed into the clear plastic tub provided. Once filled, the tub is then pushed through a small privacy door in the wall. When the door is closed, the contents are then received by security on the opposite side for screening. After a few seconds the small door is again opened, this time exposing a clear plastic container with anti-contamination wardrobe.

Striped of all clothing, visitors are instructed to step onto the bright yellow footprints painted on the floor, guiding them to Peeping Tom. After a moment, the machine begins to spool up, making a loud buzzing noise as electrons and protons are energized.

The 7 foot long by 4 inch wide brightly-polished aluminum scan panels hang 3 feet apart from each other from an overhead rotor. Once the subject steps into the center of Peeping Tom and the machine is activated, the scan panels rotate around the body with a howling scream. When Peeping Tom has completed its operation, the panels slow to a stop and the buzz of the energizers subside.

Then, a green light flashes on the wall indicating it is time to step clear of the machine and dress. Special paper fiber disposable underwear, along with a bright yellow fiber-paper anti contamination suit is provided. Also provided in the container is a hair net, face-mask, and foot wear.

The white rubberized anti-static, slip-resistant booties are to be worn at all times while in the facility. Anyone dressed in bright yellow is easily recognizable as a visitor and considered a possible threat.

Once screened for explosive devices and biological contaminants, only the person's glasses and false teeth are returned to the owner when entering the holding area just inside the bay.

Depending on the level of security, a color-coded badge is to be worn around the neck at all times via a black-banded lanyard. The Security ID badge is handed to each visitor upon entering the 'Iron Box,' the final holding cell located out in the lab's bay on the catwalk.

Four of the seven visitors stand in their bright yellow decontamination suits wearing their purple badges just inside the Iron Box. Everywhere one looks, there is the strange hieroglyph representing those that work at M-PAC, referred to as the Sign of the Shafutah.

The four dignitaries look over the immense facility in awe. Scientists and engineers work below. Bustling about, they weave around the bay of electrical equipment, monitoring equipment and shiny stainless steel test tables.

From a separate steel door, a man wearing white anticontamination pants and a dark blue lab coat enters the cell from a second side door. With a thick German accent, he introduces himself.

"Hello everyone; my name is Wilhelm Avercamp. I will be your guide today. As soon as security arrives, we will begin our tour."

Byron Sutter looks at the people present in their party and notices that Kevin, Amanda, and Lon Thompson are not with them.

"Excuse me," Byron interjects. "There are three of our group that are not with us yet."

"Yes Mr. Sutter," Avercamp politely explains. "They will be joining us a little later. Since they are already familiar with the facility, they will sit this first part out."

Just as Avercamp finishes his introductions, two armed guards enter the Iron Box. Avercamp smiles and with a wave of his arm he gestures the party to proceed. One guard unlocks the cage door, walks through, and steps to the side. Following the other guard, the group exits as he stands holding the cage door. Bringing up the tail is Avercamp and the Iron Box guard.

"Please follow the guard and he will lead us below. Once on the floor of the bay, please stay behind the painted purple line," Avercamp instructs.

As the team walks slowly along the length of the catwalk towards the stairs, Byron looks back just in time to see Kevin, Amanda, and Lon walking on an adjacent catwalk heading the opposite direction. Also dressed in anticontamination suits, they are being led by a well-built gentleman in his fifties. Byron can't help but wonder where they are headed and why.

Operations Tech Supervisor, Doctor Edward Stiner, leads the three down the catwalk. He walks quickly as Amanda, Kevin, and Lon follow closely behind.

Reaching the other end of the bay, Doctor Stiner approaches room 216. Raising his right hand just in front of the door, it automatically slides open exposing the control room. The same room Doctor Hess often oversees when he's there at the facility.

"Doctor Hess has had to give up some of his precious office space, but I'm sure he'll adjust," Stiner says with a chuckle.

Just beyond the control console is a newly-installed, high-tech door, but still in need of paint. Again, Doctor Stiner raises his hand and a second door slides open. Offering an invite with his lanky arm, the three enter.

The room is about half the size of a basketball court. It is a theater that has a large viewing screen on one end. The room has black walls, red theater carpet, indirect lighting and an upper and lower level of plush black leather couches. The couches sit towards the back of the room and can seat up to 12 individuals comfortably.

The indirect purple lighting illuminates the perimeter of the floor as well as the ceiling above. The glow is minimal, but enough to reveal obstacles in the dark theater for safe maneuvering.

The theater resembles a private Hollywood executive type viewing room. With a control console located in the center of the room, it consists of monitors, keyboards, buttons, and knobs.

Doctor Stiner instructs the three to find themselves a comfortable place to sit on the leather couches. "It'll be just a minute," Doctor Stiner says while taking a seat at one of the console's three swivel-back desk chairs.

Within a few moments, another gentleman enters through the door. The 6 foot, 4 inch man is strikingly good looking. His high cheekbones and olive-colored complexion compliment his athletic build.

He is dressed in a black silver thread suit that appears to radiate a bluish glint as he moves about. The upper left crest of his jacket has a subtle dark shiny green insignia. It is the same insignia that is posted on doors walls and floors throughout the M-PAC Laboratory.

He doesn't acknowledge the guests, but instead stands stoic in front of the console facing the large screen. Without hesitation or warning, Amanda immediately stands and greets the strange man with a kiss on both cheeks.

Amanda turns back to Kevin and Lon. "This is Adiv, Adiv Zahim. He'll be showing you something I think both of you will find fascinating," Amanda says as she places her hand on Adiv's shoulder.

Adiv and Amanda both take a seat at the console. Kevin and Lon look on, puzzled by the man they have never met. Stiner takes his seat next to Amanda and begins flipping switches and turning knobs.

As a few privately whispered unintelligible words are exchanged between Amanda and Adiv, Kevin looks on intently, realizing Amanda has a man in her life.

No wonder she continually turns down his advances. Looking over to Lon, Lon shrugs with a shake of his head, also seemingly surprised.

"If you're all ready for the show, let us begin," Edward Stiner says with a huge grin.

Stiner flips on a final switch. The large 10 by 20 foot screen immediately begins to illuminate. The projected image is as vivid as though looking through a large picture window.

Recognizing the geographic area they are viewing, Kevin and Lon are riveted by what can only be described as awe-inspiring.

GOD, GIANTS, AND DARWIN

Biblical accounts of Fallen Angels that were upon the earth during the days of Noah are spoken of in the book of Genesis Chapter 6, verse 4. It was these so-called 'Fallen Angels' who saw earth women were fair and desirable and subsequently had relations (sex) with them.

Not surprisingly, they had children. It is those off-spring who became the giants of the earth. The Bible is quite clear about the existence of these giants. Take the story of David and Goliath, for example. These were the 'Men of Great,' the 'Nephilim.'

Interestingly, these biblical accounts have long been disputed or dismissed as nothing more than mytho-logical fairytales, allegorical teachings, or just plain nonsense written two thousand years ago. Ironically, most of the dispute usually comes from the scientific community.

'Where's the proof?' has always been the big question. Darwin wrote the Theory of Evolution and his philosophy took root in the mid-1800s, which propagated the notion that mankind evolved throughout time, starting as a single-celled organism, and was not created by intelligent design.

Transmutation of a species was not just a passing interest of Darwin, but indeed a subject he wrote and spoke much of. Notwithstanding, his theory not only took root, it soon grew from mere theory to scientific fact. A belief still revered today.

In fact, this is a belief that has been supported by many scientists of the Smithsonian Institute for more than 130 years. To their dismay, proof of giants was discovered in the early 1900s. Hence, the beginnings of a huge cover up. The idea that giants once roamed the earth supports biblical theology, not evolutionism.

If a society of giants once existed, it would certainly be a huge chink in the evolutionist chain, to say the least. For years, the Smithsonian has led the American people to believe there never was such a species of these so-called giants.

Their argument? There has never been any trace evidence found. In other words, there are no archeological findings to substantiate such. Since there is no proof, evolution can therefore be a valid theory worth backing scientifically.

That was, until the American Institution of Alternative Archeology (AIAA) made allegations that the

Smithsonian Institute intentionally destroyed archeological findings. The Smithsonian, hoping to protect their prestigious reputation, sued the AIAA for defamation. Hence, the Smithsonian and the AIAA had their day in court.

The Supreme Court demanded the release of classified documents, which not only settled the case, but proved beyond the shadow of a doubt that there was indeed a cover-up. It came to light that in the early 1900s, the Smithsonian Institute surreptitiously destroyed tens of thousands of skeletons ranging from six to twelve feet in height.

The American people were led to believe that the first colonization of the North American continent was by Asians that came through the Bering Strait some 15,000 years ago. And most people bought into that theory until archaeologists began to dig a little further.

Natives claim that the hundreds of thousands of burial mounds that are still being found all over America today have been there long before their arrival. In fact, this 'Giant' civilization was proven to be highly developed for their time.

Their intricate use of metals and other forms of modern types of tools have also been discovered at or around sites where the giant human skeleton remains were found.

The fact that human remains of a Giant civilization had been uncovered and purposely destroyed borders on absurdity. The question must then be asked. Why the cover-up? The answer is actually quite simple.

It was a strategy implemented in hopes of protecting the new growing scientific belief that man is nothing more than a transmutation of species. This theory of transmutation supports evolutionism. Therefore the discovery of an ancient civilization of Giant humans supports the Bible as a reliable historical document.

If one early historical slice of evidence in the Bible is proven credible, the Bible as a whole must be accepted as credible; thereby supporting the science of creationism.

However, there are the spirit world and alternate dimensions to consider. Alien beings and alien craft witnessed by millions of people are another subject that once again questions man's origins.

AND THEN
THERE'S JOHN

"Go north on Double 'A' Ranch Road and then take Quarry Road. There's a turn off to the left, before getting to the quarry. It's marked by a large boulder. Take that for about three hundred yards. That'll get us to another road that looks more like a wagon trail that leads to John's place," Lewis says, navigating for Baggs.

"Are you getting directions from GPS coordinates or from the map you got from the store?" Baggs asks as he carefully drives north on the snow-covered Double 'A' Ranch Road.

"Both," Lewis replies as he unfolds more of the map.

"How are we going to see a large boulder? Everything is covered in snow.

"I don't know."

"Let's just follow the GPS. I think it's a safer bet so we don't get lost."

There's about two feet of snow along the sides of the dirt road with a decent six inches of packed snow on the road itself. This is making navigation a bit more challenging.

After Lewis and Baggs made it to Flagstaff, they traded in the tiny yellow egg for a more suitable rental vehicle. For the remainder of their trip, they're driving a sangria red, all-wheel drive SUV.

Baggs' idea was to choose a color that didn't look like something the government would drive. Also, a bright color will stand out better just in case they get stranded somewhere in the snowy high desert.

It's January and the elevation in Ash Fork is approximately 5,000 feet, give or take a few hundred feet depending on how far out of town they'll be traveling.

Although it's not actually snowing, the weather is bitter cold with dense low-lying freezing fog that considerably limits their visibility. It's becoming plenty obvious to them; John doesn't live anywhere close to paved roads, stores, or civilization.

After a solid hour of 5 to 10 miles-per-hour driving, Baggs reaches a fork in the road. Going left leads them onto Quarry Road. As luck would have it, there is indeed a huge boulder at the junction. Baggs looks over to Lewis who shrugs an 'okay' for Baggs to proceed down the narrow trail.

Tire tracks in the packed snow lead the way once

again. Slowly, the two men drive the narrow road which looks more like a wagon trail. At only a couple of miles per hour, their trek is an arduous journey. As they creep along, Lewis continues to give GPS directions. Another half an hour, Lewis finally shouts, "Here!"

"Here! Here where? I don't see anything," Baggs replies.

"According to this, we turn left, right here and his place is just to the right up ahead."

"I don't see a road here. Are you sure?"

"That's what it says."

Baggs stops the vehicle and carefully looks around, investigating the geography of the area. Just to the right and below it appears there is indeed a building nestled within a grove of short stubby trees.

Due to a heavy low lying fog, it's hard to make out much detail, but Baggs thinks he sees a stream of smoke possibly coming from a chimney.

Baggs mumbles, "How do we get down there." He slowly drives another 50 feet. There to the right is a drivable path leading down into the small valley.

Baggs makes the executive decision to make the turn and drive down what he believes could be John's driveway. Winding into a small punch-bowl valley, nestled in trees, is an older looking manufactured home with a fairly large pole-building shop located behind. As they get closer, it is confirmed it is indeed smoke they see. It's coming from a stove pipe exiting the roof of the house.

An older two-tone brown and tan four-wheel-drive truck is parked out front. It's obvious it has been well used, as every piece of sheet metal is either rusted and/ or dented. Mounted to the front of the truck is a rather large steel bumper and winch. The huge off-road tires are evidence that the truck is all utility.

Also painted brown, a fairly good-sized covered wooden porch is attached to the front of the home. By the front door on the porch is an old wooden rocking chair.

As the two drive up closer to the house, the tires of their SUV make a quiet drive impossible as they crunch through the snow. Sure enough, the front door of the manufactured home opens. A grizzly-looking man wearing coveralls, brown flannel shirt, baseball cap, and big black boots emerges onto the porch.

The man's beard is salt and pepper brown and grey just as his shoulder-length hair. Reaching the porch railing, he stops and stares intently as Baggs brings the SUV to a stop. What is thought at first to be a possible stand-off is soon put to rest when the man cracks a huge smile and politely waves.

"Did he just wave to us?" Lewis asks.

The two men are a bit perplexed. They were expecting a bit more of a hostile reception. Sy did say to them to watch out for possible gun fire. Baggs and Lewis are thinking that maybe this isn't John's house, after all.

Lewis pushes the power window switch lowering his window. He stops the window about 3 inches from the top, giving him just enough of the outside to hear if the grungy looking man says something.

"Baggs and Lewis, right?" The man hollers from the porch.

With a befuddled whisper, Lewis turns and asks Baggs, "It's John. How does he know it's us?"

"I don't know, but I say we get out. I don't see a gun," Baggs replies, opening the driver side door. Baggs steps out of the vehicle to greet the man.

"John? John Gussman?" Baggs shouts.

"One and the same. Well don't just sit there! Come on in, it's freezing out here." John shouts back. Baggs drops his head back into the SUV.

"I guess we're here. Let's go in," Baggs says to Lewis. Shutting off the engine and grabbing his briefcase from the backseat, Baggs exits the vehicle as Lewis follows his lead.

"I was wondering when you two were going to get here," John announces, holding his hand out for a friendly handshake.

This is obviously not the greeting Baggs and Lewis were expecting. They each shake hands as John leads the two into his home. Shutting the door behind him, John offers Baggs and Lewis a seat on the couch.

John walks straight to the woodstove and grabs the percolating pot of coffee from the hot stove's surface. He grabs a couple of cups that hang from pegs on the paneled wall just to the side of the stove.

With coffee pot in hand, John brings the cups to

Baggs and Lewis and sets them down on the table in front of the couch. With the room not being well-lit, the furnishings blend into the woodwork with pale shades of plaid.

Brown is the predominant color scheme in the living room; at least for the furnishings and John's flannel shirt. A wagon wheel chandelier hangs from the knotty pine vaulted ceiling in the center of the living room. Old Wild West style lamps mounted on majestic brass horse bases are set on vintage maple wood end tables. Along with a plethora of pictures, a variety of animal skulls are mounted on the dark paneled walls.

With a deep breath, John blows the dust out of each of the coffee cups before pouring the coffee. Baggs and Lewis look on as they realize a less than sanitary standard is being offered them. John pours coffee that is not only the blackest they've ever seen, but the thickest.

"Hope you like it black, don't have cream or sugar," John says apologetically. Baggs and Lewis look on anxiously as John pours the hot black paste from the pot.

"Black is fine," Baggs responds with gratitude. Lewis looks over to Baggs and smiles. He knows good and well Baggs is lying through his teeth.

"You boys hungry? Want some stew? I got a lot left over from yesterday," John politely offers.

"No, we're good. We're still full from this morning," Lewis immediately replies, hoping not to offend him.

"So how'd you know it was us, if you don't mind me asking?" Baggs asks John.

"Sy told me you were coming."

"You have a cell phone, way out here?" Lewis asks.

"Yeah, of course I do. There's a cell tower less than a quarter mile from here."

"We thought maybe you were completely off-the-grid," Baggs says. John smiles as he places the coffee pot back onto the stove.

"Yeah, well you're partially right. We are a little off the grid, so to speak. I generate my own power, provide my own heat and pump my own water, that sort of thing. But we still go grocery shopping and buy gas and stuff. Gotta live, you know. We do stock up on supplies so we can go off the grid when the time comes," John grabs his cup of coffee and takes a seat in front of Baggs and Lewis.

"Sy warned you have guns and told us to arrive cautiously," Lewis says, embarrassing Baggs.

"Yeah, had he not of told me you were coming, I would have shot you both," John chuckles.

"We? Are there others that live with you here?" Baggs asks.

"My kids, Madison and Cory. They'll probably be coming in, now that you're here. They're out in the shop," John replies. Just as John finishes his response, the two children come in through the back door and enter the kitchen.

"Sure enough. This is my boy Cory and my daughter Madison. Kids, this is Commander Walter Baggerly. He was once a very famous astronaut back in his day. And this is his friend, Lewis. I don't know your last name,

I'm sorry," John regrettably replies.

"Warren. Lewis Warren. Hi guys," Lewis responds while greeting John's kids with a nod.

"Hello," Baggs says, also greeting the siblings.

Both Madison and Cory say "hi" and wave as they both turn to raid the refrigerator.

"You guys can go back to getting the wood cut, and don't eat up all of the cheese," John instructs.

Turning to his guests, John informs, "Madison is 11 and Cory is 16, they're good kids. Fun to have around."

"I didn't know you were married," Lewis remarks.

"I was. I'm a widower now. Lizzy died nine years ago from cancer."

"I'm sorry for your loss," Baggs sympathizes.

"Yeah, me too," John says softly.

After a moment of uncomfortable silence, John continues, "Sy tells me you were at Los Alamos."

"Yeah, well I was. What a huge complex!" Lewis responds.

On the coffee table are a stack of old geological magazines and a couple of three-ring binders among other pieces of literature.

John picks up one of the binders and thumbs through the plastic document inserts, opening it up to the fifth page. Turning the binder around and laying it flat on the table, there is a picture of the Devil's Halo hovering over the Grand Canyon.

"Sy told me you were interested in this."

Baggs and Lewis look on, somewhat surprised at

the photo. Taken from a different angle, it is the same anomaly they have seen in their own newspaper clippings. Baggs removes the yellow manila folder from his briefcase. He places the folder on the coffee table and opens it, revealing Lewis' photo.

"So, what is it?" Lewis asks.

"Some refer to it as 'The Devil's Halo,'" Baggs says.

"You went to Hess's deal at the Laboratory?" John asks.

Lewis looks over to Baggs and then back to John before answering, "Yeah."

John begins the process of show and tell, slowly turning the pages of the plastic document sleeves in the binder. It contains pictures of the Grand Canyon, plants, rocks, petroglyphs, and even more pictures of the strange anomaly.

"It's an honor, Commander Baggerly, having you here in my home," John says with a big smile. Baggs beams.

"So, you do know of me?" Baggs asks.

"Not a lot of black astronauts. Besides, Sy has been telling me a lot about you two."

"So how long have you known Sy?" Lewis finally asks. Certainly a question both Baggs and Lewis would like answered.

"Quite some time I guess. He's an interesting guy. So, does he live in Springboro by you two?"

"Gated community. Only gated community in Springboro. He and Norma do pretty well for themselves. Do you know his wife?" Baggs asks.

"I don't. Either of you want anything else? More coffee or something to nibble on?" I'm getting a little hungry.

John stands and heads to the kitchen. With an open concept floor plan, he doesn't venture too far. John opens the refrigerator and rummages.

He removes a small jar of pickled herring. Opening the jar, he takes it back into the living room. With his fingers he pulls out a chunk of the fish delicacy and slurps it down. Taking his seat again, he holds the jar out and offers Baggs and Lewis a bite.

Both Baggs and Lewis respectfully decline his kind offer, holding up their hands with a 'no thanks' motion. Neither Baggs nor Lewis is particularly fond of eating pickled fish from a jar.

"So, you know all about the Devil's Halo stuff, then? Lewis asks, trying his best to refocus the conversation.

"Oh yeah, I guess you could say that. I didn't start out looking for the thing. It was after my hike down to the bottom of the canyon back in 96, that I got interested."

After a couple more bites of the herring, John begins telling the story of his bizarre hike to the bottom of the canyon with his longtime friend, Arnie Swinth.

"I thought he was a goner. But, by the time Arnie and I made it back to the top of the canyon, he was like a new man.

"Within a couple of days of returning from the canyon, Arnie saw his doctor. I didn't know it at the beginning of our trip, but he was a guy who just a few days earlier had diabetes and was dying of pancreatic cancer. In fact, he told me he had it set in his mind that this was his last big adventure. Doctors thought he'd be dead within a year.

"After our return from the trip, not a trace of cancer, no sign of being diabetic, nothing, the guy was as healthy as a horse. I knew it wasn't the Catclaw Acacia leaves the Indian gave him. It was what he had added to the leaves.

"I made it my quest in life to find out what that was. What else did the Indian have in that pouch? It looked silvery. It was a powder of sorts.

"I did a lot of research. The Anasazi, who were an ancient civilization that lived in the canyon, spoke of a cloud of dust that would encompass their tribe once or twice a year. Not a dust of dirt or sand but a dust made up of a very fine metallic particulate that would sparkle during certain light conditions. This metallic dust would occasionally rain down upon them.

"According to lore, it was this metallic dust which was responsible for healing their sick and wounded.

"After thousands of years, many other civilizations began to appear, and that is when they say the Star People subsequently stopped visiting.

"Hundreds of petroglyphs found in caves and carved along the canyon walls depict these Star People and what could be considered their craft or mode of inter-galactic transportation.

"One of the petroglyphs depicts a drawing of what

could be interpreted as a space craft-looking thing with particulates falling from it to the ground. The Anasazi became somewhat of a legend. Whether absorbed by other tribes, or they became extinct, Sani told me the Anasazi no longer exist.

"After several trips to the canyon floor, I became more acquainted with Sani, the Indian who gave Arnie the healing powder mixed with the leaves. We spent a lot of time together and became friends. It was Sani that showed me how and where to mine the metallic dust. Hence, the discovery of Unibihexium Carbon Particle.

"Because of my position at the National Science Lab in Los Alamos, I was able to pool together a team of scientists and resources, making possible the extraction of the particle using a method I personally invented, Radio Magnetic Electrolysis.

"The process was expensive and was not at all easy to operate, especially at that time. Furthering developments later made the extraction process much simpler. I will tell you this, there is no such element like UBH indigenous to our planet.

"Over years of testing, I found that there were many significant, unintelligible properties associated with the substance. Unibihexium Carbon is dangerously unstable. Once someone begins taking it, they have to stay on it. That meant any long term effects, positive or negative, were anyone's guess. Also, if taken improperly; wrong dosages or wrong intervals, one was susceptible to seizures or heart attacks."

John sits back in his seat and eats another mouthful of pickled herring. Baggs and Lewis wait as patiently as they can, anxious to hear the rest of the story. After John swallows, he continues.

"Have you heard of CTS-235?" John asks. Baggs and Lewis turn and look at each other, nodding.

"Yeah, we just heard about it from that Doctor Hess guy. I recorded it. Well part of it," Lewis confesses.

"CTS-235 is nothing more than a form of paint thinner for DNA. All it does is assist in breaking down the natural human DNA molecules to better accept synthetic biochemical agents such as Unibihexium Carbon. It's actually been around for years."

"Yeah, I kind of got that from his speech," Lewis responds.

"Did he also talk of DNA mapping in regards to synthetic DNA?"

"Yeah, but I was sort of pre-occupied with being invisible," Lewis admits.

"Well I'll tell you, you're only getting part of the story. Unibihexium Carbon alters the human DNA. It recreates the 23 pairs of chromosomes into a synthetic version. In other words, natural human DNA is replaced with a duplicate synthetic version DNA. The question I have is; can one still be considered human when that takes place?

"Of course, this is something scientists have wanted for years. With a synthetic DNA, humans could possibly live twice as long. They could virtually be impervious to disease.

"Not to mention, they could possibly be reprogrammed to take on herculean characteristics. Strong enough to carry around that SUV you drove up in. Or be reprogrammed with superhuman knowledge. It all sounds great, until you look at the dark side.

"Like I said, with a synthetic DNA, one's metabolic make-up is then, in a sense, reprogrammable. My question is what happens to the soul of mankind if human DNA is altered beyond natural form? You know, we're the only species on the face of the earth that debates the realities of a God figure. The creator of all mankind, if you will.

"You also know we're the only species that places value on artistic capabilities. Humans are the only ones who can logically reason with quantitative skill. Yeah, we can teach monkeys to fly in rockets, but when's the last time you've heard of a monkey actually building a rocket. It is these reasons that for me substantiates the likelihood of a deity.

"When I discovered what Unibihexium Carbon actually does and where I believe it came from, I filed my report. If Hess and his goons could turn Unibihexium Carbon into a vaccine, I knew we'd be screwed, as a human race. I left the project and the science field all together. Ironically that's when MK-Ultra was reestablished," John says, and takes a sip of coffee.

"What's MK-Ultra?" Lewis asks.

John opens his other binders and spreads them out on the coffee table. Article after article, and picture after picture, tell of a very scary MK-ultra history.

"Take 'em with you, read for yourselves what their plans are. There's a storm headed our way like nothing you could ever imagine. Sy told me of your interest in this stuff. It's dangerous what they're planning. The Shafutah rises!" John exclaims with a lift of his cup.

Baggs and Lewis sit in silence, dumfounded. They are at a loss for words.

"I'm surprised you haven't heard more of this; especially considering you're an astronaut," John says.

"I've seen a lot. Of course, that was quite a few years ago. And, at that time I wasn't able to talk much about it," Baggs responds.

John smiles at Baggs and Lewis as he stands. He offers them more coffee as he walks back over to the woodstove. Baggs and Lewis both decline.

"So, does that mean the Indian and your friend Arnie, aren't human?" Lewis asks, intrigued.

John refreshes his cup and walks back over and sits.

"Code name 'Lothar.' Albert Hess was a top German physicist who was relocated from Germany to the southwest Owl Mountains of Poland in 1944. His job primarily was to work on the Bell Project; you know, Hitler's flying saucer program?

"However, he gained interest in genetic reengineering because of what he discovered working with atomic radiation there at one of the underground facilities.

"Because of his work linking gravity to quantum physics, he was chosen for Operation Paperclip as one of America's top biochemist scientists. This group of scientists included the famous Werner Von Braun of the V-2 rocket program and his technicians. You know what I'm talking about.

"Operation Paperclip was implemented in 1949, bringing over 1,500 scientists to the United States. These scientists, engineers and technicians came to work primarily on our fledgling rocket propulsion program.

"However, others were allocated to the Air Force's school of Aviation Medicine. Albert Hess found himself working at Wright Field as their lead scientist heading up aviation medicine.

"He reportedly performed one of the first atomically administered, biological autopsies on one of the aliens brought up from the Roswell crash of 1947. The alien is supposedly still there, cryogenically frozen.

"Mysteriously, Albert Hess fell over dead in a diner in Lebanon, Ohio in 1951. It is thought he may have accidentally stumbled onto a Top Secret government program. The government may have already been working with extraterrestrial entities with ideas of world domination.

"In other words, Albert possibly heard word of population control by atomic radio wave. After all, he was supposedly the scientist who successfully developed the mass disbursement system for Nychlorithiazine-B by high-altitude aircraft. Chemtrails? It is this bacterium that conspiracy theorists believe, induces Anti-Immune Syndrome.

It's what GMO theorists believe is causing the exponential spread of deadly disease. Especially over the past 50 years.

Understand, many of these scientists didn't have a clue as to what they were working on or why. Until it was too late. A few actually committed suicide.

I can tell you this. Something big is going on. Dante's Descent, also known as the Devil's Hole, just a few miles from here has just been closed to the public. At 275 feet deep, it was a popular hike site that suddenly got quarantined by the government, with no explanation.

The government is taking over green spaces and making land grabs all over the country. Why? Something is going on. That's why I'm out here in the middle of nowhere. I may not even be safe anymore. I understand there's also an atomic RFID chip in the works," John says with a final pause.

"They have the chip and yeah, it is supposedly powered atomically. That's what the seminar at the National Science Lab was partly about. They were giving out certificates of appreciation to all of the scientists that worked on the thing, I guess.

I went as Sy and they wanted to take pictures of all of us scientists that had something to do with Chryzinium and the RFID chip. Evidently Sy has something to do with some of this," Lewis interjects.

"You look like Sy. An older version," John comments.

"So I've been told."

John continues. "Sy's interest has more to do with dark energy, black lightning stuff; things to do with reverse engineered propulsion systems. He has done extensive studies on the Devil's Halo, where its energy source comes from.

"The Devil's Halo is as real as this house and it has an energy system like nothing you could ever imagine. Sy's interest began to turn to fear about two years ago, when he stumbled onto what the government knew and what he learned about their ultimate plans," John says quietly.

"This Doctor Hess guy implied you were dead. He referred to you as the 'late John Gussman,'" Lewis remarks.

"Let's just say it's a deal we have. I'll play dead if they leave me alone," John responds with a raise of his eyebrow.

Baggs flips through the binders, being unusually quiet. Everything he has just heard is very disturbing. As an astronaut, when he saw things that were unexplainable, he was told to keep quiet about them. He has seen unidentified flying objects firsthand while he was in space, but he was sworn to secrecy. Still, Baggs has never heard anything this outlandish.

"So what happened to Arnie and what about the Indian?" Baggs asks.

John takes a moment to answer, almost wishing the question hadn't been asked.

"Arnie was killed in a plane crash that same summer.

As far as Sani, he was alive and well the last I saw him, three years ago."

John flips open one of the binders to the back page. It is an image of a Navajo tribe taken during the Civil War sometime between 1861 and 1865. John points to the man on the very right. "That's him there, Sani."

Baggs pulls the binder closer to get a better look. After a moment of studying the old picture, John reaches over and flips one page back.

"That's him there again three years ago. I took the picture myself," John takes another sip of coffee.

Baggs and Lewis are astounded as they see Sani is the very same Indian portrayed in both pictures, yet taken more than 150 years apart.

M-PAC, ROOM 216, SAME DAY

The reflected light from the screen glows in the eyes of Kevin and Lon as they sit on the leather couch in M-Pac's theater. As they look intently at the image projected on the screen, their mouths begin to open in awe. The well-defined image and sharp resolution depicts a vivid live shot of the east end of the Grand Canyon. From edge to edge, the image is as brilliant and as crisp as being there in person. The only thing missing is a light breeze blowing through their hair.

Stiner pushes a small white button on the left side of the control panel. The image on the screen begins to shift in color to a subtle greenish hue. As it does, off in the distance a large grey metallic circular shape appears to hang in the sky just beyond the eastern side of the Grand Canyon.

It appears to hover at about 15,000 feet above the ground. The position of the object, in relation to the landscape, places it over a part of the southwest topography that is often referred to as the Painted Desert. Kevin and Lon are so taken by the image, they can do nothing but sit speechless.

Doctor Stiner then pushes a small red button on the right. A very lightly frosted clear glass filter, slowly lowers from the ceiling directly in front of the main screen. As the filter lowers, it produces a slight 3D effect of the image. The filter also exposes fine, shiny micron-sized particles gently falling from the grey circular anomaly like crystal rain.

"Chryzinium," Stiner announces.

Amanda looks back at Kevin and Lon and smiles. "Shatahaham," she says with her perfect smile.

Kevin returns her glance and asks, "What?"

Amanda stands and slowly walks back to Kevin. She leans down and kisses him on the cheek. She whispers into his ear, "Bael hie Shatahaham." She runs her fingers across his cheek teasingly as she stands. Adiv stands and Amanda returns to his side.

Speaking to each other softly in an undistinguishable language, Adiv and Amanda both stand and exit the theater, leaving Kevin, Lon, and Doctor Stiner behind.

"Where the hell are they going?" Kevin retorts.

"You'll meet up with Amanda later," Doctor Stiner responds, reassuringly.

"What was that all about? What's going on here?" Kevin asks as he springs to his feet.

DEAD GIRL
WALKING

HILLSDALE FALLS, THE SHAES' HOME

It is extremely cold this February, and Hillsdale Falls is experiencing more snow than they've had for years. In fact, today another five inches of snow is expected to top the thirteen already accumulated.

For Christmas, Mark surprised the family by purchasing a new, dark green SUV. With all-wheel drive and heated desert tan leather seats, among many other luxuries, the family is certainly not at odds when it comes to traveling in foul weather. Of course, Rebecca has taken ownership of the new ride, leaving her old SUV for Mark to drive.

Mark has been able to take extra time off from work this month, which has been a big help for Rebecca. Because it's another snow day, Emily and Taylor are at home from school. And that's a good thing since Emily has another doctor appointment scheduled.

Unfortunately for Rebecca, she hasn't been feeling well for the past couple of days. A flu bug has settled into her digestive system, making her feel less than optimal. Understandably, she's not looking forward to leaving the house.

Emily has been doing remarkably well since returning to school from her brain tumor scare. Surprising all of her teachers, Emily has brought her grade point average from 1.9 to 3.7 almost overnight.

It appears her scholastic improvement is due to her newfound ability to concentrate and apply herself efficiently. At least that has been the reasoning, not only by her teachers, but also by her doctor. It is now a foregone conclusion that Emily's tumor did indeed affect not only her disposition but also her studies.

However, Emily is still experiencing some odd character traits that have been well noted by everyone who spends any time at all with her. It is mostly Rebecca and Mark who bear most of the brunt of her strange behavior.

Approximately every 7 to 10 days, Emily has her appointment with Doctor Heller. Within 24 to 48 hours after her doctor's visit, Emily will do something that would be considered odd or off the wall.

Three times now, she has been caught eating raw hamburger straight out of the package.

Twice, she has been found standing, frozen like a statue in some part of the house during the middle of the night. Her eyes are wide open and yet she appears to be asleep, or in some trance-like state of mind.

At only 15 years old, Emily doesn't yet drive, nor has she ever learned to drive. But, the morning following her last doctor's appointment, she grabbed the car keys off the hook, got into the old SUV, and drove out of the driveway sweet as you please.

While eating breakfast during Christmas break, and dressed only in pajamas, slippers and a robe, Emily walks right out of the side kitchen door jumps into the SUV and drives away. Of course, Mark immediately drives off after her; catching up with her in the parking lot of Suzette's Donut Shop.

Mark reported that she drove as though she'd been driving for years. Had Mark not caught up with her, she could have easily grabbed a dozen donuts and took off across country.

Last Tuesday, Emily insisted she was to fly to New York later that afternoon. She claimed she had a previously scheduled meeting with Marla Kennedy at the prestigious Cole-Webber Advertising agency. Strangely, there actually is a Marla Kennedy that works for Cole-Webber.

According to Doctor Heller, Emily is experiencing a rare form of Extra Sensory Delusion Syndrome. This, he says is no doubt caused by bits and pieces of information that she has gleaned from TV, magazine advertising, or other forms of media. Heller insists her odd behavior will pass with time.

On the other hand, there has been the 180° trans-formation in her overall disposition. No longer is she mean-spirited and short-tempered. Certainly, this has been one of the more desirable of her character changes since the miraculous vaccine.

Notwithstanding, today is yet another appointment with Doctor Heller. 'I wonder what quirk will Emily bring home from that?' Rebecca wonders.

This all may be a great source of amusement for Taylor, but for Mark and Rebecca, her idiosyncrasies are frightening.

HILLSDALE FALLS MEMORIAL MEDICAL CENTER

After a 55 minute drive in the snow, the Shaes finally arrive at Doctor Heller's office. And just like with Emily's past appointments, it's the same team of doctors waiting to examine her.

As Mark, Rebecca, Taylor, and Emily enter, the group again greets the Shaes with handshakes and smiles. Without wasting a moment of time, Nurse Maggie Sprague whisks Emily off to her examination. Doctor Heller stays behind in his office and offers the Shaes refreshments. Not feeling too well, Rebecca excuses herself to use the restroom, leaving Mark and Taylor behind to visit with the doctor.

Not exactly the exciting day the 13-year-old is hoping for, Taylor negotiates with dad for a trip down to the hospital cafeteria. At least there, he can maybe snag a soda and hopefully a piece of chocolate cake.

Eager for Taylor to be out of his hair, Mark obliges. He hands him a few dollars so he can go horse around somewhere else. Emily's exam usually takes about 45 minutes, but after discussing her progress with the doctor, they can sometimes have an hour and a half cut out their day.

"Stay in the cafeteria, no wandering around," Mark orders, as he hands Taylor the money. Taylor wastes no time running out of the doctor's boring office. Heller watches as his office door slams shut. He looks at Mark and smiles.

"You okay with all of this?" Heller asks.

"Yeah, I think so."

Before being able to continue with their conversation, Rebecca enters the office. With her face drawn and pale, she slowly enters and takes a seat next to Mark.

"Where's Taylor?" Rebecca asks.

"He's down in the cafeteria. You okay?"

Rebecca doesn't show any emotion one way or the other as she sits in discomfort.

Taylor stands at the elevators waiting forever; at least that's what it seems like to a precocious 13-year-old boy. Finally, one of the elevator doors open. Not paying any attention to the up or down arrows, Taylor hops inside and presses the button for the first floor, where the cafeteria is located. Much to his chagrin, the elevator goes up instead of down. At the eighth floor, the elevator doors open.

Just then, a gurney rolls by being pushed by a male nurse. Covered by a white sheet from head to toe, the body must be dead. This is way too cool for Taylor to pass up, so he immediately disembarks the elevator. Sneaking along the wall, he follows to see where the unfortunate corpse is off too.

The long corridor is much narrower than the regular hospital hallways. They are painted stark white. Bright fluorescent lights run across the center of the ceiling. No fancy artwork or health-related signage dress the walls. Had it not been for the gurney, Taylor would have never known he was still in the hospital.

The hallway doors are painted a drab gunmetal grey. Each has a tiny square window centered in the upper half of the door. The doors are recessed into the wall by 3 to 4 feet and are unmarked.

There are no room numbers or designation as to where they lead. Some are rooms and some are passages or hallways to other areas of the floor. No matter, they are perfect alcoves for Taylor to hide in just in case someone appears.

'This must be the floor where the hospital keeps the dead people,' Taylor thinks. The man pushing the gurney stops at a door about 50 feet down from the elevators. As he does, Taylor tucks himself into one of the recessed doorways, being careful not to be detected.

Slowly, he sticks his head out and around into the hall to see what's happening with the gurney man. He watches as the dead person is wheeled into the room just ahead to his left.

As he hears the door slam shut, Taylor quietly and quickly makes his way to the door. Carefully he cranes his head so he can see inside through the small glass opening.

The room is larger than he thought, and is packed with all kinds of medical machines, computer monitors and colored algorithms and flashing numbers. To his disbelief, in the room are the same doctors that took his sister away just a few moments earlier.

'What are they doing there?' he wonders. As two of the doctors step aside and walk toward the barrage of medical equipment, Nurse Maggie reaches over and pulls the sheet back, exposing Emily's lifeless body.

"Oh no!" he gasps. He quickly drops down out of sight and freezes, fearing he was heard. Beginning to hyperventilate, the shock of what he's seen overwhelms him like a flood. He can't believe it. His sister is dead.

After a moment, Taylor begins to relax. No one has come to the door. Maybe he wasn't too loud after all. Gathering his composure he slowly rises up and carefully takes another look through the door's window. Just then, he sees the nurse who wheeled Emily into the room heading toward the door.

Ducking out of sight, he runs back down the hallway, tucking back into the same alcove he first hid in. Hearing the door open and close, the male nurse begins to walk towards him. Frozen against the wall, Taylor hopes he doesn't get noticed. Sure enough, the nurse walks by without so much as a glance his direction.

"I'm outta here," Taylor mumbles to himself as he slowly sticks his head out to see if the coast is clear. The nurse passes the elevator alcove and continues walking down the hall. Just as he turns the corner, Taylor runs to the elevators and pushes the button.

The light comes on, but no elevator just yet. "Come on, come on," Taylor says nervously. Finally, the elevator door opens. He immediately jumps inside and begins banging the number 5 button, hoping his actions will help speed the door's closing. The door eventually shuts and the elevator descends.

'How do I tell mom and dad Emily's dead? Maybe they already know,' he thinks. Tears begin to well up in his eyes, just as the elevator comes to a stop.

Not waiting for the door to completely open, Taylor rushes out and heads down the hall. Nothing looks familiar. What's going on? Oh, he's gotten off on the wrong floor!

Taylor runs back to the elevator, pounding on the button impatiently.

An adjacent elevator door slides open, and he hurriedly crosses the hall and enters. Taylor is angry and in shock. His tears that were glistening as they welled up in his eyes are now streaming down his cheeks. Oblivious at first, he now notices there are others in the elevator with him. Using his coat sleeve, he wipes the tears from his cheeks.

"What floor do you want sweetie?" A female hospital employee asks. She observes that the teenager is crying as he reaches out and pushes the button for the fifth floor.

"What's wrong, are you okay?" She asks.

"My sister is dead," he says, beginning to cry again.

"Oh my dear, I am so sorry. Where's your family? Is your mom or your dad here?"

"They're in Doctor Heller's office."

The woman is obviously confused and asks Taylor, "I'm not sure who that is. Do you know where is office is?"

"Yeah."

As the elevator door opens, Taylor exits and walks somberly towards Doctor Heller's office, three doors down on the left. Once he reaches his office, Taylor reluctantly opens the door and steps in. Rebecca and Mark both turn around. His wet, puffy eyes tell all. Despite not feeling well, Rebecca is the first to respond.

"What's wrong, come here," she insists in a soft, mothering tone.

"She's dead, Emily's dead."

"What? Who told you that?" Mark quickly interjects.

"I saw her. They had a sheet over her. When they pulled the sheet down it was Emily," Taylor says as he breaks down again in tears.

"What?" Rebecca screams as she spins back to Doctor Heller looking for immediate clarification.

Pulling his phone from his pocket, Doctor Heller makes a call.

"How's Emily? Uh huh. Yeah! Uh huh. Thanks," Doctor Heller speaks into the phone. After which he abruptly cancels the call.

"I don't know what you saw, but I can assure you Emily is perfectly fine. They're bringing her back as we speak. Where were you that you saw her?" Heller asks Taylor.

"On the eighth floor."

"I thought I told you to go straight to the cafeteria. What were you doing on the eighth floor?" Mark interrogates.

"I got on the elevator and it went up; even after I pushed the first floor button. The doors opened at the eighth floor and I saw this guy wheeling one of those rolling stretcher things down the hall and it had a body on it all covered with a white sheet. I thought it was a dead guy or something. I wanted to see, so I followed him. It was Em.

He pushed her into a room with a bunch of wires and machines in it. I looked in the window and they were pulling the sheet down off of her face. It was Emily. It scared me so I ran back to the elevators and came straight here," Taylor explains.

Just as Taylor finishes telling of his terrifying experience, Emily and Nurse Sprague enter the office. Taylor immediately turns and greets his sister with a huge bear hug.

Emily is somewhat unresponsive as Taylor holds on to her with all his might. She smiles slightly with a distant kindness and places her right hand on Taylor's back. However, her actions appear to be more mechanical than affectionate.

"See? What'd I tell you? Emily is just fine. I don't know what you thought you saw, but I can assure you, we'd never do anything to hurt your sister," Doctor Heller says.

Mark and Rebecca both look on, befuddled. The fact that Taylor and Emily have never been close magnifies the weirdness of all that is happening. Taylor regains his composure and steps back from Emily with a smile. He again wipes the tears from his cheeks onto his coat sleeve.

"I think it's time you all go and have an early dinner together. Everything is okay," Doctor Heller consoles.

Without a word, Mark and Rebecca stand. Embracing their two kids, Rebecca leads the way as they exit. Mark is the last to leave. As he does, he turns and glares harshly at Doctor Heller before shutting the door behind him abruptly.

Doctor Heller's halfcocked smile immediately turns to anger as he looks at Nurse Maggie Sprague.

"What the hell happened? How'd that little dummkopf get up there?" the enraged Heller shouts.

"I have no idea, doctor. I didn't even see him."

"Well, he most certainly saw you, all of you."

Doctor Heller slams his fist on the desk.

"Get out!" he demands. Nurse Sprague abruptly turns and exits.

Subdued, the Shae family stand patiently waiting for the next available elevator. Taylor is beginning to feel embarrassed. With his head down, it is evident he is not ready to make eye contact with anyone just yet.

Finally, the sound of the elevator's bell rings its arrival and the doors open. First checking to see the elevator is going down, they make their way into the car.

"You said you were on the eighth floor. There's only seven floors, see!" Rebecca informs Taylor.

"I don't know. The number up there said 8 and the doors opened. That's all I know," Taylor responds defensively.

DEVIL'S HALO

Purportedly, it was President Harry S. Truman, in 1947, who formed Majestic 12 (MJ-12) by executive order. Operation MJ-12 was signed into existence to empower a select government committee for the sole purpose of the retrieval and study of alien spacecraft and/or alien beings.

Debunked at the time by the FBI and other government entities to the American people, the existence of MJ-12 was reported to be nothing more than a fictitious rumor run amuck. However, there is now documented proof that the surreptitious operation did indeed exist.

Secretary of Defense James Forrestal was shrewdly selected for the unique position of heading up MJ-12 because he was not an elected government official. His placement was strategic, because he would only answer to the Commander in Chief. He thereby kept any possible discoveries away from the public.

However, James Forrestal was a man of scruples. He

believed wholeheartedly that the public had a right to know if there was proof of any extraterrestrial activity. Although he adamantly opposed government secrecy concerning these matters, he was still appointed to the position. Coincidentally, the MJ-12 project was formed soon after the alleged 1947 Roswell, New Mexico space craft crash.

The Roswell incident in 1947 was reported to the public as a downed high-altitude weather balloon. It was one of the first of a profusion of government cover-ups that sparked public awareness and outrage.

Forrestal, although sworn to secrecy, reported to the public that he had an encounter with an alien life form from the Roswell crash. He claimed he had witnessed the alien during an autopsy procedure. The entire ordeal caused him severe mental anguish, and he began to emotionally unravel.

He was forced to resign from the MJ-12 project. Soon after, Forrestal was admitted to Bethesda Medical Memorial Hospital. For more than a month, he was locked in a room and only allowed to see visitors if they were prescreened and sworn to secrecy.

By the time his brother managed to secure visitation rights, Forrestal had supposedly leapt to his death from his sixteenth floor hospital room. It was determined to be a suicide, despite evidence suggesting otherwise.

Forrestal's brother found dozens of small but distinctive scuff marks at the base of the window. He demanded a private forensic examination. It was verified that the scuff marks had come from Forrestal's shoes thereby confirming signs of a struggle at the base of his window.

Reports of public UFO sighting increased significantly in the years 1951-1952. These incidents led to the formation of Project Blue Book, a government program created for the sole purpose of propaganda to restore the public's faith in the government. 'We're on it!' was their mantra with respect to the public's perspective.

In 1966, there were hundreds of reports of disc-like objects in Washtenaw County, Michigan. Also known as 'the great UFO chase of Washtenaw County.' Hundreds, if not thousands, of people witnessed the sightings, including many of the town's law enforcement officials. The phenomenon lasted for six days.

After a UFO was witnessed landing in a nearby swamp, Dr. Hineck, a government scientist, was sent to investigate. His final report suggested it was nothing more than swamp gas.

Not satisfied with the scientist's conclusions, Congressman Gerald Ford (later to become President Ford) demanded further investigation. However, an elite group of government officials determined that the government had no business dabbling in UFO investigations, and Project Blue Book was terminated.

This so-called 'shadow government' was successful in covering up yet another UFO phenomenon. Save for eyewitness accounts, any and all evidence of the sightings were either destroyed or buried deep in bureaucratic archives, never to be seen again.

Harry S. Truman is reported to have said, "Lay to rest these... UFO sightings as fictitious and explain them away, now!"

ASH FORK ARIZONA, JOHN'S HOUSE

It is early afternoon. Baggs and Lewis listen intently to John's description of mysterious, life-sustaining dust particles and a Native American who is still alive and well after 150 years. It is an unbelievable story, if it were coming from anyone but John Gussman.

"So I take it you've actually seen the Devils Halo?" Lewis asks John.

"Anytime I want. Well, anytime I'm there at the canyon."

"The sightings are pretty rare, right?" Baggs interjects.

"Follow me," John says standing to his feet.

Baggs and Lewis also stand and stretch the kinks out of their limbs. John leads the way past the kitchen and down the hall a few feet. They make a right turn and out the back door.

A well-worn path on the sandy desert ground usually leads the way to a large pole building shop. Now it's a narrow trail carved into the snow. It's the same building Baggs and Lewis first saw off in the distance. Though, the building was mostly obscured by thick freezing fog. Less than 100 feet from the house, John leads the duo in through the side man-door.

The overhead fluorescent lights flicker and buzz. Not terribly bright, but enough to see the enormous size of John's shop. Cory and Madison are heard stacking wood, laughing and talking deep in the background. Just inside the building and dwarfed by the size of the interior is John's pride and joy. A black and white high winged single engine airplane.

"Magpie," John says.

"What?" Lewis asks.

"Magpie. That's what I call my plane. You know the Magpie is the most intelligent animal on the face of the earth. The only non-mammal that can recognize itself in a mirror," John pats the plane's fuselage.

Baggs and Lewis are surprised to learn John owns a plane. Lewis is especially surprised. John doesn't look like a typical pilot. With his grey scruffy hair and beard, he looks more like the cover model for 'Old Miners of the Past,' magazine.

"You have a pilot's certificate?" Baggs asks.

"Nope. My medical certificate expired seventeen years ago. I don't need Uncle Sam telling me whether I can fly or not. I can fly just fine. With the big tundra tires I don't need an airport to take off or land, and if you look close, the plane's registration numbers aren't valid. They belong to a scrapped 1962 Boeing 707. Besides, they're too small to read without a pair of real strong glasses. And that's if you're standing on the wing. Never been an issue. As long as we don't crash into anything it's all good."

Hearing John and his guests, Cory and Madison walk up from the back of the shop.

"You two done with the wood?" John asks.

"Yeah pretty much. Just gotta sweep," Cory admits.

"Maddy here can fly the Magpie as good as any pilot I know. Can't you?"

Madison smiles proudly. "You're not taking her up now are you, the weather is terrible?" she asks wisely.

"No, no, of course not, just showing her off to the Commander and his friend. Lewis, right?"

Lewis nods 'yes' with a smile.

"So you can fly?" Lewis asks Madison, surprised.

"Oh yeah. Daddy taught me how to a long time ago. When the weather's nice I always go flying."

"By yourself?" Lewis asks.

"No, Cory comes along. We like to catch rattle snakes and stuff."

"So you don't fly, Cory?" Baggs asks.

"Nah, not interested in learning. Besides, Maddy does as good as dad and she likes it, so no big deal," Cory replies.

Baggs and Lewis are wowed.

"So you can reach the rudder pedals?" Baggs asks Madison.

"No, Daddy made blocks that slide over them. I just put them on before I go up."

You are one amazing little girl. There's someone I'd love to introduce you to," Baggs remarks, astonished.

"I guess they make little girls a lot different than

when I was a kid; so much for the 'Easy Bake Oven' generation," Baggs continues shaking his head.

"Why don't you two go finish up? I wanna show these guys the 'looky loo.'"

Cory and Madison head off towards the other side of the building, laughing and joking like one would expect from two kids. Madison turns back and waves with a big smile. Baggs can't help but be amazed. "Another Marty," he remarks fondly.

John opens a side compartment on the plane's fuselage just behind the cockpit. After digging around, John emerges with an odd black plastic rectangle tube. Open on both ends, the device is heavy with layers of lens glass much like the insides of a pair of binoculars.

"We call it the 'Looky Loo.' It's a scope that allows me to see the Devils Halo. You're heading to the canyon right?"

"Well, when we heard that it was nothing but a cloud anomaly we kind of nixed that idea. But now after what you said…" Baggs responds.

"Well, you're here and you really need to go to the canyon and see it for yourselves. Pretty darned impressive. Not to mention pretty hard to comprehend. Here, take this with you," John hands the device to Lewis.

Lewis turns the device over examining the strange invention with a look of bewilderment.

"You made this?" Lewis asks.

"Yep. It's a kind of polarized beam-splitter. I built it so I could better study the Halo."

Lewis begins looking through the device like a kid looking through a kaleidoscope.

"I don't think this thing works," Lewis remarks as he walks around the hangar with the scope held up to his face.

"Oh it works. You'll see a lot more than what those stupid magazine pictures show. Come on, let's go back in the house, I'll draw you a map."

Leaving the cold outbuilding, the three make their way through the snowy path back into the warmth of John's living room.

After teaching both men how to use the Looky Loo, John spreads a detailed topographical map out on the coffee table. Using a yellow highlighter, he draws a line as he describes the route.

"Okay, first, head back to I-40 and then take Highway 64 north. It'll take you all the way up to Grand Canyon Village. Highway 64 goes east along the south rim of the canyon. Just follow it to Comanche Point.

"It's only about an hour and a half from here. You can see the Devil's Halo from Comanche Point."

"But we're not coming back this way, how do we get the scope back to you?" Baggs asks.

"You'll see me again. Give it back to me then. Besides, I've seen all I care to see for now."

"Thank you, Sy was right. You've been a big help."

"Don't mention it. You two better get rolling if you plan on seeing that thing before dark."

GRAND CANYON, COMANCHE POINT

CHRYZINIUM   333

The drive to Comanche Point takes a little more than two hours because of the sporadic snow and icy conditions. Baggs and Lewis drive as far as they can off the main highway. It becomes four-wheel drive country within a couple of hundred feet. After the short but extremely cold hike, they reach the spot designated on the map.

"This should be it. Take a look through that thing and see what's out there," Baggs says, double-checking their position.

"I don't have it. I thought you grabbed it," Lewis retorts.

"Are you kidding me?"

Lewis smiles and pulls the Looky Loo out from under his jacket."Gotcha!" Lewis declares with a big grin.

Baggs glares at Lewis, annoyed but also relieved. Even though he's wearing his leather flight jacket, it's no match for the frigid wind blowing through the walls of the canyon. As beautiful as it is, this is no place for a couple of old men in the dead of winter, no matter what the motivation.

Lewis takes the scope and holds it up to his eyes. Looking east, he begins tweaking the small adjustment knobs on the side of the device.

"I'm not seeing anything," Lewis says discouraged.

"It may be too cloudy. Let me look through it," Baggs says, taking the scope.

Baggs does exactly as John instructed. Focusing first

on the cloudy sky straight above him, then loosening the knobs on the scope's side, he adjusts the panes of optical glass back and forth. As each lens becomes finely tuned, he brings his head down and looks east through the device. Carefully he pans the sky while continuing to adjust the last of the lens knobs.

He gasps. Dropping the scope and stumbling backward, he lands unceremoniously into a fresh snowdrift. Lewis rushes over to help Baggs, who is now almost buried in fresh windblown powder.

"Are you okay? What? Did you see it?" Lewis helps Baggs stand up and dusts the snow off his back. "I'm fine. Just get the scope."

Retrieving the scope, Lewis holds it up to his eyes. Looking in the same direction, he intently pans the panoramic view off in the distance.

"Are you sure you saw it? I can't see anything," Lewis whines.

"Yes. I saw it. That thing has lights!" Baggs takes the scope from Lewis and begins the focusing process all over again. He looks towards the east. As the Halo comes into focus he carefully steps aside while holding it steady for Lewis to take a look for himself.

"Look!" Baggs exclaims.

Lewis looks through the scope as Baggs holds it carefully in place. Lewis slowly puts his hands on the scope, cautiously taking a firm grasp of the device for himself. As the Halo comes into focus, Lewis's mouth gradually falls open as he stands in utter disbelief.

The freezing wind whistles and swirls fresh snow in drifts around the two men. But they are not feeling the cold. Each take turns using the scope to view the massive craft hovering over the canyon. So incredibly massive, they feel as though they can reach out and touch it.

It appears as a solid metallic disc when seen through the scope, yet invisible to the naked eye. Even though the immense object emits no distinguishable sound, bright lights appear to emanate from its circumference. With the scope, it makes both men feel very aware of its close proximity.

"I'm going to try and get a photograph of it," Baggs says while fumbling for his phone.

He positions his phone in front of the viewing end of the scope while Lewis holds the scope steady. After several tries he finally manages to get a distinct image. At least, it's fair enough for them to investigate when they get home.

The air temperature begins to drop as the day wanes and the two make their way back to the SUV. Baggs is contemplative as he tries to wrap his head around what this means, and more importantly, what this thing is. Lewis, however, can't stop talking.

"I think I'm going to buy a motorhome. I think we should come back here this summer. I think if I sell my plane and some of my other stuff, I could easily pay cash for a real nice motorhome for us to travel in."

"I'm not riding around with you in a motorhome," Baggs mumbles.

"Are you kidding, it'd be great. What else have we got going on? I bet there's a lot more for us to see. We can be like UFO chasers."

"You sound like a ten-year-old. You got rocks in your head."

They make it to the SUV and Baggs starts the engine to get the heater going. He takes another glance toward the canyon rim, half expecting the Halo to appear, now that its secret is revealed. The snow blows afresh from another gust of wind, and the canyon rim is obscured from sight. Baggs puts the SUV into gear and heads back to the main road.

FOOD FOR THOUGHT

M-PAC, THE PAPILLION

Just off the east wing of the main bay catwalk is the cafeteria. Resembling a prison visitation area, the stark, two-tone white and light green rectangular lounge and cafeteria area is named 'The Papillion.'

Some say it was named after a small town located in Nebraska. Others say the room got its peculiar name because of the hundreds of colorful butterflies painted on the south wall. Large dark gold and green symbols of the Shafutah adorn the remaining 3 walls. Under each symbol is written in black lettering, Health, Peace, and Unity.

Fluorescent lighting bathes the uninspiring area with a bright white institutionalized glow. The monochromatic utilitarian furnishings consist of ten round tables that are meticulously surrounded by eight metal stools. Each piece of furniture is securely bolted to a highly-polished concrete floor.

A lavish spread of delicacies and refreshments fill the serving area along the far wall. Gourmet coffees, pastries, fruit and veggetable trays, candies, assorted deli meats, rolls, bagels and breads of almost every variety stretch from one end to the other. In addition, a variety of the finest gourmet cuisines is prepared daily. Plates and silverware are stacked on carts at both ends, easily facilitating those visiting the self-serve buffet.

Strictly enforced rules concerning contraband plainly state absolutely no lunch bags, lunch boxes, or food from outside the facility. That is why sustenance provided at the Papillion far exceeds any bagged lunch cuisine possibilities.

It is 4:45 PM, and four of the seven visitors from Washington D.C. have concluded their tour and are now seated in the Papillion along with their chaperone, Wilhelm Avercamp.

The group sits at one of the tables eating their respective lunches. Byron shifts uncomfortably in his chair, annoyed by the snubbing they all got from Kevin, Amanda, and Lon. For more than three hours, they have been led around like sheep.

Sure, they've been introduced to the wonders of the manufacturing of Chryzinium, but only from a distant hands-off perspective. So far, they haven't really been shown anything that they didn't already know about the super-vaccine.

Byron is less than impressed and is feeling as though this entire trip has been a complete waste of his time. His personal reason for this visit was to see the production process of the Vul-Stream RFID implant chip. As yet, it has not even been mentioned.

The door to the Papillion swishes open, and Doctor Edward Stiner leads Kevin Rhodes and Lon Thompson into the Papillion. They join the others and take a seat at the table.

"You enjoy the fine food we have here, yes?" Stiner asks with a polite smile.

"Where's Amanda?" Byron asks bluntly.

This is the same question both Kevin and Lon would like to have addressed. The last they saw of Amanda was when she left the theater with Adiv more than an hour ago.

"She's with Mr. Zahim and will be joining us soon," Doctor Stiner informs.

"Mr. Zahim? Who's Mr. Zahim?" Byron is losing his patience.

"Adiv Zahim is the executive administrator for all of this."

Kevin is beyond disturbed as he walks straight to the coffee dispensers. Why hasn't anyone mentioned to him or Lon about the spaceship hanging over the desert? And adding insult to injury, Amanda and this Adiv guy come off as lovers or something. Kevin's mind is swirling with all sorts of thoughts.

"Kevin, what's going on? Who's this Mr. Zahim guy? I

thought we were supposed to remain as a group. At least that's what was told to all of us. And then you, Lon, and Amanda take off to who knows where, and three hours later you two come back without her. We get some dry, uneventful tour of M-PAC and nothing was even said about the RFID implant. So what's really going on here?"

"Calm down, Mr. Sutter." Stiner asserts. "We had something else we had to do, and as far as Ms. Sykes is concerned, her whereabouts are on a need to know basis, and right now, you don't need to know. Please, follow me. All of you," Doctor Stiner stands, trying to pacify the situation.

Stiner leads the group to the door of the cafeteria to demonstrate how the RFID chip works. While they watch, Stiner holds his right hand in front of the door sensor. The door slides open with a soft swish. Momentarily, Stiner repeats the procedure and the door closes and air-locks into place.

"That is the Vul-Stream RFID chip in action. I know you've all seen various staff, including myself, using the implant this way. Other than various ID capabilities, that's about all it does for now. The reason we didn't get into much of Vul-Stream is quite simple. We are not finished with programing the registry. You must understand that we don't manufacture Vul-Stream here at this facility. What we do here is research and development, and we provide the atomic electro linear infusion biometrics to an off-site plant. And, of course, we manufacture the Chryzinium vaccine."

By the looks on the dignitaries' faces, Doctor Stiner can tell they're not impressed.

"Chryzinium and Vul-Stream in combination is what makes up the Lazarus VI Project, am I correct?" Secretary of Defense Charles Hunt asks.

Leading the way, Doctors Stiner and Avercamp walk the team back to the table. "Yes, you are correct. The entire program: Chryzinium and Vul-Stream is the Lazarus VI Project," Doctor Stiner continues.

"You do know President Parkston is announcing this to the Nation day after tomorrow," Hunt reminds Stiner.

"No, he's not. That is what our meeting was about. That is why we weren't with you today. Like I said, Vul-Stream is not ready. It will be at least another three to four weeks before any of this is ready. I do apologize," Doctor Stiner concludes.

The door to the Papillion swishes opens and Amanda enters the room, her high heels tapping on the concrete as she walks to the table. She nods politely to the visitors seated at the table and then stands next to Dr. Stiner. "Gentlemen," greeting them with her perfect smile.

Without missing a beat, Kevin walks over and snatches Amanda by the arm, dragging her to a private part of the Papillion. Amanda doesn't resist his forceful manner and in fact goes along compliantly.

At the wall, Kevin spins Amanda around and whispers angrily at her, "What the hell is going on? What was that all about?"

Amanda places her index finger on his lips making a

'Shhh' sound. "It's okay. I've been a part of the program for some time now. I'm sorry, I couldn't say anything until we unveiled the All-Ray Vision Scope projection system. We knew it would have been difficult for you to understand without seeing it for yourself."

Amanda smiles at Kevin. Leaning in closely she whispers into Kevin's ear, "Keep it together." After which she brushes his cheek gently and walks back to the table, joining the others.

WASHINGTON DC, KEVIN RHODES' OFFICE, 41 HOURS LATER

Kevin rushes into his office, balancing his morning coffee, computer bag, and briefcase. The meeting is in fifteen minutes and he has no time to prepare.

Lon taps on Kevin's door, "You're here. We're running late." Kevin frantically opens the drawers of his desk looking for an important flash drive he's misplaced.

"Come on! We gotta go," Lon is anxious, not wanting to be late.

Kevin sees the small flash drive tucked alongside a stack of papers. Picking it up, he holds it up for Lon to see.

"Found it!"

He shoves the drive into his pants pocket. Gathering his things, he sprints to the office door. The two leave Kevin's office and walk at a brisk pace down the long hallway.

"You heard, right?" Lon asks Kevin as their shoes

tap in unison on the polished floor.

"Yeah, I heard. A lousy shame. So, you cool with all this now?"

"I'm in too deep, now, as you always say," Lon replies.

In attendance at the top-secret meeting are those whom have just returned from the recent field trip to M-PAC. Also included is President Parkston, Secretary of State, Pat Vance, Congressional Budget Office Representative, Paula Slater, Chairman of the Federal Reserve, Colin Franky, and White House Press Secretary, Hayden Ross.

Kevin and Lon enter the small Senate Rotunda, shutting the door behind them. Everyone is already seated and waiting. The mood is somber as the news of Phoebe Wescott's death has sent out shock waves on the Hill.

At no other time has a Republican or Democratic House Leader died during their term. Rumors are flying, speculating as to what might have happened. What they were told, however, is that she was on her way to Maine when she crashed her car.

She had gone to visit her older sister whom had suffered a sudden stroke. On her way there, Phoebe allegedly fell asleep at the wheel. Witnesses say her car went off the road and crashed in a shallow ditch.

However, they say the crash was not at all serious. Paramedics and police all arrived. They even had her standing beside her car and talking to her. The next thing, they take her away on a stretcher and she's pronounced dead three hours later. There was no autopsy and her body was immediately cremated.

Byron cannot help but think her death was at the hands of something more sinister. She did tell him she was going to the press.

President Parkston stands and addresses the group. "I'm sure that all of us here are grief-stricken over the loss of one of our own, Phoebe Wescott. I can assure you, she will be sorely missed. She was a wonderful public servant and a true patriot. If we could, please let us take a moment of silence to remember our dear friend."

The room is quiet as they take a moment to remember their fallen colleague. Kevin takes the opportunity to glance at Amanda who meets his gaze intuitively. He looks away quickly, silently cursing himself for not better understanding her or her role.

He was really hoping to be able to speak with Amanda in private before the meeting. He too has deep concerns over the project. He feels as though things are spiraling out of control and he's caught in the middle. He's only had a brief conversation with her on the flight home from M-PAC, but nothing was really resolved.

The plane was certainly not the time to discuss the complexities of Vul-Stream and a profusion of other concerns he now has. Not to mention, his concerns about Phoebe's sudden death.

"Kevin, would you be so kind and give us a heads up

on Lazarus VI? Kevin is our spokesperson due to his background with the project. Mr. Rhodes?" President Parkston offers Kevin the floor.

Kevin stands front and center and addresses the room in a soft, humble manner, unlike the boisterous personality they've previously seen.

"Ladies and gentlemen, we are very close to launching Lazarus VI. From what we've learned, there are just a few more procedures that need to be signed off on. I believe Amanda will be managing that directly. Am I correct, Amanda?"

Amanda smiles coolly.

Byron Sutter shifts uncomfortably in his chair. He is concerned. His growing suspicions about the project are slowly manifesting. And now that Phoebe has died under mysterious circumstances, his fears are magnified that much more. Still in shock, he was not buying the car crash story. Things are not adding up.

And why did Amanda have free access to the M-PAC facility? The rest of them were made to feel like bugs in a jar. The entire project was making the hair stand up on the back of his neck. He can sense something is askew and it's beginning to make him sick.

Secretary of Defense, Chuck Hunt raises his hand.

"Yes Mr. Hunt. You have a question?" Kevin responds.

"One question. How long will it be before Vul-Stream can be used for ID security purposes? We have close to a million untraceable temporary visa's floating around, millions of undocumented aliens and I think

Vul-Stream could be the answer to solving some of those issues."

This is exactly what Byron and Phoebe have been afraid of from the beginning. What starts out as a completely innocent volunteer program becomes a federal mandate. Phoebe had said as much, "A chip would be the beginning of the end for our privacy."

National Security Advisor, Steven Van Noy interjects. "How hard would it be for someone to dig the chip out of their hand? I mean really. How secure of a system is this? What if someone was to just pop the thing out with a pair of pliers?"

"They die," Amanda responds bluntly.

The room falls silent and all eyes shift to Amanda. Her expression remains pleasant and motionless.

President Parkston hastily interjects. "I think what Amanda is saying, is that removing the device could result in bodily harm and/or possible death. We all know there are risks with every medical procedure; even little tiny RFID chips."

'Nice save,' Kevin thinks. Why would Amanda say something like that, especially knowing how volatile this whole thing is to people? But, maybe she's right. Maybe if people think it is too deadly to remove, then they won't even try.

"What about them cutting their hand off?" Secretary of State, Vance asks.

"I think we've gone over this before, but there may be a few who, for whatever reason, would actually be stupid enough to amputate their own hand. But, I think those instances are slim at best. Besides all we would have to look for are those few that are missing their right hand," Kevin chuckles at his own wit. Some snickers are heard in response, but are quickly subdued.

"M-PAC would know," Amanda again interjects.

"What about previous amuptees? Where would the chip be inserted then?"

"In the neck below the right ear"

"What?" asks Steven Van Noy.

Amanda remains quiet.

Kevin continues, quickly saving Amanda from having to answer. "You have to understand. All the chip does is track by scanning ID. If someone is on the list, without the chip they can't so much as buy a loaf of bread."

"Uh, that's not entirely true." Steven Van Noy interjects. "It does have the capability to transmit. We saw it open doors by using some sort of sensor and from what we were told, they're still working on additional programming."

"To answer your first question," Kevin addresses Van Noy, "The chip is a transmitter. It has some fairly unique features as it is the very first atomically-powered RFID. That being said, it has to be properly programmed. Unfortunately, that is something that is taking longer than expected. However, it is an issue we are handling as we speak. Am I correct Amanda? And as far as additional programming, it's just like a computer, it needs to be programmed."

Amanda's sterile expression gives no indication to her thoughts.

President Parkston clears his throat. "We have a much bigger issue on our hands. While you were all at M-PAC, we received word from the World Health Organization. I have to make a most disturbing announcement to the American people, and Hayden here has made arrangements for me to give a Presidential address to the Nation, hopefully taking place this Saturday evening."

Parkston signals for Hayden Ross to pass out a one page transcript to the attendees.

After reading the transcript Kevin looks over to Amanda.

"I take it you'll be traveling to the Vul-Stream plant and expediting the project? We don't have three or four weeks," Kevin says to her directly.

Byron abruptly stands and exits the room.

ULTERIOR MOTIVE

Socrates wrote, "He who is not content with what he has would not be content with what he would like to have. While it is in man's nature to ask 'what is in it for himself?', it is the man who asks 'what is in it for others?' who will experience true happiness."

HILLSDALE FALLS, SHAE'S HOME

With Emily and Taylor at school and Mark at work, Rebecca is looking forward to an eleven o'clock brunch with Alesha at Steamers Café. But she is running late as usual.

Trying to maintain routines amid the disruption of home renovation is beginning to take its toll on Rebecca's patience. Add to that a daughter who is recovering from a serious medical scare. It will be a relief to finally be past this point in their lives when at least some semblance of normalcy is restored.

Rebecca finally finds her keys under a box of kitchen tiles and runs out the door.

Alesha has already been seated at a table for two. The table is tucked away in the corner and far from the front entrance. It is much too cold outside to sit by the drafty door. Alesha waits patiently until Rebecca finally arrives. She is flustered and out of breath.

"So sorry I'm late," Rebecca says as she drops her dusty purse and keys on the table and hangs her coat over the back of the chair.

"You're covered in dust. You look like you've been in a saw mill," Alesha teases.

"That's right. You haven't been around since all the remodeling started. What a mess. The whole house is covered in dust. Stacks of wood and tiles, plastic tarps, sawhorses, and construction workers traipsing in and out all day long, argh! It's like living in a war zone."

"Yeah, I can imagine. I ordered you a latte, I hope it hasn't gotten cold."

"Thank you. It'll be fine. I haven't had a decent cup of anything for so long, I really don't care. As long as it doesn't taste like hospital coffee."

Rebecca takes a sip from the cup. "It's delicious. So how are you, Leesh? How's Dave?"

"Fine, I told you he lost his job, right? So much for my new car."

"I know. I'm so sorry."

Alesha nods and smiles with a slight shrug as she tries her best to be gracious. She can't help but have some resentment over the sudden stroke of good fortune Rebecca and Mark seem to have run into. A brand new car and now the home remodel. But, they have all been through so much. They deserve a little something good in their lives.

"How's Em doing?" Alesha asks empathetically.

"She's doing well. In fact oddly well. Her first progress report for the semester went from a 1.9 to a 3.9 grade point average." Rebecca says with some pride in her voice.

"What do you mean, 'oddly' well? I mean, I know the raw meat thing was pretty weird. There's more?"

"Behavioral things. Her disposition went from bride of Satan to Mother Teresa almost overnight. Not to mention, she can drive a car. We never taught her how to drive. She just 'knows.' And, without any lessons, she can play the piano at well above an average level. We don't even own a piano."

"Are you serious? Have you mentioned this to her doctor?"

"Yes, as a matter of fact. He says she's fine. Something to do with Extra Sensory Delusion Syndrome. He says she's able to pick things up from media sources at a much greater level of understanding and at a much higher rate of retention. In other words, she's able to learn things really fast. She's got 2 more examinations then she gets a clean bill of health, whatever that means."

Alesha looks on with a slight smile and pats Rebecca's hand. "Well, the main thing is that she's okay, now. I can't imagine what you all are going through."

"So did Mark get a raise? I mean, you did say he was freaking out over paying the fifty thousand dollars for Em's procedure. Now you have a new car, and you're finally getting that remodel you've always wanted. I mean, it's either a raise or you won the lottery," Alesha giggles.

"He got a huge bonus. The SUV, we put a big chunk down on and we got a second mortgage on the house."

"I thought he was against going into debt."

"Yeah, I don't know. He made like 30K for his bonus and he decided we should go all out. I think he feels bad about what has happened with Em and all."

"I'm sorry, I didn't mean anything. I'm happy for you," Alesha says, taking a sip of her coffee to hide her embarrassment.

"Leesh, listen, if you and Dave need any help with anything, anything at all, please let us know, we'd be glad to help out."

"No, No, I'm sorry. I'm fine. We're alright. Dave may be getting a job at SpiresGate. He'd be working with Mark. Well not working 'with' Mark, but working in the same building. That's if he gets the job."

"I tell you what, I'll have Mark put in a good word for him. Dave's a smart guy. Any company would be lucky to have him."

"Thanks so much, Rebecca. That'd be great."

"Everything will work out fine Leesh. And the offer still stands if you need anything in the meantime, okay?"

Alesha smiles, "Okay. Hey, let's order."

"Absolutely! And this time it's on me."

THE HILLSDALE WESTIN INN, 1:15 PM

For a small city of 81,623 people, the 4+ star Hillsdale Westin Inn is fairly lavish. Built only five years ago, its primary function is to accommodate SpiresGate Technology's sub-contractors who frequently come to work for the corporation.

It is 1:15 PM and Mark is seated alone in a rear booth of the hotel's dimly lit Tiki Thai Lounge. Red, green, and purple lights illuminate the cascading water feature near the stone wall adjacent to Mark. The establishment is not well known for its drinks or cuisine. But it serves an appropriate private location for the meeting he has scheduled with Carol Hoecker.

The tapping sound of high-heels announces her arrival as she enters the lounge. Mark pokes his head out from around the high-back leather booth. Carol walks directly toward him, taking a seat.

"Hello Mark. And how are you today?" Carol asks while scooting in closer to him.

"You want to know how I'm doing? I'm scared out of my wits; that's how I'm doing. We get caught and we're both dead, you know that don't you?"

"Oh come on Mark, we're not going to get caught. That is unless you do something stupid like talk to

354   Rick Lord

someone about this. And I told you what would happen if you did that, right?"

"I don't know. I wake up at night sometimes in cold sweats and my heart pounding. I feel like I'm going to have a heart attack."

"You need to calm down. Everything is going to be fine. As long as this is kept a secret, then there's nothing to worry about."

Carol places her hand reassuringly on Marks arm. "I'm starved let's eat something, okay."

"Yeah, fine. Okay," Mark waves at the waiter.

Carol dominates the lunch conversation with light-hearted anecdotes and small talk, making Mark feel more at ease. After a few glasses of wine and a light lunch, he is feeling much better.

"Mark, I need to get back to the office. Will you be a dear and give me a ride?" Carol smiles.

"Oh, yeah, sure, I can do that." Mark agrees and grabs the check.

"You know Mark," Carol says sweetly, "I hate to be the bearer of bad news, especially now. But things have changed, and we need you to get stages two and three done this week. Can you please do that for us?"

"That's the kind of pressure I don't need. I've got a lot on my plate right now," Mark replies.

"You'll be just fine. I'll be by your side through the whole process, okay?"

"Alright, alright."

With their lunch date over, Carol slides out of the

booth. Leaving a large tip on the table. Mark follows and they exit the Tiki Thai Lounge.

Carol runs her arm through Mark's arm to help steady her walk.

"A little too much wine for me," she says with a smile. They make their way through the parking lot of the hotel.

Mark is wishing he had driven the new SUV as opposed to the old one. No doubt the candy wrappers, popcorn, and Taylor's sports gear in the back seat will cut his masculinity in half.

Center Street runs through the middle of Hillsdale Falls. Connecting the east side of town to the west side, it is predominantly retail stores, shops, and fast food joints. The hotel has a strategic location at the corner of Center and West 66th. SpiresGate Technology is to the east and the airport is to the west.

Mark's SUV is parked in the hotel parking lot facing the corner of West 66th and Center. Unlocking the passenger side door, Mark politely opens the door for Carol. Just as he does, he looks up and sees Rebecca stopped at the light. She is looking right at him as Carol's long legs swing into the passenger seat of the family SUV.

Mark's heart stops and then slides into the pit of his stomach. Trying his best to save face, he waves at Rebecca with a big smile. Shutting the passenger side door, Mark walks around the vehicle and watches Rebecca speed off. Before he gets to the driver side door, his cell phone begins to ring.

"And so it begins," he mumbles. Removing the phone from his coat pocket he answers it sounding as innocent as he possibly can.

"Hello. Oh hi sweetheart. Yeah, I just picked up Carol and I'm taking her back to the office. How about we talk later, okay? Okay, I love you," Mark ends the call. "I'm so dead." With his face becoming flush and forehead beading up with perspiration, he climbs into the driver's seat of the SUV.

"That was Rebecca, my wife. She called to tell me how excited she was to see me here at the hotel with you."

"What?"

"She saw me letting you in. She was at the stop light."

"I'm sorry Mark. Would you like me to talk to her?"

"Yeah, I don't think that would be my first line of defense. I'll just talk to her later. She'll be fine. I hope."

"If you insist." Carol shrugs and begins to apply lipstick using the visor mirror.

Starting the SUV, Mark heads to SpiresGate.

SHAE RESIDENCE, LATER THAT EVENING

Rebecca has been fuming the entire afternoon. It's almost 7:00 PM and Mark is finally pulling into the driveway. Rebecca is so angry she is ready to confront Mark with all the indignation she can muster. Mark sheepishly slips in through the kitchen side door carrying a dozen long stemmed roses.

"I'm sorry I couldn't talk when you called," he explains.

"Had your hands full with, what's her name? Oh yeah, Carol?" Rebecca spats.

"That's not fair. I had to pick Carol up from the hotel and bring her back to the plant. You just happened to drive by at the same time. Nothing happened."

"My sediments exactly. When it comes to dinner, nothing happened. You're on your own."

"No worries. We already ate."

"So you two had dinner together?"

Rebecca glares at Mark with daggers in her eyes, turns, and storms out of the kitchen. Mark follows close behind and mumbles to himself, "Stupid, stupid, stupid." Mark sets the flowers down on the table and takes hold of Rebecca by the shoulders.

"Listen! I love you. I just work with Carol. There's a lot going on at work. A lot of litigation due to some government implemented regulations. Come on. Why are you doing this? There's nothing going on. I'm telling you the truth. Please believe me," Mark gently turns Rebecca around so he can face her.

Rebecca relaxes and begins to soften. Looking into Mark's eyes, she can see he is being genuine. She starts to tear up as the emotions and uncertainty of the afternoon wash over her. Mark wraps his arms around her tenderly.

"So there's nothing going on?"

"No. And their never will be. I would never do that to you," he lifts her face up and gives her a tender kiss.

"Where are the kids?" Mark asks softly.

"Upstairs doing homework," she changes her tone and wipes the tears from her cheeks.

Mark picks up the roses and hands them to his wife, "These are for you. You're the only woman in my life." Rebecca tears up again and takes the bouquet.

"Thank you Mark. They're beautiful. I need to put these in water."

Mark watches Rebecca arrange the roses in a crystal vase and tries to be nonchalant.

"I got a call from Doctor Heller today. They need to see Emily first thing tomorrow morning. They have to finish all of her examinations before the end of the week. All of her tests have to be completed and back on Doctor Heller's desk by Friday. They want to make Chryzinium available to the public as soon as possible," Mark interjects.

"What? Why? Emily was supposed to have two more exam sessions over the next two or three weeks. Why didn't Dr. Heller call me? You know we have the countertops coming in tomorrow. I thought we were allowed to schedule Emily around our schedule?"

"I know. I was as surprised as you. Don't worry, I'll take her, okay? You stay here and oversee the construction guys. It'll be fine."

"I should go up and let her know. I think she had something planned at school. I hope it isn't going to be an issue for her. She's doing so well now."

"Let me. I'll tell her. She has to be ready at 5:00 AM. The tests are going to take all day."

"Okay. Thank you."

Mark gives Rebecca a quick kiss and heads upstairs.

From downstairs, Rebecca hollers up to Taylor that it's time for breakfast and that he's running late for school. Taylor stumbles downstairs, half asleep but dressed and dragging his backpack behind him. It makes a muffled 'thump-thump' as he descends the stairs into the living room.

Since the remodel began, the family has had to be creative during meals. This morning's breakfast is served in the living room on one of the end tables.

Taylor plops on the couch as Rebecca hands him a bowl of cereal. "Don't spill a drop! I mean it!" Taylor takes the bowl and begins wolfing down the soggy flakes.

"Where's Em?" he asks between bites.

"You're dad took her to the doctor early this morning. She's getting the last of her exams today. I'm staying here with the contractors."

Taylor's eyes open wide. "Mom, you gotta see what they're doing to her. It's freaky. I can take you there. I know exactly where she is. It's on the eighth floor."

"Nice try mister. You're going to school. Eat!"

"No, seriously! I'm not just trying to get out of school. I'll even draw you a map."

"We went through all of this the last time. You scared the living tar out of me when you said she was dead."

"Look, I'll draw you a map."

Taylor pulls out a notebook and a pencil from his backpack and draws a crude map of the hospital. And a big black 'X' on the top left hand side. Tearing the sheet of paper loose from the binder, he hands it to Rebecca.

"Here. If you don't believe me, go see for yourself. She'll be in that room there. I marked it with an 'X'. I'm telling you, she looked like she was dead. I'm not kidding mom!"

Exasperated, Rebecca snatches the map, "Go, you're running late."

"Fine!"

Rebecca is genuinely concerned that what Taylor is insinuating might be true. She folds the crude map and puts it in her pocket.

The first of the construction workers finally begin to arrive. Hustling about they set up for another day of remodel. Terry Birch, the construction foreman, is late as usual.

As the morning wanes, Rebecca cannot stop thinking about Emily and what might be happening. She should not have let Mark take her to Doctor Heller. She should be there, not Mark.

Terry finally arrives with blueprints in hand and Rebecca has decided that she must go to the hospital to be with Emily.

"Hi Terry. Would you mind watching over things today? My daughter is having some important tests at the hospital and I really need to be there."

"Sure thing Mrs. Shae. We can handle things fine around here no problem."

"Thanks a million, Terry. I should be back later this afternoon."

Rebecca can't get going fast enough. No makeup, hair a mess and in her house clothes, Rebecca is out the door.

HILLSDALE FALLS MEMORIAL MEDICAL CENTER

The elevator stops on the 5th Floor and Rebecca exits. She just needs to know for sure that Emily is indeed in good hands. It's not that she doesn't trust Mark, but Taylor is not one to be this tenacious, especially concerning his sister.

Reaching Doctor Heller's office she starts to open the door. She stops herself. She hears Mark and Doctor Heller speaking. And another voice she doesn't recognize. Rebecca leans in to the doors small window and looks in. Sitting behind his desk is Dr. Heller and Mark in the adjacent chair. Sitting in the chair next to Mark is Carol Hoecker.

Rebecca feels a knot in the pit of her stomach. Her mind races with 'what-ifs', jealousy, and anger. 'What is she doing here?'

Reaching into her pocket, Rebecca takes out the map that Taylor drew for her. Backing away from the door she opens the piece of paper and tries her best to decipher where she is in reference to Taylor's big 'X'.

He said eighth floor. She makes her way back to the elevator. As the door opens she steps inside and sees that there is no eighth floor. At least, there's no button for floor 8. Frantic, Rebecca pushes the 7th floor button figuring she'll get off there and maybe find another elevator that goes up one more floor. After exiting on the seventh floor, Rebecca waits for the elevator doors to close. There are 3 more elevators to choose from, she pushes the 'up' button.

The doors of the elevator behind her open and she steps inside to take a look. The panel has one extra button. Eight. She pushes it.

The elevator door opens and Rebecca steps out. Looking at her map, she makes her way towards the big 'X' on the map.

There is not a single person on floor 8. Odd, but to Rebecca's advantage. She arrives at the room Taylor marked on the map. As with all of the other doors in the hospital, it has a small window. She steps up to the window to take a look inside.

Emily is lying on a gurney. A sheet covers her from the neck down and a multitude of wires and cables are connected to her. The wires are laced like a web across the room to computer monitors and equipment that display odd looking codes and programming language.

There are several doctors in the room, including Nurse Sprague. She checks each of the displays making notes on her clipboard. Emily has an ashen grey pallor. Taylor was right. She looks dead.

Overwhelmed, Rebecca barges into the room and screams. "Get away from my daughter! What are you doing to her?" Nurse Sprague spins around dropping the clipboard and makes a grab for Rebecca. The other doctors rush to assist Nurse Sprague in restraining Rebecca and drag her from the room kicking and screaming.

Emily remains lifeless and unresponsive. Doctor Mintle pushes the intercom button on the wall by the entry door shouting out "Code India, Code India." Responding to the alert are 6 armed guards who relieve the doctors and restrain Rebecca, easily overpowering her.

"Take her to 8-C." Nurse Sprague demands. She follows close behind.

DOCTOR HELLER'S OFFICE

Mark sits in a chair across from Doctor Heller drinking his fourth cup of coffee. He's been there for more than two hours and is getting restless due to the circumstances and the caffeine.

"You know, you don't have to stay here. If you want to go back to your office, I can give you call when we're done," Doctor Heller says. Just then, Doctor Heller gets a call on his land line. Answering the call, he responds with "Okay."

Hanging up his phone he directs his attention to Mark, "We've got a problem."

FROGS AND CHIPS

The trip south has come to an end. Now finally home from their excursion, both Baggs and Lewis are wiped out. Notwithstanding, Baggs can't seem to tear himself away from the computer.

Comparing the photographs he took of the Devil's Halo and the images that others have captured haunt him. Like a forensic scientist, Baggs scrutinizes every detail, hoping to come up with some rational explanation for the weird-looking object that looms over the Arizona/New Mexico desert. Not to mention, he has the plethora of material John gave him to peruse.

A sudden knock at the door startles Baggs, shaking him from his deep concentration. At 9:20 PM he wonders who would be disturbing him at this late hour. Sliding back from his computer desk, Baggs stands.

Wearing his pajamas, bathrobe, and his favorite slippers, Baggs reluctantly makes the journey to the front door.

Looking out the peephole he sees nothing, yet again there is another stern knock. Since the knock comes from low on the door, he guesses who it is on the other side. Without hesitation, Baggs opens the door, and just as expected, there stands Marty. Dressed in overalls, sneakers and her new jacket, the consummate tomboy reels with disdain. Tapping her foot she lets into Baggs with her fury.

"You come home after being gone for a week and you don't call? If you're hiding from me, you're not doing a very good job of it. I saw your lights on," she accuses.

"I got home less than an hour ago. Besides, what are you doing up so late? Don't you have school tomorrow?" Baggs responds with defensive kindness.

"It's not too late for you to at least call."

"Well it's late for me. Is everything okay?"

"Yeah. I'm glad you're home. I missed you," she says with sincerity.

She breaks into a smile and reaches over and gives Baggs a big hug. Letting go, she looks up at him with her big brown eyes.

"I really am glad you're back."

"You get any flying in while I was gone?" Baggs asks.

"Sunday they closed the park. It's all fenced off with a bunch of 'Stay Out' signs."

"What?" Baggs responds, perplexed. "Who closed it?"

"How the hell should I know?"

"You're right, you wouldn't know. You should know to watch your mouth little better, though. You shouldn't be talking like that. Not becoming of a lady."

Marty stands for a minute thinking. No one has ever corrected her language before. This is a side of Baggs she hasn't seen. He's starting to sound like a father figure; and in a weird way, she's okay with that.

"Well, let's find out what's going on at the park tomorrow, okay?" Baggs suggests.

With a single thumb pointed up, Marty cracks a slight smile as though saying 'You got it.' Then, Marty turns and runs back down the walkway. Baggs watches to make sure she gets home safely before closing his door and making his way to bed.

WEDNESDAY MORNING, 7:15 AM

Although it's cold in Springboro, the skies are clear. It certainly isn't like the snow storm Baggs and Lewis experienced at the Grand Canyon. Baggs makes his morning coffee while observing the sky from his kitchen windows.

Under normal conditions, Baggs would be preparing a trip to Grass Park. It doesn't take much arm-twisting for him to take to the skies with one of his prized planes. But unfortunately, today is much different. Not only is Baggs waiting to hear from Sy, he needs to talk to Lewis, and neither are answering their phones. Not to mention, he now has yet to discover why Grass Park was closed.

After gulping down his morning coffee and eating a little cereal, he wastes no time jumping in his truck to head straight to the park. He slows as he drives up onto the dirt drive that precedes the vacant lot. He is stunned by what he sees. Sure enough, Marty was right. Chain link fencing topped with barbed wire surrounds the seven-acre field.

Every twenty feet or so, there are large white signs with red lettering stating 'Stay Out' and 'No Trespassing!' It is quite obvious that whoever wants the park area closed means business.

So why the big 'Go Away' fencing and signage, Baggs wonders as he exits his truck. He walks up to the fence and looks out and over the field. Nothing he sees suggests any type of land development project coming soon or any environmental danger to people. Just a lot of fence and a lot of signs. He figures now is a good time to pay a visit to his friends at city hall.

SPRINGBORO CITY HALL

The building is not terribly grandiose. In fact it looks more like a DMV. Springboro City Hall is neatly tucked away off the main drag, making itself somewhat obscure. After parking his truck in the small lot, Baggs wastes no time getting to the bottom with what's going on with Grass Park.

Beverly not only serves as city clerk but also acts as receptionist, bookkeeper, and janitor. She, just like everyone else in Springboro knows of Commander Baggerly. After all, he's the towns' only celebrity. Albeit an astronaut celebrity, he is a celebrity nonetheless.

Just like with many small mid-western towns, many folks never venture off too far. Some of the more restless move away from the community, but not many. Baggs enters the newly constructed building. With a ring of its doorbell, he approaches the counter.

"Beverly, do you know what's going on with Grass Park? It's all fenced off with barbed wire and 'stay out' signs."

"Hi Commander, it's good to see you," she grins.

"Good to see you too, Beverly. So, what's the deal?"

"The Bureau of Land Management came in along with the EPA and quarantined the whole area."

"Why?"

"It has something to do with an endangered frog species. It's not the only open space that they've closed off either. Have you read the paper?"

"No, I've been out of town."

"They've even got the military involved. Military trucks all over the place, now."

Beverly opens the newspaper and thumbs through it a few pages. She folds the paper in half and lays it on the counter in front of Baggs. He picks up the paper and looks at it carefully, reading the small headline at the top. 'Massive Land Grab or Environmental Catastrophe?' Baggs scans the story briefly. Disturbed by what he is reading, he asks Beverly if he can keep the paper.

"Take it. It's old news, now," Beverly says while loading paper into the printer tray.

"Thanks Bev," he says as he exits the building.

Extremely frustrated, Baggs gets into his truck and drives off. Now would be a good time to swing by Sy's place and see if he's able to able to answer more questions concerning the Devil's Halo, among other things.

Pulling his truck up onto the circular drive, Baggs slowly comes to a stop. Exiting his vehicle he walks up to the massive front door and rings the doorbell. After a minute without response, Baggs rings the bell again. No answer. Without any signs of life he retreats to his truck and leaves for home.

Along the way he calls Lewis.

"Hello?" Lewis' voice is heard over Baggs small speaker phone.

"Hey, it's me, Baggs. You busy right now? I've got something here you need to see. Did you know the BLM closed Grass Park, and a few other open spaces?"

"No, I didn't, I'm posting things to sell right now. How about I come by this afternoon?"

"Works for me," Baggs says as he ends the call. Since the only thing he can do now is continue on with his investigative research, Baggs heads for home.

"Great, if Lewis is selling things, that means he's serious about buying a motorhome," he says out loud.

LATER THAT DAY

Now 2:30 PM and still no Lewis. Baggs has spent his

morning and early afternoon poring over conspiracy theory material on his computer. Most of what he's been studying is the UFO phenomenon which has grown exponentially over the past 75 years. There are a couple of interesting pieces of information he has gleaned during his research. But there are never any artifacts or evidence that justifies aliens ever being here.

One other thing that perplexes him; is the fact our very own Hubble Telescope hasn't picked up any extra-terrestrial craft flying around outside earth's atmosphere. So where do these things come from?

It's been no surprise that the interstellar Voyager mission launched in 1977, announcing "Greetings from Earth" in 55 languages, has been all but a bust, so far. Maybe the silence is a good thing.

Baggs, however, knows firsthand UFOs do exist. He's seen objects in space that cannot be explained. But never have they been seen in deep space, only within earth's atmosphere.

And now his experience with the Devil's Halo really boggles his mind. He can't help but feel something is amiss and hopes to get to the bottom of these things, whatever they are.

There is a knock on the door, which startles him. Departing from his office, he opens the front door and sees it's Lewis.

"Come on in," Baggs offers.

Leading the way, Baggs walks straight into the kitchen. Starting the coffee pot, Baggs has Lewis take a seat at the table where he has left the paper he got from Beverly that morning. Baggs unfolds the paper and opens it to the page that has the article about the closure of Grass Park.

Lewis hunkers down and begins reading the article. Within a minute his head raises looking over at Baggs who is still fiddling with the coffee pot.

"Frogs? They closed the park because of frogs?" Lewis asks incredulously.

Baggs stops what he's doing and walks to the table. He spins the paper around so he can see it better.

"Not that, this. Read this," Baggs says pointing to an article at the bottom of the page. He turns the paper back for Lewis to read. After a moment, Lewis looks up. Baggs has a grin from ear to ear.

"She's still alive and only twenty minutes from here. You think she knows anything?" Lewis asks with a child-like sense of wonderment.

"Don't know, but I say we go have a talk with her."

"When?" Lewis asks, thinking now would be a good time.

"Tomorrow," Baggs responds just as another knock at the door is heard.

"Marty," Baggs says under his breath as he makes his way into the living room to answer the door. He opens the door and sees his young friend.

"Come on in, Lewis is here; he's in the kitchen," Baggs welcomes. Marty quickly makes her way into his house.

She darts for the kitchen, leaving Baggs behind to shut the door. Going right for the cookie jar, she grabs a handful of cookies. She stands on a lower drawer to reach for a glass.

Not acknowledging Lewis, sitting at the table, she grabs a carton of milk out of the refrigerator. With goodies in hand, she sits at the kitchen table across from Lewis.

"Wait, the milk is bad and the cookies are stale. We just got back and I haven't gone shopping yet," Baggs informs Marty. She pushes her long awaited snack to the side, disappointed.

"You know I was really looking forward to some cookies and milk with you."

Lewis is amused by what he is watching and smiles at Marty. "Don't you have friends you can play with?" he asks.

"Don't you?" Marty snidely replies.

"You're not going to win this one," Baggs informs Lewis.

"I can see that," Lewis concedes.

Baggs takes a seat at the table with his two friends and can't help but smile. Two old dudes and a ten-year-old tomboy make a pretty unexpected team.

"Would it be alright if I had a cup of coffee?" Marty asks.

"So you drink coffee?" Baggs asks.

"I didn't see any beer."

"Never mind. The cups are above the coffee pot."

"So did you have fun on your trip?" Marty asks while getting for herself a cup of coffee.

"It was interesting," Baggs responds without giving details.

"They're going to put an RFID chip in all you kids, so we can keep tabs on you monkeys," Lewis says sarcastically. Baggs looks at Lewis sternly for making such a remark.

"No they're not, Marty. Don't believe a word he says," Baggs says while scowling at Lewis.

"Yeah they are. My teacher told us all about it and how the government will be able to track us and watch everything we do. So if we do something wrong they can lock us up in jail."

Baggs and Lewis look at each other, shocked by what she just said.

"And, how do you know all this?" Lewis asks.

"My teacher said she knows someone who knows some secret stuff. She told her the, you know what, was about to hit the fan. And that we're all going to be turned into robots because of a computer chip they're going to put into us." Marty sits back down at the table with her cup of coffee. She takes a sip and smiles at the two.

"Wow, that's some tale. Let's hope that doesn't really happen," Baggs says, trying to diffuse the hearsay.

"Oh it will. It'll be happening real soon, she told us," Marty says authoritatively.

"So what teacher told you this?" Lewis asks.

"My teacher. Ms. 'K.'"

"How old is she?" Lewis asks, continuing to pry.

"She's real old, like you."

"Okay, I think it's time I go grocery shopping and I'm sure Lewis has somewhere he has to be. Right, Lewis?" Baggs says, ending Lewis's interrogation.

"As a matter of fact I have a guy interested in buying my plane. I have to meet him at the hangar when he gets off from work," Lewis announces.

"If you're still thinking you're going to drag me around the countryside in a motorhome, I can assure you, you're barking up the wrong tree," Baggs declares.

"Can I go?" Marty asks.

"You're not going with Lewis either."

"Not Lewis. I mean can I go with you to the grocery store. I think you need a woman's touch when it comes to shopping," Marty correctively interjects.

Baggs looks down at her, relieved, and offers to take her along, as long as it's okay with her mom. Baggs stands and walks out of the kitchen and into the living room to look out the window. He sees Roxanne's car sitting in the driveway across the street.

"Marty, come with me. Lewis, lock up when you leave," Baggs hollers. Marty quickly comes running and out the door they go.

Marty starts to head for Baggs truck, but Baggs instead walks across the street to Marty's house. Marty being a bit confused, quickly follows.

"What are you doing?" she asks.

"Going to have a talk with your mom," Baggs replies.

Not knowing how to respond, Marty goes along to see what this is all about. Reaching the door, Baggs rings the doorbell.

"It doesn't work. I'll get her for you," Marty says as she barges into the house hollering for Roxy.

Within a minute Roxy and Marty both come to the door. As expected, Roxy arrives at the door with a cigarette hanging from her mouth. She's wearing overly tight gold lame pants and a black blouse. Her hair is tasseled about and she is not wearing makeup. Seeing Baggs, she smiles at him, unaware she is missing her top center tooth. Usually she wears a bridge. The false tooth usually fills the empty void.

"Hey, what's up fly-boy?" She asks while at the same time exhaling cigarette smoke. "Don't tell me she broke something? Did you break something of his?" she accuses Marty.

"No," Marty barks.

"She didn't break anything. I was just wondering if it'd be alright with you if Marty went with me to the store. I need to pick up a few groceries and thought she'd like to come along. If there's anything you'd like for me to pick up for you while we're there, by all means, it'd be my pleasure," Baggs politely asks.

Roxanne looks down at Marty and then back up to Baggs as if she's actually giving it some maternal consideration.

"I don't know why you'd wanna bring the brat along, but if you want, be my guest. And, I could use a six pack of beer, I guess. I won't have time to pick any up before I leave for work. I'm running late and busy ironing my uniform. Runt knows what I like, she can show you," Roxanne says with another puff from her cigarette.

Baggs smiles and looks at Marty, "Well then, if you're ready, then let's go do some shopping." Marty makes her way back out the front door and runs across the street towards Baggs' truck, leaving him behind.

"Well, I guess we'll be back in a little while, I'll send her home as soon as we get back," he says, ready to get some fresh air.

"No worries, she knows what to do when she gets home," Roxy says while closing the door.

"Oh and thanks, mighty nice of you," she continues as she shuts the door with Baggs still standing there on the porch.

Baggs smiles and turns. "Maybe she'll pay me for the beer later," he mumbles to himself.

REVIVING ALBERT

It's only a twenty minute drive south to get to Lebanon, and Lewis is making great time as he drives a bit faster than Baggs. Baggs, however is not too pleased with himself, since he has agreed to let Lewis drive.

Lewis's car is just like everything else he owns; it's a piece of junk. Not one square inch of the body has a smooth, straight piece of metal. Rust bonded to other pieces of rust is all that holds the old convertible Chrysler LeBaron together. At least the faded red paint blends well with the color of rust. The discolored white convertible top is ripped in several spots making for an extra chilly ride, especially at 75 miles per hour.

"You were a C5-A pilot, for crying out loud, this is the best you can do for transportation?" Baggs asks, showing disdain for Lewis' car.

"I sold my plane last night to Harvey Thorp. In fact, he bought the entire hangar, all of the stuff, too. He says he can either use it or resell most of it online. Whatever, it worked for me. He gave me what I wanted," Lewis says, ignoring Baggs' insult.

"You're not seriously buying a motorhome are you?" Baggs asks.

"Maybe. You got the GPS, where do I turn off?" Lewis asks.

"Just ahead is the next exit. Take it and go right," Baggs instructs while looking at the GPS.

From right turns to left turns, the two weave the quaint streets of Lebanon until they come to East Mulberry Street. Slowly, they drive down the street looking at the houses on both sides.

"There it is," Baggs shouts. Of course, Lewis is driving too fast and passes the house, slamming on the brakes. Slowly backing up, Lewis parks his heap at the curb directly in front of the house. The quaint white bungalow sits nestled neatly amongst the Mulberry trees that line the narrow street.

"Are you sure that's her house?" Lewis asks. His LeBaron rumbles as it creates a slight haze of blue smoke in front of the house.

"I'm not sure of anything, but shut this thing off before we die of carbon monoxide poisoning," he says, coughing. Taking a moment he looks closely at his notes, confirming the address.

"Well, let's go see," Lewis says as he gets out of the car. He slams the door shut, announcing to the entire street they have arrived. Embarrassed, Baggs begrudgingly exits the passenger side and they walk up the steps to the porch.

"A door to door salesman, I'm not. I don't know how those guys do it," Baggs says meekly.

"Really? You can ride on a rocket, but you're afraid of a little old lady?"

"Never mind," Baggs says, hoping Lewis would just be quiet.

Lewis knocks on the door lightly. Standing patiently, there is no answer.

"What kind of knock was that? She wouldn't have heard that if she had her ear to the door," Baggs criticizes, shaking his head.

This time, Lewis pounds on the door like he is with the FBI demanding immediate entrance.

"Are you kidding me? Now you're going to scare the poor lady to death. Have lost your mind?" Baggs says in a loud whisper just as the door opens.

"Yes?" An elderly lady asks as she cautiously sticks her head out from behind the door.

Lewis stands there frozen. He doesn't say a word. Baggs can't believe it, thinking to himself 'Now he gets stage fright.' The little woman opens the storm door and sticks her head out a little farther. She looks up and down the street and then looks at Baggs and Lewis, carefully scrutinizing the two.

"May I help you?" She says softly.

"I'm sorry ma'am," Baggs says as he unfolds the newspaper from the day before. "Is this you? Are you April Konekelovski?"

April is in her mid-eighties and is as spry and energetic as someone half her age. Realizing they are not a threat, she opens the door farther.

"Come on in. I'm sure you're not here because of me being the winner of the Lebanon cake baking contest."

"No ma'am, this is Lewis Warren and I'm…"

"I know who you are, you're the astronaut fella."

"You know of me?" Baggs asks surprised.

"It's plastered all over your jacket. You're like a walking billboard for NASA. Only an idiot wouldn't recognize you. Have a seat. You two want some of the best chocolate cake you've ever tasted?" she asks as she wipes her hands on her apron.

"Sure," they both respond sheepishly.

Baggs looks over to Lewis. "Now you speak," he whispers sarcastically.

April walks back to her kitchen as Baggs and Lewis take a seat in her living room. The house is adorned with dozens of family photos. Ticking away in the corner of the room, is a majestic Seth Thomas grandfather clock.

Her furnishings are dated, but in pristine condition. Couch and chairs all match with their floral print design of years past. Her house is the quintessential representation of grandma's house, right down to the fine china.

With serving tray in hand, April enters with plates of chocolate cake, cups of coffee, and all of the necessary condiments.

"Here's coffee, cream, and sugar, and of course, my famous chocolate cake," she says with a sweet chuckle.

"Thank you very much," Baggs and Lewis each say politely.

It doesn't take long for them to devour their treats. They wash down their cake with sips of coffee. After finishing, Baggs gets down to business.

"This is the best chocolate cake I've ever tasted. I must confess though, as good as your cake is, we're not here for your desserts," Baggs admits.

"Oh I know that. I figured that article would bring someone sniffing around here before too long."

"So you are the April Dunn that saw that Albert Hess guy croak back in 1951?" Lewis asks, irreverently.

"I can't take you anywhere?" Baggs says under his breath.

"That's me. Of course 'Dunn' is my maiden name," she proudly informs the gentlemen.

Baggs and Lewis look at each other and smile. "I don't imagine you can tell us much about the guy, can you?" Lewis again interjects.

For decades, April has been hounded by the CIA, the FBI, the FAA, the NSA and every other government agency. Often, she couldn't leave her house without seeing a government vehicle parked somewhere in the vicinity, with 'G-Men' watching her every move.

"Well, I can tell you boys are way too old to be working for the government."

"No. As a matter of fact, we don't. We're just a couple of retired pilots who like to research government cover-ups. We think the scientist that died in your coffee shop was an important scientist that was into secret UFO stuff," Baggs says.

"Evidently, the flying business doesn't pay too well. I saw what you drove up in. That thing doesn't even look legal."

"My friend here is cheap. What can I say? Did this guy say anything significant before he died?" Baggs asks apologetically.

April is quiet for a moment, then takes a deep breath.

"What do you want to know?" she asks.

"We think there is a government plot to put ID implant chips in everyone. Lewis heard Albert Hess's son, Doctor Sigmund Hess, speak at a conference at the National Science Lab last week. In fact, he recorded it and I have it with me if you want to hear any of it.

"In your cake article, you said the last time you were in the newspaper was when Albert Hess died. Just so happens we live in Springboro, so we thought we would come and pay you a visit."

"Who would have guessed a cake baking contest would have dug all of this back up again," April says, amused.

She excuses herself and walks out of the living room. After a few moments, April returns carrying an old worn manila envelope.

"I've been hiding this stupid thing for decades. I'm an old woman and I don't need the drama. I don't know what to do with it anyway."

With that, she hands the envelope to Baggs. "You

can have it. Maybe you can make something out of it. Besides, there hasn't been anyone snooping around here for years." Out of respect, Baggs stands and takes the envelope.

"It's all strange technical stuff. It was all in a Top Secret envelope. That Albert guy handed it to me and asked me to hide it. Thick German accent, he scared me. I had no idea he was such a big deal scientist man till later. It was like a page out of a science fiction novel. There are a few weird drawings you might find interesting. There is a drawing of what I thought might be an implant chip of some kind.

"Some of those highfalutin government officials thought for sure I had something. Funny thing is, I did. But they never could find anything." April says proudly.

"May I open it?" Baggs politely asks.

"Be my guest," April says as she sits.

The manila envelope is stuffed fat with an assortment of Top Secret documents. Some are loose leaf while others are multiple pages stapled together at the top left corner.

"The envelope isn't stamped with anything designating where it came from," Baggs states.

"I left the envelope on the floor with the body. That's my envelope."

Baggs reaches into the envelope and removes the contents. Three of the loose papers inside are drawings. One drawing depicts a two inch by three inch strange-looking symbol drawn in pencil.

Baggs looks at the drawing with Lewis looking over his shoulder. Just as Lewis begins to say something, Baggs nudges Lewis, signaling him to keep his mouth shut for once. Baggs discretely lets the drawing drop back into the envelope.

Being careful not to reveal his enthusiasm, Baggs carefully folds the manila envelope shut.

"Did you tell anyone about any of this?" Baggs asks April.

"Yeah, my husband and my daughter."

"Where are they now?" Lewis asks.

"Carl passed away eight years ago, but my daughter lives up in Springboro."

"Do you talk to her often?" Baggs asks.

"You bet I do. I just talked to her Friday."

"Do you mind me asking what her name is?" Lewis asks.

"Lois, Lois Konekelovski. She never married, hence the same last name. Carl was a Polish immigrant, horrible name, I know. What can I say? She's an elementary school teacher. Kids call her Ms. 'K,' easier for them to pronounce."

Baggs looks over to Lewis and together they say, "Marty."

"Marty, who's Marty?" April asks.

"Nothing, it's a long story," Baggs says casually. Trying not to appear anxious, they both keep their cool and remain unassuming. April has no idea what she has had in her possession all these years.

"Do you know how Albert died?" Baggs asks politely.

"I think he had a heart attack, but I'm guessing. They were all pretty hush-hush about everything. They bagged the guy up and carted him off. No one said anything to me after that," April confesses.

Thanking April for the cake, coffee, and most importantly the Top Secret documents, they make their way to the door. Not in a million years did they expect a score such as this. Trying their best not to hastily rush off, the two politely dismiss themselves with gratitude.

"Thank you so much for everything. If we come up with anything interesting, we'll be sure to let you know," Baggs says to April.

She watches from her front porch as Baggs and Lewis drive off in a cloud of blue smoke.

DAY OF DARKNESS

Proverbs 29:11, KJV

"A fool uttereth all his mind: but a wise man keepeth it in till afterwards."

The twenty minute drive back to Springboro, albeit cold, is unusually quiet. It is fair to say that Lewis and Baggs have much to contemplate. Rather than going to Polinka's Café as originally planned, it is determined the sensitive information they now possess is better discussed in private. Lewis drives straight to Baggs' home.

BAGGS' HOME, 1:45 PM

Swiftly entering his office, Baggs clears off a chair for Lewis and pulls it up to his desk. Lewis takes a seat next to him. Baggs opens the aged manila folder and removes its contents. Carefully he lays out the stapled

27-page classified document, the drawings, and a small photograph.

Even though they've been sealed in an envelope for decades, the documents are yellowed, brittle, and stained. Carefully, Baggs and Lewis analyze each of the pages. For them, it's like stumbling onto the Lost Dutchman gold mine. What they have is a treasure trove of government information.

"April had no idea what she was holding onto all this time," Baggs says as he scans the documents.

"She knew enough to keep them hidden away; gotta hand her that. Frankly, I don't know how she did it."

"Frankly, I can't believe she gave these to us."

"You never got to go into Hangar 18 did you? I know I didn't," Lewis asks.

"Nope, nobody ever revealed to me what was actually in there. Of course, I heard the same rumors everyone else heard."

Though both Baggs and Lewis were once highly revered pilots stationed at Wright Patterson Air Force Base, they were considered to be little more than flyboys. The air wing is the air wing, as they say. And pilots have but one job to do: fly planes.

Both men have heard rumors of alien craft and alien beings hidden away at Wright Patterson AFB. Hangar 18 and extraterrestrials have always been at the forefront of UFO conspiracies. Although, for those who are actually stationed at Wright Patterson, any talk of alien craft or alien beings is adamantly discouraged.

Anything reported unidentified in space by Commander Baggerly was instantly and surreptitiously debunked. It was made quite clear to him and any other pilots that rumors of UFO anomalies seen were to be immediately silenced.

Certainly, neither Baggs nor Lewis was ever privy to any of the information they now possess. Before them is definitive proof there are indeed alien space craft and alien beings.

According to nineteen of the twenty-seven Top Secret pages, Doctor Hess was a Project Paperclip World War II scientist brought here from Berlin, Germany. The other frightening fact is; Doctor Albert Hess was the pioneer of chemtrail disbursement of Nychlorithiazine-B (NZB).

Speculated but never proven, NZB had been rumored for decades as being the contaminant responsible for the near pandemic levels of disease the world is experiencing today.

But, here in front of Baggs and Lewis is proof that this deadly chemical did, in fact, exist. Not to mention, two of the pages dating back to 1927 show early plans of inducing and propagating disease by means of infectious-laden microbes added to grain, vegetable seed, and water.

Even back then, 'bean counters,' the scientific mathematicians of that time, calculated there would not be enough food to support more than eight billion people living on earth simultaneously. However, with every chemical breakthrough, the same drawback kept arising, the infectious chemicals invented could not be controlled. They were creating rat poison. Once ingested, people would merely get sick and die.

This would obviously become globally catastrophic, wiping out the entire human race in a matter of years. These early attempts at controlling population were understandably scrubbed. But, the search continued over the years for something more predictable and controllable.

Hence the development of NZB. This man-made bacterium works differently as it attacks the immune system gradually. In other words, it's an immune-altering agent or chemical that once ingested, destroys cells in the body's autoimmune system over time.

It induces Anti-Immune Syndrome (AIS). The human race wouldn't die off immediately. They would simply be more susceptible to contracting deadly diseases, thereby controlling euthanization by a predetermined dissemination rate.

The propagation of NZB could be initiated easily by simply impregnating seed and feed, one bag at a time. Over the course of decades, it was originally designed to take full effect between 2015 and 2020.

However, that was not efficient enough. Mathematicians realized they needed a proficient way by which to spread the bacterium. They needed diseases to propagate worldwide by the early 1970s. Doctor Albert Hess initiated the idea of aerial disbursement. Chemtrail technology was born and has been in use ever since.

With NZB and Chemtrail technology, they knew they could stall the population at around seven billion people by 2020. According to the documents, Doctor Albert Hess was instrumental in formulating NZB. He was contracted by the government to have the chemical ready for disbursement by the end of the summer of 1949. August 25th, to be exact.

NZB is now contaminating food sources at every level. Greens, meats, and dairy are globally infected. The median age for those plagued with a disease has also drastically dropped. Cancers, diabetes, Parkinson's disease, multiple sclerosis, et cetera are now at record levels among pre-teens and teens, just as calculated.

As Baggs and Lewis continue their investigation, three pages stand out in particular. Not considered formal documents, these pages are drawings. The first drawing is what Baggs removed from the envelope in front of April. The artwork is that of a bold, black, strange symbol resembling Arabic.

"That's what I saw on the screen at the science seminar. That's the symbol that was titled 'Shafutah,'" Lewis reminds Baggs.

"So what is Shafutah, again? Is that a drug or something?"

"I don't think it stands for any particular product. I think he said it means 'Health, Peace and Unity.' I don't know for sure. I only saw Shafutah associated with the symbol. I do think it has something to do with the Lazarus VI Project."

Baggs is distracted by another drawing. As he picks up the sketch, he realizes it has similar characteristics to the Devil's Halo. Though crudely drawn in pencil, it has shading and landscape features, eerily matching the disc that Baggs and Lewis have seen. 'Vul-Helix' is scribbled in pencil at the bottom of the drawing.

The drawing is, for all intents and purposes, from around the period of 1951 or earlier. This would substantiate Lewis's theory concerning the 1956 mid-air collision of United Airlines flight 718 and Pan American's flight 2 over the Grand Canyon. Lewis looks on at the sketch with Baggs.

"I'm telling you, that thing, whatever it is, is what those pilots saw just before they crashed into each other," Lewis reiterates.

Baggs is on to the next drawing. His eyes widen as he gazes intently at the artwork. In meticulously drawn artistry, the Vul-Stream RFID chip is represented in full detail.

Though not titled, the specs depict an enlarged concept drawing of the tiny micro-chip that Lewis also saw projected at the National Science Lab. Strange as it may seem, the artwork must have been designed and drawn during Albert Hess's time, maybe even earlier.

Stunned, Lewis carefully takes the drawing from Baggs. He is amazed to see something with this kind of technology dating all the way back to 1951. He saw identical images at Los Alamos, and now again, only a much older rendition of the same thing. It's like seeing an old tin photograph of the 1890s with its subject using a cell phone.

"This is the Vul-Stream implant Doctor Hess was talking about. How'd they have the technology for something like that way back then?" Lewis remarks, astounded by this realization.

"Maybe the technology was given to them by Martians," Baggs responds jokingly.

Recollecting something, Baggs slides back in his chair, stands and walks to one of his bookcases. With his right forefinger he peruses the many books he has in his collection.

After a moment, Baggs finds what he is looking for. Carefully pulling a very old book from the shelf, he makes his way back to his desk and sits.

Carefully opening the book, he begins leafing through its delicate pages. The book is titled 'Tah.' With the binding broken and pages tattered, it is a book of Middle Eastern teachings of historical, satanic ritual.

The 'Tah' is at least an inch and a half thick and is filled with many drawings and various written teachings. Scouring the pages carefully, Baggs is in search of something. With a smile he sits back in his chair.

"There, I knew I saw the word, 'Shafutah,' somewhere. Look here," Baggs says, pointing to the word within a paragraph.

"Wow," Lewis comments as he gazes on. He begins

to read. In the meantime, Baggs reaches over and grabs his Bible that sits on top of a stack of magazines on the corner of his desk. He opens it up to Genesis 1:1-2.

"Shafutah has nothing to do with peace and health or any of that," Baggs announces as he begins to read.

"In the beginning God created the heavens and earth. And the earth was without form and void and darkness was upon the face of the deep. And the Spirit of God moved upon the face of the waters," he reads out loud. "How much time do you think passed between darkness on the earth and God creating light?" Baggs asks Lewis.

Baggs continues his keen observation.

"There were all these fallen angels that were cast out of heaven along with Satan and onto earth before inhabitable earth was completed, right? I think that may have taken place during the time the earth was without form and void. Those same fallen angels are said to be demons, and it's those demons that supposedly have the ability to come up from the deep, ever since man fell to sin. Underground, under the sea, or whereever down below, I think they have the ability to manifest themselves as humans and space craft and who knows what else.

"One of the mysteries I find interesting, is that none of these so-called UFO sightings seem to ever be seen in deep space by telescope or anything. You know that? But there sure is a lot of activity with the little devils around this planet.

"The Shafutah are what they are called. The leader

or Satan, Adramalech is considered the Commander of Hell. 'Wierius' is who he was referred to in Assyria and was actually worshipped and written of in ancient script referred to as 'Strikes' or hieroglyphs. Read here what it says in the 'Tah.'

Lewis reads the passage out loud, "They burn their children at the stake and sacrifice them to the abyss."

Lewis looks on intently at the old writings. Baggs continues, pointing again to the paragraph on the next page.

"See there, the Shafutah are referred to as demons. Adivamalech Nauru Zaheem or 'keeper of darkness' is another name for him," Baggs explains as he points to both the Bible and the 'Tah.'

Lewis turns the page, and there in full color is a picture depicting Adivamalech, The Zaheem. Lewis immediately recognizes the picture.

"That's him. That's Adiv. That's the man they refer to as the architect of the Lazarus VI Project. His name is Adiv Zahim," Lewis says as he jumps up from his chair.

"Are you sure?"

"Ya I'm sure. The only difference is the picture here is a painting. That guy is like Satan or something.

Lewis reaches over and abruptly slams the 'Tah' closed.

"Hey be careful, would ya? That book is old," Baggs scolds.

"What are you doing with it, anyway?" Lewis asks.

"I use it to cast spells on people I don't like," he

jokes, cracking a smile. "I've had it for years. Ever since my first trip to space, I saw things I couldn't explain. I found this at a garage sale. I got it so I could do some research. That was years ago. I forgot I had it until a few minutes ago."

"Yeah, well I think you should burn it. Way too freaky for me," Lewis says while fighting off the goose bumps.

A banging at the front door scares Lewis causing him to jump. Another round of bangs startles him even more. Baggs is also startled.

"Are you sure you're not black? You know it's us black folk that don't cotton much to the things on the dark side."

Baggs laughing as he makes his way to the front door. Lewis follows close behind.

"You're kidding. Are you afraid to be back there alone?" Baggs asks shaking his head and laughing.

"No, I just wanna see who's at the door, that's all."

"Hmm!" Baggs quips sarcastically.

In usual fashion, Baggs takes a look out the peep-hole, only to see nothing.

"Marty!" Baggs exclaims.

Baggs opens the door and to their surprise, Marty is standing there drenched in tears. Her eye is cut, and bleeding. With a bruised and bloodied lip, she hollers.

"You gotta help, please help. It's my mom."

Pushing his way through the door, Lewis makes a dash for Marty's house. Baggs grabs Marty and sits her down on the couch. "Don't move, I'll be right back."

By the time Baggs reaches Marty's house, the front door is already open. He enters and sees Roxanne sitting and leaning against the wall between the kitchen and the living room. She is shaking like a leaf and looking dazed.

Lewis is standing just inside the doorway, looking into the kitchen, shocked. Blood is splattered throughout. From under the kitchen table, blood is beginning to stream across the floor.

Crumpled against the lower cabinets is Vernon's lifeless body. Both Baggs and Lewis are frozen as they look at the grotesque scene.

Cautiously, Baggs walks over to Vernon careful not to step in any of the blood. Vernon's head is bleeding profusely from several spots. Placing his 2 right fingers onto Vernon's neck he checks for a pulse.

"What happened?" he asks as he examines Vernon. As he stands, he turns toward Roxanne. Lewis pulls his cell phone from his pocket.

Looking over to Baggs, he realizes by the look on Baggs face, Vernon is dead. "I need to call 9-1-1," Lewis says, bringing the phone up to dial.

"No, please not yet." Roxanne says. She slowly stands to her feet. When she does, Baggs and Lewis can see she is tightly gripping a bloodied laundry iron.

"What happened?" Baggs repeats.

With muscles involuntarily relaxing, she releases the iron, dropping it to the floor. "I walked in and the son of a bitch was beating the crap out of Martha. I picked up the iron and hit him with it, and hit him, and hit him, and hit him. I couldn't stop. He's not ever going to hurt her or me again."

"Ya, you pretty much solved that problem," Lewis says tactlessly. "I need to call the police."

"No, not yet."

Baggs carefully makes his way over to Roxanne. "Why, it's self-defense. They'll understand. We can witness to that," Baggs insists.

"No, you don't understand. Where is she? Where's Martha?" she asks, looking around.

"She's at my house. I gotta see that she gets medical attention," Baggs says, trying to get the situation under control.

"Please no, they'll take her away for good this time. I need her hid away for a while, can you keep her for a few days till this settles down?"

"This isn't going to settle down. You got a dead guy in the kitchen and whether its self-defense or not, you're going to be kind of busy with a couple of legal issues," Lewis informs her.

"He's right," Baggs interjects.

Baggs and Lewis know she's right. The state will come and take Marty away.

"Listen, she loves you Baggs. Just take her and hide her at your place for a while. I'll just say she ran away. She's run away before. They'll buy that. Besides they'll be more freaked out over this, rather than Marty. Please."

"She's got a point. He is suffering from a slight case of dead. The police are going to be expending most of their energy here for a while," Lewis says.

Baggs stands, still in shock. He considers his options carefully.

"You're not actually considering keeping the kid are you?" Lewis asks Baggs.

"She would be better off with you. I'm no good for her," Roxy says.

"What if we had her stay with you?" Baggs asks Lewis. "What if we take care of her at least until the dust settles. Only be a few days."

"What?! Have you lost your mind?"

"Leave Roxanne here to deal with all of this. Marty returns as if returning home from running away. I think we owe her at least that," Baggs argues.

"What? We don't owe her anything. I'm calling the police."

"No, you can't, they can ping your call. They'll know it's coming from here."

Lewis realizes Baggs is right. He finds himself contemplating the situation. After a moment Lewis sighs. "Only for a few days," he concedes. Baggs smiles at Lewis and Roxanne.

"When we leave here, give us twenty minutes to check Marty out for any serious injuries. If she checks out okay, we'll get her out of here. When you see Lewis leave, then call the police and not a minute sooner. I'll make contact with you in a few days. You don't try to contact me. I'll contact you. Understand?"

Roxanne smiles and reaches over and gives Baggs a huge bear hug. "That little girl loves you to tears. She'll be in good hands with you. I know it. Thank you," Roxanne softly says. Releasing from the hug, Baggs nods to Lewis, letting him know it's time to go.

Together Baggs and Lewis leave Roxy and Marty's house as inconspicuously as possible.

"If I end up in prison over this, I'll hunt you down and smash all your precious model airplanes," Lewis threatens.

Not too badly injured, Marty is out of Baggs' house and placed into Lewis's Chrysler LeBaron. With Marty lying down in the back seat, Lewis drives her off to safety.

AND THE DEAD
AWAKEN

The blinking life support monitors on a small cart and a desk lamp dimly illuminate Room 8C. A heart monitor sounds rhythmically in the dreary room. This is not a room that is intended for patients.

The door opens and Doctor Heller enters followed by Nurse Sprague and Mark Shae. Rebecca lies semi-unconscious on a hospital gurney covered by a white sheet. A clear intravenous tube extends from the top of her right hand to a saline bag hanging from an intravenous infusion pole. She has been securely restrained with leather straps at both her ankles and wrists.

"We had to sedate her," Nurse Sprague informs Dr. Heller and Mark.

Mark is visibly upset as he approaches Rebecca's bedside, "Is she okay? Is all of this necessary?"

"She's okay," Dr. Heller assures. "She's just mildly

sedated. She is in a state of twilight, as we call it. She can hear, but she can't really respond to anything."

"When will she come to?"

"I can have Maggie shut off the flow of the anesthesia at any time. Do you know how you want to handle this?"

Mark is becoming pale and pasty looking. A sheen of perspiration covers his face, and he grips the rails of the gurney to steady himself.

"You're not looking too good, are you okay?" Heller asks.

"No! I'm not okay! My daughter is being robotized like some kind of alien and my wife is lying here in a drug-induced coma. I guess you could say I'm a little freaked out right now!"

"Please keep your voice low, she can hear everything that's going on. Do you want something to calm you down?" Doctor Heller asks.

"No, I don't want anything to calm me down. I'm fine," Mark snaps.

Doctor Heller turns his attention to Nurse Sprague.

"How's Emily doing?" Heller asks.

"It's going to be a while," she says.

The door opens and Carol Hoecker enters.

"Hello Amanda," Dr. Heller acknowledges. "You can see what we're up against."

"Hi Amanda," Mark nods.

Amanda smiles her perfect smile and walks languidly to Rebecca's bedside.

Rebecca twitches and mumbles incoherently as if

she were talking in her sleep. Her eyes remain closed.

Doctor Heller asks, "Amanda, how about we disconnect Emily for just a few minutes. We can bring her here so that Rebecca can see that she's okay? Maybe we can get this mess under control with Emily here by her side. I can't keep Rebecca sedated like this all day. It'll take at least an hour for her to completely bounce back to normal as it is."

Amanda replies, "I'm fine with that. But, you'll want to check with Doctor Mintle. They're in the middle of the Psycho Stenosis Telepathy process, and we may not be able to interrupt the procedure. Emily has a lot of equipment connected to her."

"It won't take that long. I'll speak with Dr. Mintle and see what we can do. Besides, I think it's worth the down time. We can't afford to have this blow up in our faces, not now. Come with me Maggie," Dr. Heller and Maggie exit the room.

Amanda walks over to Mark and takes his hand into hers, "I know what you've had to go through and I can't begin to thank you enough. Your daughter is a queen, you know that?"

"I should have asked for more money," Mark says plainly.

"A deal is a deal, you know that, Mark. Besides, you'll do fine. I promise, we're not going to leave you, or forsake you. What you did was a true act of selflessness. Do you know, your daughter will be at the left hand of Adivamalech Nauru Zaheem. When her transformation is complete, she'll be like a new creature, like a butterfly that has emerged from its cocoon."

Mark is beginning to feel the burden of his guilt. He sold his daughter out like Judas, who betrayed Jesus for 30 pieces of silver. He was handed an opportunity of a lifetime. Who could have guessed, that of all people, it would be his daughter who would collapse from a brain tumor.

Go figure. Just as M-MAC and SpiresGate Technologies were looking for a prime candidate for Vul-Stream and the new Chryzinium vaccine, Emily becomes their queen recipient. The financial reward was too great to pass up. How do you turn down $1.5 million dollars? But, now his remorse is surpassed only by his fear over how Rebecca will respond to all of this.

Within an hour of him paying $50,000 for Emily's treatment, he received the call from Amanda that changed everything. Not only was he off the hook for the 50K, he was going to receive a tax-free check for 1.5 million dollars, all in the name of science.

Rebecca is an expensive, high-maintenance wife. She requires a lot. New clothes. Home remodeling and a new car, with lots of cash left over for vacations and college for Taylor.

He worked insane hours to try and keep up with her constant financial demands. It was just too good of an offer to pass up. But the light at the end of the tunnel has turned into an oncoming train. How will Rebecca even begin to understand? Mark contemplates his options. Even suicide.

The door opens and Nurse Sprague leads a dazed and confused Emily into the room along with Doctor Mintle. Doctor Heller enters last, closing the door behind him.

Emily is wearing a hospital gown. She is still sedated, but walking. Yards of coiled cable are draped over her shoulder. With only six feet of lead, she is plugged into a silver handheld device that Doctor Mintle is carrying. The device is about the size of a toaster and has bright blue monitor lights that flash sequentially next to the handle depicting her vital status and progress.

"Hi sweetie," Mark says, greeting his daughter. Emily acknowledges her father with a disconnected, pro-grammed smile. Emily looks at her mother and smiles at her with the eyes glazed.

"I think we can wake up Rebecca now, so if you would Maggie, stop her anesthesia," Doctor Heller instructs and leads Emily close to her mother's bedside.

"It'll take just a few moments and Rebecca will start to come around," Heller continues. Not sure what to expect, they hope Rebecca sees Emily first.

Rebecca's eyes blink open and she begins to stir. After a few moments she recognizes Emily standing by her bedside and manages a smile. Doctor Heller steps in close to Rebecca.

"Rebecca? Can you hear me?"

It doesn't take long. Rebecca's smile soon turns into

anger as she begins to remember why she is here and what she has seen.

With a gravelly, hoarse voice, Rebecca tries to speak, "What are you doing with my daughter?"

"She's right here next to you. She's perfectly fine. There's nothing for you to be upset about. You know we're trying something totally new on Emily and she has to go through some things that might appear a little odd. But I can assure you, we mean her no harm. You can see she's right here, alive and well."

Rebecca calms down for a moment. She tries to lift her hand to touch Emily and realizes she has been strapped down to the gurney.

"Why do you have me strapped down? Let me free."

"Please, Maggie, would you be so kind as to unbuckle Mrs. Shae. It was for your own good. You were in a bit of a rage and we had to restrain you so you wouldn't hurt yourself or anyone else," Dr. Heller continues in a calming tone. Becoming more alert, Rebecca takes a moment to look around the room. "Mark? You're here."

Mark walks to the other side of her bed and smiles at her. "I'm here. Are you alright?" Rebecca looks past Mark and sees Carol Hoecker standing behind him. Scowling, Rebecca asks, "What is she doing here?"

Not knowing how to answer, Mark looks at Amanda for help.

"Hello Rebecca. Everything is okay, I'm here with Doctor Heller. I work with SpiresGate Technologies along with your husband. They're the manufacturer of the RFID chip that was implanted into Emily's hand. I'm just overseeing her progress on behalf of the company."

"Why did they call you Amanda? I heard Doctor Heller and Mark call you Amanda. I heard. Who are you really? What's going on here? Mark?" Rebecca asks.

Doctor Heller steps forward and takes Emily's hand and places it in Rebecca's hand. Rebecca refocuses her attention on Emily and holds out her arm for her daughter to embrace her. Emily dutifully responds. Rebecca wraps her arm around her neck, giving Emily a gentle squeeze.

"I love you so much," she sweeps Emily's hair back from her face just like she always does. With Emily's neck exposed, Rebecca notices a glowing green tattoo, a small, oddly-shaped Arabic symbol. It is the sign of the Shafutah.

"What's this?" Rebecca demands.

Doctor Heller gives a visual cue to Nurse Sprague. She responds immediately and turns the small plastic valve so that the intravenous sedative can begin flowing again.

"What are you doing to my daughter? Why does she have this on her neck? Would someone please tell me what's going on here? Mark?" Rebecca shouts and looks at Mark for answers.

Mark says nothing, but his vacant stare speaks volumes. The room is dead quiet as Rebecca begins to fade away again into an unresponsive state of twilight.

LAZARUS VI
UNVEILED

It is just minutes before President Parkston makes his address to the Nation. Flat panel cool lights flood the podium from which Parkston will speak. From behind the quartz counter at the back of the room, camera crews from a multitude of news organizations ready themselves for the speech.

Due to the gravity of tonight's address to the people, it was decided the speech be made directly from the White House press room. President Parkston's last address to the nation was done from the Oval Office, but not this time.

It is the first Presidential address to the Nation in fifteen months. Unlike the last time, this will be televised on every broadcast network coast to coast. The Saturday primetime address is designed to hopefully reach every American before the end of the weekend.

Press teams, from almost every news outlet nationwide, wait patiently, in and around the press briefing room. Like ants swarming the west wing of the White House, reporters flood the Brady room, anxious to hear what Parkston has to say. Even the offices below, what used to be the White House swimming pool, now stream with photographers and journalists. From television and news print to internet, tonight is as important as it gets.

White House Press Secretary, Haden Ross will be handling all questions from the press after the President's address.

The President's chief of staff including CDC Director Corina Mendez, Lon Thompson, Pat Vance, and Kevin Rhodes, among others, meet with Parkston inside the Oval Office to go over last-minute details. No teleprompter and no memorized talking point speech, the president is making this vital announcement to the public from his heart.

Nothing can be left to chance for this most important life-changing event. The American people have been inundated with rumors. The sudden death of Republican House Leader Phoebe Wescott has sparked outrage from some. But mostly from those who entertain conspiracies and hypotheticals. Many believe that this is what the address is about.

Finally Press Secretary Hayden Ross steps up to the podium. The room immediately falls silent as he announces the President.

"Ladies and gentleman, the President of the United States."

President Parkston enters from the left side door leading onto the stage of the press room, and steps to the podium. Members of the press applaud, as he stands behind the microphone. As the room quiets, Parkston begins.

"Thank you all for coming and thank you America for sharing a few minutes of your Saturday evening with me. As a country, I know that we all grieve the untimely loss of one of our own, Republican House Leader, Phoebe Wescott. It is indeed a sad day and our prayers are with her loved ones as they also mourn the loss of such a dear soul.

"Whether we agreed or disagreed, we always valued her opinions and firm stance concerning those beliefs. She was tough, she was tenacious and she was knowledgeable. When it came to understanding our founding forefather's hopes and aspirations for this great country, the Constitution, and what this country should stand for, she was in a league all of her own. She will be sorely missed."

Parkston lowers his head and pauses for a moment, to gather his thoughts. After which, he lifts his head, and continues.

"But, that's not why I stand before you today as Commander in Chief of this great Democracy. Why I'm here and what I have to say grieves me even more.

"During the past six hours, we have been receiving

vital intelligence briefings from Doctor Alana Bahat-anari, head of the World Health Organization, concerning a deadly virus that is quickly making its way to our shores. As of last count, it has been verified that there have been eleven individuals who have contracted the deadly virus, known as Titan H-C, right here in the United States.

"Fourteen people in Lahore, Pakistan have died from Titan H-C, and 64 People in New Delhi, India have also contracted it and perished. Unconfirmed reports are surfacing that the virus has even made its way into the United Kingdom. Titan H-C is swift and lethal. It has been referred to as the '10-Minute-to-Eternity' virus.

"It is not a question of if; but when? When will it take the lives of those here? Those closest and dearest to us? Make no mistake about it, this virus is as dangerous as it gets.

"Just moments ago, I spoke with Doctor Corina Mendez from the Centers for Disease Control. She informed me that this could be classified as a category four pandemic, in as few as six weeks. We as a country have not experienced anything this destructive since the Spanish Flu of 1918.

"However, this is not all bad news. Eight months ago, a super-vaccine was developed and is proving to be quite extraordinary. It is called Chryzinium. We believe this vaccine is the answer to the Titan H-C Virus. It is fast becoming recognized by scientists as the cure-all for a plethora of diseases.

"Tests are showing this vaccine is completely eradicating many forms of cancer, diabetes, multiple sclerosis, and a whole host of other killer diseases. It is believed that Chryzinium will ward off the Titan H-C Virus if taken quickly.

"Two weeks ago, behind closed doors, I signed into action by executive order, a program code named 'The Lazarus VI Project.' Our hope at that time was to make this super-vaccine available for those who are presently classified as terminally ill, as early as this coming summer.

"That was until now. With the onslaught of the Titan H-C virus, it is a foregone conclusion that this virus will not only become a threat to us as a people, but a threat to our National security. That is why I have been prompted to push the Lazarus VI Project forward and make Chryzinium available to all Americans within the next four to six weeks.

"We have been working close with the lab responsible for developing the vaccine and have been assured that Chryzinium will indeed kill off the virus. By design, it will put a wall up around the immune system.

"A super-vaccine such as Chryzinium can only be activated via Electro Linear Infusion. In other words, those taking the vaccine would also be required to have a small E.L.I. activation computer chip implanted to properly stimulate the vaccine. The small implant known as Vul-Stream will also monitor and transmit vitals to the host lab.

"I am well aware of the ramifications of suggesting such a program. I know skeptics will insist we are implementing a device, misconstrued as a diabolical government ploy to track and control our people.

"I can assure you this is not the case. The 14th Amendment as you know it remains intact. You have my word. We all value our privacy, and Vul-Stream will do nothing more than track the recipients' vitals to FHP and M-PAC the hosting lab. The upside, if one was to have a heart attack or seizure; emergency response would be on the way before the person hit the floor."

President Parkston pauses and takes a sip of water.

"We have been working diligently, securing distribution outlets through sponsored medical facilities coast to coast. My promise to you is to ensure the Chryzinium vaccine is available to every man, woman and child.

"We are asking everyone to connect with your FHP consultant and primary care provider as soon as possible to arrange for vaccination. Titan H-C is a killer and we ask for your complete cooperation. Thank you!"

President Parkston ends his address to the Nation and walks out of the press room. Hayden Ross steps to the podium to answer questions.

MERRIFIELD, VIRGINIA

House Ways and Means committee leader, Byron Sutter sits in his chair watching the Presidential address. With his remote in hand, he clicks off the power to the TV. As if in a hypnotic trance, Byron stares at the black screen, stunned by what he has just heard.

Like many other U.S. citizens watching the Presidential address to the Nation, he has just witnessed the biggest scam and cover-up since the Roswell crash of 1947.

Byron knew they were going to announce the implementation of the Lazarus VI Project tonight. However, he had no idea they were planning to go so low as to scare the people into the program with such deceit.

As Byron sits in the dark, he puts the pieces of the puzzle together in his head. He now knows exactly what happened to Phoebe. She was shut up. They knew she would be going to the press. He searched high and low for her thumb drive. Her 'coincidental' death was a message to everyone involved in the project. 'What you know, and what you say, could kill you.'

"Someone took it, I know it. It's my fault she's dead," he says remorsefully, before putting his gun into his mouth.

SOUTH BOUND
AND DOWN

As Baggs passes by his front window, he can't help but vividly recollect the horrendous scene he witnessed just six days prior. Crime scene tape still encompasses the Milner house as police and detectives painstakingly examine the property.

Baggs has had to become an academy-award winning actor overnight. Three times now, he's been questioned about the event. "Did you see anything? Have you seen or know the whereabouts of ten-year-old Martha Milner?"

With every attempt from authorities to garner any useful information from him, he's managed to keep his composure, begging them, "Please find her." As with every other house on the block, they've even asked if they could search his dwelling. Of course he's obliged. After all, he has nothing to hide.

Just before leaving the window, he sees another official-looking sedan pull up in front of his house. Sure enough, now it's the Feds. Marty's disappearance has become national news. In fact, Marty's disappearance has almost overshadowed Saturday's Presidential address to the Nation. An amber alert went out for the little girl within hours of the police arriving at the crime scene.

Baggs can't stop wondering, 'Will Roxanne change her story? What if she breaks under pressure?' Baggs may have had the cojones to let the lowest bid rocket builder launch his butt into outer space but, even that doesn't compare to the stress he's under now.

Sure enough, the two men in drab grey suits are walking up to his door. "Now what?" he mumbles to himself. Three loud knocks at the door and once again, it's show time.

Opening the door, he greets the gentlemen with a nonchalant smile and big hello. One of the men identifies himself as detective George Steinberger while throwing open his black leather Federal Bureau of Investigation badge holder. The other identifies himself as detective Will O'Hearn, but shows no ID. He is obviously the muscle.

"Commander Baggerly, Walter Cecil Baggerly, is that correct?" Steinberger asks.

"Yes, that's me," he politely responds.

O'Hearn, the quiet, mean-looking guy holds up a picture of a lady, while Steinberger asks the questions.

"Have you ever seen this woman?"

Baggs brings up his reading glasses that hang from a lanyard around his neck. He takes the picture to get a closer look.

"Yes, I've seen her, I don't know her name but she works as a clerk at the grocery store I often shop at," he says while handing the picture back to the quiet guy.

"Her name is Kelly Stevens. She says she saw you last Monday or Tuesday, with a young girl. That was Martha, right?"

"Yes, Marty, she likes to be called Marty. She came with me to the store. She hangs around here quite a bit. She likes to fly my model planes. I already told the police all of that. I didn't know anything until I saw all of the cops show up over there. I ran across the street to see what was going on.

"They wouldn't let me get anywhere close, but I could see there was something serious going on. I knew it had something to do with that Vernon guy. Marty hated him. He had beaten her up pretty good at least one time that I know of. That was just before Christmas. When I found out it was Vernon that got killed I'll tell you, I wasn't too surprised."

"I'm really sorry Commander. I don't mean to keep rehashing all of this. It's just that we can't find Martha, or Marty anywhere. No trace of her whereabouts and forgive me for saying, we haven't found her body either.

We don't have anything but a statement from Ms. Milner. She is saying Vernon may have had something to do with her disappearance, that's why she killed him. So you haven't seen her?"

"No. Everywhere I go, I look for her. I'm always hoping she'll turn up. I really like her. She's a good kid. She just had a bad home life."

"I promise we're doing everything we can to find her. You have a good day. If you do come across the little girl would you call me?" Steinberger asks as they turn and head back across the street to Marty's house.

"Absolutely," Baggs replies, complying with the detectives' request. Baggs closes his door. As soon as he does, he runs into the kitchen and grabs his phone. For the third time today he calls Lewis.

After what seems like an eternity of rings, Lewis finally answers.

"Hello."

"Well?"

"Well what?"

"The feds were just here. How far along are you?"

"Just now filling the water tanks."

BAGGS HOUSE, 4:00 AM, TUESDAY

Baggs' alarm sounds and with military routine firmly entrenched, he swings his legs out from under the covers and slides his feet deep into his slippers. One last shower and one last cup of coffee, Baggs is dressed and gathering the last of the things which mean most to him.

For his entire life, Baggs has lived in the old Crafts-man home. With bitter sorrow he has no choice but to leave. The situation with Marty has grown into some-thing he can no longer control. And now with the implementation of the Lazarus VI Project, he realizes the America he once fought for and loved so dearly is gone. Corruption, greed, and a new generation of entitlement dwellers have finally ruined this great land.

Baggs begins the arduous task of loading every-thing he has meticulously set out into the back of his truck. He has room for only one of his planes. He walks the length of the table that displays his airplane collection. Picking up his twin engine B-25 Bomber, a tear drops from his eye and onto the wing. Taking the plane carefully, he packs it into a special box and slowly departs.

After the last of his belonging are secured in his truck, and the front door locked, Baggs stands in his driveway and looks back at his home. Tears again well up in his eyes as he reminisces. All of the years he has enjoyed here at 1414 Havelock Lane are now coming to an end. From the old swing in the back yard to his low fly-over in an F-4 fighter to show off for his mother. 'She was so proud,' he remembers. Baggs has so many fond memories in this place, including his recent Christmas with Marty.

In the driver's seat, Baggs' starts the old truck. Once it's warmed up, he puts it in gear and slowly pulls out of his driveway for the very last time.

Baggs drives his truck to the back of the parking lot. Waiting for Lewis has always been an issue. "Late again." He mumbles to himself.

After waiting there for about ten minutes, Lewis finally enters the parking lot, driving his newly purchased motorhome. Not new, but new enough. Lewis brings the coach to a stop and climbs out from behind the wheel and opens the side door. Lewis and Baggs haven't seen each other since the incident at Marty's house a week prior.

"Everything is in the back and on the seat," Baggs informs Lewis.

"Well let's get this truck of yours unpacked and loaded into the mo-ho," Lewis says.

Grabbing a handful of Baggs belongings, he heads straight to the coach. Within twenty minutes, they have successfully unpacked Baggs truck and reloaded his meager belongings into the motorhome.

"You bring the dough?" Lewis asks.

"Three hundred and sixty two thousand in gold and silver coin. That's what was in the foot locker you helped me carry to the front room."

"So how did you carry it by yourself to your truck?"

"I carried everything one bag at a time."

"You kept all of this in your house?"

"Not necessarily," Baggs says, carrying a small bag of toiletries.

Baggs locks his truck for the last time. He knows

the police will be looking for him, and they'll no doubt find the truck abandoned. He hopes they'll think he's been kidnapped for ransom.

As he makes his way to the motorhome, bright headlights race toward them. The sports car comes to a quick stop. Sy steps out.

"I have three suitcases, a backpack, and a sleeping bag in the trunk. Can you give me a hand?" Sy asks, opening his trunk.

Baggs looks up at Lewis, surprised to see Sy.

"I didn't know he and Norma were coming along too," Baggs says to Lewis.

Lewis smiles.

"He's going to follow us down to Nashville. He'll ditch the car there. A Russian chop shop is taking it."

"What? What's going on? And where's Marty?" Baggs continues.

"Marty's in the back, she's asleep on the bed. She's okay."

Sy walks up, carrying one of his suitcases and asks, "Are you going to give me a hand?"

Baggs says, "I hadn't heard a word from you since we got back. I thought you and Norma had already left town."

Sy looks up at Lewis who is still standing in the doorway. "There is no Norma. Never has been. My real name is Arnie Swinth."

Baggs looks on in shock, "Faked deaths, Russian chop shops? Are you kidding me? You're Grand Canyon Arnie?"

"John helped me stage my own death. With a new identity, we were able to reinvent me. If anyone knew what that stuff did to me back then, I would have become a lab frog. John taught me how to fly and with a few fake credentials, I got a job with the government. Keep your friends close, Keep your enemies closer. Right?"

"Why didn't John say anything?" Baggs asks.

"I asked him not to."

"We're heading down to John's place. We're going to hide the mo-ho in his shop," Lewis announces.

"You knew about him?" Baggs asks, sounding somewhat perturbed.

"Well, not until yesterday. I thought about calling you and letting you know, but I thought this would be more fun. Speaking of which, I hope you all didn't forget to destroy your cell phones."

Baggs is speechless as he finds it hard to take all of this in. He helps Arnie carry his heavy suitcases. Baggs turns to Arnie and asks.

"You haven't aged that much. Not compared to John. Is that because of Chryzinium? That means you got the Vul-Stream implant?"

"No implant. So much for their lies about needing Vul-Stream to activate Chryzinium, huh? That's why I'm leaving with you all. They're not putting any chip in me. That's where I draw the line," Arnie responds.

After loading the heavy suitcases and backpack into the motorhome, he climbs back into his car.

Rick Lord

"See ya in Nashville," Arnie shouts as he drives out of the parking lot.

Loaded and with the coach door shut, Lewis climbs into the driver seat and they drive off as well. Turning around and looking towards the back of the coach, Baggs breaks into a grin as he sees Marty sit up from the queen bed and look at him with a big grin.

"South bound and down. Arizona, here we come," Lewis shouts with an excited chuckle.

SHAFUTAH RISING

M-PAC LABORATORIES

The theater in room 216 is lit only by the reflected live image of the Devil's Halo projected on the large screen. It glows with a subtle shade of pale green. Sitting at the console in the center of the theater is a silhouetted Adiv Zahim.

The door of the theater slides open, and in walks Amanda Sykes, giving her perfect smile. Sitting next to Adiv she puts her hand on his shoulder.

"Biel Hie Shatahaham," she whispers into his ear. Then she kisses him on the cheek.

"No longer Amanda; I am Asharana once again."

Adiv turns and smiles at her, placing his hand on her shoulder.

"Our Queen, she comes to us soon."

Asharana leans into Adiv as they look to the screen.

The majestic Vul-Helix hovers, rotating slowly counter-clockwise over the Grand Canyon. The dark metal sheen has become brilliant. The pale green glow pulses like a rhythmic heartbeat. Finally, after all the centuries, the Vul-Helix slowly begins its transition from hologram to physical mass. The world is being transformed for the Shafutah to rule once again.

Nothing is as it seems. Albert Hess was not Sigmund's father, but in fact, Albert Hess is Sigmund's son. Sigmund has been injecting himself with the Shafutah's Unibihexium Carbon since the late 1930's. When his son overdosed on UBH, the clock of annihilation began ticking.

The governments are on stage to provide an illusion of freedom and democracy. The people follow like sheep to their slaughter. Their greed and lust for power has cost them everything. All that they covet is but barren waste. It is cinders upon cinders in a fiery furnace that they build for themselves.

The Shafutah shall deceive the government and the government shall deceive its people and the people shall deceive their offspring and their offspring shall deceive their offspring.

A Queen comes to bear a son; a son who will rise to become the ruler of darkness. Before the ages of man, the Shafutah reigned from the depths of earth. For millennia, she has been sleeping.

But now, the Shafutah rises to power. She will devour, taking her spoils to the abyss with her. Greed and lust for power have brought the Shafutah back from the pit of hell. It is the era of a new empire of evil. The Queen of the Shafutah is groomed for her throne.

Rebecca sits at Emily's vanity looking into the mirror. Her eyes are puffy and red from crying. She knows now what has happened to her daughter. 'Mark was right. They used her as a lab rat, and now she's gone. What went wrong? How could I have allowed this to happen? How could Mark have done this to his own flesh and blood?'

Bowing her head, Rebecca gazes down at Emily's make-up, perfumes and jewelry. Holding items here and there, they all have become heirlooms, memories of her daughter. Trying to understand what has happened, she reels with despair.

Emily's blue iridescent MP3 player lies off to the side of her vanity. Rebecca places the earbuds into her ears. She turns it on.

The sound of telemetry pings out its rhythmic code. While imbedded with a low register drone, the strange music plays. It captivates and mesmerizes as the soft female voice hypnotizes with her repetitive unearthly chant.

"Biel Hie Shatahaham, Biel Hie Shatahaham. Biel Hie Shatahaham. Emilia, Emilia you are the exalted Queen of Shafutah, you are promised a place in the Vul, where darkness prevails. You will be worshiped and revered forever and ever."

TIME OUT

They have become the defiant establishment and the resistant fighters; defending their freedom from oppressive control. From the very first appearance of the Shafutah, they have refused to be seduced by their empty promises. They have accepted the natural rhythm of life and their God given natural lifespans. Because they maintain freedom from control and embrace self-reliance, the Shafutah and their followers irreverently refer to these people as 'Timers'.

The Shafutah now control the majority of earths' population. Time is afforded now only to the 'New Solution' believers. They are promised, 'Health and Life. Forever'.

Baggs, Lewis, Arnie, John and the children could not remain in Ash Fork. After only 2 years, it became increasingly difficult to live in the high desert.

Without Vul-Stream and their obstinate refusal to join the 'New Solution', they could no longer purchase basic provisions such as food, fuel or electricity. The high desert is not geographically suitable for agriculture, so they set out for the Pacific Northwest. The location is a temperate region where other Timers have gone to live out their lives. Small clandestine Timer communes, dot the green valleys and lush hillsides of Oregon, Washington, and Idaho.

Farming is their livelihood. Trading and bartering with each other is how they survive. They have created their own way of life. Their very existence requires a commitment to helping and guarding themselves, and their neighbors, whatever the cost.

No schools for their children, no churches to attend, no police to protect, Timers are forced to survive in secret. With underground operations in place throughout their communities, they provide secret learning centers for the young, storage facilities for their supplies, and underground churches for the faithful. All of which are now illegal; according to the Shafutah's 'New Solution' governance.

The Shafutah and their followers make the Timers existence painfully difficult. They are constantly ridiculed and persecuted. Trading and supply buildings, when discovered, are pillaged and burned to the ground. Schools, homes, and churches are often raided. Men, women, and children are occasionally kidnapped, and sometimes even killed.

The power of the Shafutah continues to expand and seduce the world's governments with their 'New

Solution' doctrine and absolute control over the masses.

THE VUL-HELIX ON THE MOVE

For years, conspiracy theorists, ufologists, and locals referred to it as the Devils Halo. It was an anomaly periodically seen hovering over the Grand Canyon. The mysterious cloud formation produced untold rumors and widespread speculation. Just after the announcement of the Titan HC virus, the true identity of the Devils Halo was revealed.

At 3:00 AM mountain time, a brilliant glow emitted from the Devils Halo, and lit up the night sky; the likes of which had never been seen. With the blinding lights streaming from its circumference and a ground vibrating low register drone, every eye and ear within 600 miles of the anomaly was witness to the ominous craft coming to life. After millions of years, the evil had finally manifested itself in tangible form.

Adorned with hieroglyphic Shafutah markings, the massive metallic structure hovered over the Painted Desert at approximately 30 thousand feet. The vile presence spanned the sky 12 miles in diameter with the massive letters, 'Vul-Helix', etched into its ominous glowing hull.

The world forever changed.

THE RELOCATION OF A SUPER POWER

Conspiracy theorists are all aware of the High Frequency Active Auroral Research Program referred to as (HAARP), located in Gakona Alaska. The facility has been thought to have ties to such bizarre activities such as weather modification, contrails, disabling satellites, and even employing mind control. It was even thought to have control over the earths tectonic plates, causing a melee of volcanic and earthquake disasters.

It is however the Ionospheric Research Instrument (IRI), the Shafutah was mainly interested in. HAARP does have at least one valid non-conspiracy function. It is the home of (IRI). IRI is a high-power radio frequency transmitter instrument that operates in the high frequency (HF) band. It is an instrument designed to temporarily excite the ionosphere to study the effects of the aurora borealis on radio transmission waves.

For the Vul-Helix to function as a global communication transceiver, power distribution hub and optimal operations, the New World Order decided that it must be relocated. The Willamette Valley was chosen due to its proximity to the Alaskan HAARP facility. Using the HAARP station as a transformer substation, it will allow the Vul-Helix to operate and control globally from one central location.

On June 25th the Vul-Helix slowly relocates, maneuvering its behemoth mass across the sky at less than one mile per hour. Its menacing shadow relentlessly creeped along the landscape below casting a shroud of darkness under its monstrous hull. The Vul-Helix' destination: 56 miles south of the 45th parallel, near Salem, Oregon. Paradoxically, the same area many of the Timers have migrated to.

Not far from where John, Baggs, Lewis, Arnie and the children reside, the Vul-Helix comes to the end of its journey and hovers. Day in and day out, it cycles its massive generators, emitting a constant mind-bending hum. Bright bluish white lights illuminate the country side like malevolent eyes, spying. Constant reminders, we are being watched.

The fight for freedom and life is now at the forefront for the Timers. They are at the precipice of extinction. This is the time of the rise of the Shafutah.

THE END

THE AUTHOR

Born and raised in the Los Angeles area, Rick spent most of his childhood in Chatsworth, California. Many old Hollywood westerns and TV episodic shows, including *The Lone Ranger, Roy Rogers* and *Little House on the Prairie* were shot in that area. He attended Chatsworth High School, the same high school attended by Val Kilmer, Kevin Spacey and Mare Winningham.

It only seemed natural that Rick found himself drawn into the glitz and glamour of movie making. However, his Hollywood career didn't take off until he moved to Portland, Oregon, where acting classes and voice lessons landed him bit parts in movies, TV commercials and radio spots.

The motion picture biz was entrenched deep into his DNA, and he discovered that his real passion behind the lens. He worked his way up the ranks from film crew to director of photography, and he remains active in the movie-making business today. Writing the *Chryzinium* novel series, screenplays, and teaching on-camera acting satisfies his thirst between projects.

A BRIEF HISTORY OF CHRYZINIUM

Rick was recruited by two men from his church to help teach them the ins and outs of filmmaking. An avid writer and filmmaker, Rick did his tutoring by doing. Proceeds from the sale of his Harley, along with additional financial assistance, allowed them to produce short films as a practical classroom experience, and Matchlight Films was born.

Growing to more than 170 members, Matchlight began filming in and around Salem, Oregon. The little city embraced the process. Initially, location permits were non-existent, but the "Lights, Camera, Action" aspect of the whole spectacle was well received by the residents.

After months of planning, ten days of filming, visual-effects design and hundreds of hours of editing, *Chryzinium* the short film, debuted September 22, 2014 at the Grand Theater in downtown Salem, Oregon. The 26-minute feature was a hit—the theater was packed with 352 people.

Matchlight Films planned for a feature length version of *Chryzinium*. However, even after copious fanfare from the press and awards from film festivals, raising the funds for a full-length film was still a far reach.

A Hollywood producer friend of Ricks presented him a challenge. "Write the book and then let's talk."

The rest is history, as they say. One year to the day after the auspicious prompt, the challenge was met. Rick did his part. *Chryzinium, The Lazarus VI Project* is in print and in full distribution.

"It's funny, in the book I have a cast of 51 characters, of which, not one has ever complained about grueling days on the set or lattes being too cold. Nor have they demanded luxurious on-set accommodations. Book characters are much easier to work with. They eat when I eat and go to bed when I go to bed," Rick jokes.

Rick is currently at work on *Chryzinium*, Book II. The dream of making *Chryzinium* into a movie is still an ember that burns deep within his soul. *Chryzinium* on the silver screen is a vision that is fast becoming a reality.

CHARACTER CAST
BY STORYLINE

BAGGS AND LEWIS

Baggs – Commander Walter Cecil Baggerly – Astronaut retired

Lewis Warren – Baggs' close friend – C5-A Pilot retired

Sy – Simon Lazlo – Friends with Baggs and Sy - Scientist

Marty – Martha Milner – Baggs' neighbor girl

Roxanne Milner – Roxy – Marty's mother

Vernon Kootsmier – Roxanne's boyfriend

April Dunn/Konekelowski – Waitress – Pastry chef

Albert Hess – 1951 Scientist

Lois Konekelowski – April's daughter - School teacher

John Gussman – Grand Canyon - Retired Scientist

Arnie Swinth – John's friend - Grand Canyon – Scientist

Sani – Navajo Native American – Grand Canyon

THE SHAES

Rebecca Shae – Mother and wife

Mark Shae – Father and husband

Emily Shae – Teen Daughter

Taylor – Preteen son

Alesha Mason – Rebecca's best friend

Dave Mason – Alesha's husband

Mr. Alverez – Emily's world history teacher

Samantha – Emily's best friend

Carol Hoecker – Marks' work partner

Christie Lee – School Administrator

Paula Slater – Congressional Budget Office
    Representative
Hayden Ross – White House Press Secretary
Bob Martinson – FDA
Margaret Billings - FDA

THE DOVE

Joe – Fight Attendant – Security
John – Flight Attendant - Security
M-PAC (Mk-Ultra Passive Atomic Chemical)
Dr. Sigmund Hess – M-Pac Director
Dr. Edward Stiner – Operations Tech Supervisor
Wilhelm Avercamp - M-PAC's Chief Electronics
    Engineer
Adiv Zahim – M-PAC founder
Asharana – Shafutah Matriarch
Bill – M-PAC Elevator Guard

Made in the USA
San Bernardino, CA
04 August 2016